ROYAL BOROUG

Follow us on twitte

Greenwich
Centre
Library
02037950600

Please return by the last date shown		
8/25		

Thank you! To renew, please contact any
Royal Greenwich library or renew online or by phone
www.better.org.uk/greenwichlibraries
24hr renewal line 01527 852385

B

GREENWICH LIBRARIES

3 8028 02533909 1

First published in 2007. This edition first published in Great Britain in 2023 by Boldwood Books Ltd.

Copyright © Lizzie Lane, 2007

Cover Design by Colin Thomas

Cover Photography: Colin Thomas and Unsplash

The moral right of Lizzie Lane to be identified as the author of this work has been asserted in accordance with the Copyright, Designs and Patents Act 1988.

All rights reserved. No part of this book may be reproduced in any form or by any electronic or mechanical means, including information storage and retrieval systems, without written permission from the author, except for the use of brief quotations in a book review.

This book is a work of fiction and, except in the case of historical fact, any resemblance to actual persons, living or dead, is purely coincidental.

Every effort has been made to obtain the necessary permissions with reference to copyright material, both illustrative and quoted. We apologise for any omissions in this respect and will be pleased to make the appropriate acknowledgements in any future edition.

A CIP catalogue record for this book is available from the British Library.

Paperback ISBN 978-1-83751-862-3

Large Print ISBN 978-1-83751-861-6

Hardback ISBN 978-1-83751-859-3

Ebook ISBN 978-1-83751-863-0

Kindle ISBN 978-1-83751-864-7

Audio CD ISBN 978-1-83751-855-5

MP3 CD ISBN 978-1-83751-856-2

Digital audio download ISBN 978-1-83751-857-9

Boldwood Books Ltd
23 Bowerdean Street
London SW6 3TN
www.boldwoodbooks.com

1

Beth Dawson climbed on the guardrail and leaned against the cabin roof of the brightly painted narrowboat until she was high enough for everyone to see.

'It's only two days old,' she shouted, waving a newspaper above her head.

Women gossiping, men smoking and children playing hopscotch with lumps of coal all stopped what they were doing and turned towards her.

'Thought you was off,' someone said.

'There's plenty of time. We're off up the Avon and Kennet.' The Kennet canal joined the River Avon in Bristol to the Thames in London. 'We'll be halfway there by teatime tomorrow.'

It wasn't necessarily the truth, but it didn't matter. The newspaper was spread in front of her. She was ready and everyone was crowding around.

No point in getting her best green skirt dirty, so she hurriedly placed sheets of religious tracts on an upturned barrel before sitting on it. The Baptist minister who'd given them to her would be mortified to see pages of holy words pressed against her bottom, but she gave it no mind.

Patting the newspaper flat, she smiled at the gathering crowd. Most were women, their nut-brown faces shaded by bonnets, a style lingering from the last century. Eyes bright with interest, they waited for her to read out loud what they could not read for themselves. One or two children, their breath warm and sticky against her neck, peered over her shoulder, pretending to read. She knew they couldn't, thought it a shame and was thankful her mother had taught her well.

Front-page stories were read out first. 'Mr Ramsay MacDonald is reported to be thinking of forming a coalition government although at present this is not confirmed.'

'Never mind 'im. What about 'is Majesty? What's 'e up to, then?' The speaker was Mrs Bryce. A clay pipe jiggled at the corner of her mouth, gripped with the few teeth she had left. Always knitting, not once did the clickety-clacking of her needles falter.

A murmur of approval ran through the crowd and Beth obliged. 'His Majesty the King and Queen Mary are at present staying at Windsor with Prince Edward, the Prince of Wales, and their younger son the Duke of York.'

Someone asked if there was a picture of them, and if there was could she cut it out and stick it up somewhere.

'That wouldn't be right,' exclaimed an indignant Mrs Bryce. The needles stopped clicking. She was obviously shocked. 'You only have proper pictures of the King and Queen on walls, not fuzzy ones from newspapers. It's disrespectful.'

Beth thought about it. 'I suppose it's better to have any sort of picture than none at all.'

Mrs Bryce sucked her lips into her toothless mouth and snorted. The needles resumed their clicking.

The other woman smiled triumphantly. She was younger than Mrs Bryce, though you'd hardly know it. The hard life of providing food and comfort to a large family had taken its toll. The living accommodation barely measured eight by ten and sleeping arrangements were like a Chinese puzzle. Wages were low, charity sporadic and supplies were supplemented from the fields passed en route between Gloucester and the Midlands. Long gone were the days when the boatmen had a cottage as well as a boat. That was before the railways. A carrier had to be competitive in order to survive.

One item after another was read, including advertisements for patent medicines, boot polish and even ladies' corsets. She knew the precious moment was over when she heard clothes rustling and a whisper, a mutter, then a full-blown exclamation running through the group of listeners: 'Daddy Dawson. Daddy Dawson. Daddy Dawson.'

The louder it got, the quicker people dispersed. Her father was respected rather than liked, even by his own family. She sighed and, despite her fear of him, remained reading.

He called to her from the other end of the boat. 'Elizabeth!'

He was on his way.

Of the crowd that had listened, only her mother remained, her eyes and her feelings hidden behind the broad brim of her bonnet. Other bonnets and the tousled hair of the smaller listeners melted away, the adults back to their boats or to fill their Buckby cans (tall tin jugs) with fresh water. The children, their boots clattering on the loose concrete, ran among the machinery and played at boats with bits of wood in the oily puddles.

'Elizabeth!' His boots clunked the length of the boat. 'Are you deaf? Answer me when I call ya!'

She quickly folded the newspaper and her mother snatched it from her. 'He's getting himself into a temper,' she murmured as she hid the newspaper among the folds of an old cardigan that was in the process of being unpicked and reused.

His shadow fell over them.

Her mother looked up at him as meek as you like. 'I'll have a fresh brew ready for when you get back.'

'You'd better have!'

Like bullets, his dark eyes shot to Beth. 'Are we off to the wharfinger?' she asked.

'Why else would I call you, you stupid lump! Now get off yer backside and next time move a bit faster when I shout or you'll get the back of my hand. Now! Are you ready?'

Her blue eyes regarded him from beneath the dark hair that framed a face turned nut-brown by sun, wind and rain. 'Of course I'm ready,' she said, more defiantly than she should.

'Move! I don't have time to waste.' His voice was as sharp as his looks.

Many times she'd wondered how a man with such looks as his could possibly be her father. His nose was hooked, his mouth wide, his eyes dark and piercing. A gold ring hung from his right ear and a red kerchief circled his neck. No wonder the land people called them gypsies.

Bells hung from the straps binding his corduroys just below the knees and tinkled as he walked in front of her. Ignoring the black water that splashed up from dirty puddles and on to her skirt, she glared with silent resentment at the angular shoulders, the riot of hair on the nape of his neck. Menacing to face, he seemed less so from behind. She looked at him as she pleased.

A sharp wind blew off the water. She hugged her green cardigan around her. Despite the weight of her work boots, she strode proudly. No one noticed a frayed cuff or a torn hem if you moved fast enough.

In the shadow of the red-brick warehouses, men were piling crates, sacks and tubs on the quay.

'Well hello, me fine young girl!' called one sweating stevedore as he straightened from his task.

'Now what could you do with a girl like that?' said another.

'Plenty!' called a third. 'A tramp dressed in rags seems like a lady in silk as long as it's dark!'

The men all laughed just as they always did. She gave them no regard. They were the same on a dozen wharves the length and breadth of England, rough men brutalised by a hard job and dire living conditions. She could tell by the set of her father's shoulders that he was bristling.

It was all her fault, of course. 'That's the way of women,' he'd told her enough times. 'The sooner Elliot Beaven marries you, the better! Like all women, you're fit only for warming pans, pots and beds!'

Her cheeks dimpled. Soon she'd be married like any respectable woman of eighteen and things would be different. It would fall back on her mother to read the manifest and show him where to sign. For the second time that day, she glowed with pride and didn't care tuppence if pride was a sin!

He slowed as they approached the office door, took the cigarette that lodged behind his ear and shoved it into his pocket. 'Don't want 'im to think I earn too bloody much,' she heard him mutter.

The office walls were a deep shade of brown. The wharf manager sat behind his desk, corn-coloured hair flopping limply over a pink forehead. Although he must have heard the door opening, he did not acknowledge their presence.

Beth hung back as hat in hand her father stepped forward, shuffling his feet.

'Dawson from Jenny Wren, sir, loaded and ready to go.' His

voice was low, his words softened by the need to appear subservient.

The wharf manager continued to write. He would bide his time.

Her father stood rigidly, eyes downcast.

At last, the wharf manager threw his pen down on his desk, sprawled back in his chair and looked up. 'Dawson?'

'That's me, sir. Dawson. Daniel Dawson. At your service, sir.'

The wharfinger, as the wharf managers were called, was new. 'Been here before?'

'Many times, if you please, sir. I used to see Mr Turner.'

'He's dead. I'm Mr Allen. Mr Harry Allen.' He smiled.

'You can continue to call me sir.'

A nerve quivered in her father's cheek. Anyone seeing him for the first time might not notice it. But she did. She knew it well.

The wharf manager blinked in her direction, looked away then as if unsure whether he was seeing things, took another look. 'Well, hello. What, or should I say who, have we here?'

His eyes lingered on her face, dipped to her bosom and came back again as he pushed the manifests across the desk.

Her father acted as though he hadn't heard, though she was sure he had.

Well, her father might be afraid of this man, but she wasn't. After all, she told herself, he was only being friendly. 'I'm Beth Dawson,' she said brightly.

Harry Allen raised his eyebrows. 'Related to this man?' He sounded almost surprised.

'My daughter, sir,' her father muttered. His reluctance to introduce her was painfully obvious in the clenching of his jaw.

'Good morning, miss.' Mr Allen gave her a slight incline of his head before addressing her father again. 'You don't need to read the manifest. I can assure you it's precisely as loaded, and you don't need to write your name. A cross will do.'

There was veiled sarcasm in his voice. His smile was oily, but Beth didn't mind that. He'd given her a cue. It was her turn to take charge.

'I'm here to read this for me father and then I'll sign it on his behalf just like I used to for Mr Turner. Is that all right? Sir,' she added.

Harry Allen raised just one eyebrow now as he lit himself a cigarette. He smiled at her as if she mattered.

She smiled back, nervously at first, then more openly because he made her feel special.

The chair squeaked as he slid it away from the desk. 'Is that so? How very unusual for someone from the canals. Reading and writing, I mean.'

Beth didn't care that her father was giving her sour looks. Someone was interested in her. 'My mother taught me to read and write, sir. I'm named after her. I'm Elizabeth really, but everyone calls me Beth.'

'My, my. Can read and write and is pretty with it! What more can a man desire? Pleased to meet you, Beth. We don't often see such prettiness in this dull place. Your presence is most welcome.'

Much to her surprise, he stood up and bowed stiffly. He brushed back a lank of pale blond hair that had fallen forward and straightened to his full height before sitting back down again.

During that short moment, he had towered over them both. He was not a heavy man, neither was he handsome, but he was amenable. Beth felt special.

'Beth,' he said, continuing to address her in preference to her father, 'would you be so kind as to sign where indicated?' He said it so courteously as though she were one of the ladies she saw getting on and off the train at the station on the other side of the canal.

He reached for the pen at the same time as she did. As his hand covered hers, a warm flush exploded on her cheeks and seeped down her neck.

'Just there,' he said.

As she signed she felt his eyes on her. The flush that coloured her cheeks intensified.

'There!' he said. 'Well, that wasn't too painful, was it?' Leaning back again in his chair, he picked up his pen and his gaze returned to the papers he'd been perusing on their arrival. 'You may go now.' His change of tone was instant. They were blanked out.

Just as they reached the door, he called out. 'Dawson!' Her father stopped and turned round. 'Yes, sir.'

'Make sure you bring your daughter with you again, Dawson. I prefer our manifests to be read, understood and signed properly.'

Beth held her breath. The redness on her cheeks was nothing compared to that of her father. There was anger in his eyes and his jaw was set like iron. He'd been humiliated.

'Yes, sir. I will, sir.'

'Goodbye, Beth.'

'Goodbye, sir,' Beth stammered.

Gripping the manifests, he wrenched the door open, sending it crashing against the wall.

Outside he turned his anger on her. 'You've said too much for yourself, me girl!' He strode on.

With a sinking heart she followed and guessed what was coming.

There was an indent in the warehouse halfway along. At one time it must have been a door. Now it was just a deep niche dug into the side of the building.

He grabbed her arm. 'Clever girl! Pretty girl! Well, don't you go taking on any airs and graces after that sort of talk! Don't you go thinking you got somewhere better to go in life, because you haven't! You was born on the boats, you'll be marrying and living on the boats, then you'll die on the boats!'

She tried to wriggle free. 'Don't, Dah. Please don't.'

But he wasn't listening. He was a hard man to understand at the best of times. Humbling himself on the days he had to go into the canal office was totally against his nature. To make matters worse, a steam locomotive of the London and Midlands chose that moment to slide past on the nearby viaduct, its trucks piled high with coal. Eyes hard with hatred followed the creeping crocodile of clanging, clattering trucks.

'Look at that!' he said, jerking his chin to where the coal dust from the trucks stained the sky with a gritty black fog. His cheeks fluxed in and out like angry bellows; his eyes stayed fixed on the train. 'Them railways have damn near killed off the canals and now these damned motor trucks are hammering the nails in the coffin.'

His eyes glittered as he watched wagon after wagon pass by and fade into the mix of steam and smoke left by the engine. 'Bloody railways! Bloody railways, bloody lorries, and bloody Gatehouse Carrying Company! Between them they're killing us all. They're bloody killing us all.'

2

Abigail Gatehouse straightened her tie. It was green with hazelnut flecks, a perfect match to tweed jacket and trousers. She glanced at Anthony before opening her mouth. He was the one above all others that she wished to impress. 'There has to be a strike. There's no way the boatmen can survive on what's been offered.'

Anthony Wesley eyed her through the smoke rising from his pipe as though daring her to continue. 'There's no way they can survive on fresh air either, and that's all they'll have once they strike.'

'Perhaps you'd like to donate a bit more to the strike fund,' one of the other men said. 'Seeing as you've reaped the benefit of their labour all these years.'

Abigail fidgeted in the seat of the high-backed chair, refusing to feel intimidated or guilty. 'Just because my father owns the carrying company doesn't mean I've got money to throw around. Besides, I get nothing until I marry.'

'Just what I wanted to hear!' said another wag with sandy white hair and rustic cheeks. 'I'll tell the wife I've 'ad an offer I can't refuse!'

There was more laughter, and the more there was the angrier Abigail got. 'Look here. I'm here to help.'

Anthony regarded her coolly through a cloud of pipe smoke. His voice was deep. 'I hope so, otherwise we'd think you were a spy.'

'I'm not!' He winked.

She blushed, realizing he'd been joking. 'I'm not just playing at this in order to pass the time until I get married,' she exclaimed. 'I really want to help these people.'

Anthony winked again. 'Well, thank God for that.'

The comment was forgotten as the main reason for the meeting was discussed further. It was simple: the carrying companies wanted to cut the boatmen's money.

'It still goes back as to how we feed ourselves during the strike,' said the man with the yellow-white hair.

Anthony leaned forward, his dark eyes fixed on the pipe he balanced on his fingers. 'Abbie is right. There has to be a fund.'

'And we all have to contribute,' Abbie said, pleased that he'd referred to her so favourably.

It was inevitable that one of the men sitting there would criticise. She readied herself.

'All right for them that's got money,' grumbled a ruddy-faced man with a hare lip and a starched collar.

She sprang to her feet, slapped her hands down on the table and spat out exactly what she was thinking.

'Just because I was born into money doesn't make me heartless. I care how people are treated. I care when men are exploited, women are forced to live in drudgery and children cry because they've little in their bellies. Is it only the poor that care for the poor? Can you honestly say that every union official or Labour Member of Parliament is rich and therefore uncaring?'

There was a shuffling of feet as she fixed them with her clear blue eyes, her mouth set in a hard line. One or two coughed nervously. Some – all men, of course – averted their eyes. They didn't like looking at her. It was bad enough that she could hold her own in their company. Worse still was the way she dressed. In an effort to gain respect on an equal basis in a male world, her preference was for trousers, shirts and jackets, plus a suitable tie and hat to complement the outfit. She sat down slowly, her lips slightly parted and her chest heaving with the passion of concerned argument. The room above the bar of the George Inn, a small watering hole set behind the gasworks at the side of the canal, fell to stunned silence.

For a moment she felt foolish. What did she really know about the situation? Why didn't she go home, put on a silk frock and sip tea with the rest of her kind?

The urge to take flight was overwhelming, but something deep inside, something she believed in with every fibre of her being, forced her to stay. She cared what happened to people.

Suddenly there was clapping, a slow appreciative sound that gradually quickened then gained in tempo. They were applauding her? She could hardly believe it.

Her eyes met Anthony's. Judging by the look in them, it was him that had started the clapping. He was smiling, his pipe still gripped in the corner of his mouth. More hands followed his lead. Basking in their appreciation, she blushed again. All she had ever wished for was for her opinions to be respected – especially by Anthony. At long last it appeared her wish had come true.

The sound of shouting and the bar door crashing open from beneath them stopped everything.

Anthony sprang to his feet and took charge. 'Everybody out!'

'A stoolie! We've got a stoolie!' someone cried.

Anthony flung open the door then closed it quickly. 'They're heading for the stairs.' He began piling furniture against the door.

Abigail held him back before he'd gone too far. 'Let me out this way. Perhaps I can persuade them to go away.'

'I said there was a stoolie,' shouted the man again.

Abigail winced as he threw her an accusing stare. She immediately retaliated. 'Stupid man!'

'Do what you can,' said Anthony. He took her arm and guided her out through the door. 'We'll pile furniture against the door once you're out.'

She held on to the doorknob. 'You have to get out, Anthony. You know it's you they're after.' Her voice was full of fear.

'I'll climb out the window. Now go on. Get out.' He pushed her out on to the landing.

'I'll bring the car round.'

He nodded then closed the door.

Taking a deep breath, she patted her hat down firmly on her head and smoothed her jacket. Her legs were shaking, though if anyone asked, she'd never admit it.

Oh, I'm just doing this very brave thing because I feel the likes of us should lead from the front.

The bravery in her mind failed to travel to her legs. Hearing loud voices, she dashed down the stairs.

A crowd of bullies, the usual brutes prevalent around dark streets and dockside taverns, rushed out from the bar.

Though her legs were still shaking, she summoned up all her courage. 'Gentlemen,' she shouted. The sound of her own voice stunned her. It was a highbrow voice, the sort swiftly adopted by those like her father who had risen from humble beginnings. She looked at them down her nose. 'Am I right in thinking that you work for my father?'

The men exchanged dumbfounded looks with each other. 'Depends who your father is,' one of them muttered, a look of puzzlement on his face.

'My father owns a carrying company,' she said, preferring not to divulge her father's name, just in case one of them might recognise who she was.

'Begging your pardon, sir, or madam, whatever you are,' said the man who appeared to be their leader. He jerked his head. 'Go on. Get out of here.'

He moved aside to let her pass. Although they touched their forelocks, she knew he was making fun.

'Sir? Are you sure that's a sir,' said a less quick-witted of their number. 'I swear I smelled perfume.'

She ran to her car. The men behind her began to laugh. 'Fetch 'im back. I'm still not sure whether it's man or a woman.'

'Oi!' someone shouted after her.

Glancing over her shoulder, she saw them hanging out of the pub door. Two looked about to give chase.

Her courage left her. Using both hands to turn the starting handle, she prayed that the crabby engine of the Austin would start quickly. Sometimes her car seemed to have a mind of its own. Tonight, grumbling and choking, it rattled into life. 'Thank you, car,' she said, sliding into the driving seat.

The men were banging on the roof and the windows. Their faces were ugly and distorted like monsters in dreams. She put the car into gear and found herself driving along the alley that ran between the gasworks and the pub.

It was wrong! So wrong! The window Anthony would have had to climb out was in the opposite direction.

Just as she was about to slam the car into reverse, she saw a red glow from a lit match. Someone was standing between the pub and the corner of the road that led from the canal into the town. Someone was lighting his cigarette. Suddenly, she glimpsed his face. It wasn't Anthony, but it was someone she knew. A cold fear took control of her mind. Although passionate about Anthony, the union movement and socialist politics, she didn't want her family to find out. She knew what they might do to protect their good name. They'd put her aunt away because they'd said she was mad when she fell in love with a merchant seaman. Who knows what they might do to her?

Forgetting to turn on the headlights, she dashed for the only escape route open to her and drove like the devil until she was far enough away to stop, take stock and feel thoroughly ashamed.

Finally, once she was sure she'd left them behind, she came to a halt.

Beneath the fragile glow of a gas street lamp, she got out of the car, flung herself against a brick wall and was violently sick.

3

By the time they'd got back from the canal-side office it was evening and her father had decreed that they would not leave until the morning. In the meantime he was making up for his humiliation at the hands of Harry Allen, and his family were the only ones in the line of fire. Her mother bore the brunt of his bad temper.

'These potatoes are too floury. This meat's too tough! Can't you get anything better than this, woman?'

With what? thought Beth. Pennies? Do you buy best steak with farthings? But she kept her eyes lowered as she spooned mutton stew into her mouth.

Robbie, her brother, was two years older than her. He said little to his father. They'd argued when he'd been younger, but not now. It was as if there was some kind of truce between them, sensible considering that her brother was considerably taller. He also kept talking about leaving the boats and getting work in a factory. Her father was doing everything to get him to stay.

Robbie kept his head down, food disappearing into his mouth as fast as the spoon could travel.

'And the tea's stewed!' her father shouted suddenly, making them all jump. He slammed the cup down into its saucer.

'Now, now, Daniel. I'll get you a fresh one, shall I?'

'Too bloody right,' he grumbled.

Her mother lifted the heavy brown teapot from the small range that provided all the hot water, cooking and heating for their needs.

She poured a fresh cup for him. He took a sip. 'Call that fresh?'

'Daniel, I've only just—'

'Well, it's stewed! Make another.'

'But—'

Beth looked from one parent to another.

Rob, unwilling to get involved, got to his feet. 'Be back later.' Averting his eyes from what was happening, he stepped up through the tiny door into the cockpit and was gone.

Beth shouted after him. 'Robbie?' Poking her head up out through the door, she saw his tall figure slope off along the quay, cap lopsided and hands in pockets.

Behind her, things had taken a turn for the worse. Her mother looked terrified. 'Daniel.'

'Don't Daniel me!'

He grabbed the spout of the shiny brown teapot and slammed it against her mother's arm. 'Call that hot?' he shouted.

The pot had been stewing on the range above glowing hot coals. Her mother screamed as the heat permeated the thin cotton sleeve of her dress.

As Beth leapt between them a stream of brown liquid spilled from the spout and splashed on to her mother's hand. 'No! Stop it! Leave my mother alone.'

She pushed the pot against her father's stomach as hard as she possibly could. Hot tea poured out all over his belly, staining his shirt.

'You little—' Roaring with rage and pain, he lunged to the left then cried out as his shoulder collided with an overhanging cupboard.

Beth was out of the door and over the side of the boat. She fell face down, grazing her knees and ripping her favourite skirt and cardigan.

He shouted after her. 'Come here, you little cow!'

'Leave her! It was my fault!'

She heard her mother's voice. Yet again she was taking the blame! It angered her.

'Come back here, you little bitch!'

His boots slammed the broken surface of the quay. Terrified, she ran into the gathering darkness.

The night air was cool. Shadows thrown by wharf-side warehouses hid her tears and her frustration. She walked sluggishly now, her boots dragging through the grime, her arms limp and helpless at her side.

With a sigh, she leaned against a warehouse wall and looked up at the ribbon of star-spangled sky that flowed between the building and the one opposite.

Staring at the stars helped her feel less guilty about leaving her mother alone with her father. Someone had once told her you could wish upon a star. Well, she wished now. She wished for happiness. At present, the only time she truly achieved this was within the well-thumbed pages of a book, escaping into a different world.

Later she would have to go back and face her father, but by then he would have come home drunk and fallen on to the bed behind the green checked curtain where he would stay snoring till morning. The tiny cabin would smell of his sweat, tobacco and, most of all, beer. Quietly and swiftly, she would get her bedroll from within the storage box beneath her bed and without taking her clothes off, she would get in and hope the morning and the beer he'd consumed would bring forgetfulness.

She huddled down in a doorway and waited. In time she dozed, her head resting on her knees.

She didn't hear him approach. She didn't know he was there until his shadow fell over her and he nudged her with the toe of his boot.

'And what might I ask are you doing here?'

She started, and looked up at him. 'Nothing! Nothing at all.'

'Well, well, well!' A slow smile spread across his face. 'If it isn't the little girl from the *Jenny Wren* who can read and write.'

It was Harry Allen. She wondered what he was doing here. Surely the office was shut. She attempted to get to her feet. 'Let me give you a hand, me dear,' he said, his smile sliding across his face. Slipping his hands beneath her armpits, he lifted her to her feet.

'You alone, me dear?' he asked.

She nodded. Her head ached and she felt incredibly tired.

Like a rag doll, she flopped against him.

'Well, well,' he said. 'What's been happening to you?'

'I was hiding.' Her voice was muffled against his jacket. He slid his hand beneath her chin. His fingers gently touched the bruise on her cheek, the result of a slap she'd received days ago.

'I take it your father did that?'

She said nothing.

'Answer me, girl. Why did he hit you?'

'I threw hot tea over him,' she said in a cracked, low voice. She couldn't remember the real reason it had happened. The event with the teapot was more recent and seemed as good a reason as any.

He seemed amused. 'I bet that pleased him.' He smiled and shook his head. 'But trust Harry, my pretty young Beth. He'll kiss it better for you.'

He kissed her forehead. It felt good. She remembered how good he'd made her feel earlier that day.

'How about having a cup of tea with old Harry here and telling him all about it. What say you?'

He didn't wait for an answer, but cupped her elbow in his palm and led her past the warehouses and the silent machinery. Eventually they entered the office where she'd been earlier. She went willingly.

It was very dark, much darker than during the day. The only light came from a gas flame in a lantern outside.

'Does your father beat you often?' Harry asked as he closed the creaking door.

'I don't want to talk about it.'

Harry moved between her and the light, his shadow covering her like a black cloak. 'Hitting a lovely little girl like you, a girl who can read and write.'

She took steps back until she was sat on the very edge of the desk. He pinned her arms to her sides. His lips were hot and wet on her mouth. She wriggled but her efforts only seemed to make him more determined that her body should stay tightly up against his.

'Please let me go,' she managed to say between kisses.

'Now listen to old Harry,' he said, his breath wet and warm against her ear. 'Do exactly as he says, and in no time at all you'll feel better. You'll feel really good, mark my words.'

She tried to scream but only managed a whimper.

His hands clawed at her clothes. His fingers found her breasts.

She pushed at his chest with the flats of her hands. He snatched at her waist, jerking her belly towards him so that her head snapped backwards. His hand groped beneath her skirt, between her legs.

'Please. You can't do this! I'm getting married!'

'Then you'll be ripe and ready for it!'

His smell, a mix of tobacco, damp wool and male sweat, made her feel sick.

He groped beneath her underwear.

'No!'

Her cry was drowned against the dampness of his clothes. She pummelled his shoulders.

He laughed. 'I love a woman with spirit! It adds spice!'

She was helpless. As he did what he did and the pain flooded over her, she kept her eyes closed and pretended she wasn't there. Eventually it would be over; she wouldn't always be in this room. Time would pass and she would be in another place.

At last he pushed her away. As with that morning, his tone shifted from smooth to sharp.

'Go on. Get out of here. I've got important business to attend to. Get on back to your boat.' He grabbed her suddenly. 'But say nothing. Right! Or it'll be the worse for you and your damned father!'

He pushed her out of the door.

Sobbing, she tried to re-wrap her clothes around herself as she ran along the quay. There was an aching in her belly and stickiness between her legs. She knew she was bleeding and badly wanted to wash the blood and the smell of Harry Allen from her body. She'd heard of other girls ruined by men's promises. Some had thrown themselves into a lock when the waters were rising and boats were banging against each other. She'd wondered at their bravery, their despair. Tonight she understood exactly how they'd felt.

At a dark turn between warehouses, she came to a small inlet of water, a remnant of a narrow canal no longer used. She vaguely remembered that it ran towards Stroud and Nailsworth between lines of thorn and weeping willow. So pretty it used to be, not dank and dark like it was now.

Gripping her stomach, she stood so that the toes of her boots hung over the edge of the wharf. Through bleary eyes she looked down at the dark water. It looked so far off, yet so cool, so clean.

To her right, she heard drunken shouts mixed with loud singing. Off to her left and out of earshot, a number of narrowboats were moored, their small windows throwing patches of amber light on to the quay.

Her eyes returned to the water. Could she do it? How deep was it, and would she go under and not come up? Somehow it didn't seem to matter. All she could think of was what her father would say if he should find out.

Bracing herself, she stood up straight and closed her eyes.

One deep breath, a sudden jump and that was it.

On impact, she caused a splash. At first it washed over her, but once she'd found her footing it reached only to her chest. She was wet through, her hair sticking to her head and around her face. She gasped with a mix of joy and relief. She was alive.

After she got out, she didn't know how long she walked or where. Everything was a blur. Time and place melted into nothingness.

Silence surrounded her. Just at that moment, when she allowed her mind to drift and her caution to lessen, she heard a sound, then a series of sounds getting louder and louder.

She froze. Was Harry Allen following her? No. He'd said he had important business.

At first it was like the clattering of lightweight horses on cobbles. But what would horses be doing out at this time of night?

Boots! She was hearing boots, the sound of men running. Angry shouts rose above the pounding of hobnails on cobbles.

Heart racing, she melted beneath the shadow of a wooden

staircase. Dark silhouettes followed by flesh-and-blood figures fell round the corner from the direction of the town. The first looked to be running for his life. His cap had fallen off. Gaslight lit his face and the fear in his eyes.

Men in dark clothes with grim faces and heavy boots came running behind. Long sticks in raised hands waved menacingly towards the night sky. Her teeth would have chattered if she hadn't clenched them so tightly. A flickering gaslight hanging on a warehouse wall emphasised evil masks intent on violence.

The man they were chasing fell to the ground. Black water and cinders flew upwards, raining like hail against the warehouse, the handcarts and the bits of idle machinery.

'Got him! Don't let him get away.' The voice was coarse and brutal.

'Let 'im 'ave it!'

There was a whistling sound as the staves flew through the air above the dark figures. Heavy wood thudded against brittle bones. The man on the ground curled up into a tight ball.

Blow, after blow, after blow!

She covered her ears with her hands and squeezed her eyes tightly shut.

'Please, God,' she prayed softly, 'help him. Don't let him die.'

The heap of men was like a great dark monster with many arms and many backs, moving, raising sticks, beating, bending over the dark bundle that lay on the ground.

'That's enough, lads. He's learned his lesson.'

Beth froze. The voice came from somewhere in the darkness. Harry Allen!

'That'll teach him to stir up them that don't know any better!'

The staves halted in mid-air. The bundle on the ground did not move. The rough crew turned to where Harry Allen's voice had come from, a patch of darkness just beyond the halo thrown by the gaslight.

Fearful lest he should see her, she sank deeper into the shadows.

'Here's your money,' said the voice.

Coins tinkled like bells as they spun and bounced among the cinders and broken cobbles.

'Shall we chuck him in the canal?' asked one of those who had done the beating.

'Why not?' said another. ''E can swim or 'e can sink!' Another laughed.

'No,' said the voice. 'Leave him there. Go and get yourselves some drink or whatever's your fancy. You've worked well enough today.'

With murmurs and low laughter, the brutes grovelled on the ground, staves thrown to one side as fat fingers probed among the dirt and grime until every piece of silver was accounted for. Some patted each other on the back and laughed as they made their way back up the slope to the double gates that separated the canal and warehouses from the rest of the world. One man lingered and looked down at their handiwork.

'This is just for you, Anthony Wesley,' he said, his grin like a scar across his face.

The man on the ground groaned as a heavy boot divided his ribs.

Beth shoved her hand into her mouth. She felt bile rising from her stomach but now was not the time for making a sound.

Once she could only hear the sound of her own breathing Beth stepped out of the shadows. She looked down at the man they'd called Anthony Wesley. Was he dead? She couldn't be sure. Bending down she touched his face. It was sticky with blood. Cinders and dirt were caked in his hair.

'Are you alive?' She said it softly, endearingly. 'Please, God,' she said closing her eyes and raising her face to the stars. 'Please let him be alive.'

Her heart jumped as a sudden sound made her look towards the darkness beyond the pool of light thrown by the flickering gas. She saw nothing. Just rats, she thought. Just rats and they were certainly less dangerous than the men who had done this.

The man on the ground groaned and tried to move.

'Wait,' she said and felt stupid for saying so. After all, the poor man was in agony and hardly likely to hear her or to run away. But all the same, she had to say something. 'Wait. I'll get help.'

4

Hitching up her skirt, she ran like the wind back to *Jenny Wren*. Mud flicked up from her heavy boots, but she gave it no mind.

In the distance her father's angular frame leaned on the tiller. He was talking to her brother. A familiar figure stood with them.

Elliot! Elliot was here! 'Elliot! Dah!'

Her father turned towards her. 'Back, are ye! Like the bad penny, you always turn up!'

Elliot looked puzzled. 'What's up, girl?'

On hearing the commotion, her mother's head bobbed out from the cabin below.

'A man,' Beth gasped, her chest heaving with racing breath. 'He's back there.' She pointed behind her. 'A group of men beat him with sticks.'

Her father's dark eyebrows met above his nose. "Tis none of our business. Get inside, woman!' He reached out to grab her.

'He's hurt! We have to help him. Elliot?'

Her fiancé looked as though he was trying to come to some kind of decision.

'All right. Who is this man?'

'They called him Anthony Wesley.'

'The union man!'

The men exchanged looks of alarm. Suddenly they were all action.

'Stay here,' her father said, pushing her aside.

'But you don't know where he is.' Without waiting for any response, Beth turned and began to run.

Elliot, her father and brother were running too and although they were strong and their legs were long, they did not overtake her.

'Around here,' she shouted. Elliot was right beside her. 'That's him,' she said, breathless. 'I don't think he's dead.'

'That's Anthony Wesley all right,' said Elliot as they knelt beside the beaten form. 'He isn't dead.' He shook Wesley's shoulder but only gently. 'Wesley?'

The man on the ground groaned.

'We've got to get him to *Jenny Wren*,' Beth blurted. 'Ma will know what to do. She'll take care of him.'

Elliot frowned at her. 'What were you doing out and about, anyway?'

The truth flashed through her mind. Harry Allen. Her blood pulsed with shame. No one would know. She adopted a confident air.

'Well, there you are,' she said cockily, determined to keep what had happened a secret. 'It pays for a woman to do what she wants now and again, doesn't it!'

He frowned. 'Not once she's married. Just bear that in mind.'

She told herself he didn't mean it. She'd known him a long time.

'So what now?' muttered her father.

The sound of whistling preceded Robbie's arrival. He looked to each of them in turn and then to the man on the ground. 'What's going on? Who's he?'

Elliot explained the basics, then went on to fill in a few details. It was well known that Elliot had had more to do with the union than the rest of them.

'These thugs were hired by the carriers. Just goes to show that Anthony here was certainly really putting the wind up Mr Gatehouse. We've got to get in touch with his people. They were meeting down at the George.' He pushed at the peak of his cap. 'Someone had better go and find someone to collect him.'

'I'll go,' said Robbie. Without waiting for agreement, he was off, kicking up stones from the heels of his boots.

Elliot addressed her father. 'Look, I'd have him on *Agincourt* but I'm off up to Worcester within the hour. Can your missus do something for him until his people come?'

Beth's father slid his cap back on his head, spat to one side then nodded. 'We'll get him sorted.'

Supported between the two men, Anthony Wesley was carried back to the boat. Beth walked behind. In a strange way, she was glad this was happening, though sorry for the man it had happened to. But at least it had taken her mind off Harry Allen and what had happened to her – except that he'd been there. Two alarming incidents and Harry Allen was responsible for both. She shivered. She couldn't tell anyone.

Between them, her father and Elliot manhandled Anthony Wesley on to the boat.

'Beth!' Elliot disembarked and caught her arm before she climbed aboard.

He saw her eyes follow Anthony until he was out of sight. 'He'll be all right once he's fixed up. I'll be seeing you when I gets back from Worcester, then.'

She started as though she'd been daydreaming. 'Yes. Of course you will.'

'And we'll post the banns. Won't be long now.' He said it gruffly, matter-of-factly; Elliot had never been one for sweet talk.

She looked up at him, her face shiny in the moonlight. 'No. Not long.'

Quick as a flash, he planted a kiss on her cheek. She gasped and stepped back. He frowned. 'It was only a kiss.'

She smiled. 'You surprised me. But I liked it.'

He nodded. 'Good.'

Beth watched him go and although she could not describe what she felt as being in love, she did feel something.

Once he was out of sight, she climbed over the side of the boat and down into the cabin. Wall-mounted oil lamps glazed the wooden walls with a honey-coloured glow. Her mother was pouring hot water into an enamel bowl perched on a ledge beside the range.

Anthony Wesley lay on the floor with a patchwork quilt over him.

'We couldn't get him into the bed,' her mother said by way of explanation. The bed lay beam-on but was half obscured by cupboards on both sides and a curtain hanging from the space in between.

Wedging herself between the man and a side seat that doubled as a cupboard, she studied the rugged face, the strong chin and the dark hair that fell into soft waves around his temples. Tentatively, just in case he should jerk with pain, she touched a raw spot on his cheek. A muscle quivered in his jaw but he did not stir.

'He's very brave,' she whispered.

Her mother sighed. 'Some men are. Most just think they are. But there... Let's get on with it. You lift him and I'll take his jacket and waistcoat off.'

Heavy as he was, Beth wrapped both arms around his torso. It was a struggle to raise him from the floor. Her father had the strength to do the job better, but there was only room for two to kneel in the tiny cabin. Besides, this was women's work. He'd left them to it and gone for a smoke.

Hands turning pink from warm water, they bathed his wounds. Beth unbuttoned his shirt and rolled up his vest. She paused before attempting to pull both off over his head, staring at his body, its attraction enhanced by the smell of the shirt she held against her chest. She sensed her mother looking at her questioningly. Their eyes met.

'I've never seen such a smooth chest before,' said Beth. 'Dad's hairy. So's our Robert. Like apes if you think about it.'

'Keep your voice down. Your father wouldn't like being called a monkey.'

They giggled. When it was just the two of them, the cabin of the Jenny Wren was a warm, happy place. When her father was there... it was a different matter.

It was hard not to stare at him as she bathed his chest. At the same time she breathed in his smell. There was no hint of stale sweat that one almost got used to in the close confines of a narrowboat. It was pure maleness, fresh and enticing.

'I'll get more water,' said her mother.

Left alone, Beth touched the sore spots on his ribs where dark bruises were forming. His flesh shivered in response. His ribs needed to be bandaged. She reached for the long strips that had been torn from an old sheet.

His eyes suddenly flickered open. 'Where...?' He stared as he said it quickly then shut them again.

Beth leaned closer, gazing into his face. Soon he would regain consciousness, but not yet.

Holding him in a close embrace, she ran the ripped-up cloth behind his back, taking it beneath him from the left side and bringing it out from the right.

He opened his eyes just as both her arms embraced him. 'Where...? Who...?'

Very gently, she pressed her hand against his shoulder. 'Lie still,' she ordered. 'You've been injured.'

A pained smile slowly creased his lips. 'Am I in heaven?'

'What makes you think that?'

'I thought you were an angel.'

She shook her head and flushed because she was still holding him in that close embrace. 'I don't have any wings. How can I be an angel? And what with these boots...' she said and flushed again as the smile came to his face.

He chuckled and began to cough and splutter. A worrying gurgling sound came from his chest. Acting swiftly, she heaved him higher and hugged him closer.

'That's nice,' he said between splutters.

'Less of your sauce.' She reached for the bowl of water. 'Spit in here,' she ordered.

His head rolled slightly but a wicked smile played weakly around his lips. 'I'd prefer to kiss you.'

His bravado was short-lived. Retching and spluttering he leaned over and spat a mix of phlegm and blood into the warm water. The effort drained him.

'Save the kisses and get to sleep,' said Beth.

'Yes, my angel.'

His eyes fluttered and closed then opened again. 'Will you hold my hand, angel? Only until I fall asleep. Perchance to dream,' he added softly.

She slipped her fingers around his and looked down at his

hand. Despite it looking so strong, it seemed weak lying there in hers as though the bones had fallen on to the floor without her having noticed.

'Stay with me,' he said with a sudden flickering of eyelids. 'Even if I die, stay with me.'

Whilst his eyes fluttered, she sat watching him. Once they were closed, she reached for the book she had been reading between chores. It was a ragged thing, newly acquired from some Salvation Army handout and was called *One Thousand and One Arabian Nights*. It was about a queen who told stories in order that her new husband would be too enthralled to execute her.

Once she'd decided she could do no more, her mother took her own pipe to smoke out in the cockpit.

'I'll keep an eye on him whilst I read,' Beth called after her.

Absorbed in the wonders of Arabia, she did not realise for a while that Anthony Wesley was staring at her.

'You're reading.' He sounded surprised. Reminded of Harry Allen's attitude, she looked at him with as much disdain as she could.

'I read quite a lot. Not just books. I read newspapers aloud to people who can't. And when I can, I teach the little ones to write their names. Us boat people are not all illiterate, you know.'

'I'm sorry. I didn't mean to offend you. Folk must appreciate you reading to them.'

'They do. The grown-ups like being read to and the children like to learn.'

'But they don't go to school too often. Is that right?'

She shrugged. 'They're lucky to get any schooling at all. None of us are in one place long enough. My mother taught me. She came from the town.'

'Was she a teacher?'

She shook her head. 'She would have liked to have been. So would I.'

Her thoughts drifted.

'A penny for them,' said Anthony.

'Hmm?'

'Your thoughts... your dreams too. I'll give you a penny for them.'

She laughed, the most joyous sound she'd made all day.

Would it matter if I told him my dream? 'I haven't even told Elliot my dream.'

'Who's Elliot?'

'The man I'm going to marry. I'm not sure he'd approve of it. He might think it's stupid and that I should concentrate on being a wife.'

'Then tell me what it is – only if you want to, that is...'

Suddenly the words were pouring out. 'I would like a little house at the side of the canal with a room where I could teach children to read and write.'

He didn't say anything. She looked down at her hands.

'That's a wonderful dream.'

'I think so.'

'I used to read a lot when I was at sea,' he said. 'Miles and miles of endless ocean with no land and no loved ones. So I read and I read, and I read. I used to buy second-hand books in every port I visited. In Montevideo I bought the complete works of William Shakespeare for two shillings. The shop owner looked relieved to get rid of them.' Anthony chuckled again. 'Mind you, he was really taken back. He'd never met a merchant seaman who could read, let alone appreciate the works of Shakespeare!'

'I've never read Shakespeare,' she said, and felt ashamed for admitting it.

'You'd love it,' he said, his voice dreamy, his eyes thoughtful. 'Beautiful words, timeless stories of lovers, liars, scoundrels and saints.' Then he raised one hand and ran his finger gently down her cheek. 'And fairy queens who fall asleep in enchanted groves and wake up to find they have loved those who do not deserve it.' Then he recited a piece about wild thyme.

The touch, the look, the silence hung between them for a moment. Was it her imagination or had her heart stopped beating for one tiny instant? She felt her face reddening for fear she might have been mistaken or that he might be playing games.

Suddenly flustered by his presence, she pushed him back down. 'You'd better sleep now,' she said bossily, embarrassed by the effect he was having on her.

'Yes, my angel,' he said, his voice fading to a hushed breath, his eyes closing and his head falling to one side. 'Anything at all as long as you stay by my side.'

Even though she'd bidden him sleep, she found herself hating it when he closed his eyes. They were so blue, so attractive, and she liked gazing into them as he talked to her.

The book resting on her lap, she sat staring into his face, saving his features to memory and thinking about the texture of his voice. No one had ever spoken to her with such a voice and in such a manner, taking her far away with sweet words alone.

Although she willed him to, he didn't look up at her. His eyes stayed closed and he seemed so still, so silent. Suddenly she felt panicked. Was he paler than he had been?

'Are you all right?' She shook him gently. There was no response. *I'm not panicking*, she told herself, then accused herself of lying. She shook him. He just lay there, still and silent. She told herself it was anger stinging her eyes.

'I've taken too much trouble for you to go and die on me,' she said petulantly. 'You should damn well make sure you get better. Dying would be downright ungrateful!'

Still he lay there, without a muscle stirring, without the slightest sign that he had heard her.

She leaned closer, her ear next to his mouth. His breathing seemed so shallow. But suddenly she detected a gurgling from deep in his lungs.

Alive!

She sighed with relief and patted him gently. 'That's it. Sleep now and don't give me any more bother.'

Because his hand was very large, she wrapped both of hers around it and held it tightly to her warm, soft bosom. Suddenly his eyes flashed open.

'You'd be good running a little school somewhere,' he said. 'Or better still, take the schooling to them. Get a boat and follow where they go. Go to the quiet places where you can hear the birds and smell the clover.'

Enthralled by what he was saying, she was hardly aware that her mother was peering down through the hatch immediately above them until she spoke.

'His woman's coming for him,' she whispered.

Anthony raised himself up on his elbows. 'If it's Abbie, tell her it's about damned time.'

There was a sudden dryness in Beth's throat. 'I need some air,' she said, got up and went outside.

The tyres of Abigail Gatehouse's Austin Seven squealed as she came to a halt beside the Jenny Wren. Slamming the car door behind her, she marched along like a clockwork soldier about to play at battle.

'Are you Dawson?' she said, addressing Beth's father.

'Yes.' He eyed her with undisguised disapproval. 'Well, that's something. Where is he?'

She was wearing a tweed jacket, brown jodhpurs, a matching hat and very shiny boots. There was something formidable about her, as though she was about to take on the world single-handed. Beth had already persuaded herself to be impolite to this woman. She'd imagined someone pretty in pastel pink, not the sort of woman who ran Girl Guide troops or physical education in public schools.

'Who do you think you're talking to?'

'You, my good man. Who are you?'

'Daniel Dawson!' he said firmly, as though he was laying one brick on top of another.

'Then I might as well speak to you, Daniel Dawson. Don't feel too privileged; the fact is I'll speak to anyone who's likely to answer. I've come to collect Anthony Wesley.'

'Have you now!'

Abigail Gatehouse was not a fool. She sensed hostility, especially when it was written all over a man's face. This man would not make a friend. Instead she addressed the dark-haired woman in the green skirt.

'Hi there, bright eyes. Am I at the right boat?'

Beth nodded. 'He's here and he's alive – just.'

A voice came from the cabin. 'Is that Abbie's sweet tones I can hear?'

The upper torso of Anthony Wesley appeared at the tiny door, his chest now wreathed in bandages and his jacket thrown over his shoulders.

Abigail winced. 'My! You have been in the wars!'

He grinned. 'I'm not too bad, thanks to Beth, my guardian angel.'

The way he looked at the dark-haired girl grated, but Abbie knew better than to protest. She'd abandoned him back at the George. There were bridges to rebuild.

All the same, she couldn't help being brusque. 'Fine. You're good people. All of you.'

She saw the animosity in the men's eyes as Anthony climbed off the boat. They didn't like being ordered about by women. Women should be meek and mild, she thought, her eyes landing on the dark-haired girl with the surprisingly blue eyes.

Beth was looking at him in a way that alarmed her. What, she wondered, was in her mind?

The moment Anthony was sitting in the front passenger seat, Abigail went on the offensive. 'Pretty little thing, that girl who looked after you.'

Anthony looked out of the window at the passing scene and saw his own reflection grinning back at him.

'I owe her a great debt of gratitude. She saved me.' She felt his eyes studying her face and knew what he was really saying.

'I'm sorry, Anthony. I don't know what came over me.' She brought the car jolting to a halt. 'I apologise.' Resting her forehead on the steering wheel, she burst into tears. 'I'm sorry. So sorry.'

He shook his head. 'You were frightened. It's understandable, but never mind. We have to put this behind us. Your father must be about to declare the tonnage cuts. There must be figures to prove this. It's your job to find them.'

She sniffed and dabbed at her eyes. 'I'll do my best.'

He put his arm around her and gave her a hug. 'Come on, old thing. No need for that. You're still my favourite girl, you know.'

She smiled through her tears. She liked it when he talked to her like that, as though they were more than colleagues. One day she hoped they would be. In the meantime her confidence was restored.

She started the engine and they rolled away.

He closed his eyes and leaned his head against the window. Tired out, he was asleep in minutes. Abbie eyed him sidelong between peering through the rain and the windscreen wipers. In his sleep he smiled and her heart leapt with joy. She reached across and touched his face.

'My angel,' he said.

She snatched her hand away and her heart filled with jealousy.

5

Hands stuffed deep in the pockets of her tweed trousers, Abbie marched up the steps leading into the offices of Arthur Albert Gatehouse, Canal Carriers.

Her brain was buzzing with a well-rehearsed lie. Could she carry it off? She wasn't sure. Her stomach felt as though she'd swallowed a brick. But it mustn't show. She adopted a happy face.

A quick knock, a deep breath and she entered the decidedly masculine surroundings. Shelves full of ledgers, books and files almost obliterated the dark green walls. The curtains did the same to the windows.

The fractured leather of her father's chair creaked as he looked up. A pile of papers and a brass inkstand sat in front of him. A dozen pieces of paper fluttered on a metal spike to his left.

Penmore, his trusty office manager, stood at his shoulder. His fingers were stained with ink, his shirtsleeves dulled by resting his arms on sheets of carbon paper. Abigail addressed him first. She knew her presence unnerved him and she badly wanted him to leave.

'Penmore! Are you still office manager? I thought you were dead!'

'Now, now, Abigail,' said her father with a warning look. Penmore sniffed. She sensed he trembled – with rage? Distaste? She decided on the latter.

He kept his dented nose pointing towards the papers and muttered a greeting. 'Good morning, Miss Gatehouse.'

Abbie sighed. 'How would you know if it were a good morning, Penmore? You're dead. You've been dead for years.'

'This won't do, Abigail.' Her father eased himself back in his chair without putting down his pen. 'Be a good little girl and leave Mr Penmore alone. He's a useful fellow, after all.'

She wanted to say, *I understand, Father. He's useful. Just like a dog, he does exactly as you tell him.* But that might jeopardise her mission. 'Father, I want to talk to you.'

His eyes dropped to the paperwork. 'You can talk to me.'

'Alone.'

'Penmore is my man. Whatever you want to say, you can say in front of him. I trust him implicitly.'

'It's a family matter.'

'Is it now.' He took his pocket watch from his waistcoat, checked it then put it away. 'I have an appointment. I can let you have five minutes. That's all,' he said without looking at her, his gaze fixed on the piece of paper he held as if it was a target and he was adjusting his aim.

Abbie rested her hands on his desk and leaned closer until she could look straight into his eyes and smell the hint of whisky on his breath and cheap perfume on his shirt collar. Did her mother never notice any of it?

'I was down at the wharf yesterday.'

His face clouded and the loose cheeks began to burn red. 'No daughter of mine should be frequenting such places, and what's more, I know the people you frequent with.'

She frowned. 'How do you know? Do you have me followed?'

A secretive look passed between him and Penmore. Abbie nodded. 'I thought so. Do I worry you that much, Father?'

He looked her up and down. 'No. You embarrass me. Look at you. Call yourself a woman?' He held up a warning finger. 'Tread carefully, my girl. At times I wonder you're not heading towards madness.'

She remembered the aunt who had been sent to the asylum simply for falling in love with the wrong man. Fear prickled at the nape of her neck but she recovered her confidence. She had to get him out of the office whilst the papers were still here. She knew his habits, knew that important papers only lingered a while in his desk before being stored in the safe.

She glanced at Penmore and back to her father before deciding to continue.

'You're quite right. I mix with the wrong people. Just like Caroline did. And they trust me. That's why they tell me things that neither you nor that spy of yours is ever likely to be told. I hear things – like the whereabouts of a well-brought-up young lady who ran off with an unsuitable man.'

Her father's face drained of colour and the pen fell to the desk.

He was hooked! Deliberately turning her back on him, she folded her arms across her chest and walked to the window. That should annoy him!

'Are you trying to tell me you've heard something about my daughter?'

Abigail tensed. It was as if she'd been stabbed in the heart. *My daughter*, he'd said, as though he'd had only one, as though she didn't really exist.

'Well?' He got to his feet, his eyes like rivets pinning her to the wall.

She took her time. He was in her power, in her thrall. The delicious part about it was that he would fall on this bone of knowledge and suck it dry because he wanted to believe he would find Caroline again.

She took her cigarette case from her pocket, flicked at the silver lid and took out an ebony holder and a cigarette. She took her time lighting it, relishing the impatience that he tried, unsuccessfully, to hide beneath his anger.

'If I get my hands on that man, I'll make sure he pays for the pain he's caused me for the rest of his life, I swear to God I will!'

She smiled, slipped one hand in her trouser pocket and with leisurely ease, blew smoke rings up into the air.

She walked close to her father, so close that the residue of cheap perfume on his jacket made her feel sick. There was a cut-glass ashtray on his desk. She purposely avoided it and let a measure of ash from her cigarette fall on to the highly polished floor.

'I met a man,' she said carefully, watchful for his reactions. 'He thought he'd seen someone answering Caroline's description. In fact, he was sure he had.'

His knuckles rested on the desk.

'Yes,' she went on as a description of the imaginary man fermented in her brain. 'He assured me he had seen her at Brentford hanging around the Grand Union depot. Told me he got into conversation with her and she told him she was off to the railway station to take a train to the West Country, to Dartmouth, I believe.'

'Dartmouth? Why Dartmouth?' Her father's eyes shone with false hope.

'She told him she had an acquaintance there. A military gentleman.' She lied and enjoyed doing it.

'Who was this man? Not the collier, surely?' His voice trembled with anger.

Although she felt a sense of triumph, the life-long feeling of being second best resurfaced. How could he have loved her sister so much more than her? Wasn't she cleverer than Caroline?

'Father!' She leaned across the desk. 'Perhaps I shouldn't have told you. Perhaps you should take a breather and leave the office to Penmore this morning.'

For a moment he seemed incapable of speech. His eyes flickered as though thoughts she could not possibly understand crossed his mind.

'Perhaps I should go down and see this man again, in case I've got the facts all wrong.' She made as if to move, to walk as briskly out as she had briskly walked in.

'Stay where you are!' The deep bass of his voice echoed around the shelves and green walls.

Abigail stopped and stood looking out at the street, the canal and the viaduct beyond where a plume of white steam rose from a passing train.

'And this man's name?'

'I think it was foreign.'

'I don't care if it was bloody Zulu. Tell me his name.'

'It wasn't Zulu. I'm pretty sure of that.'

'Tell me!'

She closed her eyes and swallowed quickly as she fought for the name she had made up earlier.

'Romanov,' she said resolutely as though the name and the man really existed. 'His name's Peter Romanov.'

'That's Russian!' he exclaimed. 'Is he one of those bloody

Bolsheviks over here to cause trouble for this country the same as he's done in his own?'

'He might be,' she replied quickly. 'He's something to do with some foreign church down on Brentford Wharf. You know how many Bible-bashers frequent the wharves. The boat people must get fed up with them. Perhaps this man Romanov was brought in to intrigue them. He certainly has a way about him.'

The man really did exist. She'd read about him in some literature sent over by comrades in the new Russian regime. Had her scheme worked?

'Well!' The sound of her father tapping his top hat on his head followed his exclamation. 'I certainly know how to deal with the likes of him! Religion or politics, it's all the same when it comes to stirring up trouble.' He growled low and angrily to himself. He opened the office door and shouted. 'Boy! Get me a cab!'

Abbie turned to the window. A train rumbled on the rails on the viaduct opposite. The loud blowing of a horn and the rumble of an engine diverted her attention as a motor lorry stopped outside a warehouse opposite and began to offload. By the time her gaze went back to the viaduct, the train had gone. Only the lorry remained.

Her father paused before leaving the office. 'Do you know,' he said, more softly, 'I worry about your sanity, but your concern for your sister convinces me that your behaviour is a reaction to her disappearance. It has unbalanced your mind slightly, but all will be well once she is found.'

He came close. She smelt his breath and again experienced that pang of regret that he did not love her as he had loved, and still loved, her sister.

'At first I thought you had something to do with it. Was it you that persuaded her to leave? Was it, Abbie?'

Although she did her best to hide her true feelings, her words were bitterly spoken. 'You were not the only one who loved her. I loved her too. Why would I drive away someone I loved?'

'No. No. I suppose not,' he said sadly.

He made a point of locking his desk before leaving.

'Are you expecting thieves?' she asked.

'Penmore suggested I lock my desk. Good idea, don't you think?'

No! No, it was not, but she kissed him dutifully, smiled and said nothing.

'Are you going home now?'

'Shopping,' she said as though it was the truth. He shrugged. She doubted he'd noticed.

She stood watching him go. His cane tap-tapped along the cold tiles towards the double doors, he shouted something to Penmore then he was gone. She watched as he crossed the road to where the arches ranged beneath the grey stone of the railway bridge.

A cab stood waiting, its polished headlights gleaming in the dullness of day. A sudden gust of wind made him clutch at his hat and turn up his collar until only his red-veined cheeks showed between the two. Then he was in the cab and gone.

She knew he wouldn't only be going to instruct Harry Allen to make enquiries. She had timed her visit well. Wednesday and Friday mornings he visited a certain lady who lived in a house with white-painted window frames and roses growing around the door. The roses climbed profusely over a trellis that listed slightly to one side, in severe danger of collapsing under the weight of blushing pink blooms. She'd followed him there once; that's how she knew.

Her thoughts returned to Caroline. She smiled to herself as she remembered the secrets they'd kept as children together. Running away was one they had not shared. Even as a child, her sister had expressed a longing to leave home. She closed her eyes. Long-ago summers.

It had become a habit on warm summer days for the children to play croquet and the adults to sit drinking something clear and strong that was poured from a decanter. At her father's specific suggestion, the adults had joined in the children's game of hide and seek. With cries of laughter, girls and women in snowy white organza had run across the lawn and hid in the shrubbery, the greenhouse or the far end of the conservatory where the plants had big leaves and threw pan-size shadows. It was here that she had found her sister sitting underneath a particularly large palm, a huge leaf of which rested on her head. In turn her chin was resting on her arms, and they were resting on her bent knees. It was plain to see she'd been crying.

'I'm going to leave home as soon as I can.'

Abigail laughed. 'Why would you want to leave? It's me who should be thinking like that.'

'I want to leave because…' She paused and covered her head with her hands as though afraid she was about to divulge a secret too dreadful to speak of.

Abigail persisted. 'Because of what?'

'Because I don't want to stay here. I don't want to be treated like this any more.'

Abigail could still feel that confusion she'd felt then.

'I don't want to be with father!'

Abigail hadn't time to question the statement. Two boys who lived in the solid stone residence opposite came crashing into the conservatory, their boots skidding as they slid to a halt.

'Caught you!' they shouted.

When Abigail tried sometime later to ask Caroline what she had meant, she merely laughed it away. 'I was just being silly,' she said. 'I should never have said anything.' But the look on her face said otherwise.

Once she had the office to herself, she tried the desk drawer. It was locked and wouldn't budge. Her father had taken the keys, but there were others and she knew where they were kept.

She made her way quietly down the corridor to the batch of cupboards clustered at the back of the building. The cupboard in which spare keys were kept smelt of mothballs and mice. The spare set she wanted was not there. She shut it quietly and muttered a vulgar oath under her breath.

'Can I help you, Miss Abigail?' Penmore! Damn!

Whatever you do, don't look guilty. She straightened and shoved her hands in her pockets before speaking. The only thing she couldn't do was smile. Penmore brought out the worst in her.

'The desk drawer is locked and I appear to have left my own set of keys at home. Do you have a spare?'

She saw the hint of suspicion in his eyes. If she had been made of lesser stuff, she might have crumbled and admitted she didn't have a set of keys.

'Well, man! Have you or haven't you?'

'Miss Abigail. You are not allowed access.' He fumbled in his pockets as he said it.

She lowered her gaze. 'Have you got an itch in a very difficult spot, Penmore? Go on. Give it a scratch. I'm broad-minded.'

At first he reddened. Once he had collected himself – and taken his hands out of his pockets – he rallied enough to repeat what he'd already said.

'You're not allowed access. I'm only repeating your father's instructions.'

'I beg your pardon!'

She adopted her mother's favourite words and favourite stance – hands on hips, head held high. It was the servants who bore the brunt of her attitudes. When her father was within earshot, she was a mere watercolour to the vibrant portrait she presented to some unlucky servant.

Penmore was made of sterner stuff. 'I have to adhere to your father's orders. You are not allowed keys,' he said with tongue-slapping relish.

She pretended to leave the building, the heavy brown doors swinging behind her. She waited a few minutes, sure that Penmore had watched her leave and breathed a sigh of relief once he was sure she was gone.

Not yet, though, she thought with impish glee.

Ensuring the door opened silently, she went back inside the building, and slid into a recess between a long-case clock and a coat rack. Then she waited.

Penmore came back out through the office door, retrieved a watch from his waistcoat, looked at it then put it away again.

'I'm out back,' he shouted over his shoulder.

Abigail flattened herself further into the recess. His footsteps pattered along the corridor and down the three stairs at the end that led to the yard and the outside privy. A door squeaked on its hinges before slamming shut.

The time had come! After straightening her jacket and adjusting her hat, she marched determinedly into the general office. The eyes of clerks and other underlings glanced up then were swiftly lowered.

Her brightness returned. 'Good morning, chaps!'

With dogged determination she marched swiftly in the direction of her father's secretary, Miss Stansonbrick, then leaned very close as though what she had to say was much too important for the likes of mere clerks. 'I have a secret to share with you.'

A pale flush seeped over a complexion that was rarely exposed to either the kiss of natural sunlight or the assistance of a little powder.

'Miss Abigail,' she said, her voice little above a whisper, 'what can I do for you?'

'I need your help.'

Poor woman. It was so easy to convince her that she had inadvertently locked her mother's birthday present in her father's desk drawer. 'It was a secret, you see,' she said. 'I'm sorry, but I appear to have left my spare key at home. Do you by any chance...'

Yes! Of course she did and, of course, she was so happy to help her out even to the point of standing outside the door to her father's office 'just in case he should return'. Poor Miss Stansonbrick was sworn to secrecy not to reveal that Abigail had forgotten to collect the present and had enlisted her help. Being a meticulous man, Archibald Gatehouse had stored everything she wanted in a buff-coloured folder with *Disbursements* written on the front.

Disbursements! She opened it. There before her was a list of costs incurred – payments to Harry Allen for 'attention to agitators'. Aware that her hands were shaking, Abigail let the papers and the folder they were in slide back into the drawer. And so it starts. So far only Anthony had been beaten. But it wouldn't stop there. Her blood boiled so hotly she expected steam to come from her ears and down her nostrils. What should she do? She needed a copy, but this one would be missed. Now who was likely to have one? Miss Stansonbrick!

Abigail had no wish to see the poor woman lose her job, a position that obviously gave her more status in life than a spinster such as her could ever dream of. And she was so efficient. Her father had said so. And if she was efficient...

A sudden thought came to her. She rummaged in the file again and felt the piece of paper she had just been reading. The front was smooth, best-quality paper. The back, however, rustled as she rubbed her fingers over it. Miss Stansonbrick, efficient as she was, had thoughtfully produced a carbon copy! Moving more quickly now, Abigail retrieved the carbon copy, folded it and shoved it into her pocket. She never carried a handbag. Men didn't so why should she?

'Many thanks,' she whispered passing the keys back to her father's good and faithful servant. 'Now. Not a word to anyone.'

'Not a word! Pleased to oblige,' she said in a hushed whisper.

Then she tapped her lips, her face for once a picture of pleasure. Abigail thanked her again then made for the door. Once she was safely outside, she pushed her hat back further on her head and whistled like a man, although her hips still swayed like a woman.

Penmore saw her leave. She did not see him. 'Bitch,' he muttered.

'Language, Mr Penmore.'

He turned to see Mrs Brown the cleaning woman putting her mops and buckets away in the cupboard under the stairs.

'Bitch,' he said again. 'Treating me like any common servant.'

Mrs Brown eyed him a little ruefully. She viewed single men of his age with something akin to suspicion. After all, it wasn't as though there weren't eligible women waiting for someone to propose. The Great War had seen to that.

Although she was ready to make her way back to the little terraced house she shared with her husband and the crippled son the war had left her with, she lingered and listened.

'I'll take you down a peg,' Penmore muttered quietly, his small eyes glazed behind the thick glass of his spectacles. 'You'll find it ain't all fun and games getting mixed up in working men's business, Miss Abigail Gatehouse!'

6

Catkins were hanging like lambs' tails and wild flowers were bursting into bloom when Beth told her mother about Harry Allen and what he'd done. They were pulling the teats of a cow, one eye on the farm gate in the corner of the field. If the farmer caught them they'd be for it, but likely as not they'd be away before then.

Aware that she was no longer being pulled on, the cow wandered off to join the rest of the herd. Beth continued to kneel on the ground; her mother rubbed at the small of her back as she straightened. She looked older than her forty-five years. Work and worry had done that. She was doubly worried now and Beth felt terribly responsible for it.

'So. Did you bleed this month?'

Beth shook her head. 'And I feel different. I don't know how, but I just do.'

Her mother shook her head slowly and thoughtfully. 'Yer father'll go mad.'

'I didn't encourage him, Ma, honest I didn't.'

Her mother continued to shake her head. 'Not just with you,

but me too. He'll blame me for teaching you to read and letting you run wild.'

Reading and running wild seemed far removed from each other, and rightly so. She'd loved running through water meadows thick with clover, through woods carpeted in bluebells. She also loved reading.

'We'll have to bring the wedding forward,' said her mother. 'We can tell Elliot that the baby's come early when it finally happens. He'll accept that. Men know little about the ways of women. He'll think it's his. But you don't tell him,' her mother added suddenly. 'You know that, don't you?'

Yes, she knew. 'But what if Elliot finds out?'

'Who else knows about it?'

'Just you, Ma.'

'Then it's a trick worth doing. Your babe gets a name, Elliot gets a bride and a ready-made child, and the pair of us escapes yer father's bad temper.'

Beth persuaded herself that her mother was right, but in her heart of hearts she worried about the repercussions.

'Sooner the better,' said Elliot when they met up with him on a stretch of the Gloucester and Worcester Canal. 'The boy that 'elps me is off to Wales to help on his uncle's farm. I'm going to be short-handed.' He grinned at Beth as he said it. 'Could do with an extra pair of hands.'

She knew from experience that he meant what he said. This was no veiled hint of romance. Elliot was nothing if not practical.

'Then we'll shake on it and post the banns,' said her father. The two men shook hands. No one asked her opinion. She was just about to open her mouth and say so but spied a warning look from her mother. It swiftly crossed her mind that one day she wouldn't be around to curb her reactions.

Then what?

'That's that,' they said, and went up top to smoke and talk about the wage situation. Her brother Rob joined them.

'They didn't ask,' she murmured angrily to her mother. 'It's as though I'm a carthorse changing ownership.'

There was a sad look in her mother's eyes. 'Aye. I know how you feel. But it's a woman's lot. Don't you see that? And bearing in mind the other matter.' She threw a telling glance at Beth's stomach. 'It's for the best, me dear girl. For the best.'

Since that night in his office, Beth had tried hard to thrust Harry Allen to the back of her mind. It wasn't easy. A new life was growing inside her, a reminder of what he had done. She also thought of Anthony Wesley and the way he'd looked at her and encouraged her to read. The verse about the wild thyme made her think differently about the countryside through which they passed. No longer was it just an expanse of muddy fields and cows ready for milking. It was something to see with different eyes and hear with a more finely tuned ear.

* * *

On the day the marriage details were agreed, Anthony Wesley turned up again.

There were many chandleries, shops and pubs lining the canals, a chance to stock up on what was needed or desired. Beth pushed open the door of the canal shop that was ordinary on the outside but inside shone like a jewel.

She drank in the smell of Indian hemp, kerosene, leather, freshly baked bread and a stew simmering in a black three-legged pot above an apple-log fire. Metalware, buckets, tin trays, dippers and Buckby cans painted with all manner of castles, roses and birds sat next to boxes of dusty white crockery, the sort produced in profusion in Stoke on Trent. The latter were white merely because they were awaiting the sweep of Ned Wheeler's horsehair brush and pots of paint. Ned had once had his own boat. Now he ran the shop and was a fountain of gossip and news for everyone who plied the canal.

In a floral rainbow, the results of his labour jostled for position from the shelves to the tar-blackened beams of the ceiling where dried thyme, sage and rosemary hung in bunches beside kerosene lamps and bits of bridle.

Ned didn't acknowledge her. He was sitting to one side of the fire where a black kettle continuously puffed a curl of white steam. His unusually fine hands were clasped tightly together and his head was bent close to the man sitting opposite him. His pale face was lined with concentration, his brow so furrowed it was almost impossible to see his eyes. The other man sat with his back to her and had dark hair that curled over his coat collar. 'I need a post box, Ned,' he was saying.

Beth started at the sound of his voice. She saw Ned frown then look away again. The other did not move.

'Use the Royal Mail like everyone else,' said Ned flippantly, and he turned and spat into the fire. She heard it sizzle.

'You know what I mean, Ned. This strike has to be planned properly if it's to succeed. Everyone on the canals has to know what's happening and boats don't have letterboxes!'

Ned was still frowning. At last he sighed and pulled at his fingers until each made a loud crack. 'You mean trouble, Anthony. You always mean trouble.'

'This is a cause, Ned. I'm fighting for people's livelihoods. People's right to a fair wage.'

Beth wanted to applaud.

Ned raised his head and the pale eyes looked across the fireplace to the man sitting opposite. 'What about my livelihood, Anthony?'

'You've broad shoulders, Ned.'

'But only one head!'

'I'll not knowingly put you in any danger, Ned. I'll not have you lose out on our part. All I'm asking is that you pass on dates and times of union meetings and the action itself when and if it ever happens. Putting up posters would help too and reading them out for them that can't read would be even better. What do you say?'

Anthony clasped Ned's shoulder as if he would not let go until he had an answer. Just as Ned opened his mouth to speak, he looked up and saw Beth.

Anthony smiled and got to his feet. 'If it isn't my guardian angel.'

'Me dear!' said Ned. 'What can I get you, me dear? Here. Have a chair. Is yer mother well? And yer father? Yes, he would be. And Rob. Ever the ladies' man that one, why I remember seeing him.'

'I'll do the reading of the posters,' she blurted, her eyes bright with interest. 'You know I can read,' she added, looking directly into Anthony's eyes.

They sparkled, but it was his lips on which she fixed her attention. What would it be like to be kissed by him? The thought made her flush. Why was she thinking like this?

His smile was light with amusement. 'How's the book?'

'Very good.' Her blush lessened.

Ned took his stool with him and set it down just before the ramshackle table that doubled as a counter. Glass jars full of bulls' eyes, liquorice sticks and peppermint rock balanced precariously on its uneven surface. Next to them were boxes of bootlaces, buttonhooks and tins of shoe polish.

Anthony was slow in getting to his feet, perhaps because he wasn't too sure of the ceiling height and whether his head might hit the low beams. He stood over her, his knuckles resting on his waist.

'Well, young Beth, my angel, if everyone were as keen as you this fight would be won.'

'I want to be like Abigail,' she said, remembering the red-haired girl who she'd presumed was Anthony's sweetheart.

He laughed. 'I don't think there's room in this world for two like Abigail.'

Beth looked appalled. 'How can you say that? She's such a kind lady.'

'I didn't mean it like that,' he said, his voice warm and compassionate. 'I only think that you should be satisfied with who you are. You're quite magical, Beth. Quite magical.'

She felt herself blushing, and although it might not be her place to speak out, she felt the need to do so. 'I only thought that I might get involved with some of the union work. That's all.'

She liked the way he smiled, the ends of his mouth seeming to disappear into his cheeks. And he had a dimple in his chin. She'd never noticed that before.

'How about you come to a meeting this evening upstairs at that pub along by the tea warehouse?'

'The Navigator?'

He nodded. 'Will you?'

Would she? Of course she would.

'Over my dead body! You're goin' to no pub!' Daddy Dawson was adamant.

Beth dared to protest. 'But Anthony Wesley invited me. I met him when I went to fetch a loaf of bread from Ned's shop.'

'Unions are for men and so are pubs. Your place is here with the dishes and the duster!' He pointed at her threateningly. 'Now you stay 'ere with yer mother.'

Seeing her mother's worried expression, she turned back to the dishes. Later, once everything was done and put away, she combed her hair, put on her best cardigan and went up top.

'He'll not like it,' said her mother, the permanent frown she'd worn for years creasing her forehead with ruts beyond her years.

'I have to go, Ma, I have to. This isn't just about unions and wages. It's about fairness, and isn't it time us women received fairer treatment?'

Her mother stared at her blankly, then nodded and with a sad expression turned away.

The men were gone and her mother was dozing by the time she got away. The Navigator wasn't far. She was there in minutes.

Stiffening her spine and her resolve, she pushed open the door enough to smell the sweat of men, stale beer and a sawdust floor just on the point of turning rancid.

It was as far as she got. Slam went the door as a hand grabbed her shoulder and she was spun round to face the other way.

'Where the bloody hell do you think you're going?'

She cowered as she turned, half expecting her father with his hand ready to belt her. Instead she was face to face with a set of big arms crossed over a plain black waistcoat.

'Elliot! I weren't expecting you.' She beamed at him, flushing slightly. She hadn't seen him since they'd posted the banns for the wedding. 'Do I get a kiss, then?' she asked tilting her chin and closing her eyes. None came so she opened them again.

Elliot was looking at her in the same all-knowing way as when they were children. 'I asked you what you were up to, girl. Are you goin' to answer me?'

'It was like this, Elliot, I was going to go in and listen to that man.'

'No wife of mine's doing any such thing!'

'I'm not your wife – not yet!'

He looked surprised at her defiance; she'd always been so agreeable. Well, we'll soon sort that out once we're wed, he thought. And now was as good a time as any to put her in her place.

Towering over her, he raised a finger and held it just inches from her nose. 'Men's business, not women's, so you be on yer way and leave men's business to men.'

In the past she would have complied, but somehow she felt different. It was as though a curtain had been drawn back and a little light was filtering in. Was it the child, or was it because Anthony Wesley's words had unlocked something in her mind?

She was infused with a sudden longing to read whatever was

in the political pamphlets that sat on the pub tables. It made her brave, even reckless. 'But I think—'

He interrupted, his eyes narrowed. A nerve throbbed in his cheek just above his clenched jaw. 'It doesn't matter what you think. No wife of mine is going into a pub full of blokes and getting involved in matters that are not her concern. It ain't right. Clear, girl?'

Her first inclination was to repeat that he did not own her, that she was not his wife and wouldn't be if he carried on like this. Thoughts of her mother, the baby and loss of reputation softened her voice. She became cunning. 'I could at least get one of the pamphlets and read what they've got to say. There's plenty there. I can see them on the table.' She smiled sweetly and stroked his arm. 'And I could read them to you if you like.'

She was reminded by the look on his face of the time she had tried to teach him to read. He'd found it difficult, lost patience and torn out the offending pages leaving them fluttering through the fields at the side of the canal.

His jaw hardened. He jerked a thumb over his shoulder. 'Get on back with yer mother.'

Out of necessity, she swallowed her anger, but it was still simmering beneath the surface. How dare he order her around like this! She held off scowling. Arguing would not get her what she wanted. She smiled sweetly though it almost hurt to do it. 'People will listen to you, Elliot, and be more willing to fight if we get a few pamphlets and give them out to folk. If there's going to be trouble, everyone should know about it even if it has to be read out to them. What do you think?'

She saw the square chin soften, the straight line of a mouth relax.

'I've made me mind up that we have to be prepared.' His big hand came to rest on her shoulder. Firmly but gently he eased her out on to the pavement. 'Now get on back and leave this to me.'

'I want to help, Elliot, and I'm not a child.'

He paused and grinned. 'No. I can see that.'

He looked so sure of himself, so confident that it was a man's world and women should know their place.

'I'll see you with the pamphlet later, then,' she said.

'You'll see me when you see me. Go on. Back to your mother,' he said firmly.

With a toss of her dark curls, she walked away, every fibre of her being protesting that this was not what she wanted, that perhaps even Elliot was not quite what she wanted.

Wait until he goes into the pub. Then go back? Was that possible?

She glanced over her shoulder. There he was, standing guard, a dark silhouette against the light glowing through the etched glass of the pub door.

The smell of coke dust, oil and mildew shifted on the breeze replaced by the perfume of wildflowers blown from a distant meadow.

No such smell should have existed here, and yet it did. She became overwhelmed with a great desire to be elsewhere, to be where she wanted to be, not where someone had ordered her to be.

Setting her jaw, she turned away from the direction in which *Jenny Wren* was moored and towards the town. She would not go back to the boat just yet. She would go where she pleased and no one would stop her!

8

Scuffed shirt shoulders rubbed together in the dimly lit bar of the Navigator. Lively eyes in weather-worn, work-hardened faces turned to Anthony Wesley.

He was standing on a chair that rocked when he moved, his presence as firm and strong as his face. His heart thudded with zealous passion as he surveyed the gathering. Though his background was not as theirs, these were his men; their rights were his mission in life.

He brushed a loose wave of dark hair back on to his head and surveyed the gathered men. There was a quickness about his movements that seemed slightly out of place on a man of good height and strong proportions. His voice matched his looks. There was depth to its sound and eloquence in his words.

'Mark ye well why you're here!'

The last rumblings of conversation ceased. He had their attention and it warmed his heart. Abigail passed him a piece of paper. She was dressed in a tweed jacket, brown cord jodhpurs and a black fedora. Those gathered regarded her with critical eyes and even more critical comments.

He waved the paper above his head. 'I have here the proof that wages are to be slashed yet again. At present you have trouble affording butter to put on your bread. Before long you'll be hard pushed to afford bread!'

A murmur of concerned comments coupled with a few blasphemous expletives rolled from one side of the bar to the other. Their faces grizzled by weather and age, the boatmen turned sharp eyes towards him. Some gripped blackened pipes in equally blackened teeth. Most had a look of God-given health about them. But he knew full well that their outdoor lives gave them the look only but not the actuality. Malnutrition kept them lean. He could even smell their poverty, that odd mix of stale sweat, tobacco and well-worn clothes. Their smell he could cope with, along with their deep distrust of anyone who wasn't of their clan. And a clan it was: people who over the years had become closer both by blood and by sweat. They laboured hard. None could know how hard unless they had done the same themselves.

Anthony's voice rang around the hall. 'Negotiation is what we must have. The day will come when this union will be recognised as a responsible body that only wants to make the lives of their members that bit better. We want fairness, not favours.'

'But will we get it?' shouted a small man in a deep baritone.

'Only by fighting for it,' Anthony replied. His gaze settled on the man with a mix of fascination and amusement. He had a large head and a scrawny, misshapen upper body. His clothes were more noticeable than his deformity. An ornate waistcoat heavily woven with clambering dog roses and blue and yellow kingfishers covered his barrel chest. A red scarf adorned his neck and gold hoops dangled from both ears. These, Anthony knew, were by way of pension. All boatmen wore them, something put back for when a man couldn't work any longer.

Comments about what should and shouldn't be done rumbled around the room.

'How do you fight if you've got mouths to feed?' was the most common question.

'United we shall stand and achieve victory,' cried Anthony. 'We must stand together as one.'

'United? How can we be united? You need to keep in touch to be united and we are spread wide all over the country.'

Anthony recognised Daddy Dawson, a man of dark looks whose tanned arms bristled with swathes of black hair. It was thanks to him that his ribs had healed, though they jarred now and again when he coughed.

His exuberance was somewhat punctured. Unwittingly, Dawson had latched on to the problem that had been plaguing him for quite a while.

'We will have to pick a time and a place,' said Anthony without really knowing what was planned by the powers at union headquarters with regard to a strike. 'All of us.'

'All of *us*, you mean,' said the small man with the highly embroidered waistcoat. 'We're the ones whose livelihood is at stake, not yorn!'

Loud murmurs once again ran through the room.

'We can set up some kind of communication. Pass word from boat to boat throughout the system. Well,' he asked amid rumblings of misgivings, 'are we to strike or not?'

It was Elliot Beaven who cleared his throat and spoke his mind. 'If striking has to be done, then we'll do it. Nuff said about that!' and the room erupted again into conversation as men with empty tankards surged towards the bar.

Anthony exchanged a pained look with Abigail as he got down from the rickety chair. 'Why do I do this?' he muttered.

'Because you care,' she whispered back. 'That's why I admire you so much. You really care.'

He pretended that there was nothing else lurking behind those hazel eyes and her honeyed voice, but knew he was only fooling himself.

'I agree with what you say.'

The voice was gruff and recognizable. He turned to face Elliot Beaven. Daddy Dawson was with him. The fierceness of his face made him flinch for a moment but he quickly recovered. 'I'm glad someone does.'

'Sure. I'm no coward. I'm game for a fight.' As if to prove the point, he cracked one set of knuckles against the other.

Anthony flinched. 'That wasn't the sort of fighting I had in mind. I was referring to a withdrawal of labour.'

Beaven sneered. 'Then you're a fool if you think it won't come to it.'

Dawson added, 'The owners won't stand for it. They'll fight us all the way, chuck out the masters of company boats and bring in scab labour. Then they'll try and starve us out. They'll beat us down if they can. I guarantee it.'

Anthony looked at the two men. These were stronger than most. He shuddered at the thought of crossing either of them. They both had fists like navvies' shovels.

As he sought the right words, he eyed the pinched faces of weaker men. 'There's a good chance the carriers will agree to our terms,' he said, but questioned his own honesty.

Abbie interrupted. 'I've still got all of these left,' she said, running her fingers through the bundle of flyers. She ignored Dawson's disparaging gaze. She'd seen it all before.

Beaven drained the dregs from his tankard, his throat heaving like a thirsty horse. 'If you ask my opinion, you're goin' to need a few men with strong arms. No matter all the jawing, things are likely to turn nasty – with you before it do us.'

Anthony stared after him as he strolled away. He became aware of Abigail's nervous glance.

'That man could take on an army. Not that we will take on an army – will we?'

He looked down, his expression grim. 'The trouble is he could be right. Unite the boatmen, and the carrying company have got trouble. At first they'll suffer the inconvenience but once they start to lose money then we're the ones with the trouble!'

'They'll be after you as the ringleader.'

He nodded. 'Uneasy lies the head that wears the crown.'

Abigail sighed. 'Shakespeare always did know how to say it.'

* * *

Moisture and mist covered the windows of the King's Arms, a public house a mile or so into the town centre on the corner of cobbled streets where terraced houses stood in tight rows and shadows fell like black sheets between the street lights.

The air inside was thick with the smoke from cheap cigarettes and black shag navy tobacco smoked in old briar pipes. The floor was slippery with wet sawdust and the effluent spat from the mouths of men with no learning and no regard for social graces.

One or two women sat with groups of men at tables, their looks and laughter betraying their trade, their thick makeup doing little to hide their age.

The two men at the bar whose shoulders rubbed close together had no time to notice the less-than-convivial surroundings. Their heads were almost as close as their shoulders and their conversation was meant for no ears other than their own.

'As agreed. Ten shillings.' As he spoke, Penmore, the smaller of the two, passed Harry Allen a clutch of silver.

'Daylight robbery,' he added, his voice not much above a whisper.

'You gets what you pay for,' said Harry, his mouth a surly grin as he shoved the coins into his pocket.

'I trust these men I've paid you for really exist.'

'Take a look for yourself.' Harry jerked his head to where a woman with red hair and lips was laughing loudly. A number of broad-shouldered men sat with her, their chins as grey as the clothes they wore, their eyes hard as buttons between folds of flesh. One of the men was fondling the woman's knee and gradually easing her skirt a little higher with his fingers. Her stocking, Penmore noted with a mix of embarrassment and disgust, was laddered and stained. But he kept looking, not just at her but at the ugly crew with whom she kept company.

Penmore felt Harry Allen's eyes boring into him. He swallowed hard. Violence made him feel sick. Setting this up hadn't been easy and the sooner he was out of here, the better. He turned quickly away, glanced at Harry then cast his gaze back on the mirror. 'Brutes to do a brutish job, I suppose,' he muttered.

'Well, that's the way it is. Wesley should have taken more notice of the first warning. Applying a few more should help persuade him to keep his nose out of canal business. Strike at the root of the problem and the rest wither.'

'He knows too much.'

'Ah, yes. Now what about old man Gatehouse's daughter? You say she's passing Wesley details,' said Harry, a wry smile curling his wide mouth. It had pleased him to see Penmore's face turning slightly green.

But Penmore managed to collect himself now he was on a different subject. 'I say so. She can fool the old man, but she doesn't fool me. I know what she's up to, her with her hoity-toity ways!'

'Stuck up, is she?' said Harry with an accompanying leer. All women were fair game to him, no matter what their breeding. He thought of the girl Beth, smiled and corrected himself. All women were the same but some were better than others and Beth Dawson was one experience he wanted to repeat.

Penmore sipped at his beer. 'She's that and a lot more.'

'Miss Abigail Gatehouse. High-class name. High-class tart. "The Colonel's lady and Rosie O'Grady are sisters under the skin." Ever heard that saying before, Penmore?'

'Can't say I have,' said Penmore. He didn't want to hear more of Harry's sayings. His aim was to get things over and escape from both Harry Allen and these tawdry surroundings. 'Everything where it's best placed, is it?' Harry Allen sounded off-hand, yet anyone just a little discerning and not entirely sober would have seen the sly look in his eyes. He could paint women with his mind, never clothed of course, but what good were they when they were dressed?

Penmore frowned. 'In what way?' He didn't like Abigail but he liked Harry even less and he recognised lust when he heard it.

'The only way, man! What does she look like? Is she worth a second look?'

Penmore downed his drink at last and looked glad that it was gone. 'If you like women that dress like men and look as though they might throw you a left hook, then she's the one for you.'

'A real Percy of a woman?' Disappointed more so than surprised, Harry Allen lifted his eyebrows and whistled through clenched teeth. He liked a challenge but by the sound of it, she was well worth avoiding, nothing at all like the sweet little thing he had groped in the office recently. Beth Dawson was worth a guinea to a rich punter, and he had in mind just the place that would make use of a young gal looking like her. And of course it wouldn't be that hard to get her away from that brute of a father. What did she have to lose? He had already made up his mind to seek her out again. She was young, fresh and too vulnerable to escape someone as worldly wise as him.

'Sounds like the back end of a tram,' laughed Harry. 'Best viewed from a distance!' He laughed again at his own joke. Penmore did not join him.

'No. That's just it. Abigail Gatehouse is a handsome woman. It's more as though she's got something to prove – especially now her sister's gone. Left home she did and no one can really understand why. The old man's never stopped missing her. If you ask me, he cared for t'other sister more than he did for her.'

Harry Allen put his arm across the bonier shoulders of Arthur Penmore. If he noticed it, he ignored Penmore's instant shiver.

'Well, you tell the old man that any time he wants that daughter of his taken off his hands, I'm the one to tame her.'

'Tame her? You talk about women as though they were animals,' said Penmore, who took the opportunity to brush at the shoulder of his pin-striped suit now Harry's arm had left it.

Apparently ignorant of the other man's aversion to his touch, Harry leaned closer to Penmore and patted his arm like a long-lost friend. 'They are, mate. You have to train them, stroke them when they've been good and beat them when they've been bad. Stands to reason.'

Penmore straightened and put his empty glass back on the bar. 'If you say so, Mr Allen. But I won't be getting near to her, I'll tell you that. I'd prefer her to be out on her ear. She's mad, she is, though that's not too surprising. It runs in the family. But she goads me she does, and that's what I'd like to put paid to. A know-all. Always telling people what to do. Had enough of that in the army, I did.'

Arthur Penmore put on his hat once he was outside, glad to stop and breathe the chill night air. He didn't look back as he drew his collar up around his neck. Harry Allen was an evil necessity of life. He had to deal with the man, but having one pint with him was more than enough. The man both frightened and revolted him. Women did not possess the stronger qualities of men, but surely they deserved to be treated better than beasts? He only hoped that Harry Allen never got too close to Abigail Gatehouse. He'd like to see her brought down a peg, but only with regard to wounding her pride, not her body.

9

The warehouses threw pools of blackness across her path. Occasionally, the flickering gleam of a gaslight lent a splash of brightness, adding its own peculiar smell to that of iron filings, rotting wood and blackened brick.

She sang as she walked. Now and again, she even danced a bit. Defying Elliot about going back to the boat was one thing; coping with the darkness following the assault by Harry Allen was another. At the sound of footsteps, even a rat sliding into the water, she melted into the shadows.

Eventually she came to the very edge of the canal compound and the song became no more than a hum. Beyond the stout railings shone the lights of the city. A church tower speared the sky. Her route went past the back of the Navigator towards the dock gates.

She asked herself why she wanted to do this. She could imagine the scene, the men talking amongst themselves, dissecting what they had heard and what should be done.

Neither Elliot nor anyone else would see her pass by. She would keep to the rear of the premises. Men would be staggering out of the front door, full of talk, bravado and pints of dark stout.

Tobacco smoke drifted out from the bar each time the door swung open. Both the smoke and the sound excited her, as though the ideas discussed inside the pub were drifting on the night air.

At first, the feeling that she was not alone was purely instinct. It swiftly became fact. Like a bright red firefly, the glow of a cigarette danced in the darkness.

Beth paused, her heart thudding against her ribs as though attempting to escape her body. Harry Allen?

She took a step back, her heart racing with fear. 'Leave me alone.'

A figure moved in the darkness and came into a bead of light falling from a chink in a curtain.

A vast sigh shivered through her body as she recognised Anthony Wesley.

'I'm sorry,' he said. 'Did I startle you?'

Her breathing resumed. 'I thought you were someone else. And you're not.'

She saw him smile. 'I'm glad of that. You sound as though you don't want to meet whoever you thought it was ever again.'

'I don't.'

He put out his cigarette, grinding it into the earth with the toe of his boot. 'I'm doubly glad it isn't me. I wouldn't want to think I could never meet you again or that you detested meeting me.'

'I love meeting you,' she blurted and felt her face reddening. How could she have been so forward?

'I'm glad of that.'

She expected him to sound amused. He didn't. He sounded warm, like people do when they respond to something without having time to think about it. Spontaneous, she thought the word was: instant and straight from the heart.

'I wanted to come to your meeting.'

'It was all men there.' He thought of Abigail. In a strange way, she would have liked his oversight. 'I asked Elliot Beaven to bring me some pamphlets. I thought I could hand them out and read them to people. You have pamphlets, don't you?'

'We do indeed.'

He wondered at the energy in her voice, the same passion for action that he harboured himself.

'I want to get involved with this,' she said as though she had read his thoughts. 'After all, it's the women and children who suffer in the long run when the money's tight. It's us that starve, that have to do without.'

He saw the blueness of her eyes, stars in the night. 'You have passion in your soul, Beth Dawson.'

'You remembered my name.'

'You're the girl who tended my wounds. Remember?'

She blushed more deeply. Oh yes, she remembered all right. Sometimes dreamed she was doing it all over again.

She sensed rather than saw his sudden frown.

'Who did you think was waiting in the shadows?'

'The wharfinger.'

'Which one?'

'Harry Allen. I saw the cigarette glowing in the dark, just like when...'

'When I was being beaten up?'

She nodded.

He sighed as though the weight of the world was on his shoulders. 'I owe you a lot, Beth Dawson.'

She wanted to hug him like she had when she was bandaging his ribs.

'Can I have some pamphlets?'

'Of course you can. I'll go in and get you some then I'll walk you back to *Jenny Wren*.'

'No! I'll walk back alone.'

'I'm disappointed, but if that's what you want.'

'I enjoy walking alone.'

She said it exuberantly in order to hide the truth. Elliot's boat was moored next to *Jenny Wren*. He would not approve of another man walking her home. And besides, he'd promised to bring her pamphlets. He wouldn't like to think that someone else had done the same.

10

It was late August, but September was already waiting in the wings with sharper mornings and white mists that shrouded the canal like a winter bride's veil.

They'd pulled into the Victoria Wharf at Market Drayton to offload freshly sawn wood from the Worcester Sawmills and to buy white poplin with which to make Beth's wedding dress. Beth didn't need to be told that this was the most important day of her life, the destiny of all good women since time immemorial. And suddenly she was a good woman again; she bled that month.

'At least we don't have that to explain.' Beth heard the relief in her mother's voice, though of course it was only partial. 'You'll still have to cry out on your wedding night as though it's the first time.'

She was expected to feel pain. 'How do I know it's the first time for him?'

'That doesn't matter. He's a man. It's different.'

Leaving *Jenny Wren* was going to make a small difference to her parents' lives. 'You'll 'ave to come and do the writing with me once our Beth is gone,' her father had said to her mother.

Mother and daughter had exchanged looks that silently asked

why Robbie couldn't go. Robbie could read and write too. But Robbie seldom spoke or offered to do anything. He rarely used the waterside pubs either but made his way into the towns. Her father said little except that the boy had to become a man sometime or other and a man bided his own business.

It had been a long while since Harry Allen had found her in a warehouse door in Gloucester. Just the week before they'd been there again and Beth had trembled as she'd followed her father through the gaping men and gigantic machines. She had wanted to close her eyes as the door opened and for the floor to open up and swallow her whole, but found to her surprise that Harry Allen wasn't there, only a man who silently and efficiently dealt with everything that was needed.

Unwelcome memories were swiftly brushed away as she tied up the tiller and looked along the mooring. An autumn sun sat low in the sky so she had to shield her eyes to see who had arrived before them.

She knew the next boat and the one beyond so nodded a welcome at both, but it was the next again that drew her attention: the *Sadie G*, a smart boat owned by a man named George Melcroft that was painted in the most royal of blues. Bands of red tulips ran in wavy rows along its sides. George was middle-aged. His wife had run off some time ago and although he wasn't exactly divorced, he had married a refined kind of girl called Carrie, who was very near to Beth's own age. It was his business whether he'd told Carrie or not. No one on the boats mentioned it. The men stuck together and the women minded their own business.

'It's Carrie,' she said as her mother came up from the cabin, her hands raw from all the washing she'd done the day before. 'I wonder if she'd like to come with us to the market?'

'You'll only find out if you ask her.'

Her mother smoothed her skirt and straightened her bonnet.

Beth guessed that, like her, Carrie made her feel shabby and poor. Carrie always looked trim, her clothes that bit better. Beth had once asked her where she got them. 'I've had them a long time,' she'd answered and then she said, as if she was remembering something important, 'I bought them a while ago in Birmingham when I used to live there. But that's all in the past. Let's talk about something else.'

Beth didn't question why Carrie didn't want her prying into her background. Valuing her friendship, she warily avoided touching on the subject.

'I've been there before with George,' Carrie said, 'but I'll enjoy it better today because it's special. It's the day we buy your wedding dress.'

'Only the material,' Beth corrected her; although she felt embarrassed to say it to someone like Carrie, with her well-tailored clothes, she felt a need to be honest.

It was half an hour's walk to the market and they never stopped talking all the way there. Only once they'd arrived were they stunned into silence.

The square and the long street that led off from it were packed with stalls selling everything you could possibly think of. Their eyes opened wide with delight and their mouths began to water as the air filled with the smell of ripe cheeses, fresh fruit and bread just taken from the oven. Among the stalls beside the kerb sat round-bodied countrywomen with great baskets of fresh eggs in front of them, trussed chickens, geese and ducks and vegetables picked that morning or at least no more than the day before. The air was filled with the cackle of poultry and the equally loud cackle of continuous conversation and raucous laughter.

The inns were filling with country folk who must have been up before dawn. Yeoman farmers in old-fashioned spats drank ale and talked about livestock, market prices and the likelihood of a hard winter. Their wives, with ruddy faces, big behinds and breasts that rested on their bellies, drank rum that they replenished from a kettle above the innkeeper's fire. Shepherds and cowherds still sporting their grandfathers' and great-grandfathers' voluminous smocks sat with their dogs and compared their skills with their neighbours'.

At the end of the square beyond the stalls were the animal pens: sheep, cows, pigs, but predominantly horses. Market Drayton was famous for its horse fair, and moving among the foals, cobs, geldings and mares were a motley collection of buyers, from gentlemen farmers to dark-eyed gypsies.

Beth, Carrie and her mother took it all in, the younger women talking excitedly, their eyes bright. Her mother was more reticent, as though a married woman had no right to laugh too much. Beth briefly wondered whether she'd end up the same once she was married. Women who had married boatmen were either reserved like her mother or like Fanny Bennett: big as a barn and with a mouth to match. That wasn't to say that her mother wasn't interested in her surroundings; her eyes opened wide as she took in the food, the animals, the wares and the people, but her interest was controlled.

'What about this?' said her mother, her work-worn hands gently fingering a bolt of white poplin.

'I'm watching you,' the stallholder said with a heavy frown. 'I know you be from the cut, and I know what you people are like.'

The cut was what local folk called the canal. He had almost accused her of stealing. Bowing her head, she withdrew her hand and retreated behind the brim of her bonnet.

Beth glared haughtily at the stallholder as someone like Abigail Gatehouse might do. She felt the poplin's softness. 'I think I might buy this,' she said, at the same time throwing another angry glare.

She was suddenly aware of Carrie wrinkling her usually straight nose. 'Is there something wrong?' Beth asked her.

'I think this will crease easily.'

Mother looked at daughter and both looked at Carrie. Without comment all three moved on. The stallholder grabbed the bolt and sat it more firmly between its companions, then spat on the ground, his eyes following them until they were lost in the milling crowd.

Satin, silk, cotton and muslin hung in billowing drapes from the next market haberdasher. Beth, still indignant, jostled the crowd aside as she homed in on a bolt of muslin that had small daisies scattered all over it. She hesitated about touching it but glanced over her shoulder preferring to see what Carrie, who appeared to have a more select taste than most, would favour.

'This is nice,' said Carrie softly. Her long white fingers caressed the equally white cloth. Beth wondered how her hands had stayed so soft and white whilst working and living on a narrowboat. Her hand roamed along behind Carrie's. 'I like this.'

The plain part of the material was very fine, very soft; the daisies were machine-stitched with yellow centres that felt like tiny buttons beneath her fingertips.

With wary watchfulness, her mother reached for the price tag then gasped. 'It's much too expensive. You'll need at least six yards to get a decently full skirt out of this!'

Carrie and Beth exchanged glances. The dress design both had in mind was completely at odds with that of Elizabeth Dawson.

'I want a modern design,' said Beth. 'I've seen them in the newspaper advertisements. It's just a straight shift – almost an oblong – with no gathers at all.'

Her mother looked at her askance. 'You don't mean one of those flapper-type things?'

'Just like the ones at the pictures and in the papers. You know the sort I mean, Ma.' Beth was embarrassed by her mother's attitude, especially in front of Carrie, but she was determined to have her own way. 'I want a modern dress, Ma. I want a straight shift with a broad sash around my hips.'

'And a lace collar at the throat,' Carrie interjected, her enthusiasm for the modern design blatantly obvious. 'And it should be fairly short. Perhaps just below the knee – or perhaps just above it.'

'Just below it? I see,' said her mother, but it was clear from her face she didn't see and that she preferred to keep to the traditionally acceptable rather than chance something new. Rather than argue, she turned her attention elsewhere. 'Now what about a veil?'

Again Beth exchanged a glance with Carrie and they both turned to one particular spot.

There were small scraps of more expensive material strewn on top of the piled bolts, remnants of the yards already sold to people more able to afford it. One piece above all others caught Beth's eye. 'This is lovely!' she said as she leapt on a piece of Nottingham lace that was plain and fragile but heavily decorated around its borders.

'It's very narrow,' said her mother with a frown.

Beth draped the yard-long piece over her head. Her mother was right. It was barely twelve inches wide but somehow Beth knew that it suited both her and the modern vogue for slim outlines.

'It looks perfect,' said a smiling Carrie. 'I've got two pearl hatpins we can pin it in place with. A clutch of white anemones and a rose or two would make a very suitable bouquet; you'll look lovely.'

Knowing she was outvoted, Beth's mother paid. As she was counting out the coins carefully saved in a brown jug she kept beneath the range, Beth looked up and saw a familiar face. Abigail Gatehouse was giving out pamphlets, the self-same ones as those hidden beneath Beth's pillow. Elliot had brought her a few; Anthony had brought her even more. She'd distributed them among the boat people, reading them aloud to the illiterate.

'Hello there!' She waved enthusiastically. 'It's Abigail Gatehouse,' she shouted to her mother.

'My word! She looks like a man!'

Abigail was wearing a rust-coloured jacket, matching trousers and a dark green waistcoat. Beth thought she looked outrageous – so did most of those around them, their expressions a picture of shocked intrigue as they took the leaflets she so swiftly handed out.

'She's incredible!' exclaimed Beth, her eyes shining with admiration. Leaving her mother to complete the purchase of the muslin and the lace, she made her way through the stalls, moving sideways and elbowing aside the jostling crowds.

'Abigail!' she called. 'Do you remember me?'

Holding on to her hat, Abigail's intelligent eyes turned and looked into hers. 'Well, if it isn't the fair maid who rescued our battered Sir Lancelot!'

'Is he here?'

Abigail lowered her eyelids and hesitated before replying.

'Of course not. He's got better things to do than saunter through a common market.' She started to turn away.

'Is he very far away?' asked Beth.

Abigail shook her head. Amazingly, Beth noted that her red locks barely moved from her face. Were they stuck there with glue?

'No, not very far. Are you shopping for anything in particular?' She sounded keen to change the subject.

'I'm just buying some material for my wedding dress.'

Abigail's attitude changed instantly. A broad smile lit up her face. 'My very best wishes. And when is this to be?'

'Next week.'

'Gosh, will you get the dress done in time?' There was genuine concern in her eyes that Beth could not quite understand, as if her news had raised some deep-seated worry.

'We'll manage.'

Abigail shook her head and a mix of copper and dark red hair flicked forward on to her face. Her red lips smiled. 'You people have been managing for too long and in this case my dear, you don't need to manage. Are you getting married at Gloucester?'

'Yes,' said Beth.

'Then give me the material,' said Abigail. 'I'll get my seamstress to make it up and have it waiting for you at Gloucester. She'll have it done in no time at all.'

Beth looked at her with a mix of wonder and curiosity. 'But I can't possibly pay her.'

Abigail's long fingers folded over her arm in an unexpected show of affection. 'No need to, my dear. My wedding gift to you. I own the shop, you see. My father bought it in the mistaken belief that it would stop me frequenting the rougher parts of the world and mixing with the basest of people – his words, not mine, so don't take offence. He said it was either a little shop or the lunatic asylum. I choose to think he didn't really mean it, but I can't be sure. He can be quite mad himself at times.'

Beth closed her gaping mouth. She could hardly believe what she was hearing, although one nagging doubt still remained. 'I want something modern,' she blurted. 'And the skimpiest, simplest of headwear.'

Abigail listed exactly what was in Beth's mind. 'Flapper-style dress, sash at waist, lace collar at throat, little lace skullcap with a few streamers hanging down. Goodness, you're a difficult customer. And there was me thinking we were friends. Do I get the job or not?'

'Yes!' said Beth, feeling privileged that Abigail should consider her a friend. 'Yes, oh yes!'

'And you can meet the price?'

Beth's smile froze. What price could she pay? What price did Abigail have in mind?

'Invitations to the wedding for Anthony and me! Can you afford that?'

'Yes!' Beth laughed loudly. 'Yes!' Although aware of shocked looks, she threw her arms around Abigail, who stood there in her mannish clothes and hugged her back.

'They ain't right!' someone shouted.

'I think we'd better move on,' said Abigail, looking bemused. 'Dressed like this and showing affection? Goodness me, what will the honest burghers of this town think?'

'You don't care what they think,' said Beth, and knew it for the truth. Being a rebel gave Abigail immense satisfaction. She'd probably remain rebellious all her life – unless she found something that satisfied her more. 'Come on. We've got to tell my mother.'

With wary fascination, her mother's eyes alighted on the shiny-faced Abigail and Beth explained her offer, then turned to Carrie. 'What do you think...?'

Carrie was gone.

The morning was growing old and more people were pouring into the square. Getting carried away by the throng was easily done.

'Then I'll see you at Gloucester,' said Abigail once the material, wrapped in brown paper, was tucked under her arm.

Mother and daughter watched her go. Like a changing sea, the crowd swelled and surged around them until they were in danger of being swept away from the direction of the towpath and their waiting boat.

They met Robbie and Elliot going in the other direction. 'Hope you ain't spent all the money,' Robbie said to them both.

'We'll be going on, then,' said Elliot. 'Market Drayton's the place for me, what with the pubs being open all day and me future brother-in-law's offered to buy me a pint.'

'Reckon I might have to,' said Robbie, wearing the sort of look that warned her of teasing when she'd been a child, 'she's been out spending your money already, Elliot. Mark my words, you'll never be a rich man when you've got my sister on board the *Agincourt*.'

Elliot shrugged his square shoulders. 'As long as there's food on the table and—'

'A bun in the oven?' interjected Robbie.

Beth reddened. 'Robbie Dawson! I'll thank you to mind your language in the company of ladies.'

'Ladies?'

Robbie resumed his laughter until Elliot laid his hand on his shoulder. 'Shut yer mouth, Rob, and have a care. 'Tis my future wife you're talking about. I'll not have even her brother insult her.'

For the second time that day, Beth was overwhelmed with warmth that someone held her in high regard. Whatever doubts she might have felt were washed away. Perhaps it was love or perhaps it was just familiarity.

She'd heard some men could tell if they were getting damaged goods. But she smiled up at him brightly and hoped that he was not experienced enough to notice.

'Let's be off, then,' said Elliot to Robbie.

'I'll go take a look at the horses first,' said Robbie.

Elliot raised his eyebrows. 'You're turning down a beer?'

'I'll catch up with you later.'

Elliot agreed and the two went off in separate directions.

Her mother frowned. 'Has our Robbie got a new girlfriend?'

Beth shrugged. 'Not that I know of. Perhaps he's getting religion.'

Her mother laughed. 'Now that *would* be a miracle!'

* * *

It was mid-afternoon before she heard her brother's voice again. To her great surprise, he didn't sound as though he was drunk.

She was filling a brightly painted can from a standpipe. Droplets of water were spraying up into her face, a pleasant experience on a warm afternoon.

Along with her brother's voice, she heard the sound of girlish laughter.

'You're a wicked man, Robbie Dawson, and your flattery will get you nowhere.'

Beth looked up. Carrie waved, her face wreathed in smiles. Beth pretended to concentrate on filling the water can, but her eyes kept straying back to them. There was something about the way they stood, the poses they struck as they talked to each other.

Later, when the two had parted, she pushed what she had seen to the back of her mind and asked Carrie where she had got to in the market.

'Where were you? We looked for you.' It was all she could think of to say.

'I've had a wonderful day,' said Carrie, brushing her hair back from her face as she smiled. The setting sun behind her turned her blonde hair red. 'Did you get everything you wanted?'

Beth told her all about Abigail Gatehouse and her wonderful offer. 'And she's coming to the wedding with Anthony Wesley. Isn't that wonderful?'

Carrie's smile was less than enthusiastic at first and it occurred to Beth that perhaps she was jealous of her new friend. But no, the familiar smile returned. Obviously Carrie was very tired after such a long day at Market Drayton. Perhaps she was expecting the baby she'd always wanted.

'You're going to be a wonderful bride,' Carrie said, her face slightly pink with the sunset.

She became aware that Robbie had returned and was standing, kerchief at throat, swarthy complexion wreathed in smoke from a glowing Woodbine. His gaze was firmly fixed on Carrie. The look in his eyes was unsettling.

Only later did that look truly register. Harry Allen! The burning desire in Robbie's stare reminded her of that night.

11

On her wedding day she wore forget-me-nots in her hair and carried a mix of lupins, lilies and roses picked from the garden of her proposed father-in-law, a lock keeper on the Worcester to Birmingham Canal.

The Petersons, the Abners, the Spockets and many other old families that had travelled the canals since the height of the industrial revolution had all worked their schedules so that they arrived at the Navigator prior to going to the church. Men and women had donned their best, the men's Yorks tied just below the knee with velvet bands embroidered with flowers, small brass bells tinkling when they walked. The women had done their best with Sunday-best dresses of linen or cotton, pressed with a hot iron, or sewn and patterned on the latest fashions they'd seen in town stores, out-of-date newspapers or even a picture house. Some of the older women still wore the high-necked, voluminous dresses of the last century, complete with white apron and starched black bonnet. They had worn white bonnets but when the old queen had adopted black on the death of her consort, Prince Albert, they had followed suit out of respect. Even the children whose parents carried coal or tar products had been scrubbed clean, the black dust soaked, soaped and vigorously brushed from their pores. Once their skin was pink, ears were cuffed to emphasise the stern command to keep away from the coal.

They were to be married in a small Baptist chapel just outside the dockyard gates in Gloucester and, as promised, Abigail arrived with the dress. The sight of it took Beth's breath away, its beauty filling the tiny cabin like the gleam of a magic lantern.

The men were ordered off the boat whilst she tried it on. Her mother and Abigail stayed to say the right things in the right places and make sure nothing was tucked up, in or drooping.

A funny little boatman named Goblin Coombes had lent them a long mirror, all that remained of an old wardrobe. It was tarnished in places but if she positioned herself just right, she could see the lovely vision in creamy white, scattered with daisies.

The dress had turned out exactly as she had wanted it. The veil of Nottingham lace sat on her piled-up hair at a saucy angle. She had thought of having her long locks chopped off to the same length as Abigail's – Carrie had offered to cut them in a fashionable shingle for her, similar to the style she'd seen worn by one of Valentino's leading ladies – but something within her wanted to cling to part of the past. Her mother had not approved of the dress design. Having her hair cut would have been too much.

Everything was perfect. Only one thing, or rather one person, was missing.

'I only wish Carrie Melcroft was here,' she said wistfully to her reflection.

'P'raps I'd better go 'long and see where she is,' her mother offered. She tapped at the walnut clock fixed to a nail above a cluster of porcelain plates. 'Mustn't leave it too long. though.'

Abigail fussed with Beth's appearance.

"Ello there...!' George Melcroft appeared in the upper half of the cabin door. 'Sorry to tell you this, Elizabeth me dear, but ma missus is none too well. I trust you'll forgive us if we're absent from your weddin'. We're dead sorry to miss it. Dead sorry, we are.'

'Oh no!' Beth couldn't help looking and sounding crestfallen. Carrie was her best friend. She was counting on her to be there to approve of how she looked and what she was doing.

George nodded at the two other women. To Beth's surprise, he didn't bat an eyelid at Abigail's striped jacket and white Oxford bags. Her straw boater sat on a side seat.

'Anthony can't be here either,' added Abigail suddenly. 'And, I'm afraid, neither can I.' With a serious expression, she pushed back the sleeve of her blazer and glanced at her watch. 'Almost eleven. I have to run along and pick Anthony up...'

'From right here!'

They all looked up to see George Melcroft's moon-shaped face nudged slowly to one side as Anthony appeared next to him. He grinned broadly.

'Is it bad luck for me to see the bride before the big moment?'

'No!' Beth exclaimed. 'You're not the bridegroom so you can see me any time.'

There was something ominous about the words and yet they still smiled at each other. She had spent so little time with Anthony Wesley and yet both his voice and his looks stirred her as if she had known him forever.

He paused when he saw her. She fancied his jaw dropped slightly and his eyes sparkled as he viewed her in the slim white dress and pert veil, with the flowers she clutched in her fist.

It wasn't so much a pause but more as if his breath had suddenly been snatched away by something unfamiliar, something alien to his nature.

He quickly collected himself. 'You look stunning. I'm sure your husband will be proud of you. And that dress is...' He paused again and shook his head. 'Wonderful!' He turned to Abigail, who had been standing very still and very silent. 'That woman of yours did a wonderful job, Abbie. She's to be congratulated.'

Abigail too had seen the look in Anthony's eyes and the answering echo in Beth's. Her mood changed. 'She did what she could with what she had!' she snapped. 'It was only a very cheap piece of material.'

Beth was hurt. 'No one asked you to make up my dress. No one asked the likes of you to come down here and interfere in our lives. Why do you do it? Does it make you feel good to have so much when the likes of us have so little? Is that it, Abigail? Is that it?'

The cabin fell silent. Abigail's superbly made-up face turned pink.

Beth was persistent. 'Well?'

She heard the husky voice of Anthony Wesley. 'There's a lot that might ask you the same question, Abigail.'

When he called her by her full name, Abigail seemed to become smaller, less masculine and much softer.

'I...' she began, looking at Anthony. Suddenly, she pulled herself together. 'I'm sorry, Beth.' Her smile was slow and almost painful. 'Materially, one has a great deal. But you have much more than I have. Today you are getting married. You've got what any woman wants.'

In an effort to rebuild their friendship, Abigail squeezed Beth's hand before disappearing. Anthony moved aside to let her pass. His head reappeared at the cabin door.

Beth presumed he was going to apologise for his colleague and prepared herself to be forgiving because today she could forgive anybody anything.

His smile was slow. 'I think your dress is beautiful, Beth, but Abbie knows as well as I do that it doesn't do you justice. You outshine it, Beth. Keep shining, Beth, just like an angel. And keep reading. Here. I've bought you a small wedding present. Just for you – from me.'

He handed her a book with a red cover and gold lettering faded by time.

As she turned the book over to read the spine, she felt its warmth, the fact that its cover was less than perfect and that the gilt lettering was worn away.

'*A Midsummer Night's Dream*,' she said. 'Thank you. I can feel that it's been very well loved,' she added.

He smiled. 'I've read it a lot. It's not new but it's one of my favourites.'

'It's yours? And now you've given it to me?'

He nodded. 'Love it,' he said. 'Just as I've loved it.'

Moved by his generosity, she nodded.

'Be seeing you. I hope you'll be happy.'

The sound of his voice stayed with her after he and Abigail had left. But there was no time to mull over them further or be upset that they hadn't been able to stay. Today was her wedding day.

George Melcroft came back to tell her that Carrie was feeling much better and they would be attending. Not even the weather could dampen her high spirits.

The day started dry but by the time the service was over and bride, bridegroom and guests were on their way to the Navigator, a slight drizzle had begun to fall.

Encouraged by a bevy of intoxicated guests, Elliot danced with her to the sound of a wheezing accordion and the jollier squeal of a jig played with great flourish by Goblin Coombes on a fiddle. The little man's bowed legs jigged with the best of them as he played. Everyone was happy and even Beth forgot she had once had doubts about marrying Elliot. What else was there for her? She was married now.

Thoughts of what would happen later in the dark privacy of their cabin on the *Agincourt* were swept aside by the music and the energy she put into her dancing. She laughed and whirled as much as anyone, and although her consumption of sherry and stout had been below the average, her head was spinning.

At a lull in the music, Elliot went off to get more beer and a hunk of fish-paste sandwiches and pickled gherkins.

Breathing deeply, her face pink, Beth sat beside Carrie on a rough wooden settle. George sat opposite them.

'George doesn't dance,' said Carrie immediately, interpreting Beth's questioning look.

Carrie's slim, neat feet were tapping in time to a jig. 'I'll dance with you,' Beth offered.

Carrie shook her head. 'No. You must dance with Elliot. I'm all right sitting here watching everyone else enjoying themselves. Just look at them.'

Age seemed no barrier to those who danced to the sound of the fiddle. Even her mother was up swishing her skirts and flashing her black-stockinged legs as she did a turn with Mrs Grady. The latter had forearms like hams and when she swished, her voluminous skirts showed her tree-trunk legs covered to just below her knees by long, pink knickers.

Robbie, her brother, was also out there dancing. Beth recognised his partner as Rosie Grady, a blowsy type who spoke loudly and laughed too much. His mouth was close to her ear and they were not dancing in time with the music. Carrie noticed too.

'Your brother's whispering sweet nothings in that girl's ear,' she said with that light tinkling laugh of hers.

Beth remembered a night she'd seen him canoodling in a shop doorway with a cheap tart from a wharf-side pub. 'I wouldn't let him do that if I were her.'

'You shouldn't be so hard on your brother,' said Carrie. 'He's a fine-looking young man.'

Beth was surprised. She'd never heard Carrie make comment on any man before, except for her husband, who she appeared to dote on. George had made his way to the bar.

'He's just my brother,' she said dismissively. Although he still whispered in Rosie's ear, he was looking elsewhere – straight at Carrie. He winked and smiled. And Carrie smiled back.

The exchange embarrassed her. But why? Was it because both were revealing a side of their character she had never seen before? Even though Robbie was her brother, they'd never been close. He'd always been a loner, isolated even in the midst of his family.

She told herself to ignore what had passed. By way of distraction, she said something admiring about Carrie's dress. Carrie thanked her and smiled. 'I got married in this dress. That was three years ago now. Doesn't time fly!' She sighed heavily.

Beth knew the reason why. Carrie had often mentioned that three years of marriage had produced no children. She patted her hand. 'Some people take longer than others.'

Carrie's wide, blue eyes stared at her, then blinked in an uncommonly self-conscious manner. 'You'll have three long before I've had one. Elliot is young. George is... well... his first wife never got in the family way either.' She bit her lip and her self-consciousness deepened. 'I don't think it's my fault,' she said softly, 'if you know what I mean.'

'No man would want to hear that.'

'George isn't just any sort of man. He's different than the others. He wants whatever I want.'

'He's kind. I know that, but still—'

'He wants a child. We both do. And we will have one. I'm determined we will. We both are.'

'It will happen, Carrie. I know it will happen.'

She saw a sad smile cross her friend's face, then a look she could only think of as determined. 'Of course it will. If something doesn't happen soon, we shall be forced to do something quite drastic. We've made up our minds. Isn't there something you really want, Beth?'

Beth frowned. She knew Carrie expected her to answer that she too would like children, but there was something else; something that burned like a flame in her mind. 'I'd like to teach the youngsters to read and write. That's what I'd like.'

Carrie looked surprised but made no comment. Immersed in their own thoughts, they turned back to those dancing. Legs were now unsteady by virtue of the amount of beer consumed, the laughter louder and ribald.

Beth's eyes searched for Robbie and the girl. They were nowhere to be seen. She was strangely glad. He was with someone who suited him; Carrie was lovely, but married. He must stay away from her.

Nearby, Mr Grady was standing in the shadow of his wife, looking anxious, his one good eye scanning the floor for the errant Rosie. His wife, her cheeks red and the hairs on her chin bristling with displeasure, was looking furious.

Neither Robbie nor Rosie was anywhere to be seen and George had returned from the bar. Carrie was safe from her brother, at least for now. Rosie would be putty in his hands.

There were three people in the wedding bed that night. Elliot was fast asleep beside her, his trousers down to his knees and his hand on her breast. If he had been sober, perhaps he might have heard the thudding of her heart. Only Beth was aware of the ghost of Harry Allen.

Tonight she had escaped discovery; tomorrow might be different.

She turned her head to escape the fumes that filtered down his nose and rumbled from his mouth.

By dawn, she was up and about, glad to be out of bed and pottering around. The range glowed red and the kettle steamed. Two slabs of white bread spat and sizzled in a pan of half-melted dripping.

Before her new husband arose, she threw a shawl around her shoulders and went up on deck. The smell of frying bread and brewing tea followed her.

People waved from other boats. Some were still moored, waiting for loads, but the majority had collected loads the day before and were already pulling away from the wharf, off to Oxford and down the Grand Union, or up the Worcester Risers, a series of climbs through backbreaking locks, and into the Potteries. Her look was wistful. She too wanted to be travelling along quiet waters where the willows kissed the surface and the owls called across the fields.

At the sound of groaning, she glanced down into the cabin. Elliot was rising. His boots thudded on the floor. He swore as he stretched and his head hit the roof. Eventually he appeared in the doorway. His eyes were bleary and his chin unshaven, the look of a man who had drunk too much and slept too little.

Would he remember that they weren't yet man and wife? She hoped not. That way he would never know he wasn't the first. He would presume and presuming would be enough. But though his memory of what they might or might not have done was hazy, hers was real enough. Tonight he would be sober and would do to her what Harry Allen had done. The thought made her shiver, but she knew she mustn't show it. She must go willingly to bed and submit to his body. Hateful memories of that first time had to be overcome. She would steel herself to do it because she had to.

'I'll get your breakfast,' she said as he dragged himself up through the cabin door. Fatty bacon joined the frying bread, filling their small home with its mouth-watering aroma.

'Good girl,' he mumbled and patted her arm; such a small act, yet from a man like him, it meant a lot. A kiss would have been nice but such men as him didn't go in for showing affection in public and some, like her father, had none to give.

As she took the bread and dripping bacon from the pan and placed it on a plate, the sound of his boots scraping along the sideways told her he was going forward to relieve himself. The fact that he'd made a point of doing it out of her sight was oddly touching.

By the time she was coming up out of the cabin door with breakfast and thick, brown tea, Elliot was standing by the tiller and the engine was already chugging its single, leaden note.

'Take it,' he said without dropping his eyes.

She took the tiller with one hand and passed him the plate with the other then stood up, glad to feel the wind in her hair and to be leaving the town.

As her husband pushed bread into his mouth and swigged at the strong tea, she swung the tiller. He stooped and tickled the throttle. The prow of *Agincourt* swung out into the pound, pushing its way through the greenish, brackish water. They were away to the quieter canals where fields of clover kissed the water's edge. Ahead of them, kingfishers, moorhens and mallard made their homes among the willows and reeds. Ahead too was their married life and all it might hold.

That night, in the cosy warmth of the bed, Elliot reached for her. She tensed, afraid of what was to come and what he might say.

'Come on. It's not the first time, woman,' he said.

Her heart skipped a beat. 'How did you know?' she said, amazed he was taking the fact that she was not a virgin so calmly.

'I wasn't that drunk last night,' he said gruffly. Beth sighed with relief. Her secret was safe.

12

Abigail eyed her reflection with grim determination. 'Don't think you own me, Anthony Wesley. No one does. And no one ever will.'

Anyway, it was just sexual attraction, she told herself. 'It's not just about playing hard to get,' quipped her confidante and darling Aunt Maude, the black sheep of the family who had once been 'put away' to protect the family reputation. 'Men like clever, independent women a lot more than they admit.' She visited Aunt Maude in secret; they shared ideas as well as clothes, two rebels of two separate generations.

Maude told her all this as she lay full length on a chaise-longue dressed in an oriental kaftan and wearing a silver turban with black and purple feathers.

'Get rid of your virginity as quickly as possible – though not to him,' she added, her eyes sparkling and her crimson lips forming a warning moue around an ebony cigarette holder. 'This Anthony person has to be handled differently than most men.'

'So who do I do it with?' An awful vision entered her mind: Penmore, rutting like a stallion between her legs, his sweat dripping on her face. Ugh!

'Someone ineffectual, perhaps someone you've known all your life.'

Gilbert! He was the obvious choice.

Aunt Maude echoed her thoughts. 'Perhaps cousin Gilbert. He's available and malleable, exactly the sort of man that can be used and forgotten.'

And so it was that as part of her grand strategy to be a woman who managed her own destiny and sexuality, she'd made her plans.

Gilbert was coming to tea, invited by her parents at her behest. The gleam of favoured suitor came swiftly to their eyes. She was interested in Gilbert! She would get engaged and married, hopefully as swiftly as possible. The rebellious, quirky girl would be confined to the past.

She let them think that. Now she was standing naked in her bedroom, eyeing her reflection and deciding how best to bait and capture her prey.

First she needed to soften her look a little. The trousers she pulled up over her naked thighs were of the palest lemon silk. She slid her arms into a matching silk blouse trimmed with grey satin at the collar and around the pinched-in sleeves. The silk was cool against her skin and made her flesh tingle. As she fastened the satin-covered buttons, she congratulated herself for leaving her bosoms unfettered by any item of underwear. She fastened the last button at the soft hollow beneath her throat.

Too stuffy, she thought, and unbuttoned it.

Now why am I doing this? She stood in front of the mirror, head held high, one arm thrown across her chest as if making a pledge to King and Country.

'This is for women everywhere!' she exclaimed, her expression serious though a nervous knot tightened in her stomach.

The sound of laughter, a piano playing and the tinkling of

teacups downstairs told her that their expected guests had arrived. And Gilbert.

A little more encouragement might be needed. A signal or two that any advance he made would not be repudiated. With that in mind, she undid two more buttons of her blouse and pinched her nipples. Dutifully, they stood to attention.

Better but not beyond improvement, she decided. Bending over the dressing table, she pouted at her reflection as she applied blood-red lipstick.

'Voila! How terribly dramatic, my dear!' She laughed.

Pale skin, grey eyes, hair the colour of autumn leaves: her appearance needed nothing to enhance it except the lipstick. Lipstick was a badge of eligibility. This afternoon she was available and she had to advertise the fact.

With a determined toss of her head, she marched from her bedroom. October 10th: this was a day she would remember all her life. Today she was throwing away something that others set more value on than she did – not so much her reputation but also her conformity.

At the bottom of the stairs, she heard the library door swing open and angry footsteps come her way. She did not look round but quickened her step. Nothing could dampen her exuberance, not even her father marching swiftly along behind her. Before she could make the sitting-room door, he had grabbed hold of her arm. 'You lied to me!'

His face was red and smudges of yellow mudded the whiteness of his eyes. She'd already guessed she'd be today's scapegoat and was prepared for it.

'Oh, Daddy. What do you mean?' Her voice was childishly sarcastic. Indeed, she wanted to flaunt it, to fling everything she had once been into his face.

'Don't play with me, Abbie. You know what I mean. I wasted a whole afternoon asking about some man who does not and never has existed. You lied to me!'

She could tell him the truth about Carrie, but she wouldn't. Carrie was better off without him. She knew it. She remembered things, things best forgotten in respectable families. Retaliation was the order of the day. Her father had secrets that were also best kept hidden.

'Was that the same day you didn't get home until midnight? Are you telling me that you looked for this man right up until then? Or was it one of your henchmen doing the looking for you?'

'Cut out your cheek, girl! It's your father you're talking to!'

Surprisingly, there was weakness in his voice. More sensitive than others realised, Abbie picked up on that small hint of diminishing power. 'Could it be that you found your way to a certain little seamstress who came here dressed in cheap cotton to measure Mother up for morning dresses, but now wears satin and spends her time flat on her back with her legs in the air?'

A vein throbbed in her father's temple. His grip lessened on her arm.

'Put your own house in order, Father dear,' she said through clenched teeth.

He let her go. She resumed her progress towards the sitting room, the silk trousers swinging energetically like battle honours.

'Mark my words, I shall do that some day,' he called after her, his voice trembling with anger. 'I'll clean up this family. Mark my words if I don't!'

Normally, afternoon tea was something she went all out to avoid. But today was different, though some things had not changed. Her mother, neat in pale primrose with her legs tucked demurely in a sideways sweep, was there with a small group of women who all had rich husbands and lives full of nothing more than gossip, gardening and running up bills. Their menfolk were waiting for her father in the library where he kept an eight-bottle Tantalus of various whiskies.

Gilbert, dressed in white flannels and a blue-striped blazer, was holding court. The matrons perched like contented hens in the easy chairs, faces upturned as though awaiting his wisdom.

The moment he saw her, the cup and saucer he held rattled down to the tray and his wide mouth slid into a sensual smile.

'Abigail, darling.' He rushed to her side and kissed her on both cheeks. She responded like with like.

'Darling Abigail, how very chic you are. So now! So, so...'

'Sexy?' she said softly.

One of the older women clamped an ancient ear trumpet against an ancient ear. 'What was that?'

'Sexy. I said sexy,' said Abigail, not giving Gilbert a chance to substitute the truth.

'I was going to say super,' he said.

She grinned. 'I know. But it wasn't what you were thinking, was it?'

His smile was reflected in his eyes and the way they kept falling into her cleavage. 'I admit nothing,' he said slowly.

'You don't need to.'

She held herself slightly away from him and breathed deeply, her nipples heaving against the flimsy material.

'Do you fancy a walk in the garden?' She pouted ever so slightly in the same way as Mary Pickford before Douglas Fairbanks kissed her.

Before he could accept her invitation, Abbie's mother asked Gilbert the question she asked everyone who met her eldest daughter. 'Do you really approve of women in trousers, Gilbert?'

'Mother doesn't approve,' said Abbie. 'But then, that cannot be any surprise, can it. She doesn't approve of women going to university either.'

'A woman's place is in the home. Don't you think so?' said her mother, to murmured approvals from her flock of preening friends.

Abbie's eyes narrowed as she gazed at each of them. Of course they thought so. 'Depends whether her acumen is in her head or her hips,' she sneered, and accompanied her statement with a provocative wiggle.

A gasp hit the ceiling like a tidal wave.

Sensing the skirmish could easily evolve into a battle, Gilbert chose to side-step. 'You're right. We should take a walk to the rose arbour. The garden's looking lovely with the last of the summer roses,' he said.

Smiling as if everything at home was just as lovely as the garden, Abbie took hold of his arm. 'It is. Let me take you round it.'

The last of the magnolia blossom fluttered across their path as arm in arm they strolled towards the summerhouse that sat next to the stream and beyond the shrubbery. The smell of rosehips and ripening golden rod lay heavy on the air. Spiders were spinning silvery webs between dead stalks.

'You've never forgiven her for not letting you go to university, have you?'

Abbie sighed. 'I've never forgiven my mother for doing a lot of things. Primarily I've never forgiven her for being the type of woman she is. Till the day she dies, she will be a mat for my father to walk on. She's the woman who takes care of his house, entertains his business friends, and represents him at those all-female social events. The women there carry their husband's position in society as easily as they would a handbag or an umbrella.'

He laughed. 'Is that a type? Or is it just a social requirement?'

He took hold of her elbow and steered her beneath an arch

where rosehips hung heavily between stiff wire and sparse leaves. He had a long stride but she kept pace with him.

They stopped in the summerhouse, the doorway framing them and forcing them to be close, just as she'd expected it to.

His eyes strayed to the gaping blouse and the rounded fall of her bosom.

She regarded him with amusement, but not mockingly, smiling with her eyes as well as her mouth.

Gilbert's reaction was predictably smug. He knew he was good-looking and women were attracted to him. Seduction was his aim. What would he think if he knew she had set out today to seduce him?

He was hesitant about kissing her. She'd rebuffed him in the past. She waited her chance.

Hesitantly, he put both arms around her. 'My, but you're looking gorgeous, Abbie. Just like a film star.'

'I'm too big to be teased, Gilbert. I'm also too intelligent to be patronised.'

He laughed and threw back his head. 'Patronised. That always was your favourite word.'

He held her more tightly and looked down at her. In the past, she would have pulled away but not today. As she moved closer to him, the breeze toyed with the loosened neck of her blouse and exposed the dark areolae around her nipples. To her delight, she saw a liquid look come to his deep-set eyes and a sudden loosening occur in his facial features.

'Abbie... Oh, Abbie!' His voice trembled.

His hands ran over her ribs to her waist then on to her hips. She let him kiss her. The effect was not unpleasant. She found herself liking it, mostly because she imagined it was not Gilbert but someone else, someone who she desired more deeply than anyone could possibly imagine.

Gilbert was breathing heavily in her ear whilst one hand fumbled at her breast, his thumb tweaking her naked nipple. She felt a hardening in his loins. She would achieve her objective. Her virginity would be vanquished.

'Abbie. I think we should get married.' His voice was slurred with lust.

'Why?' she asked, her eyes wide in mock surprise.

'So I can do this all the time,' he said. His mouth moved to cover hers again, his hand diving between her legs.

A shower of falling leaves blew their way and tangled in her hair.

He rained kisses over her face. She tried not to show distaste.

'Oh, Abbie, you can't imagine how good it is to kiss you. You'll let me do everything else, won't you? You know I want you. You know I'll marry you.'

'Then let's do it. Now!' she gasped back, pretending to be as breathless as he.

'I want to have you,' he said huskily, his stomach tight against hers.

His hardness pressing against her abdomen aroused her curiosity. She ran her hand down between their bodies, gripped then stroked him through his trousers.

He gasped.

'I don't love you, Gilbert,' she said between his fervent kisses. 'And I don't want to marry you.'

His lips paused inches from hers. She could smell his breath. 'Does it matter?'

'Not to me.'

He looked amazed when she pushed him back into the hidden shade of the summerhouse. Accompanied by the buzzing of insects, she undid the buttons on his shirt then his trousers.

He gasped again and threw back his head.

She let the silky garments fall from her body and almost laughed out loud when she saw the lunge at the front of his trousers.

'Take me,' she said as she lay down and opened her legs. He fumbled with his clothes. She turned her lips from his kisses as he got on top of her. Would this hurt? For the first time since embarking on this adventure, a knot of true fear gripped her stomach.

She felt his hands fumbling between her legs, guiding the hard shaft between her surprisingly fluid lips.

She began to relax. She was doing this for herself. She should enjoy it, but in the back of her mind she knew she was also doing it for Anthony.

One short stab of pain and she began to respond, not because she loved him or really wanted him, but just because it was natural for her body to respond to his.

There was no great climax, only a torn feeling in her groin and the knowledge that she was at long last a woman.

* * *

The pain and the feeling stayed with her as they made their way back up the path to the house.

Gilbert's exuberance, which seemed to border on affection, surprised her.

'Abbie, I hardly know what to say. Gosh! What a whiz you are!'

She hated the way he spoke. It was so superior, yet at the same time so banal. Every so often his hand slid to her bottom.

'Don't do that, Gilbert,' she said. 'Just because we've had intimate sexual relations doesn't mean you can take liberties.'

He was astounded. 'After what we've just done?'

She quickened her step on the narrow path so he had to fall in behind her. '*Especially* after what we've just done. It doesn't mean you own me.'

He blustered. 'No. I know that. At least, I don't own you just yet. But I will, Abbie. I mean, you know me. I'm not a cad, you know. I wouldn't take advantage of a girl like that and then let her down. I want to marry you. I've always wanted to marry you.'

The arrogance of the man!

'I wouldn't let you down,' he said again.

'How very gallant of you.'

'Then that's agreed.'

'Yes,' she said, but because she was still thinking on what she'd just done, she didn't see her cousin beaming broadly. If she had, she might have guessed what he was going to do next.

The parents were gathering to leave, coats brought by servants, chauffeurs attending with blankets for the more needy. The woman with the ear trumpet was sipping whisky from a hip flask.

'Medicinal,' she hissed when they caught her unawares.

Ignoring her, Gilbert made for the middle of the reception hall where he stood waving his arms. 'Listen,' he shouted. 'I've got something to tell you. Abigail and I are getting married!'

A loud chorus of approval arose from the clucking hens. Abbie was astounded. 'Oh, no, we're not!'

Gilbert smiled like an idiot and shook his head. 'Don't be silly, Abbie. We have to now.'

Abigail glared at him. 'Don't be so stupid. Of course we're not getting married.'

Her mother threw her hands up in the air. 'But that would be so wonderful.'

Her father gripped his nephew's hand. 'Gilbert, my boy.'

Abbie felt her whole body growing rigid. No. This was not what was supposed to happen.

'Gilbert! Just because I had sex with you in the summerhouse does not mean that I want to marry you. I thought I made that clear!'

Turning her back on him, she marched off up the stairs.

'Oh my word,' cried her mother.

Abbie looked down from the landing in time to see her collapse in a dead faint.

* * *

Twenty minutes later, she was dressed in her usual sporty style behind the wheel of her trusty Austin, her lips pursed, her face pink and her eyes blazing with anger.

'Bloody fool!' Remembering her mother fainting and the shocked faces of her friends, she began to smile. Then she began to laugh, and laugh and laugh until the tears were streaming down her face. Just for her own amusement she said again, word for word, exactly what she had said back at the house.

'Gilbert! Just because I had sex with you in the summerhouse does not mean that I want to marry you. I thought I made that clear!'

Then she burst into laughter again until her vision was so blurred that she had to pull in at the side of the road and dry her eyes with a man-sized handkerchief.

13

Beth lived in fear that Elliot would recall their wedding night. So far he had not; her secret was safe. Everything might have gone on the same way and he might never have known about Harry Allen until the New Year and the day they pulled in to Gloucester. As before, the office windows were dull with grime; the weeds thrusting up through the concrete were taller.

'All set,' said Elliot, resolutely snatching his cap from his head. A steely resolve glinted in his eyes.

The door creaked as he pushed it open and entered, leaving Beth to follow. To some, it might appear impolite that he had entered first. But Beth knew he needed to be first. It was his boat and his livelihood long before she had come along.

Because the door had dropped on its hinges Beth found she had to push it hard then pull it back open before pushing it in again.

'It's a bit stiff, sweetheart. You have to lift it,' said a voice.

Beth froze as Harry Allen eased himself away from the window and into the doorway. 'Let me.'

She smelled his maleness, the faint odour of camphor, a hint of cheap scent and strong tobacco. Craving fresh air, she swallowed her revulsion. The last time his body had been this close, he had ripped at her clothes and explored her whilst she sobbed against his shoulder.

Imagination, she said to herself. *It's only imagination.* How often had she thought she had heard him or seen him following her down some dark wharf or staring at her out of some sightless window?

Look up and you'll see you are mistaken, she told herself. It was no mean task to gaze up into the eyes of the man who had raped her, the man who had beguiled her with sweet words of sympathy.

In one brave moment, she managed it and looked up into the face of Harry Allen. Suddenly her world was less bright, more terrifying. But she mustn't let Elliot know. Whatever else, she must not show that anything was wrong.

Swallowing hard, she passed through the door without comment, her legs shaking and her eyes darting between Harry and her husband.

'What? No thanks? And there was I thinking we had something special between us.' There was no mistaking his meaning. At the same time, his hand, unseen by Elliot, slid over her hip. Beth stepped smartly away.

Smiling smugly, Harry went back behind his desk.

Beth saw Elliot's frown and the question in his eyes. He was not a fool. Neither was he a man to be crossed. The fear of what he could be and what he could do lay like a rock in her stomach.

Harry beamed. 'Beaven! What a lucky man you are!'

His statement echoed around the dusty office. Even the little man scribbling in the corner glanced their way.

Elliot eyed Harry. 'I'm sorry, sir?'

Harry grinned. Beth shivered at the malice in his eyes. 'You married this beauty! Thought I was in with a chance myself. She and I were acquainted once. Did you know that?'

How dare he! 'There was nothing between us!'

'Wasn't there?' Harry raised his eyebrows, as if daring her to own up before he did.

Elliot was looking at her, waiting for explanation.

She prayed Harry would not enlighten him. A man's ego, she had learned, is a very fragile thing and slights or insults are not easily forgiven.

Harry hooked his thumbs into the armholes of his waistcoat. 'She's quite a catch, Beaven. She can read and write. Read and write! Not many of you people can do that, now can you!'

'Yes, sir. She can,' growled Elliot.

Beth noted his clenched fists, the way he gripped his hat.

It'll be shapeless now. What a foolish thought that was.

Harry bent to study the manifests, perusing all five sheets. She saw him scribble on the third page but only glance at the others before rustling them back into place. At last, he looked up and spoke directly to her. 'Read it carefully, my pretty girl. Your husband's depending on you.'

The insult was obvious. Elliot's tension was tangible, the heat of his body seeming to boil out and touch hers.

As she concentrated on the manifests, her anxiety lessened. It was a mixed load, wire to Worcester on the first page. All was in order. She nodded at Elliot to sign it. She did the same to the second: four cases of matches for Birmingham. Elliot signed that too, his spidery 'X' finely drawn but slightly lopsided.

When she came to the third page, her heart skipped a beat. *Rubber washers* was all it should have said. But beneath it, in Harry Allen's rounded hand, an extra line had been inserted.

I won't tell him what we did if you're nice to me. You will be nice to me again, won't you?

The curling sweep of the question mark leapt up out of the page at her. She smothered a gasp of surprise.

'I trust everything is in order, my dear?' said Harry, his voice as thick and sickly sweet as molasses.

She quickly passed the pen to Elliot. 'Sign it.'

He frowned at her and she saw the puzzled look in his eyes. If she had sought to escape any explanation when they were alone later, that was enough to tell her otherwise.

Harry was still smiling widely, his teeth exposed like a row of yellowed tombstones. In her mind she was hitting out at them and watching as they fell into jagged fragments.

It was an effort to stop her hand shaking as she read the last two pages: two more loads of matches, one for Birmingham and one for Warwick.

'All done!' Elliot flung the pen back down on the desk, his eyes fixed on Harry Allen's face.

Harry's wide-toothed smile remained but a hard glint came to his eyes.

'Thanks to your wife. You're a lucky man to have a wife such as her, Beaven. I wish I had her myself – in every possible way.'

There was no doubting his meaning. He winked at Elliot because they were both men of the world, weren't they, well used to the ways of women.

Beth's face burned with shame.

Elliot's complexion was only slightly paler than his hair. ''Tis none of your damn business Mr Allen!' His voice was cold, even.

Beth sensed his muscles tightening and saw his jaw clenching. The one thing they couldn't afford was for Elliot to lash out or even to warn him. *Agincourt* belonged to the carrying company.

Elliot, unlike her father, did not own his boat. Such people as her father were referred to as 'number ones' and had more scope than men like Elliot did.

She grabbed his arm. 'Come on. Let's be off.'

It was like moving a tree trunk. His feet reluctantly headed for the door. His glare remained fixed over his shoulder.

Harry Allen sat smug and self-assured behind his desk, daring him.

'Remember your boat,' Beth whispered.

His head swivelled round. She wanted to reach up and smooth away the rigidness in his jaw. He blinked as though surprised to see her.

'Ignore him,' she whispered again. 'He's a monster. My dad had dealings with him,' she added as if that might explain everything.

Remembering what Harry Allen had done to her brought back other feelings. Was it all her fault after all?

The door swung creaking on its hinges behind them, the dust disturbed by a passing coal truck drifting into the grimy office.

Elliot took big, angry strides along the cinder path back to the boat. She followed, the thud of his footsteps echoed by the beating of her heart.

'Never mind, Elliot. We've got our load. That's all that matters, isn't it?' She spoke cheerfully, though she felt far from cheerful inside. Her skin prickled as it did just before lightning flashed and thunder rolled at the end of a hot summer's day.

His shoulders were squared. He began to swear. 'Bloody swine!'

'I'll warm up that bit of mutton stew for tonight. It's your favourite. How'd you like that?'

'What right does he have, what bloody right!'

'And I've made an apple pie. I've a little cream...'

'Meet him on a dark night and I'd knock that bloody smile right off his ugly face!'

'Never mind him. Let's get home,' she said.

The small windows of the towering warehouses squinted down at them. They reminded her of Harry's wicked wink and the narrowing of his eyes when he looked at her.

'We'll set off tonight, shall we?'

Still Elliot did not respond, his anger bottled up for later consumption.

The sun hung low in the sky, dirty windows and puddles reflecting its orange rays. Oh, to be off on some silver strip of water where willows dipped their fingers and moorhens scurried among the reeds! Where there were no other people and the only fearful sounds in the darkness were the hoot of a far-off owl and the high-pitched bark of a lovelorn vixen. The smell of wild thyme, bluebells and clover hung heavy over the water, each in their season. Oh, to be there, far from the satanic dirt of factories and wharves!

Agincourt came into view. Beth convinced herself that all would be well.

She cried out when Elliot grabbed her arm, jerking her to a standstill.

'What was that writing he wrote?'

Her first inclination was to lie. The words rolled off her tongue. 'It was about the fire hazard of carrying both wood and matches on the same load.'

'You're lying!'

'How dare you call me a liar!'

She felt the sting of his hand across her cheek. 'Don't lie to me. I know when you're lying. The truth: I want the truth or I'll...' He raised his hand again.

She winced. 'All right!'

She hung her head, at the same time grinding gravel beneath

her toe. 'It was a rude comment.' She dared not look up in case he saw the guilt hidden behind her thick dark lashes.

'Well!'

Her thoughts raced. 'He said I could share his bed with him any time he liked.'

'I'm going to kill him!' He turned back.

Beth grabbed his arm. 'No! Leave it, Elliot. Please. Leave it.'

He stared down at her. 'Strikes me as you're taking this too gently, me girl. Why is that? Like the thought of sharing his bed, do you?'

'No! Of course not. Think of the boat. Think of what damage he could do to you. He doesn't have me, Elliot. You do!'

She felt his muscles relax beneath her hand. His flesh was warm, the hairs on his arm soft like goose down.

'You're right,' he said though his jaw must have ached as he said it. 'But I'd still like to smash his smiling teeth all the way down into his belly!'

All day he brooded. She watched, unsure of what he would do, fearful of what revenge he might take.

At dawn they left the wharves where mangy cats hunted vermin. The smell of the morning went some way to calming her soul. But her cheek still stung. It was difficult to know who to fear the most: Harry Allen or her husband.

14

There was to be a meeting at Worcester, where further plans were to be made regarding strike action for the boatmen.

Anthony had travelled up from a meeting in London and looked tired when Abigail collected him from the railway station. Once the formalities were over and the car was on the move, he fell soundly asleep. She couldn't help glancing at his rugged features, correcting her steering when she became too carried away.

'The face that launched a thousand ships,' she murmured and smiled to herself. Anthony was hardly Helen of Troy, but there were similarities. He was about to cause disruption to her father's business. The thought pleased her.

Anthony awoke with a start. He'd been dreaming that men with long staves were beating him. In his dream there was no rescue, no fair maiden bathing his wounds.

'Did you have a bad dream?'

'No. Why should I?'

'You just look as though you did.'

He had no intention of retelling the dream. He'd told no one he still dreamed of that night, and that's the way it would stay. 'You look mighty pleased with yourself,' he remarked, assessing by their surroundings that they'd almost reached their destination.

'Hmm!'

'You're purring.'

'Meaning?'

'Like the cat that's licked a whole bucket of cream.'

She smiled. 'You could say that. The fact is that my cousin Gilbert considers himself engaged to me.'

'Now what's made him think that?'

'Why shouldn't he? Don't you think I'm worth a marriage proposal?'

In two minds as to how to answer, Anthony chose the coward's path. 'Of course you are. To the right man.'

'Are you saying my cousin Gilbert might not be the right man?'

'I couldn't say. I've never met him.'

Disappointed that he showed no sign of jealousy, Abigail pressed her foot more heavily on the accelerator. Her smile became tighter. 'He's very rich.'

'But not very bright.'

She turned her head to stare at him. The car swerved. 'Steady!' He grabbed the wheel and set it straight. 'Do you think you can keep your eyes on the road?'

'That wasn't a very nice thing to say.'

'About your cousin not being very bright?'

'Exactly. That was very rude of you.'

She dared to look at him long enough to see a boyish grin. It made her tingle.

'But I'm right,' said Anthony. 'If he was rich enough, handsome enough and clever enough, you might accept. As it is he must be a bit stupid to even consider marrying you.'

'How dare you!'

'Steady!'

He grabbed the wheel again. The little car careered all over the road before straightening. A horse pulling a passing milk cart reared in fright, the churns clanking and toppling as it came to a halt.

Anthony looked back. 'The driver's shaking his fist.'

'Stupid man.'

'You can't blame him, Abbie! His milk's churned to butter!'

'Don't be so bloody ridiculous!'

Anthony laughed. It was big, throaty and spontaneous; and totally irresistible.

She burst out laughing. 'Anthony! You're incorrigible.'

'Poor bloke. Explain that to the housewives waiting to fill their jugs.'

Abigail turned serious. 'So what did you mean?'

'About the milk? Well, it's like this. Once it's shook about a bit you get butter, not that a well-brought-up young lady like you would know anything about—'

'That's not what I meant and you know it.' She cleared her throat. There was no more laughter, just an uncomfortable question for which she needed a comforting answer. 'Why would anyone be stupid to consider marrying me?'

Anthony studied her. Her eyes were fixed on the road ahead as though it would melt away if she didn't concentrate. He was immediately overwhelmed with a great surge of affection. From the very first, Abbie had intrigued him. What was a well-to-do daughter of a carrying-company owner doing attending union and Labour Party meetings? 'Because I care,' she'd answered when questioned. There was something in her eyes that made him think she was not telling the complete truth. He didn't push it. People told the truth in their own good time. It was best that way.

He looked down at the thick tartan car rug she'd placed over his knees. His voice was deep and low, the sort of voice that had captivated more than one attractive female: passing women, none that had held his attention for long.

'I just thought...' He paused, not wanting her to jump to any conclusions. 'You're a strong woman, Abbie. There's few men that would suit you. You're no fool. A man would have to be very special indeed to gain your affection or your hand in marriage. The fact you've refused him is proof enough that he's not up to much. So! There you are!'

'Would you marry me?'

He controlled his surprise. 'Now now, Abbie. I know you're only teasing.'

Abbie tossed her head the way she always did when she wished to hide her true feelings. 'Of course I am. But that does not mean you cannot give me an opinion.'

Anthony studied her features as he thought about it. There was no doubt she was attractive. But why hide it beneath men's clothes and a less than feminine attitude? He sighed and smiled. 'I think you'll be the one to choose who you'll marry, and damn what the world might think.'

She glowed in the warmth of the answer. It wasn't exactly as she'd wanted, but close: it gave her scope. 'So! Will you marry me?'

He instinctively knew she was serious and that he had to do something quickly. He laughed. 'I'm already married.'

A small frown drew her eyebrows together. 'I didn't know that.'

He leaned slightly closer. 'To the cause of the working man, and so are you. Aren't you? Say you are, Abbie. Don't let me down.'

Her laugh was brittle. She'd almost believed he was married. She couldn't have lived with that.

'Of course I am. I won't let you down, Anthony. I swear I won't. And men only marry innocent girls. I have to inform you that I've lost my virginity. I did it intentionally.' She noted his surprise and shrugged. 'Gilbert just took things too seriously.'

A silence followed, leaving them both with their own thoughts. After swiftly coming to terms with Abigail's announcement, Anthony's reverted to Beth Dawson and Elliot Beaven. Beth's eyes were the ones that made him whole again once the dream had drifted. Elliot he knew by reputation. He was handy with his fists; too handy from what he'd heard. He wondered whether he was good to Beth. He hoped so.

Abigail bit her lip. She'd let Anthony down, driven off and left his rescue to the daughter of a boatman. She remembered the way he'd looked at that girl and felt jealous.

Never mind, she's safely married now and out of his reach.

* * *

'I'm going for a pint and there's a meeting,' Elliot said.

Without needing him to say it, Beth went to the willow-patterned tea caddy that held a brown-paper bag of pennies as well as tea. She placed two pence into his outstretched hand. He glanced at the copper coins and then at her. She handed him the caddy and turned away, preferring not to see what he was taking but promising herself to check it once he had gone out of the door. Arguing about money was something to be strictly avoided this evening. Besides, she didn't want him to linger. It had been a difficult journey since leaving Gloucester; he'd asked her more questions about Harry Allen and the message he'd written on the manifests. She'd since scribbled it out in case others saw the words and read them to him.

He'd pointed a finger straight between her eyes. 'If you're lying to me, girl, it'll be the worse for you. If you dare stray from the path of a right and proper wife, then I'll teach you otherwise. Got that?'

An angry silence had travelled with them. It was stifling. Two people sharing just one tenth of the whole length of the boat and working together every day. She couldn't remember it ever being this unbearable, even with her father.

Tonight, she hungered for peace and quiet. Tonight, she would read.

Once his footsteps had faded away, she reached for the caddy and shook it before prising off the lid. A few pennies rattled around at the bottom. Hopefully he wouldn't spend all he'd taken.

She sighed. What was the use of worrying? She moved the long, flat cushion from on top of the storage unit beneath the overhead cupboard, lifted the seat and took out *The Old Curiosity Shop*.

Once the book was opened, she was standing outside the dusty exterior of an old-fashioned shop, watching as Little Nell and her grandfather closed the door. She smiled at the Marchioness, a cute little thing who everyone, but mostly Mr Quilp, took full advantage of. Nothing, she thought, has changed. The strong still take advantage of the weak and men, no matter how ugly or mad, still take priority over women.

It was only on taking a breath between chapters that she chanced to glance up at the walnut clock Carrie and George Melcroft had given her as a wedding present. She frowned. Elliot had been gone for two hours. It wasn't like him to linger in a pub, not with starting a journey before five in the morning. They had a load to pick up halfway to the Potteries.

She rushed to put the book away. Her passion for stories meant entering a world where he could not follow. When it was just the two of them, she sensed his resentment. She didn't want him to know about this book and more especially the one Anthony had given her, not after a day like today and the things Harry Allen had said. The books only came out when she was alone.

After returning it to its hiding place, she put on the cardigan she had discarded earlier.

At first she only poked her head out of the door, listening for the tell-tale sound of his boots beating on cobbles. She heard and saw nothing.

She'd go and find him. He'd appreciate her seeking him out, wouldn't he? The Navigator was the obvious choice. Perhaps he'd be in there slumped over the bar between boatmen bemoaning the state of their industry and their lives.

There was more noise than she'd expected. A group of men were milling around outside and a woman was shouting for the police.

And then a man's voice. 'The bastard deserves it! He's a liar! A bloody liar!'

Elliot! Calling his name, she ran forward.

A strong arm and a firm grip reached out and stopped her.

Abigail's voice: 'Mrs Beaven.'

Beth stared. A body lay on the ground.

Abigail explained, 'There's been a fight. Anthony's dealing with it.'

'Elliot! Is he hurt?' Beth struggled to shake off Abigail's strong grip.

'No. It's a man called Harry Allen. And serves him bloody right!'

A gnawing fear gripped Beth's stomach. Elliot wasn't hurt, but Harry was. What had been said?

Two figures approached, dark cameos against the light falling from the pub windows.

Elliot swayed. Anthony Wesley put his arm around him and whispered, then handed him over to two other men who held him between them as Anthony stepped forward and pointed to one of the crowd. 'You! That man there! Get him to a doctor.'

The small man he addressed wore a dull suit and large glasses. 'Never mind a doctor! He should be arrested for what he's done to Harry!'

Anthony grabbed the man by his collar and hauled his face close to his own.

'Well, if you're so fond of Harry Allen, you can return him to those who have time for him!'

'But that ruffian attacked—' he blurted, his arms flailing.

'From what I hear, he had every right to,' said Anthony as he let him fall to his feet.

Harry Allen raised himself on to one elbow, blood snorting from his nostrils. He pointed a shaking finger at the staggering Elliot. 'I'll have your boat off you, Beaven. Mark my words, and then I'll have that pretty little wife of yours – just like I did before!'

A horrified hush surfed through the gathered crowd.

Beth shook from head to toe. There it was! It was out! But Elliot was drunk and just maybe – maybe – he wouldn't remember.

'You keep away from my wife,' shouted Elliot.

Anthony trapped him in a vicelike grip as he fought to have another go.

The small man Anthony had dropped to the ground pushed his spectacles back up his nose, held himself very straight and wagged his finger. 'I shall report all this to my esteemed employer, Mr Gatehouse. I shall reiterate everything that happened here this evening, I promise you that!'

'So go tell your tales to your high and mighty employer, Mr Penmore. As I understand it, he may be a man who likes to get his own way. Is that not right?' shouted Anthony once he had Elliot under some sort of control.

'That's my father, all right,' said Abigail.

Beth, unsure if she had heard correctly, looked at Abigail. Was it her imagination or did she look suddenly embarrassed, suddenly vulnerable?

Penmore looked surprised. Taking off his hat, he addressed her directly. 'I do apologise, Miss Gatehouse. I didn't see you there.'

Abigail bristled. 'Well, go on. Take your tales to my father.' His abject demeanour disappeared. His thin lips stretched even more thinly as though he'd just sucked a particularly bitter lemon.

'Did you know that I've lost my virginity, Penmore? Does that make you jealous? You would have liked to have taken it, wouldn't you? Am I right, Penmore? Am I?'

Beth couldn't hear what was said but saw her leaning close. Whatever she said made the little man's face turn crimson.

Anthony was urging Elliot to get away. 'Quickly! Get going!'

Abigail nudged her arm. 'Quick. You have to go. Now!'

Beth allowed herself to be herded along the wharf. Abigail ran with her, Anthony behind prodding a loping Elliot into quicker action. 'You shouldn't have done that, chum,' Anthony was saying. 'That's a mean piece of work back there.'

Breathless and agitated, they got to the boat. Elliot, leaning heavily on Anthony's arm and stinking of ale, scrambled over the side first and fell forward towards the door. It sprang open and he fell headlong down the ladder, his boots sticking out like a pair of upturned buckets.

Beth climbed down after him and turned up the oil lamp. Somehow she and Anthony managed to heave him on to the bed.

Abigail removed his boots. 'My, but that was certainly very hard work.' Her eyes shone with excitement. 'But it was worth it, wasn't it? Did you see the look on old Penmore's face? And what about Harry Allen! Did you see the state of his nose? Blood everywhere! Your husband certainly gave him a bashing to remember! It was simply super!'

'Abbie!' Anthony's expression eddied between shock and amusement.

Beth couldn't help smiling.

Unrepentant, Abigail perched herself on the middle step of the ladder and gave him a knowing look. 'I was only praising Mr Beaven's right hook. I wish I could hit as hard as that.'

'Never mind that.' He frowned at her before turning to Beth. 'He'll have a bad head tomorrow.'

Beth glanced at her sleeping husband, whose head rested in the crook of his arm as he slept and snored softly into the pillow. She knew what she had to do.

'That can't be helped. We have a load to get delivered. Bad head or not, we must be away by first light.'

Anthony touched her shoulder. 'Beth, you don't understand. You have to leave now, not in the morning. There'll be hired thugs on their way even now.'

'Anthony's right,' added a flushed Abigail. 'You have to leave now. No arguing! I insist! Penmore will be off to tell my father and get things organised. He may look an ineffectual weakling, but he's quite nasty. Nastier than Harry Allen.'

'I doubt that,' muttered Beth. She wiped the back of her hand across her forehead. 'And how do you suggest I get him sober enough to get going?' she snapped, suddenly annoyed with her husband for being drunk and with Abigail for being so smart, so superior.

'Some women run boats by themselves,' Abigail retorted tartly.

'Well, I don't!' returned Beth. But of course she could run the boat if she had to. It was just that at this moment she didn't want to be conciliatory and she didn't really know why.

'Now, now, sweet Beth.' Anthony's disarming smile smoothed

her prickly emotions. 'I think I can give you a hand, Mrs Beaven, at least until the morning. The canal is not the sea, but some time on the water won't do me any harm at all.'

'Anthony!' Abigail exclaimed, panic replacing her earlier excitement. 'You have meetings to organise, leaflets to plan.'

'You can do it,' he said. 'Aren't you always saying you can do a better job than a man? Well, here's your chance.' He addressed Beth. 'I'll start the engine,' he said as he began to peel off his coat, then turned to Abigail. 'And you can drive off back to my place and sort out the stuff I've left there. Meet me at the first drop. Where is that, Beth?'

'Worcester,' she said.

It amused and amazed Beth to see Abigail's painted lips part in astonishment.

'You'll be staying all night?'

Anthony grinned. 'Yes. All night with a married woman whilst her husband sleeps off his hangover.' His eyes twinkled as though relishing the dismayed look on Abigail's face.

'You don't have to,' Beth said.

'I think I do. I owe you a favour. Remember?'

Her blood warmed at the thought of that night. 'I much appreciate it. You're very kind.'

15

They steered away from the bank, the sound of the engine not nearly so loud it seemed as the beating of her heart.

Her face white against the blackness, Abigail slowly melted into the shadows.

Anthony raised his hand in a last wave. Narrowing his eyes, he turned his attention to the slick surface of the canal. Straight as an arrow, it lay before them.

Accompanied only by the deep *thud, thud, thud* of the single-cylinder engine, they glided past the brick warehouses, the ships sleeping at their berths. Most were waiting to be unloaded or for the tide to come up the River Severn. The only other sounds were the wild things sliding into the water or flapping on the surface.

Lights from houses and pubs fell in squares and oblongs across sooty cobbles and pitch-black water. Anthony stood as though he was carved from wood. She had a strong urge to tell him so, but the silence was as welcome as the darkness.

Three hours slid idly by before the city was completely behind them and they were heading up the canal towards the Worcester

Risers, a great set of locks that had to be opened one after another until they were on the right level to continue.

A slight breeze rustled the grasses that fringed the canal, blowing her hair across her face. In that moment, something changed and at first she couldn't work out what it was. Then she realised the sickness was gone. I've left it behind, she thought. It's back there in the city that stinks of oil, creosote and the leaks of huge gasometers. Well, good riddance!

She took a deep breath and filled her lungs with air that tasted of fresh grass and clean water. 'I know a place.' she said softly, not meaning anyone to hear but herself.

Anthony broke his silence. '*A Midsummer Night's Dream*. You've read the book I gave you.'

'I liked that bit best. It reminds me of the quieter places along the sides of the canals.'

'It suits this place.' He spoke softly as though he was addressing the scene before his eyes. Shadows thrown by the bare branches of winter trees passed over his face. 'And here we are travelling towards Shakespeare's birthplace. They make chocolate and all manner of machines and metal things in the Midlands nowadays. They made a great playwright too. Don't you think so?'

She smiled to herself. 'My father used to hate me reading books. He can't read himself, you see. "Another book," he shouted after a new one was given to me. Sometimes he'd throw it into the canal. That's why I try and remember favourite bits.'

'Keep it in the mind. It makes sense.' He was silent for a moment. 'Say it to me now,' he said at last.

'Now?' Her heart seemed to beat more noisily.

'Now.'

> 'I know a place,
> Where oxlips and the nodding violet grows,

Quite over-canopied with luscious woodbine,
With sweet musk-roses, and with eglantine.'

The words seemed to drift on the night air along with the crisp scents of winter. Silence followed. For a precious moment it seemed as if they were the only two people left in the world. In some odd way that only a woman knows, she knew he was feeling the same way.

Like him, she looked straight ahead. To look at him was far too dangerous. What if he saw her looking? What if their eyes should meet?

'You should read more of Shakespeare,' he said suddenly. 'His sonnets are especially fine.'

She glanced at him quickly and just as quickly looked ahead again to where the darkness hung like a blanket across the next bend.

'Sonnets! Are they poems? I thought he only wrote plays.'

'Yes,' he answered.

'Unfortunately there's little room for books on boats,' she said sadly. The few she had hidden from Elliot instantly came to mind.

'You'd especially like *Romeo and Juliet*,' he said. 'It's about forbidden love between two young people from warring families and she's been promised to marry someone else. It's the way of the world. Life never ends up as you want it.'

Her thoughts were stirred. Promising to marry someone else was such an easy thing to do. The silence between them persisted. She guessed he was waiting for her to say something, but she couldn't. Her tongue seemed to have turned to glass, too heavy to lift, too smooth to form words. There was so much she wanted to say to him about books but she didn't want to appear a fool.

'Perhaps one day you'll have more space,' he said suddenly.

Unknowingly, Anthony had opened a door. In her mind's eye,

she could see that cottage she longed for, the lock shining bright before it, the windows clean and reflecting the sunlight. And there were the brightly painted boats, the children spilling over the sides to laugh and chatter as they eagerly made their way to her cottage where she would teach them how to write their names.

The image was so clear and her longing so intense that she failed to hear him say, 'Anything is possible given time.'

'Beth?' He laid his hand on her arm.

Distracted by her thoughts, she reached to brush it away. She caught her breath and looked into his face as her fingers met his.

'I said, it could happen given time,' he said. 'You didn't hear me.'

He had not removed his hand and she had not removed hers.

He grinned. Such a naughty grin, such a lovely mouth, she thought as his fingers closed over hers.

To her great surprise he took her hand to his mouth and kissed it.

'You shouldn't,' she said and made a half-hearted attempt to snatch her hand away. But the thrill of his touch travelled up her arm to cover her shoulders like a warm shawl. Even the fact that Elliot was asleep downstairs failed to halt the tingling in her blood.

'My guardian angel,' he said softly as his grin became a smile. There was warmth in his eyes and she felt no fear, no distrust.

It was hard to find the right thing to say. If only she could write words to flow like a story or a play that people would come to see or to read and comment on.

Seeing him again felt as if all the time in between their meetings had not happened. Once again, she was the girl who had found him, taken off his shirt and tended to his bruised flesh.

Was she being as stupid as she had been with Harry Allen? The guilt she had carried around since that night flooded over her and urged her to step back, to recover her hand and her emotions and even to lock herself down in the cabin with her sleeping husband.

'I sometimes dream of you,' he said.

She caught her breath. 'You shouldn't say that!'

Her hair flew out in a dark cloud as she glanced nervously between him and the cabin door. If Elliot could see this man holding her hand, if he could hear what he was saying...

'He's out cold,' Anthony said and she wondered how he had known what she was thinking. 'You won't see him up and about until the morning.'

It would have been right for her to withdraw her hand then and there but a host of warm feelings came with his touch. Signs of affection had been few and far between in her life. Perhaps that was why she could not resist him now – unless she was a slut, unless she had been responsible for leading Harry Allen into temptation.

'I respect you, Beth,' he said. 'I won't be abusing your trust.'

He squeezed her hand before letting it go. She touched the spot where his had been. It feels so cold now, she thought. And he isn't Harry Allen; in fact, he's nothing at all like Harry Allen. If only I'd known him...

'I wish I'd met you before Elliot did,' he said unexpectedly.

'I was a child,' she stammered, surprised he had again pre-empted her thoughts.

'Never mind,' he said. 'Have a happy life, Mrs Beaven. Name one of your children after me – as long as your husband doesn't take on about it, of course.'

The silence intensified. There was so much she could say but the words stayed stillborn in her throat. Instead, she stole sly glances, memorizing the slight lift to one side of his mouth, the lines at the corners of his eyes, the way his hair curled around the nape of his neck. In those cold moments when she needed sweet words and the image of a strong man, she would remember him.

Anthony was strong in a different way than Elliot. There seemed no wasted strength about him. You could almost mistake him for being slow until you noticed that everything was really done very quietly and very efficiently.

Elliot was quick to do things but not always well. Speed matched brawn and left clear thinking and methodical planning way behind.

'How did you come to get involved with the union and us people?' she asked.

'I was the second eldest in a family of eight,' he began. 'I was born in Bristol. My father was a merchant seaman on the Australian wool run. He died at sea. My mother was a widow for most of my childhood.' He paused. She sensed he was remembering and experiencing a host of emotions he had not felt in a long while. 'She worked hard to keep us clothed and keep us together.'

He told her about going to sea and sending home money so that the family could eat and his mother not work so hard.

But he'd not counted on his brother turning out to be the black sheep of the family. He gambled, worked as little as possible – at least not in any legal way. On Anthony's last visit home to Bristol, he'd found the house empty, the children in the poor house and his mother buried in a pauper's grave. Without needing anyone to tell him who had brought them to this, he went off looking for his brother.

'My anger was blacker than the night,' he said, his voice breaking with barely suppressed grief. 'I wanted to kill him. I wanted to slit his throat from ear to ear. But he'd already got word that I was home and looking for him. I heard he'd gone north. I would have followed him then and there on the train but after I made sure the younger members of the family were placed with relatives, I didn't have too much money left. So I got a passage on a flyer – you know, one of those fast boats that keep going all night and day. That's when I saw how you folk live and how the carrying company were robbing you blind. I met a man called Ernie Bevan back in 1920 who put me in the picture about things. He said I should use my anger to help anyone who was exploited or not getting the same benefits as everyone else – like education, for instance. So! That's how it was.'

The story was succinctly told. Exploited! That was the word that stood out from the rest. She'd never realised her true position in society up until now. Everything she had ever known had been taken for granted. Suddenly, she was angry.

'Why shouldn't we have our dues? Why shouldn't the children be long enough in a place to learn how to read and write!'

'No reason,' he said softly. He blinked as he studied her face. Each feature had been studied and dreamed about so many times. Why did he need to study her face yet again?

He told himself to stop thinking like a corruptible youth and looked tellingly away.

Beth broke the spell. 'Why was Abigail whispering to that man with the glasses?' she asked.

As the pale glow of dawn began to roll back the night, she saw him raise one dark eyebrow. 'I didn't know she was whispering to him. But he does work for her father, so it isn't as if they're strangers.'

'She's very rich?'

He nodded.

'Then why is she involved with the likes of us? What are we to her?'

He smiled a strange kind of smile that made her wonder

exactly what his feelings were for the young woman who dressed like a young man.

'A lifeline.'

Beth frowned.

He explained. 'Abigail believes that women are second-class citizens. She believes they should have equality with men and that anything a man can do a woman can do just as well or even better. Therefore she works for the union – unpaid, of course.'

'She'll end up an old maid,' said Beth with a laugh.

'That's the whole point,' said Anthony, still stunned by the secret she'd told him. 'She's questioning the whole thing: marriage, men, children. Why does a woman have to get married? Why does she have to have a man at all?'

'But if she wants children,' said Beth.

Anthony laughed. 'According to Abigail it doesn't have to be a permanent arrangement – as long as she's got a private income, of course.'

Beth gasped then prickled with amusement. Abigail's views were different, crazy and excitingly intriguing.

'So why doesn't the union pay her a wage?' she finally asked expecting the answer to be something to do with Abigail having plenty of money and only carrying it out as an act of charity.

'Because she's a woman,' said Anthony with obvious embarrassment.

* * *

Elliot woke up around breakfast time.

Beth smiled at him. 'Are you feeling better?'

He grunted a reply and barely glanced in her direction.

He thanked Anthony for getting him away from Harry and apologised for all the trouble caused.

'You're not out of the woods yet,' said Anthony, 'so don't think you are. Keep away from Gloucester. Not that it's likely to save your boat. But it'll give you some time to sort things out if Gatehouse does snatch it back off you.'

Elliot clenched his fist and thumped it hard below the shelves in the cabin, sending the little china plates jumping and the teacups clattering. 'That rat. I wish I'd killed him!'

'I'm glad you didn't,' said Beth.

She immediately regretted her outburst once she saw the look on his face.

Anthony sat with his elbows resting on his knees, a cup of steaming tea clenched with both hands. 'Is there somewhere you can go until things die down? If he does take your boat off you, it could be some time before you get another. I could help you, of course.'

Elliot nodded. 'My father's place.'

Beth looked from one man to another. 'We could be thrown off?'

Their silence confirmed it. She imagined their meagre belongings thrown on to the wharf. She'd seen it done to others, heard the wailing of women and children as they'd collected their bits and pieces.

She tried to convey her fear to Elliot, but he wouldn't look at her.

A loud honk on a car horn sounded from outside. 'Abigail,' said Anthony, setting the tea aside and getting to his feet. 'Or should I call her Boadicea, complete with her battle chariot!' He reached for the cap warming beside the range.

'I appreciate what you've done,' Elliot said as he shook hands. 'You must be tired after bringing the boat up for me.'

The impatient toot of Abigail's horn sounded again. She waved her arm out of the window. 'Come on. Get a move on.'

Anthony waved and shouted goodbye before getting into the car. Beth sensed the accompanying wink was just for her. She hoped Elliot didn't think so. He stood silently beside her, watching the car drive away. Then it was only the two of them. Her stomach churned. Instinctively, she knew that Elliot now knew the truth about her and Harry Allen.

* * *

'You're too fond of that girl,' said Abigail. She smoked as she drove, the tip of an ebony cigarette holder gripped tightly between her teeth. 'She's wasted on him.'

The tyres screeched as she swerved around a corner.

'You're going too fast,' said Anthony.

'So are you. I saw the look in your eyes. You like that girl too much.'

'Watch that lamppost. And that cat!' He covered his face with both hands.

'You don't fool me! My driving has never worried you before, Anthony Wesley. I know very well when someone is trying to change the subject. I happen to be very good at it myself.'

'You'll need new tyres in no time.'

'That is it!'

The car screeched to a halt. Both driver and passenger jerked forward.

'That girl is married, Anthony. I see something sparkling in your eyes every time you look at her.'

He opened his mouth to protest.

She held up a warning finger. 'Don't even think about lying.'

Anthony looked out of the window at the streets of narrow terraced houses. He'd grown up in streets like this, where you could smell the dank river water mixing with sewage. 'I can dream, Abbie.'

'She's married.'

'Should that matter? I'm only dreaming.'

It hurt. That was why, but she couldn't tell him that. 'It wouldn't be right.'

He eyed the finely plucked eyebrows; the makeup that gilded the lily yet was subtle and did not shout its presence. 'I thought you didn't believe in people conforming to what's always been.'

Her resolve seemed to flicker like her eyelids. But she recovered quickly. Abigail always recovered. He wished he could control his true feelings as easily as she seemed to.

Abigail tightened her grip on the steering wheel and stared at the road ahead. 'She looks pale. I think she's pregnant.'

'Come live with me and be my love and we will all life's pleasures prove.'

'This is no time to spout Shakespeare.'

'Marlowe.'

'Whoever!'

Anthony sighed and sat straighter. 'You're right. Feelings must be pushed to one side for the moment. These people are likely to lose their boat if Allen and Penmore have anything to do with it.'

'So what next?'

Anthony shrugged. 'Quite frankly, I don't know. The only thing I can think of is touting around the availability of a good boatman to other carriers. But it's a nasty business having your things thrown off your boat. I wish we could avoid that but I don't see what I can do about it.'

'Well, I do!' Abigail jabbed the accelerator. With a jolt and three backfires from the exhaust, they shot forward. Lace curtains stirred at sash windows.

Anthony retrieved his cap from the back seat. 'Well, that's another journey I've survived. What have you got in mind?'

'Girls rush in where union men fear to tread,' she said, smiled then winked in that wicked way of hers. 'I've got more skills than you give me credit for, Anthony Wesley.'

* * *

The gravel spat up from her tyres, the rear swaying like a drunken sailor. 'Home, sweet home,' she muttered through gritted teeth.

The spaniels, Gertie and Georgie, came running, their useless stumps wagging as if they had half a yard of whiplash stuck on to their rear ends.

She grimaced at the opulent facade. This was her father's badge of achievement, his due for exploiting others. Other people had to make do with two up two down and a square yard obliterated by dripping washing and the squat presence of an outside privy.

As she eyed the Palladian elegance of Pearcemore Park House, her father's consistent lecture rang in her ears. *I despair of you, Abigail. You have no appreciation for how hard I have worked to get all this. Why can't you behave like other young women, go hunting, play tennis, drink champagne at all-night parties?*

'And get married,' she had added with as much sarcasm as she could get away with.

That would be wonderful, dear! Her mother's words: her mother who judged a woman's success purely by the income and social standing of the husband she happened to snare. And that, in Abigail's opinion, was exactly it. Dangle the bait – in the case of a woman, her unblemished virginity – and hey presto! A man willing to offer her half of his bed and his fortune – as long as they remained married, of course. Once the novelty wore off, the little wife would have a household to run and he would immerse himself in business and other affairs!

A tall, shadowy figure carrying a tray of food was coming along the passageway at the side of the sweeping staircase that led to the upper floors.

'Miss Abigail. We weren't sure whether to expect you.'

'Fenwick. How are your legs? Still coping with the two flights down to the kitchen?'

The butler blinked nervously. Pale and misty, his eyes flitted from side to side like a lost and weary butterfly looking for somewhere to land.

'My legs are better,' he blurted. 'It's only two flights of stairs, miss. I can still manage and will do for a long while yet.'

Abigail smiled. 'You're old enough for a pension. You know that, don't you?'

'I have no need of the Lloyd George or any other charity, Miss Abigail.'

Abigail looked at him in amazement and shook her head. 'It is not a charity, Fenwick. It is structured like an insurance policy and everyone pays into it so that you can draw it out when you retire.'

Fenwick lifted his head higher, the first step already taken towards the dining-room door. 'As long as the master needs me, I shall be available.'

Exasperated, Abigail tore her hat from her head. How did you help those who would not be helped? The answer was simple. You didn't. Only when her father told him to get out would Percival Fenwick take what was his – or starve.

Two, four, six! She counted the stairs as she took them two at a time just as she had when she was a child and was trying to get to the top before her sister, Caroline.

Once in her room, she threw open the windows, looked out at the green lawns. She was about to do something completely against her nature. She was going to give hope to her parents that she might conform to their wishes – but at a price only her father could pay.

After throwing her hat and jacket on to the white satin counterpane, she took a quick bath but without disturbing her makeup. There just wasn't time to be too fussy. As she was putting on a silk kimono, a knock came to the door.

She hadn't expected to see her father. 'What are you doing home?' he asked. 'You know we have guests, don't you?'

'I wanted to see my family, Father. That is all right, isn't it?'

He looked awkward. 'As long as there's no repetition of your behaviour on the last occasion you visited.'

'Of course not.'

She caught him eyeing her body in a way no man should look at a daughter.

'I have to get dressed,' she said suddenly. Her sudden interjection seemed to wake him from his stupor.

'Yes,' he said, his eyes flickering. 'I'll see you later.'

'Father,' she said in the soft way that Caroline had used, 'I'm sorry about what I said on the last occasion I visited. I've decided I will marry Gilbert.'

His face lit up.

'But,' she added, 'there's a condition.'

A wary look. 'What sort of condition?'

'Have you seen Penmore?'

'Of course I have.'

'There's been trouble?'

'There's always trouble. Some of the boatmen are more trouble than others. But I know how to deal with them. Let's see how they manage when they've no job and no roof over their heads.'

'Ah! So you do know about Harry Allen.'

'A good and faithful servant!'

She grimaced. 'Not quite my impression of the man, but perhaps I'm as biased as you are. However, I've decided to marry Gilbert as long as you promise that my friends the Beavens will not be thrown off their boat.'

He stared at her. 'You do not interfere in the company, Abbie.'

Abigail sighed. 'Some of your employees do overstep the mark on occasion, like Harry Allen, for instance.'

She saw him frown and guessed he knew that she was angling for something.

'What's he been up to?'

'Ah. So you know he's no good.'

'He's sometimes more of a problem than he's worth.'

'He insulted a boatman, made overtures to the man's wife. What would you do in the circumstances? Disgusting, isn't it? Mother would certainly think so.'

'Don't try to blackmail me, young lady!'

'And tell Mother about the little seamstress in Hope Street or the actress in Clifton?' She shrugged. 'Mother has all she wants. What does she care if you take your physical satisfaction elsewhere? No. I can't blackmail you, Father. I know that.'

He glowered at her. 'What's between me and yer mother is our concern. As for the business, I'll thank you to keep your nose out. I'll judge whatever's happened on its merit and if there's due cause that these people you're talking about should be thrown off their boat – correction, *my* boat – then so be it.'

His reaction was no less than she'd feared. There was now only her trump card to play. 'Then give me your word as a wedding present that they won't be thrown off.'

'What? You would marry Gilbert only on the understanding that a bunch of water gypsies are not thrown off their boat?' He looked astounded, just as she'd expected him to.

'I will do before the end of the day if, and only if, you let the Beavens keep their boat.'

'Beavens, is it!' He eyed her suspiciously in the same way she eyed people, one brow up and one down. 'By Jove, but I'd like to see you married. This union stuff you're getting involved with is downright bloody embarrassing, especially to your mother.'

'So do you agree?'

'Do you know,' he said after he had pondered a while, 'I'll do this one thing you ask as long as you marry Gilbert. But mark my words, if the Beavens cause any sort of trouble again, they're out. And,' he added with great emphasis, 'if you ever get involved with their like and these union people again, I will have no recourse but to have you put away as a woman who is out of her head.'

Abigail smiled as though she was the most obedient daughter in the world, reached up and placed a quick peck on his cheek.

'I'm taking in everything you say, Daddy darling, but having me put away is a little drastic, isn't it?'

He screwed up one eye. 'I mean what I say.'

'Don't be silly, Daddy.' She laughed it off. Of course he didn't mean it. She put the idea from her mind.

Later, she walked out in the garden, thinking how uncomfortable it had been to make love in the summerhouse. Yet still she had loved it, the natural urgency of it, the feeling of being in charge of the situation and of another person.

'It's the best offer you're likely to get, darling,' her mother said at dinner.

'An offer, Mother! Goodness, you make me feel like a prize cow waiting for the auctioneer's hammer to fall on the one and only bid for a creature of dubious character and famously reckless behaviour.'

The prospect of her marrying Gilbert would buy enough time for the Beavens to get away and for things to cool down. The police would not be involved, Elliot would not go to prison and he would keep his boat. But that was all it was: a prospect. When the time was right, she would break off the engagement. She could do it easily: of course she could.

Two days after the banns were posted in the parish church, and unknown to her, her father secretly went back on his word.

16

The sickness that Beth thought she'd left behind in Gloucester returned every morning and there'd been no monthly bleeding for some time.

Elliot was having a quiet smoke when she told him she was expecting. He was sitting silently on a capstan, his back to her and his shoulders hunched. Silence was something she had lived with since the night Anthony Wesley had taken the boat up to Worcester. Once he'd left with Abigail, she'd found out exactly what Harry Allen had said. Elliot's right hand had felled her against a cupboard.

'Whore! Slut! You! My wife! Second-hand goods like from some Sally Army sale!' There were no sweet words as he'd spread her legs that awful night, his mouth and hands rough upon her body.

Their marriage had continued in uneasy silence. Whilst her bruises faded, Beth wondered whether they'd ever speak to each other again.

Now she could stand it no more. "Tis your child!' she shouted. 'It's yours! Count back from now and you'll work it out to six months or so after we got married. Hit me again and I belt you one with this frying pan!'

Her blazing eyes and the determined way she clenched the pan surprised him. His jaw dropped as he thought about it; hit her and get clobbered himself? He sloped off.

A truce developed. Gradually, they began to communicate again, stilted at first, then more smoothly. Throughout the period of silence, she submitted to what was expected of a wife. Elliot rolled on top of her without any pre-emptive kisses or caresses, rolling off again to turn and lie facing away.

The heat of anger had been replaced by a cold contempt. She coped with being used and shut out by training her mind to think of other things. When he puffed and sweated on her body, she retreated into the world of her imagination. The cramped surroundings became a palace, the tired nightgown glistened and rustled like silk or hung warmly around her body like velvet. The man was different too; he was caring and understood the woman inside the body. Like lovers in a great romance, they embraced in the glow of a purple and gold sunset, perfect people in a perfect world.

The weather turned fine as they glided into Worcester, a golden day that seemed too good to be spoilt by trouble. But looks were deceptive. Even as the first planks were lifted from the boat by a crane, a shout rang out across the quay: 'Clear that boat!'

Beth had been calmly sitting with a needle in one hand and an already well-patched skirt in the other. Even before she set eyes on the man who had shouted, she knew whose face she would look up into, what eyes would look back at her.

Just as expected, Harry Allen had a vengeful look in his eyes and a gloating sneer on his lips. There was a large purple bruise on his cheek, a parting gift from Elliot. But this time, he was prepared. Three men accompanied him, all wide-shouldered and as grey and grubby in their faces as in their clothes.

She sprang to her feet. 'Elliot! Watch out! They've come for you!'

With one mighty leap he was on the top of a crate, then speeding along the planks of wood laid from bow to stern. The planks clattered under the weight of his boots.

He scrambled up over the cabin roof then jumped down in front of her. His fists were clenched and an angry redness was spreading up from his neck and over his face.

He glared at Harry Allen. 'Get away from here, if you don't want the same as you had before!'

Harry grinned. 'I won't be having that, Beaven. I'm having your boat. The company's dispensing with your services on account of you attacking one of their employees; that's me, you see, and I have some standing with the company, which is more than what you have.'

'We'll starve!'

And it's my fault, she thought to herself. Suddenly, she wished she could turn back the clock. If only she hadn't gone walking in the dark, if only her father hadn't made her so dejected, then she wouldn't have been so easily taken in by Harry Allen's false sympathy.

She hung on to Elliot's arm, not that her weight or her strength would do much good if he decided to swing his fist in the direction of Harry's chin. 'No, Elliot,' she said quietly. 'I don't want you to get hurt.'

He stared at her as if she lied. For a moment, the knotted muscles she felt beneath her fingers eased slightly before tensing again.

'I'm taking the boat, Mr Beaven!' Harry exclaimed with a malicious smile. 'And there's nothing you can do about it. Nothing at all! Now get off! It's company property and I am the legal representative of the company. Legal! Get it, Mr Beaven? The boat is no longer yours!'

'Over my dead body!' Elliot growled.

Harry's grin widened. 'Don't tempt me, Beaven. Don't tempt me!'

'Please, Elliot!' Beth screamed and tightened her grip on his arm.

The men with the staves stepped forward. One of them, his brow a furrowed ridge over his eyes, tapped the stave into the palm of his hand. In that instant, the sickness she thought had left returned. The sound was an echo of the heavy thuds she remembered falling on Anthony Wesley's body.

The men sprang aboard with shouts and yells. 'Give it 'im, lads!'

Elliot let fly but fell under the shadow of the shabby men and their raised staves.

Horrified, Beth fell back flat against the side of the cabin then steadied herself and leapt forward into the path of a falling stave.

Elliot shouted, 'You stupid cow!' He flung himself and landed heavily covering her body. The blow from the stave cracked across his back.

Beth screamed again, though this time it was smothered by the weight of his body.

'Stay still!' Elliot ordered and covered her head with his hands.

'Chuck their personal stuff over the side. It's only rubbish anyway!' Harry Allen's voice.

She imagined her china, her metal pots, her bedding and her beloved books being flung out on to the quay. She tried to get up, seriously meaning to scratch and thump anyone in order to keep what was hers. Elliot held her down. 'No,' he said. 'Think of the baby.'

'That's it, lads. Throw it all out! Into the canal will do!'

'You'll do no such thing!' A woman's voice.

'Clear off, woman! You can't stop... argh!'

There was a thud of something hard connecting with something soft, like a man's stomach.

'Oh yes I can!'

Elliot got up. Beth slowly got to her knees, then her feet.

The darkness of bodies that had obstructed her view now shifted. Confused frowns deepened the creases on heavy brows. Harry Allen was bent. His eyes bulged, his face was red and both arms were held protectively across his stomach.

Head held high and both hands resting on a silver-topped walking stick, Abigail Gatehouse stood proud as a peacock. She was dressed in a striped blazer, straw boater, Oxford bags and two-tone shoes. Her pale complexion was beaming with healthy enjoyment. Knocking the breath out of a man like Harry Allen obviously agreed with her.

No one moved. Abigail was not the sort of woman they were used to. Give them the tart smelling of gin that called them darling without ever knowing their names as they pumped themselves into her, or their cowed wives incarcerated with a bevy of beaten children in some stinking hovel where daylight seldom fell between the high buildings or found an unbroken pane in a small square window – they could understand them. Abigail did not act like them and she certainly did not dress like them. She carried herself with confidence. She emulated their masculinity in a flamboyantly dramatic manner. Sometimes, it seemed she was mocking them.

Shifty and confused, the gruff, scruffy men glanced nervously at each other. When nothing was said, nothing was done, they looked back to Harry, who'd now managed to feel his way backwards and was sitting on a crate trying to get his wind.

'No good looking at him,' Abigail exclaimed with a light laugh and a loud tap on the crown of her hat. 'He's just one of my father's minions. You've heard of my father, no doubt – Archibald Gatehouse. I'm Abigail and I'm here to say these people have been given a second chance. I'm here to make sure it's carried out.'

* * *

The atmosphere in the little cabin was warmer than it had been for a long while. Although Elliot harboured resentment that another man had known her body before he had, he still had his boat.

'I stuck my neck out for you two,' Abigail said as she sipped tea from a rose-painted cup with her little finger held delicately aloof. 'Now don't blot your copybook, will you? I can't guarantee I can help you a second time.'

'We owe you a lot,' said Beth and although she wondered quite how Abigail had managed things the details were unimportant. They still had their boat.

With a feeling of relief, she covered Elliot's hand with hers. He looked surprised but did not withdraw. She glanced at him with new hope and then looked back at Abigail. 'We'll do our best to keep out of Harry Allen's way.'

Abigail let the cup drop into the saucer with a noisy clatter. Beth guessed it was to emphasise whatever she was going to say.

'He's trouble. Keep away from him at all costs. Why my father keeps him on...' She stopped and a strange, embarrassed look came to her eyes as though she was thinking thoughts that she could never voice. But she quickly recovered.

'Well, I know why he keeps him on. But be warned. He's evil and in more ways than one. It's not only a cut of the loads he takes from the poor fools that will stand it. He takes a cut of other trades too, some not mentioned by people of polite manners in polite society.' She turned aside and muttered, 'But some of them indulge in it anyway.'

Beth was extremely grateful to Abigail and told her so before she left.

'Think nothing of it, old girl!' Abigail said in a jolly but boyishly juvenile way.

'We'll certainly try,' said Beth and she smiled as she waved Abigail into her car and off through the gates. She continued watching until the tail lights of the car had flickered to red, then disappeared. She stood a while thinking about what Abigail had said. It occurred to her that the bluff and masculine exterior had little in common with the person within.

'Are you standing there staring after her all bloody night, woman?' said Elliot.

In the past, she would have stopped whatever he disapproved of and slipped into the role of the dutiful wife. But Abigail's presence had done something to her attitude to him and herself.

'Are you deaf?' The old coldness was back – the disgruntled Elliot had returned!

Something erupted from deep down inside. Something of Abigail had been left behind and become part of her.

'No!'

She spun round, eyes blazing, and hair falling like a shower of dark rain around her shoulders.

Whether Elliot read her expression and thought it politic to withdraw, she couldn't really know. All she did know was that she was approaching some sort of climax both in her relationship with him and in discovering the sort of person she really was.

He turned his back in an abrupt, final manner, clambered up on to the cabin roof then stepped down on to the covered load.

Beth watched silently as he stalked off to the other end of the boat, lit his cigarette and sat there, one leg crossed over the other. Still as a statue, he looked forward, perhaps contemplating the dizzying flights of waterside midges and the birds and bats that came out at twilight to feast on them.

He's thinking about me and nursing his wounded pride, she thought, gathering all the evidence and stuffing it like clean white cotton into the wound. But the wound would still be there. Would things ever change?

That night his hand groped at her body and although she seethed and wanted to scream out, *No! I'm too tired, too angry with you for treating me like something you own, like a horse or a dog*, she didn't refuse. Deep within, she knew a storm was coming. Until then, she would be calm, placid and compliant in all he wanted. Yet in her mind the emotions she felt and the words she wanted to say were falling into place.

After he'd climaxed, he rolled away from her and lay very still, very quiet in the blackness of their narrow bed.

'I'm sorry,' she said and was amazed that she'd said it. They were definitely not the words she'd had in mind.

'So am I,' he said, and she knew he was speaking through gritted teeth.

'I'll try to be a good wife. I won't complain,' she said, and again, she was surprised at herself for being too compliant, too subservient.

'I might!' He rolled back towards her. She felt the heat of his naked body against hers, and in a sudden beam of moonlight, she saw him get up on to one elbow.

'He told me you enjoyed it. He told me you cried on his shoulder and he gave you the comfort you needed.' His voice shook with emotion.

'How could you believe him! It wasn't like that! It wasn't like that at all!' She couldn't help shouting. She couldn't help venting her anger.

Closing her eyes very tightly, she bit her lip to stay any sign of sobbing. She was angry, for God's sake. Harry had taken advantage of her and it wasn't her fault. She knew now that it wasn't her fault!

'I didn't know what he was doing,' she began.

'You didn't know!' Elliot's voice boomed around the little cabin. 'You must have known exactly...'

His voice droned on, a monologue of what she should have known and how she might possibly have enticed him, and most of all, why she had fancied Harry at all.

All the beatings, the cuffings, the slaps she had received from her father, and most of all, Harry's rape and his lies suddenly combined to make her angrier than she had ever been in her life.

She raised herself up on her elbows. 'Now listen! Listen you great, stupid brute!'

Never had she raised her voice to a man, any man. She began to tell it as it really was.

'Dah had belted me and I'd curled up in a warehouse doorway. It was dark and I was crying. Harry Allen, who had been kind to me earlier that day, asked me what was wrong and offered to make me a cup of tea. I was sore and confused and I went with him to his office, glad that someone – *someone* – was paying me some attention, giving me some sympathy.' She caught at her throat with her finger, suddenly aware that she was filling up with emotion and with anger that one man could take advantage of her as he had and another man, her own husband, blamed her for it happening. She took a deep breath, glad that the moistness in her eyes was hidden by darkness because she wanted to state her case without attracting pity. She wanted to state things as they actually were.

'I threw myself in the canal afterwards but it was too big to drown in. All I could do was to wash away the scent of him and cool the soreness and the bruises he'd left me with.'

His body tensed.

'I didn't know,' she repeated in a softer voice. 'I was innocent and from what Abigail has just said, Harry Allen is anything but.'

His arm went over hers and his hand gripped her shoulder. 'He had you and you let him!'

The sound of his voice made her shiver. There was no hint of forgiveness or understanding, only hurt, selfish pride.

'He's a man. He took what he wanted! Why do you think it was my fault? Why do men always blame the woman?'

For a moment, everything about him, his body, eyes, mouth, was still. She guessed he was attempting to digest what she had just said and she fervently hoped that all would be mended between them.

Eventually, his mouth came close to her cheek. At first, she thought he was going to kiss her.

'So you're second-hand like a battered hat in a Sally Army sale. But I won't put you out on the streets. Some might. But I won't. So you be grateful to me, woman. Because if you're not, then you'll be the one to regret this marriage!'

Beth shivered. His voice was like dust: dry and stinging to the eyes, the nose and the throat.

Eventually she slept, though her dreams were fitful and full of dark shapes lurking in warehouse doorways. She wasn't sure whether Elliot slept. She could hear him breathing but not in the usual snoring, tired way she had become used to.

Reflected light from the water outside danced over the cabin ceiling and slid down the walls. But she wasn't really seeing the silent spectacle. All she could see was her life stretching out before her. Only one bright light shone amongst the gloom. In the morning the sickness would come back and she would be reminded that something better was yet to come.

* * *

Before Elliot was awake, Beth stole into a field where cattle were queuing waiting to have their udders emptied of milk. At the other side of the field, a white mist formed a convenient curtain between what she was about to do and the grey stone farmhouse in the yard beyond the fence.

Bobbing up and down between the cows, she kept an eye on the mist, willing it to stay and provide a barrier between her and discovery. Thankfully it did, its whiteness seemingly reflected by the dew-laden grass.

Experienced fingers red raw in the cold bite of morning pulled on the cow's teats and aimed a warm white shot of milk into the jug she had brought with her. The farmer wouldn't notice it gone and all narrowboat people knew how to take a little from each cow.

Holding the jug tightly to her body so that its rim nuzzled between her breasts, she trod swiftly and surely along the side of the hedge, her eyes surveying the fence and the farmhouse in the distance then returning to the field of cabbages immediately to her left.

The mist stayed with her, and although the cold and the excitement flushed her face, a great elation was with her because her mission had been successful. But once the wooden walls of the *Agincourt* surrounded her and the smell of bubbling beef dripping permeated the air, the sickness returned. Even before Elliot got out of bed, she rushed up top and sent the little she had eaten exploding into the water.

'Is this going to burn?' trumpeted Elliot from deep inside the cabin. 'You know I hate burnt bread. Burnt anything, in fact.'

Legs shaking, she climbed back down into the cabin, grabbed the frying pan and sent the two pieces of bread sliding on to his plate.

Look at it, she thought as with wide, tortured eyes, she stared at the sizzling fat spitting from the pan. It's doing that to make me feel sicker. Her hand shot to her mouth. Elliot looked up from his fried bread.

'Do you want a slice?'

She shook her head. 'I'm not hungry.'

'Oh, come on,' he said in a stupidly pleading voice. 'Have a piece of this, just a bite then.'

He got up and stood beside her, the bread in his hand, noticeable out of the side of her eye.

'No. I told you. I'm not hungry.'

Not meaning to be aggressive, but unable to contemplate the bread being so near, she struck out at his arm and hit it away. The bread flew out of Elliot's hand and on to the side seat that also served as an occasional bed.

'I don't want it!' She glared at him. 'Now please. Eat it yourself.'

'Do I get any relief with the steering today or do I do it all myself?'

'All myself! Just you? Is that what you're saying?' She looked at him angrily. 'You're speaking as though I take little part in steering the boat, loading, unloading or making sure the paperwork is correct. I've spent long hours at the tiller. What right have you to say otherwise?'

He looked dismissive. 'I know what I know.'

Her anger threatened to choke her. She'd scrambled or skipped – depending on the stability of the load – over green tarpaulin, stretching it tight where necessary and tying it down. There was nothing he'd done that she hadn't done herself.

She concentrated on pouring the tea from pot to teacup, but still her anger bubbled out. 'I always do my turn and in the months ahead I'll still continue to do my turn!'

He looked dejected as though she'd got the better of him. There was one subject that he knew would elicit reaction. 'I'm still not convinced whether it's mine or Harry Allen's.'

'Jesus!' Beth spun round on him, the frying pan in her hand. For the first time ever, she actually hit a man. Clang went the pan, reverberating against his head.

'Count! Count, you stupid, ignorant man. Count! I know you can't read and write, but I do know you can count! Count the months back from next spring back to when this baby was conceived. Count and you'll see that you and only you can be the father!'

Hand flat against the side of his head, he stared at her as if she'd turned mad.

Suddenly the little cabin seemed smaller as though the walls were coming in on them. Everything was closing in around her. 'I can't stand it any more! I can't stand it!'

Turning swiftly on her heel, she climbed the ladder. The cool morning air helped. The top of a church spire pierced a band of morning mist. She sat on the cabin roof, arms wound around her knees.

Elliot came up too and went straight to the tiller. The engine spluttered into life. 'I'm sorry,' he called out to her.

At first she thought she was hearing things. 'I'm sorry,' he shouted again.

Had he really said that?

She turned and stared at him. It was the first time she had ever heard him apologise to anyone and she didn't know quite what to say.

17

'Mrs Beth Beaven, you are fat! But then, at six months it's only to be expected. And stop talking to yourself!'

She sighed as she pushed open the door of the canal-side shop.

Two men were sitting either side of the fire, their heads close together. Not much surprise in that; men talked as much as, sometimes more than women. But that wasn't what made her stop in her tracks and wish she wasn't so fat or didn't waddle so much.

That head of hair, that certain vulnerability at the back of his neck; she knew it was Anthony talking to Ned, the shop owner. Their heads were low and their voices not much more than whispers.

'Mr Wesley?'

His head jerked up. He looked surprised to see her. 'Beth!' His eyes dropped to her belly. 'Mrs Beaven. You're looking well.'

'No, Mr Wesley. I look like a whale!'

She patted her belly as jovially as she could, but that wasn't how she was feeling. Inside, she groaned. If only she was as slim as she used to be. If only he'd look at her in the way he used to.

'Be right with you, me dear,' said Ned, getting to his feet. Beth managed to divert her attention long enough from Anthony.

Anthony picked up a poker and jabbed at the logs smouldering in the fireplace. He was sitting on a stool with his back to her.

Much as she willed him to look round, he kept his eyes fixed on the fire as though the pile of logs had some secret to spit from their sap.

Pulling her cardigan tight around her chest, she turned away and pretended to examine some plates that had fretwork edges with pink ribbons threaded through them.

'Is it bread you're wanting?' asked Ned for the second time, already making his way to the set of tin shelves that rocked as his heavy feet plodded the floorboards.

'Yes, please, Ned.'

Newly baked loaves sat on the shelves next to his oven. If he'd noticed the prickly atmosphere, he did not comment on it. Ned took hold of the bread in one beefy hand then wrapped it round in a precious piece of newspaper.

Beth eyed the newspaper with interest though it was poor consolation after Anthony's off-handed manner.

'Can you wrap two or three pieces around it, Ned? It will keep the warmth in and my husband does like to eat it warm with the butter running through it.'

'As you like it,' said Ned.

As he wrapped, she read a few words of print, enough to work out that he was using the inner pages of the newspaper, the pages where there were less articles about political events and more about ordinary people.

ST JOAN OPENS IN THE WEST END

stated one headline. A name, George Bernard Shaw, was mentioned underneath it. She espied some comment on fashion by a woman named Coco Chanel, another article about the possibility that women might soon have the same voting rights as men and not have to wait until they were thirty. Another said that women would have more machines to help them in the home of the future. And of course there were the letters to the editor about how much of a reduction the working man should expect in his wages and how strikes sapped the lifeblood of the empire and were grossly unpatriotic. In fact it looked as though one correspondent thought they should be hung for such behaviour. An alternative to starving, she thought, and pondered on how much the carrier companies were likely to decrease their wages.

Reading a newspaper at an odd angle whetted her appetite, made Anthony's behaviour less hurtful, and made her exceptionally eager to get the bread home and unwrapped. It would be placed next to the butter. Once the newspaper was flattened and folded, she might have time to read a little before supper, and then she could forget that Anthony had been so abrupt with her and that nothing untoward had happened between them.

Resigned that life would always be the same without romantic words and uplifting conversations, she sighed then slid her hand into an apron pocket. After some thorough rummaging she finally brought out a halfpenny.

'Oh! I'm sorry,' she said, looking plaintively up at Ned. 'I thought I had more. I'd better just have half a loaf. It should be enough. I don't eat a lot of it myself.' She said it bravely, but inside she curled with embarrassment. If only she'd come with more. If only Anthony Wesley hadn't been here to witness her poverty and her need.

She saw Anthony wince and look down at the floor. Ned merely blinked away his surprise and looked awkward.

Beth felt her cheeks reddening. Surely something could be worked out. Half a loaf shouldn't be difficult to sell, should it? She wasn't unique in being short at this time of the week. But she could see Ned was hopping from one leg to the other, scratching his head as he sought to make his mind up.

Anthony, who had made such a strong point of ignoring her, got up from his chair. He was rummaging in his pocket. When he smiled, her heart did somersaults.

'Take my advice and eat plenty of bread. It's good for you and good for the baby. I recommend it. Here, Ned.'

He flicked a penny and Ned caught it. Ned handed Beth the loaf.

'I can't accept,' she said abruptly. 'I don't take charity. What my man makes is what we live on. And he works hard. He works very hard.' She didn't have to convince herself of that fact. Elliot did work hard. She had no complaint about that. It was just that he had other failings, some of which reminded her of her father and the darker side of his nature.

Anthony regarded her steadily. She knew it sounded as though she was trying to convince herself as well as them. But she didn't care. Having nothing but a ha'penny in her pocket was demeaning. She'd been used to poverty all her life. But somehow, perhaps because Anthony was here, her poverty seemed more intense.

Ned sighed and took the bread back from her. With great solemnity he unwrapped it again then cut it in half. 'There you are,' he said handing it back to her re-wrapped in its layers of newspaper.

She took it quickly, lowered her head and made for the door. She had to get out. The mass of colours and the mix of smells suddenly made her feel dizzy. To avoid those feelings, she almost ran to the door. It was only at the very last moment, just before she reached for the door, that a shadow fell in front of her.

'Why didn't you let Anthony pay?'

The sight of Abigail Gatehouse standing between her and the door brought Beth to a sudden halt. Where had she been hiding?

'Abigail. I didn't see you.'

'You weren't looking for me. But I saw you come in. I was out back.'

Ah! The privy!

'So,' said Abigail, frowning at her. 'Why didn't you take a whole loaf? Even Anthony can afford that!'

'I have my pride,' she said, resolutely hugging the warm bread to her body.

Abbie shook her head and smiled. 'Our pride – women's pride – has always stood in the way. That's why men have always been able to take advantage of us and we've never taken advantage of them.'

This was getting on her nerves and made her start tapping the loaf with her hand, counting how long Abbie would go on. Abigail's continuous tirades against men puzzled her. They also got on her nerves.

'I don't know what you mean.'

Abbie adopted her smuggest expression. 'Then I'll enlighten you. As long as women allow themselves to be doormats, there'll always be men ready to wipe their feet on them.'

'Abbie, I have to go...'

Abigail didn't budge but stayed in the doorway. She nodded down at the bread she carried. 'At least they could have put it in a decent bit of white paper for you like they do in the town shops. Newspapers! It's disgusting.'

Abigail reached out.

Beth jerked it away. 'Don't do that. I want to read it.'

Abigail raised her eyebrows. 'Do you?' She sounded genuinely surprised.

'Yes!' she said with finality. No matter her poverty and feeling inferior, she would now state the truth. 'I can't afford newspapers either.' She glared into the other woman's face. 'There! I can read and write but have to wait until someone gives me something to read or write on!' Indignant and angry, she looked Abigail up and down. 'And I know I'm a woman, not a doormat!' She stormed out, the door slamming behind her.

'Well,' said Abigail. 'That's telling you, Abbie Gatehouse!' She strolled through the ranks of shelving, trailing her fingers through the dust along their edges. Anthony was taking her with him more often nowadays. She wandered back to the fireplace.

'Well, there goes a woman with potential,' she said.

'What makes you say that?' asked Anthony. He was chewing on an unlit cigarette, his gaze focused on the logs that were showing signs of bursting into flame.

'She's unnerved you, Anthony.'

Anthony did not look up. Neither did he answer.

'At least her condition has cooled your ardour somewhat,' said Abigail, smiling.

He eyed her sidelong. 'You're an antagonistic woman, Abigail. I recognised the error of my ways. All right?'

Abigail smiled. 'Poor girl. She probably thinks you're gone sick in the head.'

* * *

The winter had been wet since before Christmas. Mist clothed the towpath and rain glistened on the slate roofs of the warehouses on the opposite bank. Trailing smoke rose from rigid chimneys. Like a watercolour, the winter colours were all running into a muddy grey nothingness as though too much water had been added.

The loaf was warm against her belly. She held it close and

perceived a light movement, like feathers turning in a pillow. She smiled to herself. The baby liked warm bread too.

A boisterous breeze dried the rain, cooled her skin but did little to lessen her perplexity as to why Anthony Wesley had not shown her the warmth he had before. *But why should he?* asked a small voice inside. *He's a free man and you're a...*

She paused and looked down at her growing bump. 'An expectant woman.'

It helped that the Thomas, Kent and Rutherford children were playing close by. 'Read us a story! Read us a story!' they shouted, their voices a mix of different octaves, different ages.

'I haven't got a book with me.'

They groaned. 'Aw, come on, missus.' *Missus*. It sounded funny to be called that.

'A story, a story, tell me a story,' sang one little soul.

Beth bit her lip and glanced towards the boat. There was no movement and the door was closed. Squinting, she looked further along the quay to where two figures – two men – were standing close, obviously talking. One of them was Elliot.

'Guess what?' she said brightly. 'It's your turn to read,' and with a broad smile she pointed at each of them in turn.

'This,' she said pointing at a patch of firm black earth with a spiky stick, 'is where we shall write our letters.'

She bade them crouch down with her and as the rain began to drizzle again she formed a large, rounded letter on the ground before them. 'This,' she said as she scratched the dirt with the stick, 'is the letter "A". Who can give me a word that begins with A?'

The obvious came first. A hand black with ingrained jam shot up into the air. 'Apple!'

"Appy!' said the next.

'Animal!' said an older child, a smug smile exposing the fact that she had no front teeth.

Beth shook her head and although she tried to hide her smile she wasn't altogether successful.

'Let's start with apple. Repeat after me. A is for apple.'

Accordingly, the children intoned as directed. Beth hid her heartfelt smile as each child took a deep breath in an effort to pronounce the word correctly.

'Marvellous!' she said once they had repeated it at least half a dozen times. 'Give yourselves a hand!'

They all clapped and she joined them. It was a pleasure to see their faces, beaming with the brightness of having achieved something worthwhile.

'You seem to be enjoying that.' Abigail Gatehouse blew smoke into the air and warned the boy with jam in his fingernails not to touch the smart coat she was wearing.

'The children enjoy it,' Beth said curtly, her attention immediately returning to the dirty faces that looked so expectantly up into hers.

'Now, children. What's this letter?'

Still using the stick she scribbled out the A and replaced it with a B.

'B!' they all shouted and immediately began to buzz just like the word they automatically associated with the letter.

'You could do with some books,' said Abigail suddenly.

Beth glanced over her shoulder. 'These children could do with a lot of things. Learning to read and write isn't easy when earning your daily bread by travelling the length and breadth of every canal between Brentford and Manchester! Books are given to us but it's time to learn that we really want. A schoolroom near to the water. That would be best!'

When at last she could see Elliot returning, she got up and turned to face Abigail.

Abigail looked at her with narrowed eyes. Perhaps perception or instinct was more tangible than believed, but Beth winced at what she saw there. Even before the question came, she knew it was coming and that it dug too deeply into her life for comfort.

'Does it embarrass your husband that you can read and write and he can't?'

Beth made as if to get back on the boat. 'Sometimes.'

'You don't fool me, my dear girl. He can't read or write so he has an inferiority complex. And you have to hide your intelligence under a domesticated exterior in order to placate him. Is that right?'

Instead of confiding in the other woman, she retaliated in a way that she judged would embarrass her.

'Are you going to marry Anthony Wesley?'

Abigail's eyes sent the plucked brows shooting up her forehead. Her mouth dropped open and she laughed and laughed and laughed.

'Whatever gave you that idea?' she said when she at last stopped.

'The way you look at him,' said Beth.

The last vestige of laughter fell from Abigail's face. Only the hint of a forced smile remained and there was a new pinkness in her cheeks.

'Of course not!' It sounded convincing enough but there was that slight edge of sharpness to her voice.

Like me, thought Beth, she is merely a woman. It was only later that she realised just how deeply she had delved into Abigail's true self and just how much the woman loved Anthony Wesley.

* * *

Elliot was bent over the engine, greasing it and pouring fuel from a dark, smelly can. 'I'm hungry,' he said as she climbed aboard.

Once in the cabin where the range threw out its great warmth and the oil lamp flickered, she set down the bread. Carefully she unwrapped it and with even more care, she spread the newspaper out on the bed she shared with Elliot.

The remains of a rabbit stew simmered in a black iron pot on the range. Water steamed from the kettle on the hob. The bread was close by.

With a look on her face that was akin to love, Beth took the sheets of newspaper and gently flattened then folded them into readable form.

She sat on the edge of the bed and began to read the headlines. The newspaper was dated April. Avidly she read all there was to read about the wedding of the Duke of York and his bride Lady Elizabeth. That was definitely something to read to others even though she had read bits from other newspapers since the actual event.

So absorbed was she in reading and studying the advertisements for ladies' coats, dresses and corsetry that the smell of burning bread did not register. Just as the cabin began to fill with smoke, Elliot filled the cabin doorway.

'More burnt toast?'

She sprang to her feet. The newspaper fell to the floor. She grabbed the bread and beat its blackened end on the range. But the end she held was hot too. She yelled. The bread fell to the floor.

'Oh no!' Her eyes filled with tears which were partly induced by the smoke. It stung. So did Elliot's words.

'You stupid woman!'

He grabbed a cloth, wrapped it around the black and burning bread then flung it out of the cabin door. A splash heralded its journey to the bottom.

'I'm sorry,' said Beth, her eyes still streaming from the smoke. 'I was reading.'

Elliot, his mouth grimly set, scooped up the remains of the newspaper, screwed them up and, to Beth's wide-eyed horror, opened the range door and shoved them in.

'No!' She grabbed the handle. She screamed. It was hot.

'Leave it!' Elliot pushed her away. Just like he had outside the Navigator the night of the union meeting, he wagged a finger in front of her eyes. His own eyes bulged with anger. 'No more reading at all – *ever again*! Cook, clean and work the boat. That's what I expect from my wife. That's what you will do! Is that clear?'

'You can't mean that!'

'Get my dinner! Now!' His shouts filled the tiny cabin. She thought about climbing up the ladder and going ashore.

She thought about shouting at him. For the sake of peace, for the sake of the child she was carrying, she kept her mouth shut.

She eyed her scorched hand. It signified the burning of the newspaper, but also something else, something burning inside.

Abigail's words were still with her. She wasn't going to be a doormat! She wasn't!

She turned on Elliot. 'I'm not going to stop reading!'

'You'll do as I say.' His words almost spat in her face and his eyes were hard as buttons.

She willed herself to swallow her fear and continue. 'I'm your wife, Elliot, not your slave. I'll please myself!'

She didn't see it coming. She hadn't expected it, and when the palm of his hand landed on her cheek, it was as though it was happening to somebody else. Her head slammed to one side and she fell against the stepladder.

Reaching up she felt the burning redness of her cheek, but more than that, she'd jarred her stomach.

He wagged his finger in her face again. 'Let that be a lesson to you. I'm master here. What I say goes. Now get my dinner.'

He gripped her arm then pushed her towards the range. The iron was hot against her belly.

She stood there for a moment in shock, her breathing laboured. No more reading! She couldn't believe he would make her stick to that. It was cruel, it was unfair and it was designed, she thought suddenly, to keep her in her place. But it wasn't only that.

Numbly, she dished what was left of the rabbit stew into a soup plate. There was barely a cupful for her, but Elliot was a man. He would need that bit extra to keep him going. He ate in silence, not once asking her why she wasn't eating. His jaw rolled as he chewed. Not once did he look at her, not once did his eyes leave the plate she had set before him. And all the time she could hear his chewing and it sickened her because he sickened her. The life she had so easily slipped into was not at all to her liking.

Suddenly, she could no longer stand being in the same confined space as her husband. She dipped the cooking pot into the icy water, took it on to the bank and scrubbed it out with earth, then dipped it again. She did the actions automatically. No matter that it was dark and there was no scenery to appreciate, no water-fowl waiting for scraps. She needed to gather her thoughts.

Had he really meant it? Laying the chill of her palm upon her cheek, she detected the heat in her face and the ache in her jaw.

A sense of impending conflict descended on her as she went back into the cabin. Elliot was sullen. She waited for him to ask the question he always asked the moment they pulled up near any canal-side pub.

'I suppose we do have enough for me to have a pint?'

'Just about.' She clamped her mouth shut over the words as

though she'd really have preferred to swallow them. Until now, she had regarded it as a duty that there should be money put aside for him to have a beer. It meant scrimping on other things such as food, but making sure of a man's needs had always been a priority for the boat women and Beth had adhered to the rule.

Elliot was too wrapped up to notice her unhappiness. Accusations seemed to hang on the air between them, as if the reason they had little money was her fault and hers alone. 'Can't a man have a pint, then? Working all the hours I work, and no money for a pint!'

'I didn't say that.'

Tins, jugs and teacups were upturned in his search for a few coins.

Her stomach churned as he banged around, shouting and swearing because there wasn't enough – there was never enough.

It was, she thought, as if butter, tea, flour and bread were luxuries they could ill afford and had a lesser importance than what he wanted.

'Well, do I have some money or not?'

She closed her eyes. It was always *his* money, never belonging to the two of them.

'Come on, woman. I want to be going.'

She leaned against the range, this time for support. She closed her eyes. Go, she thought to herself, please go! The need to be alone overruled all her best-laid plans for emergency funding.

She went to an old humbug. With deep regret, she counted out the few pennies she'd managed to set aside for an emergency.

'And the rest!' He raised his hand and its shadow darkened her face.

With sinking heart, she gave him the rest and prayed it would be enough. Then she closed her eyes and waited for the blow. This time, it didn't come.

Relieved, she watched him stride off down the windblown wharf. Once he was out of sight, she delved into the storage space beneath one of the side benches and brought out the book Anthony had given her. As she read the words, the narrowboat, her life and her husband were almost forgotten. She could smell the wild thyme, and see the purple violets exploding in an elfin spring. But escaping into the world of the fairies was not as easy as it had been. The reality of life sat like an anvil on her shoulders. As she fondled the covers between her palms, she thought of Anthony and how off-hand he had been. Then she looked down into her lap because she knew that the reason was the bulge in her body.

Stroking her belly, she talked to the child. She did it all the time.

'If only I hadn't married Elliot,' she said softly. 'Then perhaps I wouldn't have you on the way and, perhaps, I might have Anthony.'

18

The Navigator was a true canal-side pub and neither so fine nor so well furnished as some of the town-centre pubs in which Abigail and Anthony arranged union meetings. The bar was little more than a trestle on spindly legs. Resting on a low wall behind it were three barrels. Shelves above and below them held bottles of brown ale and ginger beer, glasses and pewter tankards. The fire dappled the lime-washed walls and the wood and cigarette smoke filled the pub like a thick blanket. Scrawny, broad and tall boatmen jostled arms and shoulders with plump wives, and widows, who managed their own boats; children ran in to sip at a neglected mug of ale and were chased out again.

Anthony and Abigail surveyed the scene with immense satisfaction. It had never been easy persuading working people to unite to improve their lot. Evenings were always best and holding a meeting in a pub had always drawn more attendance than a church hall. Ned had reluctantly acquiesced to act as post-box and had informed every boat that had moored outside his shop of the time and place of the next meeting. Even those who preferred to keep their heads down and not annoy their employers wavered when pints were mentioned.

'The beautiful Beth,' said Abigail, catching Anthony's arm and nodding towards the corner where the wives were sitting. It wasn't often they attended either pub or meeting, but when they did, they certainly knew their place.

Anthony had been re-polishing his speech, making notes in the margin. Now Beth was present, the things he'd meant to say seemed trite and ill thought-out.

'She's getting fat. Her time must be near. I wonder if she'll still be as beautiful when she's got a baby at her breast.'

She was purposely mean, never taking her eyes off him as she awaited his reaction. If only he would look at her the way he looked at Mrs Beaven.

'She's not fat, Abbie. Don't they say women blossom when they're pregnant?'

'Hmm! Is that what they call it? Well, I call it fat.' The urge to be mean would not go away. She knew it was irritating him, but couldn't help herself.

Anthony couldn't help snapping. 'All mothers and babies are beautiful, Abbie, so I hear tell. But then how would you know? You don't know anything about being a woman, do you, Abbie? And what's more, you don't want to know.'

He didn't need to look into Abigail's face to see he had hurt her and regretted it. 'I'm sorry.'

That was when she should have apologised herself, but she wouldn't. She loved him. She wanted him, but he was being so... so... obstinate! Her expression remained frozen. Anthony shook his head. Ordinarily, he would have tried again, but he didn't feel inclined. Deep down, Abigail was a kind person. Her attitude to Beth was out of character, but then, who was he to talk? Beth made him act out of character.

Analysing people's behaviour, especially his own, wasn't one of his strengths – at least not in his opinion. Other people had congratulated him on his perception of people and situations, but he had never acquired the confidence in himself they had obviously seen. But then, they didn't know just how badly he had misjudged his own brother. Rats didn't come any bigger or more evil than he did.

As regards Beth, she was the one thing he had tried to analyse. Like the most beautiful words ever written, she came into his mind and floated there between midnight and dawn.

Of course he also had other dreams and thoughts that were not so pleasant. Nightmares about being beaten to death were an occupational hazard for someone like him. Organizing the workforce meant he was eating into the company's profits and he had to expect them to retaliate.

On seeing her condition at Ned's shop, he had told himself not to upset her life. Abigail continued to be his conscience in that regard.

Damned woman! All the same, there was no harm in talking to Beth and her husband. Elliot he remembered as being extremely grateful that he had helped out on the night he had floored Harry Allen.

He'd never mentioned it to Abigail but he wished mightily that he'd been there when she'd struck the wharfinger with her walking stick. Shame she hadn't given him a lot more than that, but fortunate that she'd been able to sway her father into letting Elliot keep his boat. He still wondered how she'd done it, but Abigail kept the details close to her chest. In time, perhaps, she might tell him.

He was aware that Abigail watched him as he made his way to the women. They were only approached by their spouses to ask if they wanted another half of sweet cider or brown stout. An

English *purdah*, he thought, similar to that which he'd seen in the East and had thought no Englishwoman would put up with. Yet here it was, watered down but shockingly obvious to the outside observer.

'Well, Mr Wesley!'

The older women were brazen in their greetings, their rough hands grasping his and their wedding rings gleaming against their brown fingers.

Beth alone was the one who kept her eyes lowered and her hands tightly clasping her glass. If he could have read her thoughts or her heart, his own might have quickened.

Abigail noted the intensity of his looks, the emphatic use of his hands and the overall stance of his body. Yet all the while, she thought, he's willing Beth to look into his eyes, to notice him there, to give him some sign that she still wished him to be something to her, even if only a friend.

'So when's this strike coming?' asked Mrs Bennett as she chewed on the pipe she held clenched at the corner of her mouth.

'Soon. Unless the carrying company agrees to a wage rise, there will definitely be a strike,' Anthony replied.

At long last, Beth looked into his face. 'And when will this happen?'

His eyes met hers and she didn't look away. 'I can't say. Ned will let you know if I'm not around.'

'Why won't you be around?' She almost shivered at the sound of her own voice. For the briefest of moments, she thought he did too.

'Good question, Beth.' The way he said her name was like running fingers through long grass. 'The carrying companies are going to do their damnedest to get rid of me.'

'Like that night when Harry Allen paid those men to beat you up?'

At the likelihood of gory details, those around leaned closer; hands cupped ears and hard, bright eyes flickered with interest.

For a moment, he looked surprised. 'Then there's a man I will get even with.'

'I shouldn't have said that. I shouldn't have mentioned him.'

Without thinking, she had pointed the finger at Harry Allen. Even though she and Elliot had kept their boat this time, there was no knowing how long it would be before he attempted revenge.

'Of course you should.' He folded his hands into tight fists. 'That's a man who could do with more than a tap from Abbie's walking stick!'

'You mustn't!' She leaned closer to him; the touch of her hand on his arm was light and yet it burned. He listened to her. 'Anthony, if he found out that I had mentioned his name...'

'I'd already guessed.' He shook his head. 'No matter. There'll be plenty more trouble from the likes of Harry Allen before we get satisfaction.' He sighed. 'In time, the Labour Party might get more seats in Parliament. Then and only then will things improve.' He laughed. 'I'd like to think I'd be one of them. Wouldn't that be grand, eh, ladies! And you can all come and vote for me and say how we supped ale together in a pub on the side of the canal. What do you think of that, then?'

The women, some advanced in years, giggled like young girls.

If Beth could have looked into his heart, she would have seen his affection for her seated beside his ambition to be a Member of Parliament in the heart of the British Empire. If she could have read his mind, she would have noted that he had met the local Party secretary that very day and his name had been mentioned for the local by-elections coming up towards the end of the following year.

But Beth could not look into either his heart or his soul. All she saw was the affection in his eyes that she hoped he could see reciprocated in her own.

As Abigail watched them, the taste of jealousy was bitter on her tongue and in her heart. Didn't he realise what he was doing? He was leaning too close to the pregnant Beth, and what a way to look at a married woman! Quite shocking!

Quite shocking!

My goodness, you sound like your mother, she thought. And you're not shocked. Not really. You're just jealous: terribly, terribly jealous.

She swallowed her sigh. How she wished it was her he was looking at. One day it will be. *I'll make it happen, I swear to God I will.*

She turned away. Her jaw was set; determination lit her eyes. Never had she felt more resolute.

It did occur to her that she had let her feelings for him – and her jealousy – show. *Am I that self-destructive?* she asked. *No. I am not. All I am doing is acting as his conscience.*

It was time to curb his inclinations!

Fixing a smile on her face and shoving her hands in her trouser pockets, she approached the women. They eyed her warily but moved along the bench so she could sit between the man she loved and the woman he had affection for.

'Hello again,' she said with easy amiability, elbowing her way between Anthony and Beth. He had no option but to move aside. She sat herself down, her smile never waning. 'So. Are you expecting?' Abigail asked her. Then she laughed and nodded at Beth's round belly. 'Of course you are. Silly question. Sorry. When is it due?'

Beth pulled her cardigan down over the large safety pin that was bridging the gap that had appeared in her favourite green skirt.

'Spring. April.'

She cleared her throat. It was difficult not to feel small and silly beside the jaunty Abigail.

'A spring lamb. How lovely.'

Beth's smile was weak. She knew Abigail was mocking her. What a strange woman she was, changing moods more often than some rich women changed their clothes. At times she liked her, at other times she did not.

Anthony was joking with the women, making them giggle some more and think they were young girls again.

'Anthony's looking well,' she said. 'But then, he does have you to mother him, handing out his leaflets and driving him around. Busy men need servants to look after them.'

Although the brim of the black fedora shaded Abigail's eyes, she saw her jaw clench. She knew if she could see her eyes, she would see jealousy there – and passion. Abigail loved Anthony. There was no doubt about it.

'He's very well,' Abigail answered. 'I expect he'll need a good bath once we leave here – we both will...'

Beth simmered as Abigail tellingly scratched at her arm.

The inference was obvious. 'I don't have fleas.'

Abigail's finely plucked eyebrows rose in graceful arches. 'I didn't say you did, Mrs Beaven.'

Beth's earlier embarrassment vanished beneath her indignation. 'We're poor, but we're not dirty.'

Abigail's smile persisted. So did the mockery. 'Well, I suppose there are exceptions. But there, your clothes are a bit the worse for wear. You could do with better. I'm gathering some old clothes from here and there including some of my cast-offs. I'm sure they'll fit you once you've had the baby.'

The words and their implication now found their mark. Beth

wanted to shrink to the size of her toe. Abigail's clothes were so well cut and so polished.

Turning away, she self-consciously tugged the edges of her cardigan together and folded her arms over the gap where it didn't quite meet. She wished Abigail would go away, but she didn't. She wanted diversion and got it.

'I've got a newspaper,' said a woman with wire-framed glasses sitting immediately next to Beth.

Abigail attempted to butt in. 'How jolly! Would you like me to read it for you?' She held out her hands.

The woman blinked like a short-sighted owl. 'I weren't talking to ye!'

Because her lips were flaccid and she had no teeth, Abigail was showered with spittle. Disgusted, she wiped it off with her handkerchief.

The old woman ignored her. 'I've got it here, Beth.' She brought out a crumpled sheet from a knitting bag and handed it to her.

Wire-framed spectacles were adjusted to sit more comfortably on her nose. 'Will you read it out loud?' she asked.

'Of course I will.'

Snubbed, Abigail leaned back. Everyone else was leaning forward, their attention fixed on Beth, their ears straining for the tiniest bit of news.

Abigail watched, a terrible tightness gripping her chest, as though bands of iron were choking the breath out of her. She looked around for something that might take her mind off how she was feeling, preferably something that would make her laugh – and breathe – and not be jealous.

Respite came from an unexpected source. The woman with the glasses poked her finger through where a lens should be and rubbed her eye.

'Can you see all right with those?' she asked the woman.

'Oh yes.' The old woman barely took her eyes off Beth's face. 'Carry on,' she ordered and took her knitting out from her bag.

Abigail's face was a picture, her cheeks ballooning as she tried to stifle her giggles.

Beth noticed, and despite Abbie's earlier behaviour, smiled herself.

Like everyone else, Abigail listened as Beth read out articles of news. She'd expected Beth to read haltingly. On the contrary, the words flowed freely. Not once did she hesitate, or trip over awkward words.

'You read well,' Abigail said once she had finished.

Beth glowed in the warmth of her praise. Suddenly, she was the confident one. 'My mother taught me. She used to live in London. She went to school before marrying.' She spoke proudly, keen to let Abigail know exactly how she was feeling.

'Shame more can't read.'

Beth turned wistful. 'A school would be nice. A little place at the side of a canal. But there's not any money...' She paused. Something flickered in Abigail's eyes. 'Are you all right?' she asked.

Abigail sat up straight. 'I've got the money!'

Hearing the outburst, curious faces turned in their direction.

'For the school?'

'Yes. The children must go to school.'

Half a dozen pairs of eyes fixed on Abigail. She met their gaze, looking steadily at each in turn. Suddenly, it was all quite clear. This would be her vocation. This would be her inroad into the boatmen's lives. She raised her voice. 'Education, especially learning to read, is extremely important. I pledge money to found a school.'

Even as Abigail got to her feet, a brief speech forming in her mind, those gathered turned away, their conversations resuming.

'What is it?' she asked, turning back to Beth. 'What have I said?'

Beth was frowning thoughtfully. 'We spend too little time moored up for our children to attend a proper school. They all know that.'

'But surely there must be a way?'

Beth nodded. 'There must be. I for one would like my child to learn. If nothing else, I can teach him or her to read. But what of everyone else?' She shrugged. 'That was my dream, but now I'm not so sure. Everyone travels around. I should have thought things out more carefully.'

Abbie sat back down, her moment of glory swiftly passed. Why was it she had never quite broken through the barrier surrounding these people? She was almost glad to feel the landlord's hand tapping her shoulder.

'Anthony is ready to speak,' he said.

Abbie left her seat to make sure the leaflets were laid out properly on the table. She was fussing over nothing, but at least it hid her disquiet. Anthony had the floor. Anthony, not her, was about to make a worthwhile speech.

He stood on two chairs, one foot on each. His hands were on his hips.

Abigail fixed her eyes on him and sighed. 'He looks just like comrade Lenin in the new Russia,' she murmured to no one in particular.

Full of zealous enthusiasm, Anthony poured forth his expositions on the rights of the working man. His hair was too long for most men, and flopped over his eyes. His eyes were full of passion for the cause.

Abigail sighed again. If only they were full of passion for her. But no matter. At least they were on the same side.

'It is your right to strike. Your right to demand a living wage.'

As he spoke, she handed out leaflets. Her task took her all around the public bar. The gaslights flickered. The flagstones beneath her feet were slick with beer and soaked sawdust. Shadows cloaked those standing around the walls of the packed pub, nodding their thanks as she pushed leaflets into their hands. Their eyes and ears were for Anthony. Their faces were pink and peach in the glowing light. They all looked hard, tired and hungry. Some were vaguely familiar. One in particular was instantly recognizable – Penmore, and he was not alone. Rough, heavy-set men were with him. She bit her lip, a pang of fear clutching at her belly. Were they boatmen? She couldn't be sure.

A rumbling of discord ran through the bar. She turned round to where Anthony had been speaking. She'd barely noticed him ceasing or getting down from the chair. She looked for him. Suddenly, he was speaking into her ear.

'I think we have trouble.'

She froze. She saw the women moving from their corner.

She saw Elliot Beaven.

'Get out to your car,' Anthony ordered. 'I can't—'

'Now!'

He was standing between her and the intruders, his body a barrier to whatever might happen.

The ruffians with Penmore began to move, their eyes dark hollows beneath their brows. They elbowed their way through the crowd, trying to get to Anthony. They found they could not move freely and the men they were elbowing were turning ugly. The crush of men and women kept them pinned to the outer edge of the room.

Anthony pre-empted their action. 'We have intruders!' he shouted. 'The bosses don't want you to have more money, men! They don't want you to feed your children. They just want you to make money for them, and look, they've sent their toadies to persuade you to think as suits them. What say you, men? What say you?'

Anger and fear rose in equal proportion; the smell of it mixed with tobacco, male sweat, coal dust and kerosene.

Anthony sprang round to face Abigail, his shoulder hitting her sideways. 'Go!' he shouted. She cried out as his arm hit her chest and she tottered backwards. She would have fallen, but a firm hand grabbed at her elbow, dragging her back and holding her upright.

'Quick. This way!'

She looked sideways and saw the dark tousled hair of Beth Beaven floating out behind her.

Shouts of anger mingled with the thud of sticks on bodies and boots against shins as man fought against man. Two or three picked up one of the intruders and smashed his head into a gas mantle. He shouted and slapped at his singed hair. The bar was in turmoil, fighting everywhere. A sea of men ebbed to and fro as though they were one creature, one cause.

Most of the women had already left. Beth remained. She tugged at Abigail's hand. 'This way!'

Abigail moved in time to avoid a body stumbling past, then falling soundly to the floor. They pushed their way through to the door, waited until the crush of bodies had moved, then pulled it open. Outside, the moon was bright and patches of light fell on to the towpath from boat windows.

Abigail turned back. 'I have to see how Anthony is.'

'He'll be all right,' said one of the women, her skirt a heaving mass of clinging children. 'Men can take care of themselves.'

'So can I,' said Abigail, now feeling breathless and irritated that she had been led out of the fray so easily – and by Beth, who was far less bold a woman than she was.

'No.' Beth's fingers gripped her arm. 'You should know better.'

'What should I know?' snapped Abigail, staring at the pub just as the other women were doing. The noise of heavy blows and bad language carried out on to the night air.

'You should know that the police will be here, so we have to go. We have to get away.'

'I'm not afraid of a bunch of silly men in uniforms!' she exclaimed. Shrugging Beth off, she began to make her way back.

Warnings that the police would appear were no big surprise. Many a dockside skirmish had been started purposely so that the police could be called and insurrection nipped in the bud.

Well, they're not going to forget me in a hurry, she thought. It was a glimpse, a mere second, but as she turned, a square-shouldered figure stepped out of the shadows that fell between the pub and the stables next door. Something about the shadow made her pause. *You're imagining things.* She'd gone no more than a few yards when Beth cried out.

In the shadowy alley, the blackness moved as though it had come alive. In a sudden light from an upstairs window, she saw Beth. The other was Harry Allen.

Back at the pub, the fight was tumbling out of the door. She shouted at those skirmishing and trading blow for blow. 'Help us! Will somebody help us?' The brawlers eyed her briefly, but were too busy with their own battle.

She ran back, tripping over something lying across the entrance to the alley.

Her ankle throbbed. She paused to bend and rub at the soreness, saw what she'd fallen over: a stave so beloved of Harry Allen's henchmen.

Never mind her ankle. Never mind the pain. She picked it up and gripped it with both hands. 'Let her go!' she shouted.

Raising the stave above her head, she ran into the alley and towards the struggling figures. 'Let her go! Now!'

Her voice echoed between the buildings and over the muffled screams and the lustful grunts of Harry Allen.

Wading into the darkness, she tuned her ears to hear where they were. She recalled that Harry was at least six inches taller than Beth. 'Aim high, it's Harry's head you want to crack not Beth's,' she muttered to herself, then shouted, 'Damn you, Harry Allen!'

His figure formed a denser blackness than the night. He ceased what he was doing and looked up when he heard her. Then he laughed.

'Come for some yourself, have you? Fancy old Harry helping you get back to being a woman again?'

She bristled. The pig. The damned pig! His words alone made her want to smash his head open. 'Let her go!'

'I'm not going to hurt her. Got a little proposition for her, in fact. Nice little job down in Blackfriars Street where she'll have plenty to eat and drink and lack for nothing for the rest of her life. Once she's got rid of this lump, that is. Marvellous little place!'

'So I hear,' snarled Abigail, her fists tightening around the stave. 'She'll get plenty of diseases too if I know rightly. And when her looks are gone, she'll be out on the streets. Is that right, Harry? Is that the place you've got in mind?'

Suddenly, the blackness was moving again. Abigail attempted to lash out but missed. Then Harry screamed. 'Bitch. She bit me!'

Beth broke free. 'Abbie! Come on! This way!'

Abigail's first inclination was to follow, but the opportunity was too good to miss.

He stooped low as he came towards her. Her heart fluttered and her legs felt weak. But she wouldn't run. By God, she wouldn't! Summoning all her courage, she gripped the stave more tightly.

He reached to grab her.

She sidestepped neatly. He backed away before she could use the stave.

Beth called her. 'Abbie. Come away. Come away!'

She couldn't. There was a job to be done and she badly wanted to do it.

'Come on. Let me give you some of what you gave Anthony Wesley,' she said breathlessly, amazed at how excited she felt and how energised.

'I've heard about you,' he said, his voice thick with lust and the confidence of a man used to bullying and having his own way. 'Come here and I'll make a woman of you!'

He reached again. She took a step back and pretended to waver.

Sensing he was in with a chance, Harry's hand clawed the air only inches from her breast. Before he could touch her, she raised the stave and with all the might of Samson she brought the heavy piece of willow crashing down on Harry's head.

He made an odd sound as he crumpled to the ground, an exclamation of surprise rather than a groan of pain.

Beth watched, astounded. 'Abigail!'

Arms still raised, Abigail was finding it impossible to move. Despite the darkness, Beth could see that she looked surprised. 'Violence is supposed to be for the ignorant,' she murmured.

'You're not ignorant. You're brave.'

'I'm unrepentant. I know that much.'

'Come on! We have to get you away from here.'

'I'm not running.'

'Of course you are. You have to before the rozzers come or we'll be for it!'

'*We'll* be for it!' Even in the darkness, Beth detected her pleasure. 'I like that. It makes me feel I at last belong in your world.'

Beth tugged at her. 'There's no time to linger. We have to go.'

Of course they did, but not before Abigail peered down at him.

The men who'd been fighting began to gather. 'Is he dead?' someone asked.

Harry Allen groaned.

'Hmm,' exclaimed Abigail. 'Unfortunately not. I've only knocked him out.'

She flung her stave into the darkness where it pinged off a brick wall before she heard a swish of stems and leaves. Nettles, she thought. How very suitable.

'Come on!' shouted Beth.

They ran like the wind, Beth surprisingly swift for a pregnant woman.

By the time they got within sight of the mooring, they were still panting but the night air swiftly cooled their faces. Their footsteps slowed considerably.

'Do you think he might yet die?' Beth asked Abigail as they walked.

'Unfortunately not. Skull like an elephant and brain of a rat,' sniffed Abigail.

'He may take revenge. You said yourself not to upset the likes of him,' said Beth. 'What if he sets the police on you?'

'He won't do that. He'll be too afraid of losing his job,' Abigail said with conviction. 'After all, my father pays his wages.'

A shiver ran down Beth's back. In response, she wrapped her cardigan more tightly around her shoulders. 'What's the place you were talking about?' she asked.

'Place?'

'The place he said he would take me. You know of it?'

'It's something I prefer not to discuss. I just know of its whereabouts. That's all.'

'Have you been there?'

'No! I have not. Now can we please drop the subject?'

Beth didn't answer. Her gaze fixed on the familiar shape of *Jenny Wren*. It was showing no lights. Her spirits fell. If it had been, she would have gone along to see her mother, knowing her father was still back at the pub. But there was a light burning on the Melcroft boat. George was obviously still up at the pub. Carrie usually enjoyed a night gossiping with the other women from the boats, but tonight she had not been there. Beth frowned. It wasn't like Carrie to stay away.

'Can I make you a cocoa?' she asked Abigail.

'That's a good idea.'

'Better still, would you like to meet my friend Carrie? We could go along and have a cocoa with her. What do you say?'

'A grand idea.' She rubbed her hands together. 'I could do with a bit of something warm and comforting, though I felt pretty comforted when I hit Harry Allen on the head.'

It was as though another bridge had been crossed. They had Anthony in common, but now they were becoming friends. 'You'll love her. That's her boat...'

Just as Beth raised her arm to point in the direction of the Melcroft boat, light blossomed on to the cockpit as the cabin door was opened. It was short-lived. A figure vanquished it for a moment before it reappeared then disappeared as the door was closed.

'Was that her husband?' asked Abigail.

Shocked by what she'd just seen, Beth didn't answer her question. Someone had come out of the cabin, got off the boat and walked away.

'On second thoughts,' she said, smiling in an effort to hide her amazement, 'let's keep it to the two of us. We can talk about Harry Allen and how sore his head's going to be in the morning. We'll go to my boat.'

Abigail agreed. If she noticed anything had changed in Beth's attitude, she did not comment. They made their way to *Agincourt*.

As she boiled milk and water, Beth kept talking about what had happened and what might happen as a consequence. But all the while she was thinking of the shadowy figure she had seen come out of Carrie's boat and walk with long strides back to the *Jenny Wren*. Did she have the guts to ask Carrie what was going on?

No! First she would ask her brother Robbie what he was doing alone on a boat with a married woman when her husband was not there.

19

Some instinct advised caution about telling Elliot how Abigail had poleaxed Harry Allen and left him out cold the night before. The mention of the wharfinger's name still sent her husband into a temper.

The drink had got the better of him by the time he got back from the pub, so he didn't question where she had been. He fell on to the bed, mumbling something about having a night of conjugal passion. Gradually, he subsided into muffled grunts and then snores.

'Hardly my Romeo,' she murmured as she eyed the gaping trouser fly and the creased shirt tails. After removing his boots and his cap, she left him as he was. Physical intimacy with someone who stank like a brewery was something she preferred to avoid.

What attracted me to him in the first place? she wondered. He's not attractive or loving. Security? She nodded silently. Security. It was what every woman had wanted since the beginning of time: security for herself and her children.

Her train of thought led her to consider young Carrie and

middle-aged George. And Robbie. Dread circulated like cold air in her stomach.

Nature was a wily affair, enticing the unwary regardless of matrimonial promises and gold rings slid on to willing fingers. A vision of Anthony Wesley came to her mind and it would have stayed there if she hadn't forced herself to open her eyes and see her world as it was and how it must be. She was a married woman and regardless of her lot, she had made her bed and must lie on it. Carrie too had to be reminded of her commitment and Robbie deserved nothing better than a severe ticking-off and a threat to tell Ma and Pa if need be.

She must go along and see her mother in the morning. She had avoided her father; he didn't approve of women in pubs and had glowered when he saw her. Thoughtfully, she patted the baby that grew big in her stomach then closed her eyes and slept.

* * *

It was still dark when she awoke with a feeling that something was not quite right.

At first, she thought a sound from outside had disturbed her. Lifting her head, she listened, her eyes searching the darkness for any shadow falling through the tiny windows. There was nothing discernible except the muted trumpeting of Elliot's breathing as he snored away his sleeping hours. She often thought that he sounded like a pig rooting up cabbages.

She fell back on her pillow and closed her eyes. Then she ran her hand over her stomach and wondered for a moment whether the child within was trying to tell her something. Perhaps he or she had moved and in shifting weight, had disturbed her slumbers.

Babies talk to you even before they are born. Some old gypsy woman had told her that.

Unable to sleep, she lay very still, very quietly and listened. There was no sound as such – unless she counted Elliot's continuing snores. But there was something else she was aware of, a sound that seemed to come from inside her head.

She rolled the patchwork counterpane away from her body and swung her legs over the side. The rough coconut matting was harsh beneath her feet. She felt for her shoes but found only her boots.

Grabbing a shawl of beige wool edged with a red stripe, she went up top into the cool dampness of the morning air.

In the odd half-light that is neither night nor dawn, the boats at their moorings were grey shapes, waiting for the light to paint them in the colours of day. Sounds of water running and the scuffling of waterside rats made the silence seem much deeper. By day, such sounds were indiscernible amongst the noise of men shouting, machinery grinding, and crate after crate and load after load being swung from quay to hold.

All movement should have been as minimal as sound and she wouldn't have noticed him at all if it hadn't been for the fact that she smelt tobacco drifting on the unsullied morning air.

Her eyes searched the quay and boats until she saw him standing like a statue, leaning on a cabin roof, his gaze focused on nothing in particular. He drew and blew on his smouldering pipe. Her father was up already.

There was only one reason her mother wasn't up and about before him or, at least, at the same time as him. She had to be ill.

At once, she felt a surge of concern, but also of anger. Why hadn't he called for her? Unlaced boots slapped against her ankles as she made her way along the quay, her eyes fixed on the man she should respect, but didn't.

'Is my mother ill?'

The pipe paused in mid-flight to his mouth. His jaw dropped and his mouth hung open beneath the thick black moustache.

'None too good,' he said and jerked his head towards the cabin door. 'She was going to shout out for me to get you if she needed you.'

Beth glared. '*If* she needed me!' All the years of abuse became like a bonfire. 'If you weren't so wrapped up in your bloody self you would have come along and got me right away!'

She didn't give him time to answer or strike out. Those days were gone and whatever happened, she was never going to put up with that kind of treatment again.

Over the side went one leg. Big belly or no, over came the other, one boot falling off to thud on the cockpit deck.

'Damn to the other one,' she snapped, kicking off the remaining boot, then stepped down the ladder into the dimly lit cabin.

Only one light burned. Even if it had been turned up full, it would not have been enough. There was a smell of sticky sweat and also of something else she couldn't quite recognise. 'Ma?'

A low mewing, groaning sound came from the main bed. The bed was half-hidden by a privacy curtain and a cupboard to the right and in front of it.

Beth reached out and drew the curtain back. Her breath caught in her throat. Without her bonnet, her mother's face seemed very small, very pale. 'I'm here, Ma. I'll look after you.'

'Beth.' Her mother's voice seemed as small as her face. 'It's coming away, Beth.'

'Coming away?'

'Like when you were small. Do you remember?' she gasped between spasms that bent her body double.

She remembered! Hadn't she been there before, as a child of

seven and again at nine? She knew instinctively what had to be done.

Her mother lay in shadow. She reached for the oil lamp that jutted out from the cupboard above the sink and turned up the flame, which fell on features she'd rather not have seen. Circles as dark as bruises hung around her mother's eyes.

Beth gritted her teeth. 'Did he hit you again?'

'No.' Haltingly, as though it weighed heavy as iron, Elizabeth Dawson pushed back the bedding. 'Take this off me.'

Beth did as she was told until the rough blankets and coarse cotton were bundled over her mother's ankles. Nothing else needed to be explained. Beth knew what was coming. Her mother drew up her knees.

A bloodstained, cotton nightdress stuck to the tops of her legs and her belly. Beth bit her bottom lip to stop it trembling. This was a time for strength and support, not blubbering weakness.

'Don't die, Ma! Please don't die!'

Struggling to find the strength, her mother eased herself up on to her elbows. 'I'm not going to do that, sweetheart, but I have to say that I'm too old for all this. Get me some newspapers.'

The weight of her own baby began to feel like lead in her stomach, but Beth did as her mother asked. Lifting up the storage bin beneath the seat, she rummaged among the useful things her mother collected, such as newspapers, odd garments for reusing and her small supply of books, pencils and paper. Her hand trembled as she retrieved the newspapers, closed the box and turned back to the bed. Her mother's breathing was interspersed with a quick gasp each time a pain racked her body.

Despite this being a dire situation, the newspaper headlines assaulted her eyes.

STRIKE THREATENS!

> GOVERNMENT TO MOBILISE THE ARMY UNDERGRADUATES
> TO BE DRAFTED IN TO KEEP THINGS GOING
> UNREASONABLE DEMANDS BY THE UNION

The important words that affected all their lives became a blur. There was no time now to find out what was going on across the country or in the world. Working-class demands were now secondary to the needs of the woman who had given her birth.

Hands trembling uncontrollably, she handed the papers to her mother. In passing them over, she noticed how cold her hands were and how thin and fragile were the fingers.

'Draw the curtain. I'll pass it out to you.'

'No. I'll help. Let me do it.'

'No!'

Her mother's back arched like a bow as another pain grabbed at her belly and her spine. 'No,' she repeated and turned her face towards the wooden wall.

Beth drew the curtains as she'd requested. It might have been best if she had gone up top to get some air rather than stay with the smell, the stuffiness and the presence of pain. It was impossible to move her feet, her hands or her eyes. As the smell of rancid blood intensified, she stared at the green and brown roses that tangled over the curtain. There was no need to be able to look through it because she could hear, and indeed feel, what was going on.

Each time her mother sucked in her breath, then mewed with pain, she had the urge to rush forward, to rip the curtain aside and to... What could she do to ease her mother's suffering, except to pull the half-formed child from her body, or to throw herself on to her and weep all over her beloved face?

Minutes passed yet they seemed like hours. Just when she

thought she could stand no more, her mother's hands appeared where the two pieces of curtain joined together.

Beth stared at what looked like an innocent newspaper parcel. Normally it would contain nothing more upsetting than a loaf of bread or a Savoy cabbage. But no loaf of bread felt as warm or as moist as the bundle that nestled against the life growing within her.

She swallowed the nausea that rose from her stomach. 'Should I burn it?'

'No. Take it out to your father. He's waiting for it.'

The significance sent a prickling sensation running over her skin. It was as though she'd been caught in a sudden frost with nothing on. She remembered now. He had done this once before when she had been considered too small for the task. Hands trembling and eyes averted from her charge, she did as asked. Her father glanced down at her and for the first time in a long while, their eyes met, but he did not smile. Neither did she.

'This is for you to deal with,' she said coldly, and although she would have liked to throw it at his feet, the fact that the warm lump had been destined to be a baby like the one she carried within her prevented her.

He grunted and gave a curt nod. 'I'll get a stone.' Without a backward glance, he climbed on to dry land, returning with a large rock that had to be held in both hands. He flung her a piece of string. 'Tie it round the parcel.'

Although her fingers seemed to have turned into toes, she managed to wrap the string around and around, careful to leave enough to tie around the stone.

Silently she rested the bundle on the side of the boat.

Without looking at her or touching the parcel, he tied the trailing pieces of string around the stone. 'Now throw it over the side.' He turned away, his broad back saying it all.

Angered, she responded instantly. 'No! You do it!'

When he turned round, there was an alien look in his eyes. His lips juddered as though searching for the right word. "T'ain't no job for a man. It's women's work.'

'Women's pain,' Beth responded.

There were things she wanted to scream at him, like why wasn't he showing more emotion, why didn't he rush down into the cabin and hold his wife's hand, ask her how she was? But what was the use?

She stared at the newsprint and her trembling fingers. It was hard to let go, yet it had to be done.

'God bless,' she said softly as the bundle and the stone splashed into the water and disappeared from view. A few ripples remained like the drifting halo of an innocent soul. Then that too was gone and there was only the flat surface and her reflection looking back at her.

She became aware that he was still there and was watching her intently.

'One less mouth to feed,' he said. 'And don't you be gettin' all upset about it, 'cos it never really lived! Bloody women!'

His eyes were fierce. He pointed the stem of his pipe at her. *As though he might stab me.*

In the past, she would never have dared done anything, but she was grown now and her anger at men in general and him in particular was too great to contain.

'Bloody men! You're all selfish! All wrapped up in your bloody selves, especially you, Dawson! Especially you!'

Whether it was being called by his surname, she didn't know, but his mouth fell open like an empty purse and his eyes widened in shock. And he was so still. So frozen.

His silence and stillness were short-lived. He raised his hand. 'No woman talks to me like that!'

The anger was still in her. She stood with her hands on what remained of her hips and shouted, 'No woman would ever want to talk to you any other way! Tell me how you ever got anyone as good as my mother to marry you. Did she think she could change you? Or did you buy her or beat her into submission like you tried with your children? No wonder we hate you. Hate you! Do you hear that?'

No one could have looked so beside himself with fury. But the moment passed.

There was a sudden movement to her left. 'What's the noise?'

Beth's anger rose higher as Robbie crawled out from beneath the tarpaulin that raked over the engine housing and the main cargo hold. He was still wearing his underwear – long-sleeved vest and ankle-length underpants. He was scratching his head with one hand and his chin with another. He reminded her of a picture she'd seen in a book.

'And *you* look like a chimpanzee.'

'No need for that,' he said between yawns.

If Robbie was expecting to be a peacemaker, the image was swiftly shot down. Beth rounded on him.

'As for you, Robbie Dawson, no money for tarts any more? Is that why you're chasing after married women when their husbands aren't around?'

She saw the surprise on his face and waited for the boasting to start. Robbie liked to crow over his conquests. But he didn't do that. His face collapsed into seriousness and for a fleeting moment, she suspected that he cared more for Carrie than she could possibly have anticipated.

His brows dipped, his face darkened. It was his father's face looking back at her. "Tis none of your business!'

'What are you both on about?' For the first time in his life, the bullying demeanour of Daddy Dawson seemed to have deserted him. Looking confused because he was in the dark, he looked quickly from one to the other, waiting for someone to apologise or explain what the hell was going on.

'No!' Beth retorted. 'It's George Melcroft's business!'

Speechless, Robbie's mouth dropped open. For the first time in her life, she saw fear in his eyes.

'You'll do no such thing. I'm warning ya!'

There was something else in his face. At first she couldn't quite make it out, but then it came to her. Robbie cared for Carrie.

She could tell from the look in his eyes that he was pleading with her. Silently, they stared at each other in mutual understanding. There was no need for words. In the midst of the silence, a small groan came from the cabin. Mother!

'I'll be right there!'

Beth hooked her leg up over the side of the boat. Her father's arm shot out to stop her. 'Oh no you don't!'

'And who else is going to help her?' she said angrily, hitting his arm aside. But he came back at her, his arm barring her way.

'Me!' he exclaimed, his eyes like chips of burning coal. 'It's always been me she wants at times like these.'

There was something in his look that stopped her from pressing the point. It was as though she would be taking something away from him if she went down to take care of her mother. Could it be that this painful moment was the only one in which he felt truly needed?

Silently, she watched as he turned away from her, not daring to disobey, not just because of the old days and her old fears. This was for now and the new fear that her mother might still have more than a passing regard for the man she had married. 'He knows what to do, I suppose,' she said quietly as the cabin door closed behind him.

Robbie only glared at the door then at her. 'Pah!' he exclaimed and before she could turn and accuse him of committing a sin with Carrie Melcroft – *her friend* – he had already ducked back down to his temporary bed beneath the heavy layer of tarpaulin.

'Men!' Beth exclaimed. Her eyes blazed with anger. Her thoughts were confused. She couldn't quite work out who was the worse of the two: the one who so callously dismissed the child born too early, or the one who seemed to have no guilt about his relationship with a married woman.

20

Whether Elliot noticed it or not, she was silent at breakfast, her mind full of how she would warn Carrie about her brother. Before they shoved off with their load, she decided she would pop along to the *Jenny Wren* and see how her mother was.

'I'll have another piece of that bread,' said Elliot, holding out his plate. He made an attempt to look pleasant or even not so sullen.

As she shook the pan to get the blackened crumbs to the edge of the fat, Beth's thoughts were elsewhere. *And I'll tell her how I saw my own brother canoodling with some tart in a dark shop doorway. Did it for money he did! Now! What do you think of that!*

'Beth! More fried bread, woman!' he said loud enough to send her thoughts fragmenting but not dissolving. The pan went back on to the hot coals of the range. She slapped his bread on to the plate along with the crumbs, sprinkled like blackened mouse droppings all over the crust. He ate it anyway.

'Come on. We've got a load to get away.'

He washed the bread down with a third cup of sweet tea. He

liked it strong. Even with milk added, it was the colour of burnt toffee.

Not yet, she thought, though she wouldn't let him know why she wanted to linger. Her eyes turned to the oblong of blue-and-white sky through the tiny door. She just had to speak to Carrie before leaving. And of course, there was her mother to think of.

'I have to see how Mother's doing.' She begged her mother's forgiveness as she gazed at her husband imploringly, using her as the excuse to do both.

'What's wrong with her?'

'Elliot, I told you about Ma last night. Surely there's enough time for me to look in on her before we leave.' For a moment, she thought he was going to refuse.

'Ten minutes,' he said at last.

* * *

Although looking pale and strained, her mother was up and about, sitting quietly beside the tiller. Beth's father was checking the ropes, holding the load and adjusting those fastening them to the mooring.

'Ma?'

A lump came to her throat and prevented her from saying any more. The dark lines beneath her mother's eyes echoed the colour of her bonnet.

Seeing Beth biting her bottom lip, she reached out and patted her hand. 'Now don't be afraid. You and your babe will be fine. It's nothing to be afraid of. It won't happen to a young girl like you. I'm older. These things happen to older women. All part of a woman's life, Beth. It's not the first time, you know.'

Her smile was weak. Beth pondered on how strong women were when it came to the natural events of life.

'You're not going to steer for very long, are you?' Beth asked.

'I promise I won't.'

Beth looked at her accusingly. She knew her mother would carry on uncomplaining unless a break was offered.

Elizabeth the elder saw the look in her daughter's eyes and knew what she was thinking. 'I promise I'll take it easy. Tell you what; in between stints at the tiller I'll do my bit of knitting. Will that convince you?'

Beth smiled and nodded. 'I'll get it up for you.'

'No need!' said her mother.

But Beth got up anyway, and put one leg through the cabin door until she felt the top step.

'Leave it, Beth. I'll get it myself!' shouted her mother. She sounded agitated. It's just the way she is, Beth told herself, and went ahead with what she was doing.

The knitting was easy enough to find. It was a large blue square that she guessed was to form part of a quilt for Robbie's single bunk – when he got back in it. One bone needle was still with it but rummage as she might, she could not find the other amongst the heavy blue folds.

Rolling the knitting over the remaining needle, she happened to knock against the water bucket. Sticking out of it was the other needle. She eyed it warily, her instinct telling her that not only was it an odd place for it to be, but that it was there for a purpose.

Once it was in her hand, her blood seemed to drain out through her toes. The needle was bloodstained and she'd heard enough from other women to know that knitting had nothing to do with it.

'She killed it,' she muttered through a bitten lip as tears filled her eyes. Why did she do that? But deep inside, she knew the reason why. Her mother was over forty. Two children and several miscarriages had happened already, whether by plan or from natural causes. She could not cope with a small child at her age.

After wiping her eyes with her sleeve and the needles with an old rag, she put them back with the blue wool and made her way up the ladder.

There was silence between them when she got back up top. She put the knitting at her mother's side. At first, she looked along the canal to where it disappeared into a low-lying haze that sat between a tumbledown barn and a copse of silver birch.

'It's just one of those things you have to deal with,' her mother said in a slow, matter-of-fact voice. 'We're too old for little ones. But they come along when you least expect it, even at my age. I'd be an old woman before it was grown. Then who'd look after it?'

Beth couldn't bring herself to turn round and face her mother because she understood her logic. Of course she was too old to be having babies. But what she found so difficult to accept was that her mother could be strong enough to kill her own child.

She looked down at her hands. She hadn't known just how tightly she was gripping the side of the boat. Now she could see her knuckles were white with effort. Before her eyes was the rounded lump that would soon be another soul entering the world. She prayed it would not be a girl.

Their goodbye included the most deeply emotional hug they had ever given each other.

'Take care of the little one,' her mother said, her blue eyes sad and large in her paleness.

Beth promised she would. She didn't leave that part of the quay until *Jenny Wren* had disappeared.

Conveniently moored two boats up from her own was *Sadie G*, Carrie's boat. She had planned to knock on the window as she passed. It had always been a recognised signal for Carrie to poke her head out and offer her tea. Elliot couldn't object to her accepting, could he?

But her mood had changed. Important as it had been for her to tell Carrie about her brother's worst habits, what had happened to her mother in the past few hours weighed heavily on her mind. Bowing to male pressure and their own fears, women could almost... She couldn't bring the word easily to mind because she didn't want to recognise it for what it was. But the word came anyway. Murder!

'Beth! Beth! Will you have tea with me? The kettle's just boiled.'

Without her needing to knock on the window, Carrie had seen her and had said exactly what Beth expected her to say. She stopped and looked into the grey eyes, saw the serene smile, the silvery, fair hair pulled so firmly away from the high forehead. At times, Carrie looked like a missionary's wife. At others, she looked homely, mostly when she was smiling and happy, with George's arm placed lovingly around her shoulders. Thinking of George made her think again of her brother and all the things she wanted to say.

Suddenly, her mission to enlighten her friend returned with a vengeance.

Beth had always admired the collection of silver and fine china placed so prettily on the lace-lined shelves in Carrie's cabin. Tea was poured from a rose-painted teapot into rose-painted cups. She offered biscuits, Garibaldis with sweet little nibbles of currants wedged between sugar-coated oblongs. Carrie always offered biscuits, which impressed Beth no end because as far as she knew, only very rich people who lived in smart houses offered biscuits with tea.

Beth sat on the small stool kept under the table that folded away when more room was needed. Carrie sat opposite her, her smiling eyes and face suddenly annoying Beth in a way they never had before.

Normally, they would tumble straight into conversation. Today things were more stilted.

'Sugar?' asked Carrie.

'Just one.'

'Milk?'

'Of course. I always have milk. Who's likely to drink tea without milk in it? Certainly not me!'

Obviously surprised at her uncharacteristic attitude, Carrie raised her eyebrows but did not comment.

Beth kept her gaze fixed on the teacup Carrie had pushed in front of her. The state of her mother and the things she wanted to say congealed like cold porridge in her mind. Yet she had to do something, say something!

Carrie broke the silence. 'Is there anything wrong? Have you got enough sugar?'

As though her neck were a spring, Beth's gaze leapt into Carrie's face. 'Of course I've got enough sugar!'

Once it was said she regretted it. Carrie looked so hurt, her eyebrows knitted in puzzlement.

'Something's wrong,' Carrie began, her voice as even and gentle as ever.

'Of course something's wrong.'

'Is the baby all right? Do tell me, Beth. Please.' Her pale eyes widened. Her pink lips were slightly parted.

Beth was taken aback. How she could sit there so innocently and talk about her expected baby when she was... Thoughts that had cleared started to congeal again. Had she come here to warn Carrie of what her brother was like or to chastise her about entertaining men when her husband was not around? She took a deep breath.

'I've come to talk to you about Robbie.'

Carrie's smile faltered. 'Your brother.'

'Yes.'

Beth watched with a sinking heart as Carrie's long lashes fluttered nervously and a faint blush seeped over her high cheekbones.

'So what has he told you?'

Now that did surprise her. 'Told me? Nothing. I came along to warn you. He's a rat. I've seen him twist every little innocent barge, factory or shop girl he's ever come across around his little finger.' She didn't add about the women he'd paid to have sex with, the tawdry tarts in the shadows around the warehouses and scruffy shops. The shamefulness of her brother's lifestyle was not an easy thing to admit to.

Carrie's hands fell into her lap. 'I don't know what you mean.'

Beth slammed her palms down flat on the table so that the teacups rattled and the biscuits jumped from the saucers. 'Oh yes you do! I saw him leaving here the other night, Carrie.'

'He came to see George.'

'George was at the meeting. I saw him there.'

Suddenly, Carrie dropped forward to rest her elbows on the table, her head in her hands. She began to weep.

This was all too much! Overcome by anger at her brother and sympathy for her friend, Beth got up and leaned across the table. This whole affair, she thought, is what comes of marrying a man twenty years older than you. But she couldn't possibly point that out.

'Robbie is a swine, Carrie. You shouldn't have trusted him. He'll tell you anything just to get what he wants. And we all know what that is, don't we!'

Carrie began shaking her head within Beth's embrace. 'No! No!

You've got it all wrong. And I didn't want anyone to find out. That's why I was so careful.'

Frowning, Beth's arms fell to her side before she slid back on to her stool. What could she have got wrong?

Tear-laden eyes looked into hers and although Carrie's smile seemed dreadfully wooden, at least it was returning. 'He's not the one taking advantage of me. I'm taking advantage of him.'

Beth stared at her. How could a woman like Carrie take advantage of a man like her brother? Was she out of her mind? Was that the reason she was keeping company with her Robbie? Had living with an older man made her daft?

'I can't see it,' Beth said. 'And why are you crying?'

With a flurry of hands, Carrie patted her cheeks then pressed her long fingers over her pale pink lips. It was a bit disconcerting to have those grey eyes looking at her. She'd never seen such confusion, such sadness in them before. All she had ever seen was serenity that she presumed mirrored Carrie's pure soul.

'I want a baby!'

It came out so fast, so unexpected.

Beth shrugged as if she did not understand because she didn't want to confront what she thought Carrie was implying. 'Then have one. Talk to George about it.'

Carrie shook her head, looked down at the table then back up at Beth. Fresh tears hung on her lashes and one more lustrous than the others split and ran unchecked down her cheek.

'George can't have babies. That's why his first wife left him. She's got five children now. I've met her. I've explained what I want to Robbie. But neither of us wants to hurt George. He mustn't know that it isn't his.'

Beth didn't have the heart to say that George was still married to his first wife, regardless of where her children had come from.

Divorces were costly and besides, they were frowned on by anyone wanting to be considered respectable and hard-working.

She could imagine them: Robbie wanting her for sex and Carrie wanting sex with him so she could have a baby. The shock of it all took her breath away and she couldn't find the right words to say because there were none.

Again, it was Carrie who broke the silence. She leaned close to Beth until their noses almost touched. 'I want a baby, Beth. And I think I've just started one.' She smiled. 'Regardless of how I got it, I'm very happy about it, Beth. Very, very happy!'

There was no doubting the sincerity in Carrie's eyes, and although some would brand her with wicked words, Beth could not find it in her heart to condemn her for what she had done. Expecting a child gave a woman a very warm feeling and made her feel different than she ever had before. The world was a different place and even the people in it were better than they had been.

'I understand,' she said. The truth was she did understand, but would Robbie? Would anyone else who found out? The answer was obvious but the truth would not come from her.

21

Abigail knew that at some time she would have to confirm to her father that she had no intention of falling in with his wishes and marrying Gilbert. Although her mother had already fainted over her declaration that she had only wanted to 'try him out', they hadn't really taken her seriously.

'She will have her little joke,' her father had told those gathered that afternoon once the smelling salts had done their job. Abigail was adamant. True, Gilbert had a great body and looked good in tennis whites, but being in bed with him for the rest of her life was something she could well do without. It pleased her to think that no man would get her entirely on his terms. She had scuppered man's traditional privilege by giving her virginity away in the first place. It was all part of the strategy she had laid down when she'd first decided to storm male bastions like pubs, unions and the right to wear trousers. What was hers she could give away as she would and it didn't have to be sanctified by a vicar spouting words at the altar. If men could wed without being virgins then so could she. Besides, her main reason for telling her father that she would marry was all to do with the Beavens and the problems they were having with Harry Allen. Their livelihood had been saved. It was too late now to throw them off their boat.

The chance to hammer home the bad news came on a Sunday afternoon when the wind was chasing clouds across the sky and the plane leaves were spiralling off the tree to fall like flat feet on the surface of the pond.

She'd come in late the night before and although the servants had tried to tell her that people were coming for tea, she was too tired to take too much notice. Besides, she was still relishing the fact that she'd half brained Harry Allen and wanted to re-enact the scene in her mind. Breakfast was an event best avoided. A tray was brought to her room but left untouched by the bedroom window.

Requests by her mother that she wanted to talk about things and make 'arrangements' were banished with, 'Not now. I'm busy.'

Throwing herself on to the bed, she smiled at the ceiling as she thought about Harry Allen and how she'd done for him good and proper! The room was warm and she dozed. In dozing, she dreamed about Anthony: how he looked, how he stood and how he spoke.

Refreshed by five o'clock, she got herself ready for tea. As this was to be a moment of truth, she wore the clothes she always felt best in: trousers, a shirt and a smart black-and-white-checked jacket and matching two-tone shoes.

To her great amusement, a bevy of relatives and friends were gathered in the drawing room. Like a flock of pigeons suddenly wheeling to the right, they raised their glasses of sherry when she entered, smiling smugly as if the battle was won and she had lost her fight to be different. A few eyebrows were raised when they saw what she was wearing.

'You should have changed, dear,' said her mother, a feathery frown creasing her powdered brow. As though in dire pain, she winced at the outfit her daughter was so fond of. Family friends merely exchanged knowing glances.

'She hasn't changed that much,' whispered one aunt to another.

'I'd lock her up,' whispered an uncle after draining his glass and pouring more sherry from the decanter the maid had left on the table. He'd pinched the maid's bottom as she'd passed by.

Abigail was aware of the whispers, but what people thought of her was of no real consequence to humanity and therefore of no real importance to her. Gossip was something everyone enjoyed and if one was slightly eccentric one had to expect to be talked about. That was all part of the fun. Besides, she enjoyed the sport and the possibilities. It stood to reason that even when she was old and grey, she would still be food for gossip and that gossip might get more and more outrageous the older she became.

After she'd taken a sherry from the tray, downing that then taking another, she approached her mother.

Her mother gave her the fish-eyed stare, which she did whenever she disapproved of her clothes, her friends, or her behaviour, which was pretty frequently.

'You have such pretty frocks, Abigail darling. Why don't you go back up and put on the one with the pink rosebuds around the waistline?'

'Because I hate it,' said Abigail and reached for a third sherry. Gilbert was a picture of cream-coloured excellence – or at least his clothes were. 'Darling,' he said, his cold lips aiming for hers but only brushing her cheek when at the last minute, she turned her head.

'I am not your darling, Gilbert. Neither am I your lover, your paramour, your whore or even your wife, and I never will be any of those! Especially your wife!'

An amazed hush echoed around the room.

'Smelling salts!' wailed her mother, her eyes closing and her knees crumpling as she wafted a lace-edged handkerchief before her face.

'Abigail!' growled her father. He grabbed her arm so tightly that sherry splashed from the glass and on to the carpet. 'What is this outrage? You have agreed to marry Gilbert. You promised me that you would, especially as you've... you've...'

It would have been easy to finish the sentence for him, but she wouldn't. *Let him stew.*

'After all,' he went on, 'you have been intimate with each other.'

Abigail smirked. 'You mean I let him have me. Sexually. Like a bride on her wedding night, a whore in a bordello. Making love, some call it. The more general term is...'

'Abigail! You will not use such words in this house!'

A muttering of conversation started up, relatives chattering like a coven of elderly ravens.

While Gilbert stood like a statue, not sure whether to speak or swig back his sherry, Abbie shook her arm from her father's grasp and rounded on him with all the venomous intent of a maladjusted cobra. 'There's been some misunderstanding!'

Her father's face reddened. His voice dropped. 'You stated in this very room that you would.'

She shrugged her shoulders. 'I've changed my mind.'

'I promised you. And you promised me. I let those people keep their boat.'

She was pert and cheeky and her laughter bordered on the hysterical.

'The time is past. You've got no excuse to dismiss them now, and even then, you almost did go back on your word. If I hadn't arrived on the scene, you would have. Besides, you've got no one left to do it if what I hear is true. Someone brained Harry Allen. Couldn't have happened to a nicer bloke, could it!'

'But, Abbie,' said Gilbert softly, his smile a nervous pretension. The smile persisted as he nodded at the family and friends invited especially to witness the occasion. 'I thought we'd agreed when we left the summerhouse...'

Her expression became scornful. 'My name's Abigail. You know I don't allow anyone to call me Abbie except my very dearest friends.'

She smiled to herself when she thought of her very, very dearest friend. Anthony. Only Anthony called her Abbie and that was the way she wanted it to be: one special name, one special person. The truth was that Beth called her that too, and so had Carrie. But for now, it was only Anthony she wanted to own that privilege.

She shook her head, the coppery hair shimmering like silk. Her complexion suffused by an angry colour that spread from her cheeks and poured down over her neck as she fought to control her contempt for him and everything he stood for. 'I never agreed to anything, Gilbert. I let you make love to me. I gave you my virginity. You should be grateful enough for that. Isn't that what every young man wants: to be the first? Well? Isn't it?'

Everyone heard. The room fell into instant silence relieved only by the sound of a slight thud as her mother, unseen until then, slipped to the floor and a sherry glass bounced on the carpet.

* * *

Abigail leaned against a crusted brick wall in the Birmingham Gas Bar, not caring about the stink of kerosene and gas oil, but puffing thoughtfully on a cigarette as she considered whether to leave home or to stay. She had enough of her grandfather's trust money to find herself a nice little place, but there was something sadistically enticing about goading her father and having her mother faint at the mere mention of sex. There they sat in their fine house, icons of middle-class matrimony – a state of contractual bliss rather than conjugal. They had separate rooms, separate lives; her mother had friends, her father had floozies. A mad existence, and yet they considered her mad. She was the rebel who found fault with everything they did, who turned her back on her class. 'I wish you weren't here and I wish your sister was,' her father had snarled in the drawing room when she'd made it clear that Gilbert could go to hell. 'Whatever she's done, I'd have her back tomorrow. But you!' he spat. 'If you leave my house, never darken my door again! And I mean that!'

'I can't say it's likely,' she'd responded. 'But be careful. Remember your little seamstress friend. I could have mentioned her in front of all our relatives. And there's that other place you sometimes frequent. Now what is it called? Can't think at the moment. Do believe it's run by a Madam Rubere, though? Is that right?'

Her father had visibly paled before exploding with anger. 'I'll have you committed! I bloody well swear I'll have you committed!'

She'd smiled. 'You'll have to – if you want me to keep your little secret!'

So she had left and now she was waiting for Anthony.

'Are you ready?' His voice was like the sudden beat on a drum, waking her from a deep sleep.

'Of course. I've been waiting for you for absolutely ages.' She pretended to be cross. She wasn't. Her whole body responded when he spoke. More and more she found herself hanging on his every word and her weakness embarrassed her. Sometimes she thought he had surmised how she felt about him. Was he looking at her with as much affection as she felt for him? Her elation had so far been short-lived. He had merely grinned broadly and slapped her on the back like he would a man and told her what a good job she was doing.

She flicked her cigarette into the canal, where it glowed for a moment before sizzling and going out.

'Have you got everything in there?' she asked as she eyed the tan-coloured, dog-eared suitcase he was carrying.

'I travel light.'

He flung the case on the back seat of the little Austin next to her own luggage: one suitcase, one vanity case containing all the trivia she needed to keep herself looking like a woman despite the masculine clothes she wore.

They were off to a place called Braunston near Leicester, where the strike they had planned was to happen at last.

'My,' she said breathlessly, inhaling the smell of leather as she slid in front of the steering wheel. 'This is so exciting.'

Anthony made no comment.

'Well,' she said as she pushed the gear stick forward, 'don't you think it's exciting?'

Anthony grimaced. 'For you it might be, but for the boat people, it's a matter of life and death.'

* * *

The midwife, an old woman named Mrs Crow who had birthed more babies than anyone had had hot dinners, so she said, delivered a beautiful baby to Beth Beaven just two hundred yards from the canal-side shop. 'It's a girl,' cried Mrs Crow, her clay pipe dancing like a Maybug in the corner of her mouth.

Beth fell back on to the pillow. 'Is she all right?'

'Fine.'

But silent, thought Beth, and wondered, just for a moment, whether the child had indeed been born alive. Chillingly, her mind went back to that morning when she had held a warm bundle wrapped in newspaper, tied it to a stone and dropped it into the water.

Suddenly a huge bellow came out of the child's lungs and took Mrs Crow – and Beth – by surprise. What a noise! What significance there was in that sound! This was a child bellowing defiance, demanding to live and have whatever this life could offer, and by the sound of it, she was willing to make herself heard and fight for what was hers by right.

'Give her to me,' said Beth, holding out her arms. In that moment, she resolved that she would do her best to grant her a worthwhile life, something better than the one she had been given. She studied the tiny face, touched the delicate fingers. 'You should lie abed now for a fortnight,' said Mrs Crow as she tucked the bundled child under Beth's arm, exposed her breast and pushed the baby's face close to her nipple. Fascinated, Beth looked down at the round pink face and gossamer-fine eyelids trimmed with dark lashes like her own. The baby needed no prompting, her small mouth puckering then clamping tightly over the hard nub of flesh and snuggling tightly to the well-filled bosom.

'I'll bind you up so that everything goes back in place.'

With that she reached for the strips of sheets that had been torn in pieces for just that purpose. 'I suppose you're going to call her Elizabeth like you and yer ma.'

Beth eyed her new daughter. Was she? At first she wasn't sure, but then she was. She wanted a different, a better world for her child. In that split second, she decided that her name must change too.

'Her name's Pamela. Pamela Agnes Beaven.'

Mrs Crow looked surprised but didn't comment. Women who'd just given birth sometimes got funny ideas. Their brain got a bit addled for a while. She'd seen it all before, giving odd names to their babies then regretting it just a few weeks later.

'Now,' she said, cascades of white cotton falling from her left arm as she approached the bed, 'let's get you bound round and proper so that yer belly goes back where it should be.'

'I don't know whether I want to,' said Beth. 'Are you sure it's not just an old wives' tale?'

'Certainly not.' Mrs Crow looked quite offended and Beth felt guilty. She held out the strips of sheet. 'Now you come on there. Let's be having ya.'

Beth's protest was drowned by the sound of boots thudding on hard ground outside then a riot of thuds and bangs as Elliot leapt over the side of the boat and pushed open the cabin door.

'Pamela,' she said gently to the baby. 'Your father's come to see you.'

Elliot's eyes glittered like chips of melted copper. His eyes flashed from child to mother. There was an unusual glow, the sort of look he got following a few beers and a pub brawl.

'The strike,' he said. 'It's on. We're off to Braunston at the end of May. We'll get in some work before then.'

Taking note of the glare from Mrs Crow, he turned his gaze back to Beth and eyed her a little more discerningly as though only just remembering that she had recently given birth. 'There's no time to waste. When can you be ready?'

'A fortnight!' cried Mrs Crow.

'I can be up and about by tomorrow morning,' said Beth, enthused with Elliot's excitement. Something was at last going to happen for the benefit of all of them. This other happening occupied his mind.

'What about the binding?' shouted Mrs Crow.

'I don't want it,' said Beth, her eyes fixed on Elliot's face because his were fixed on the child and were filled with wonder.

I'll never forget that look, she thought.

'You'll regret it!' shouted Mrs Crow before leaving, but Beth gave it no mind. For this moment at least, they were a family.

22

Sunlight and shadow raced in quick succession above the Braunston compound. For a fortnight, nearly two hundred boats had gathered, their little smokestacks chuffing black smoke. Boats decorated with castles, bluebirds and flowers glowed in the sunlight.

People beamed at each other, proud that they'd managed to do what they'd once thought was impossible. Until now, strikes by boatmen had been spasmodic, spread over hundreds of miles of inland waterways. But this time, Anthony's network of communications had done its job. Hundreds of boats were descending on the small town close to Leicester.

'They have to be in the same place at the same time,' Abigail had stated at yet another pub bar meeting. 'Leave a message with the post-box – Ned Wheeler – then chain all the boats together as they come in.'

The instruction had been passed by word of mouth. The boats slowly gathered. Each boat was chained to its neighbour so that no one could be forced away from the wharves. A man riding a Douglas motorcycle delivered an ultimatum from the carrying company. A crowd gathered, the messenger and his iron steed causing more of a stir than the actual message. Eventually the carriers issued a statement: force would be used if they did not go back to their work.

Scratching their heads and looking worried, the men gathered around Anthony Wesley.

'What'll they do?'

'What can they do?'

There were worried frowns. 'As long as it's over quickly. I've got a family to think of.'

'We've all got families to think of. Have we come this far to turn tail and flee?'

'Do we stand our ground like men or flee like rabbits?'

A chorus of voices rose up in agreement.

The compound consisted of two separate 'pounds', or man-made lakes, each filled with boats moored raft-style so folk on the outside had to step over those closest to the quay. Between the two stretches of water was a small island of raised earth connected to each bank by a single walkway bridge. A bonfire had been built in the middle of the island and people were sitting around it, their faces pink from too much warmth and their backs shivering more from the contrast than the cold.

'Glad you could make it,' cried a familiar voice.

Both Beth and Elliot looked to where the tall, square-shouldered figure of Anthony Wesley stood waving at them. Because they were at the end of a four-rafted arrangement, Anthony waited for them to come to him, Beth with Pamela clamped tightly to her breast. Elliot followed on behind.

Anthony tipped his cap at her and glanced at her only briefly. He shook Elliot's hand as though he was the most important arrival. 'Pleased you could get here.'

Elliot cracked the knuckles of his right hand into his left palm. 'There's serious work to be done. I'm the man for that, I think!'

Beth cringed. She hated him doing that. The sound of cracking knuckles made her feel sick.

Anthony noticed her grimace. 'Lovely baby,' he said.

She looked away when their eyes met. It wasn't seemly. She was a married woman. She'd seen that look in his eyes. *If only things weren't the way they were.*

Abigail came calling shortly after that. She appeared to be in her element, shouting out slogans and organizing men into groups on instructions from Anthony.

'This is a fight for justice,' she shouted. 'You deserve a decent wage and you will get a decent wage.'

'We certainly do,' Elliot said. 'And if my guts are anything to go by, it's going to be a right nasty fight, old butt.'

He said it to anyone who listened and in the cabin of a night he lectured his wife about it, tramping up and down – as far as one could tramp in such a confined space. Arms waving, he told her how much better things would be once this was over.

'Good for every man that's trying to earn a crust for his family.' He tucked a finger under her chin and raised her face to look into his. 'I believe in that, Beth. I believe in doing my duty to my family. Do you know what I mean?'

When she nodded, the baby at her breast disturbed slightly. Elliot looked down at her and ran a rough finger over the pale pink cheek. 'I want better than I had. Better than we both had.'

The forthcoming fight had lit a fire in his belly. She dared to hope his temper would improve.

'Including education,' she said blithely. Then the old fear returned. She saw the warning set of his mouth. Despite that, she carried on. 'The bosses have it. That's what makes them so strong.

You can read all about what they're up to in the newspaper. They prefer that we can't read. Otherwise we'd be as wise as they are.'

At first, she thought she was in for a beating. His eyes glittered like they did when he thought that someone was getting the better of him. It was the first time she had mentioned reading and writing since he had proclaimed that she should never do either again. But this was her personal fight and she was determined not to back down, whatever he might do.

She held her defiant look. Their eyes seemed to lock as if their minds were in competition with each other. If he didn't give soon, or if someone didn't interrupt them, there was no knowing what would happen next.

'Elliot!'

Beth recognised Anthony's voice and blessed the fact that he'd come by.

'Here!' Elliot shouted back.

Anthony's face and torso appeared at the half cabin door.

He nodded politely at Beth and looked quickly away again. She guessed he'd gauged Elliot's mood.

His voice was calm and firm. 'Elliot, I'd like you to take charge of a group of men. We're going to stand guard in shifts.' He turned to Beth. 'All right with you if I take your husband, Beth?'

She smiled, liking him asking her even though she had no real say in the matter. Elliot would do as he pleased. 'Whatever you have to do is all right by me.'

Wedging the baby against her hip, she stood to one side as a group of men marched by with shovels held like rifles over their shoulders.

'What about the women? How are they to be organised?'

'See Abigail,' he answered. 'She's probably got some ideas on that.' He set about to leave.

'So have I,' she said.

He turned back. Elliot, who had obviously overheard, bumped into him.

'Now what ideas have you got?' he said, hands resting impatiently on his hips.

She kept her gaze fixed on Anthony's face. 'The women are going to be frightened, but not as frightened as the children. I thought I might set up some kind of school where I could read to them. Perhaps we could find some old bits of paper and some pencils. Slates and chalk would be good too. At least it will keep them occupied and out of the men's way. They'll need to concentrate on their battle plans.'

She was aware of the way Elliot was looking at her. *Battle plans indeed! Another set of fancy words from yer fancy books!* That's what he would have said if there'd been no one else there.

He would stop her if he could, but she wouldn't allow it.

Shivering inside, she didn't dare look at him but kept her gaze firmly fixed on Anthony.

Seemingly unaware of the friction between them, Anthony beamed. 'That's a marvellous idea.' He turned to Elliot. 'Clever wife you've got there, Beaven. You must be proud of her.'

'Yes. I am.' Strangely enough, he sounded sincere. He might have been, but Beth found his expression difficult to read.

She followed them to the shore. Still clasping Pamela, she marched along the wharf, calling to the women she knew that she was having a meeting for women only and could they tell everyone to come along.

'This isn't going to be any Sunday School outing,' she shouted out to the sea of bobbing hats and heads, the milling children with blackened jam around their mouths and between their fingers. 'So we don't want loads of children causing problems for the menfolk. I'm going to set up a school but I need an empty boat to do it in. Who came here with no cargo?'

A sea of hands went up and it occurred to her that perhaps if they had hauled cargo in here they could have held the carrying company to ransom. But she knew these people. They were hardworking and honest and if they were going to strike, they were going to do it with no more than their just share of what was right.

Her needs were obvious. She called them out. 'We need crates for desks, something to use for seating, and a roof in case it rains. Tarpaulin would be good.'

Quicker than ants, whatever she asked for was provided by an army of women intent on helping their men by making sure their children were occupied and out of harm's way. Beth helped get all the younger children together, herding them into a boat that was covered its whole length in a thick blanket of tarpaulin that smelt of grease and coal dust. The children, excited rather than frightened, laughed, shouted, cried and dug at each other as they sat at makeshift desks made from disused crates that had once held tea, gum Arabic or spices from countries most of them had never heard of.

Beth retrieved the books given to her from their hiding place. Thumbed and loved, they were looking a bit the worse for wear, but the words were still there and her heart leapt in anticipation of reading them again. With loving care she stacked them on the crate prepared for her – the same as the children's, but bigger.

'I wish we had pencils and paper,' she said wistfully to her mother, who seemed to have blossomed at the prospect of being useful in the midst of a gaggle of children. Neither mentioned the miscarriage. It was past, out of the way, exactly as planned. They could all sleep better that way. 'Better still, slates and chalk,' she added ruefully. She patted the old books like familiar friends. 'They'll have to do. Shame we don't have some more suitable for children.'

* * *

It was a few days later when more books arrived.

Suddenly, the patch of sunlight that filtered in under the flap of tarpaulin was masked by someone's figure.

'Your library looks a little the worse for wear, teacher. And you appear to have a dearth of pencils and paper.'

A familiar voice!

'Abigail!'

Dressed in clothes that looked as though they might have belonged to a navvy, though scrupulously clean, Abigail hugged a bundle of books close to her chest. The jacket she wore had leather patches on the arms. The trousers were big and baggy, and, to Beth's surprise, leather Yorks were tied around them just below knee level.

'Father won't miss them,' Abigail said brightly as she banged them down on the crate. 'They're all children's books, favourites of my sister and me. I do hope you'll find them useful.'

'Abbie!' Mindful that she had called Abigail Gatehouse by a shortened version of her name, which she knew she disapproved of, Beth quickly corrected herself. 'I'm sorry. Abigail!' There was no way she wanted to upset someone who had shown such generosity. 'This is really generous of you. I'm grateful, honest I am.'

Abigail held up one restraining finger. 'I've not finished, my dear girl.' She turned towards the opening through which she had just entered. 'Spiky!' she shouted.

A pair of skinny white legs clambered over the side of the boat. A lean body wearing a ragged pullover followed. Finally a cheeky face topped with spice-coloured hair that stood up like a hedgehog confronted her.

'The box, please!'

'Yes, missus!' The boy swung forward a large cardboard box. Without any further instruction, he bent and snapped quickly at the string that bound it with a very sharp and very small knife.

'This should do the trick,' said Abigail as she knelt down beside the box then beamed up at Beth with a mischievous smirk. 'Scrap paper from my father's office and lots of pencils, plus sharpeners, and all brand new. His secretary thought she was letting me have them for a garden party at my parents' house. Heaven help the poor woman when my father finds out. Still,' she said with a careless wave of her hand, 'your need is greater than theirs.'

Imagining the poor woman's consternation, Beth felt guilty. 'Oh, Abigail, what if she loses her job?'

Abigail looked up and grinned. 'Of course she won't. I would do the right thing if that came about: step forward and take the blame.'

'More books,' said another figure from the opening in the tarpaulin. 'But not as many as my friend Abigail's brought you,' said Anthony, pushing his cap back further on his mass of dark waves as he set three books down on the table. 'All classics,' he said, ignoring Abigail's frown as he pushed them firmly towards Beth's hands. 'Can't have future generations not knowing Shakespeare and the like, can we.'

The children, the boat and the world around all seemed to fade away as Beth looked into his eyes. How blue they were. Her thoughts went back to the first time they'd met, when he had lain helpless in her arms.

Sensing the feelings between them, Abigail turned frosty. 'Well, that's a pathetic contribution.'

His eyes twinkled. 'My pockets are nowhere near as deep as yours. I was as generous as I could be.'

Abigail stiffened. 'You shouldn't be here. You should be out with the men!'

She smarted in response to the look he threw her. 'I'll be with them soon enough.' He paused and tipped his cap briefly. Then he was gone.

Outside, he whipped it off, threw his head back and closed his eyes. He hadn't meant to upset Abigail. He could never put it into words, but she was his trusty support. The trouble was that she would insist on acting as his conscience. She was right, of course. Why couldn't he be a sensible chap and go courting some suitable girl who'd help his career and take him where he wanted to go? He'd already been told he was political material. He grinned as he marched along. Fancy. Able seaman Anthony John Wesley a Member of Parliament. Well, anything was possible if you really wanted it. And that was the trouble. He wanted it all right. But he also wanted someone else's wife.

Back inside the boat, Abigail prepared to sulk, but pure bedlam broke out thanks to the help she'd recently taken on. 'Look what I've got,' shouted Spiky, he of the skinny white legs and bright red hair. He held up the pencils and paper.

'Come and get it! Last one's a sissy!'

The children poured forward, all scrabbling to get the same as he had, all talking at once, all arguing and crying and screaming if they thought they weren't getting their fair share. Once it was all shared out, Spiky headed for the side of the boat. Beth grabbed his sleeve and the hole already there became larger as the stitching gave way. 'And where do you think you're going?'

Freckles scattered over his face as he gave her a big toothy grin. 'Not me, missus. I don't need no readin' and writin'. I lives by me wits, I do.'

Then he was gone, grinning over his shoulder at her, his spiky hair waving like stalks of orange corn.

She turned back to her charges.

Abigail was shouting. 'Shut up, you little horrors!'

Few gave her a second glance. She looked surprised to find they were not intimidated by her behaviour as adults usually were.

'I think you'd better leave it to me,' said Beth, hiding her smile behind a fall of dark hair. 'I'm more used to children than you are.'

Abigail stood aside. Being side-lined wasn't something she liked very much, but Beth was right; she wasn't used to handling children. All the same, Beth's easy way with the youngsters made her feel jealous as well as admiring.

Abigail sighed and straightened her hat. She looked round at the assortment of small fry, whose ages seemed to range from three to twelve if one didn't count Pamela. And the smell of them! It was sweetish, yet oily and gritty as the earth. If she didn't keep swallowing, it would be easy to be sick.

Sweat began rolling down her forehead from beneath her cap as she stood there listening to Beth read the opening lines of *Treasure Island*. The children sat wide-eyed and open-mouthed. Just looking at them convinced Abigail that reading had indeed been a good idea. Judging by the looks on their faces, they were no longer caught up in the devilish manoeuvres of adults. In their minds' eyes, they were sailing on the *Hispaniola* towards warmer climes where treasure was buried on a wave-soaked beach and a parrot shouted, 'Pieces of eight!' from the shoulder of a man with a wooden leg.

Suddenly, the expectant hush was broken by the sound of Pamela crying for her feed. Abigail watched as Beth started to unbutton her blouse.

'Now, quiet all of you,' Beth said. 'Miss Gatehouse is going to carry on reading to you whilst I feed my baby.'

'I am?' said a surprised Abigail. Somehow she'd been ready for rejection.

Beth pushed the book at her. 'I'm going out there.'

With a quick shift of her hip, the baby ended up tucked under one arm, her head tucked inside her blouse. Although she couldn't see Beth's nipple, she could hear the baby sucking.

Abigail tried to stop her, reached out and grabbed her shoulder. 'It's dangerous out there.'

Beth shrugged her off. 'I want to know what's happening.'

The urge not to leave Beth and Anthony alone was too strong to resist. Abigail put the book to one side. 'I think I should come with you. Who else can read?'

'I'll do it.' Beth's mother took the book from her.

'Just a minute,' said Beth. The child took a few sucks then fell asleep again.

Abigail blushed as she noticed a pearl drop of milk hanging from Beth's nipple, which was now dark pink following the suckling of her child. Beth did not seem to notice her discomposure but merely tucked her breast back inside her blouse. 'Sometimes you want milk, and sometimes you don't,' she said to the baby. 'I should have called you Mary.'

Abigail frowned before the penny dropped. 'Oh. Contrary Mary. I see.'

A group of men ran past them suddenly.

'What's happening?' shouted Abigail, glad to turn her attention to a man's world and away from that of a mother.

One of the men, a big gangly chap with a black moustache and holding his cap flat to his head, slowed slightly and shouted, 'Rozzers!' over his shoulder.

The two women looked at each other in mute fear and understanding. 'Now it begins,' said Abigail. 'We've all got to be brave. This is a war. A class war. You know that, don't you?'

'Of course I do. God for Harry, England and St George,' cried Beth.

Abigail looked at her in amazement. 'Who taught you that little line?'

Beth avoided her gaze, her heart racing with excitement and fear. 'I read it in a book. Let's see what's going on.'

Dodging the puddles left by the overnight rain, they headed towards one of the iron bridges that led to the central island separating the boat pounds. From its central point, it was possible to see whatever was about to happen. Around the water, ranged between the boats and the growing army of blue uniforms, the boatmen huddled in groups. Nervously they eyed the broad-shouldered policemen with their pink faces, trim moustaches and buttons that glinted every time they moved.

Underfed and shabbily dressed, the boatmen looked anomalous, their skeletal features covered with taut, leathery skin tanned by wind and sun. It was an odd contrast, one the hallmark of impending starvation, the other giving the impression of well-being only gained by living in the fresh air.

'What's happening?'

Together they surveyed the situation, noting the position of each faction.

Beth felt her heart racing. An uncanny silence had fallen over them all. Silence before the storm, peace before war, softness before violence. She didn't want to guess what would happen next, but knew it would be violent. Abigail put her fear into words.

'They'll baton-charge,' she said in a matter-of-fact way. 'They always do. I've seen it before.'

Beth hardly dared to breathe the word. 'Batons?'

'Truncheons,' stated Abigail. 'No policeman would be without one.'

Beth hugged her daughter more tightly to her chest. 'I wish you didn't sound so sure about it.'

The police stood like dark-blue gargoyles, their expressions impartial. Beth felt her fear rising like water in a well.

Tension was born of the breathless silence, a taut, highly

strung awareness that ran through the mass of men and women like a current of electricity.

'I can't believe this is happening,' said Beth. Pamela awoke and gurgled in her arms. She looked down at the child and thought she might be better off back with her grandmother and the children.

'Things *are* getting ugly,' murmured Abigail as if reading her mind.

Many men and even a few women were armed – one with an axe, another with a boiler stick that was softened from many dips into hot water. Beth guessed that the police had more experience of beating people with sticks. The women only ever beat laundry.

Both women's eyes strayed to one man above all others. Abigail was almost breathless with admiration. Even though she regarded Beth as her rival, she couldn't help passing comment. 'He looks so handsome, don't you think? Like a Caesar leading his men into battle.'

Perhaps it was the emotional way she spoke that moved Beth to repeat some words she'd read that had stayed in her memory. 'Oh my Mark Antony, waiting to smite his enemies and looking like a god in the process.'

It was an amalgamation of different stories, different books. But all the sentiments of good women waiting for brave men were wrapped up in it.

Elliot Beaven was standing with his shirtsleeves rolled up and brandishing a boat hook like a pikestaff. He was like all the other men there, looking to Anthony Wesley for the command to go into battle.

She hid her feelings with a loud peal of laughter and outright sarcasm. 'Anthony is such a sham. Look how he struts around. Like a cock fowl in a farmyard.' She bent nearer Beth's ear. 'Always on the lookout for a silly little hen.'

'I don't believe you mean that.' Beth's eyes stayed fixed on Abigail's face as if daring her to say it again.

Abigail folded her arms across her chest, her attention supposedly riveted on what was happening to those in the gulley below. Inside, she was crying with disappointment, screaming with frustration. What could she offer Anthony that Beth couldn't?

Things were beginning to happen. Anthony was barking orders, waving his arms around, directing men here and there. The air was filled with the noise of boots clattering on cobbles, men shouting, the whinnying of police horses and the popping and banging of motorised police vehicles, a novelty that the boatmen enjoyed watching almost as much as the policemen enjoyed riding in them.

Against the weed-grown copings of the basin wall, the men were being directed into defensive lines, a raggle-taggle phalanx between the multicoloured boats and the dour line of navy serge. Under Anthony's direction, others were gathering at either end of the pound where an attack might be expected to force its way through.

The crowd split apart then closed up again. A figure of odd proportion with long arms and spindly legs pushed his way through and made his way towards them.

Beth recognised Goblin Coombes. Puffing and snorting like a pot-bellied boiler, he came scrabbling up the slope towards them, his under-developed, twiggy legs struggling to cope with the steep incline. 'A message!' he gasped between deeply inhaled breath.

Abigail got to him first and grabbed his arm. 'Spit it out, man!'

'Take your time,' said Beth as the small man fought to catch his breath.

Chest pumping like a pair of torn bellows, the little man nodded. One more intake of breath and he found his voice. 'Mr Wesley said to pile crates at both ends of the two bridges. They mustn't take the island. If they does, they'll be in among us during the night and free to bash our 'eads in whenever the mood takes 'em.'

Abigail sprang into action. 'The crates,' she shouted. 'Get the crates!'

Her movement away from Goblin's side was obviously unexpected. He tottered and tilted forward. Luckily, Beth caught him by the collar and jerked him upright again. The air of excitement was breathtaking. Making a quick decision, Beth raced back to the boat. She laid Pamela in an open crate just behind the one provided as a desk.

'Things are happening,' she said quietly to her mother. 'I'll pull down the flap. Keep the children here.'

Stunned to silence, her mother merely nodded and although Beth wanted to hug her because she looked so small and so frail, her heart and spirit were outside with all the others doing their bit to fight for their rights.

Pulling and lifting the crates wasn't easy. Two women moved one, three women another. The access to the bridges was blocked. The island was cut off. Abigail hedged her bets and placed a very large woman with a pickaxe at the entrance of one. 'Keep to the high ground,' she shouted.

The women quickly did as ordered, knowing that to stand at the highest point would give them the best view.

'Is anything happening?' said Beth as she came to her side. Abigail shook her head.

Silence fell as they all waited and watched.

'What will you do when all this is over?' Beth suddenly asked.

'What?'

'I know you're not married. But is there anyone at all?' asked Beth.

'No one,' said Abigail, her mouth snapping like a trap in the hope that Beth would not ask her any more questions of that nature.

Beth knew she was lying.

Abigail's eyes rarely strayed from the tall figure with black hair and deep blue eyes. Anthony was still barking out orders and directing men where he wanted them to be. She knew without looking at her that Beth's gaze was fixed on him too.

'No one,' she repeated under her breath and sighed. 'Right!' she shouted before Beth could ask her anything else. 'Those women who are armed, stand directly behind the barricades. The rest of you, move back. They won't care if you are women, so be prepared. I'll stand up here and shout when I see them coming.'

The cry was stark and sudden. 'At 'em, lads!'

A dark-blue wave of uniforms surged forwards, some parts of it marked by crests of enthusiasm, but tempered by those of a more reluctant disposition who seemed to be holding back. Not all the police were in favour of getting involved in conflicts with working men. All the same, they knew who paid their wages.

Those at the front broke before the rest and were beaten back. Fists hard and callused from pulling on rough hemp mooring ropes and loading coal, corn, wood and iron by hand connected with the stiff chins of the comparatively soft-living policemen.

Helmets flew into the air and landed in the buttercups. Some landed in the canal and others, even more unfortunate, landed in horse manure because not all the barges were yet powered by engines.

As the fighting began to dissipate and the boatmen hooted for victory, the reluctant policemen collected those compatriots who had been enthused and were now soundly beaten. Again and again they charged, each time repulsed. Those at the front who had taken the full force of the boatmen's defence were gathered up and taken into honourable retreat by those behind. Frustration erupted into anger as men with bloodied noses and cut cheeks flung their helmets and truncheons to one side and buried their heads in their hands. Finally, a loud cheer went up from the motley collection of men in dusty clothes with worn faces and bleeding knuckles.

'We've won!' Abigail shouted flinging her arms around Beth's neck. 'We've won, Beth. We've won!'

'Is Anthony all right?' Beth stretched her neck, her eyes darting over the multitude of men.

Being taller, Abigail could see Anthony and her heart pounded with obsessive pride. Beth had no right. 'No,' she said abruptly. 'I can't see him anywhere. But I can see your husband.'

The men around Anthony ebbed and flowed, finally falling away.

Beth knew immediately that Abigail had been able to see him. She didn't blame her for lying. What right did she have to make claim on him? She looked for Elliot with less interest than she had for Anthony. He was there at the front, a thick stave lying over his shoulder and triumph on his face.

Flying something white tied to a truncheon, the leader of the police stepped forward. Anthony stepped forward too. There was silence as everyone strained to pick up what was being said. Then the two men parted and the white flag retreated among the sea of dark blue.

'Where are they going?' asked Beth.

Abigail's jealousy was still upon her. 'I can only see what's going on, I can't hear what they're bloody well saying!' she snapped. 'I'd better go and see.'

'Abbie?'

Abigail paused and looked round.

It was difficult to meet Beth's knowing gaze, but she held it. Inside, she locked away her secret thoughts.

Beth was not fooled. 'Don't think I don't know how close you two are. You're so alike. You have so much in common. Whatever we achieve in this place is all down to you and him.'

Confused by her own feelings, Abigail eyed the dark-haired Beth. Deep down, she liked her and knew she was intelligent. She *had* to understand.

'You could spoil it for him, you know. He could be a Member of Parliament if he set his mind to it. You won't hold him back, will you?'

Beth shrugged. 'Why should I?'

'He could do so much good in London. He's obsessed with you. I think you know that.'

Beth folded her arms across her milk-laden breasts and looked at the ground. 'I'm not stopping him from being anything.'

Abigail pursed her lips. 'I'm not blind.'

Beth looked up at her as though she'd just been woken from a dream. The attraction between her and Anthony was out in the open. She should be covering her tracks and retreating back into the matrimonial mould, but somehow she couldn't do that. Anthony had opened her mind and her eyes to everything she could be in her life – given half the chance. But for everyone's sake, she had to make the effort. She had to deny it.

'I don't know what you mean.'

'Oh yes you do!' Abigail turned her back. Beth was beginning to irritate her. She was too wonderfully female; too obsessed with a man who didn't belong to her and never would. And it hurt.

'Anthony's opened my eyes,' said Beth suddenly. 'He gave me books...'

Abigail spun round on her. 'Books! They're just books! I gave you books too. Lots of them.'

'I'm grateful.'

Abigail's eyes blazed with passion. 'Are you, Beth? Are you? What is it you really want from him?'

Beth said the first thing that came to mind. 'He's going to help me set up a school so I can teach the women and children to read and write.'

'Hogwash!'

Beth was struck speechless. Her cheeks burned she acknowledged the truth as deep inside. As much as Anthony was obsessed with her, she was obsessed with him. But she couldn't put it into words, especially not to Abigail. 'It's wrong for people to grow up in ignorance.'

She winced beneath Abigail's accusing glare. She was not believed.

Someone interrupted saying there was a message needed sending and could Miss Gatehouse deal with a telegram. Abigail snatched the message and marched stridently towards her car.

Beth simmered and called out after her. 'What will you do when the strike's over, Miss Gatehouse? Go back to your rich family and marry someone with just as much money so you never have to do without, so your children will always be well fed, well educated and have everything they could ever want?'

Seething with feelings she did not want to admit to, Abigail stopped in her stride. Being tongue-tied had never been a problem. Now she found herself unable to speak because she really did not know the answer. What would she do and, more to the point, what could she do?

23

That night it certainly appeared as if the strike was over.

Voices of jubilation echoed around the sheds, repair yards and company offices, hands clapped and whatever metal objects came to hand were knocked together like pairs of clashing cymbals. The noise was deafening and at the same time irresistible.

Beth wanted to be down there with them, celebrating, not stuck up on a hill with the women. Leaving Pamela with her mother, she began to run. Other women joined her, all eager to get to their men and share their elation – and their beer.

A bonfire lit up the night, its sparks soaring skywards. Potatoes stolen from wayside fields were cooking in the ashes and all manner of bread, stews, hot tea and warm beer was brought out in large buckets into which tin cups were dipped and dipped again.

Turning into the compound, Abigail pulled her car to a halt. Igor, the Russian observer who she'd brought with her, immediately joined in the celebrations. 'A party,' he shouted, dancing his way from the car to the bonfire like a demented Cossack.

Abigail followed, but too slowly for his liking. He spun round; his strong arms encircled her and he whirled her round on the spot, his rough chin grazing hers as he kissed her. 'For now,' he said, 'it is over.'

'For now?' she echoed, unsure of what he meant.

'It is not over, I don't think,' he said shaking his head, his strong hands still holding her waist.

'Of course it is,' she exclaimed. 'Ask Anthony. He'll tell you.'

She turned round meaning to point at Anthony and call out for him to explain things. But only the sparks from the bonfire moved through the darkness. Anthony was nowhere to be seen. She saw Elliot Beaven, drunk as a lord and singing rude songs with other boatmen. She looked for Beth but couldn't see her either and although she told herself she was probably with the other women, some instinct told her otherwise. Inside, she cried.

* * *

Long shadows fell from the buildings that bordered the basin, and further out, battalions of poplars lined a lane leading to a churchyard and some small fields beyond.

Anthony had come to tell Beth that Elliot was all right but had volunteered to do guard duty during the night. He didn't tell her that he was already drunk, but then she probably knew that. Then, with a sombre, serious look on his face, he had asked to talk to her in private.

Weeds and tall grass snatched at Beth's skirt as she walked close to him, her thigh brushing against his and his arm around her waist. This was always what she had hoped for: to be close to him, to smell his masculinity on the night air and to have the hardness of his muscles brushing against her own.

He knew he should feel a cad. Beth was married and had a child. But he was an ordinary man with ordinary needs and his need, above all else, was for her. Why didn't he feel guilty about being alone here with her? Why didn't he feel any sympathy for Elliot Beaven, the man she had married? Elliot was no different from a lot of working men. Long hours and hard work brutalised men and they in turn became brutes to their womenfolk. All the same, it shouldn't really cloud his judgement.

He'd gone over the same arguments, purged himself time and time again of feeling that way, but his purity of thought was short-lived. If he could lie with her just once in his life, it was a memory he would take with him to his grave.

For her part, Beth's heart was beating so hard she was sure he could hear it. She knew she should be telling him they shouldn't be alone together. Married women were meant to stay faithful whether their husbands deserved such loyalty or not.

But she had been an innocent when she'd married Elliot Beaven. Physically, she had proved not to be, but mentally, she had gone to that altar without a clue of what was expected of her. All she had known was that women were loyal to their husbands no matter what, just like her mother was – just like a lot of other women.

But Anthony Wesley had changed all that. It was dangerous being here with him; she should be back in her boat with her child. But no matter how much she thought about turning and leaving him, her legs did not obey her.

'Just look at those stars,' he said, and she looked. 'Not even Solomon in all his glory...' His voice trailed into nothing as he stopped by a dry-stone wall. 'You know you shouldn't be here,' he said to her. His voice was hushed and his breath was sweet on her face.

Beth had done battle with her own guilt and won. 'It must be right because if it wasn't, you wouldn't let me be here.'

'You must let yourself do what you want, Beth.'

'Like Abigail?'

Anthony laughed strangely. 'I don't think she really does let herself do what she really wants to do. She thinks she does by dressing outrageously and doing things most women don't do, but I'm not sure she's really following her heart. That's what you have to do at the end of the day, Beth. You have to follow your heart. You have to believe in whatever you set out to do.'

'Doesn't Abigail believe in what she's doing?'

He smiled at her through the darkness. 'Abigail is trying to prove something and she's also trying to punish her father for what he is and what he does. The trouble is that by punishing him, she's also punishing herself. And that, my dear Beth, is a very sad thing.'

His hands were warm on her shoulders as he turned her to face him.

He shook his head slowly, the calm gleam of his eyes looking into hers and mirroring the guilt she herself was feeling. Yet he couldn't resist.

There was silence except for the first chirping of the nightjars and the song of the nightingale. Beth shivered. 'It's chilly up here.'

Anthony raised her chin with one finger. 'Through the forest have I gone, but Athenian found I none on whose eyes I might approve, this flower's force in stirring love... The forest is life. The flower I have found is unique and I can't stop...'

His lips moved closer to hers.

'Stop it!' She turned away. It was all too difficult. How could she deal with the feel of him, the look in his eyes and the thundering of her own heart?

For a brief moment, his fingers caressed her neck. She shivered. The effect was as if he had stripped her bare and ran his fingers down her spine.

There was no more resistance, no more denying how she was feeling, how he was feeling. Urges they could not control swept over them. His lips kissed hers gently then intensified as his passion increased. She didn't flinch. She was lost because he was with her. And nothing and no one else mattered.

They lay in the long grass, covered in nothing but the darkness of the night and the splendour of their love, limbs entwined, flesh against flesh. Male and female passions knotted and knitted together in some graceful helix whose template was laid down at the dawn of creation. And she was Eve and he was Adam, yet there was no real temptation of one of the other. It was a mutual need, just as it always had been and always would be.

* * *

From the darkness, Abigail watched them, her body rigid, silent tears running down her face. This wasn't right. This just wasn't right. Her jealousy burned more brightly than the bonfire that popped and crackled in the clearing below.

* * *

'Once more,' he said, kissing her before they returned to the gathering by the side of the canal.

'You go first,' she said to him. 'We shouldn't be seen together.'

He brushed her cheek with his fingertips, smiled thoughtfully, and left her there.

She counted to ten, watching with joy in her heart until he was no more than a shadow amongst the trees.

She looked up at the stars for one last time, wanting to remember them as they were on this night. Finally, she too headed for the narrow path back through the churchyard, the fields and the wood.

She went straight to the bonfire, confident that her mother was looking after Pamela. She found herself on the opposite side to Anthony, who was with Igor. The Russian was jigging up and down in an impromptu dance. Like the others round about, Anthony was laughing at his antics, but his eyes met hers across the dancing flames.

'A vigorous and virile man, don't you think?'

She blushed. Startled from her thoughts, she turned to the speaker.

Abigail still wore the heavy boots and clothes of a boatman, the black corduroy jacket buttoned tightly around her breasts. Outside, she was still the woman desperate to make her way in a man's world. But inside, her heart was aching, longing for the one thing she couldn't seem to get. Her face was flushed with anger.

Beth glanced at Anthony then back at Abigail. Her cheeks reddened further.

Abigail saw this. Oh, how her heart ached to tell the truth. But she wouldn't. 'I mean Igor, of course. Our enigmatic Russian preaches too much politics, drinks too much alcohol and dances like a gypsy.'

'I don't know,' Beth replied. 'I don't know him.'

'Come,' Abigail said brightly, grabbing Beth's arm. 'I'll introduce you.'

Though she didn't want to go, Beth felt compelled. There'd been a certain look in Abigail's eyes. Without her saying anything, Beth knew that she'd seen her and Anthony together. Her heartbeat thudded anew.

The Russian was red in the face and swigging a clear liquid direct from a bottle. She guessed it wasn't water.

Abigail laughed up into his face. 'Have you enough drink and food, Igor?' she asked him.

Thick, pink lips broke into a smile seeming to crack open the thick black hair of his face. 'I have good foods. Good vodka. Now all I need is bad woman! Very bad woman!'

He laughed loudly at his own joke. The men who'd heard did the same, including Elliot.

Mesmerised by the huge Russian, Beth held back. Abigail took advantage, flinging her forward to slam against Igor's chest. 'Here's one. She's all yours.'

Beth was taken totally by surprise. It was like colliding with a brick wall and the breath was knocked out of her.

'Good,' laughed Igor, his mighty arms holding her tight against him.

Beth struggled. 'Let me go.'

She could see Elliot's dark frown just a short distance away.

She heard Anthony. 'Let her go, Igor.'

'But she mine,' he protested, holding her even tighter.

'Igor. Let her go.'

Anthony gripped the big man's shoulder. 'Her husband is watching, Igor. Please let her go.'

'I fight him for her.'

'You'll do no such thing.'

Aware that his voice was betraying too much emotion, Anthony tried a different tack. He slapped the big man on the shoulder.

'Come on, Igor. We've got a lot more fighting to do yet, and not among ourselves. We've won a battle, but not the war. Isn't that what you said to me the other day? Just like the battles you fought in Russia?'

The big man's arms loosened. Beth took the opportunity to make good her escape. Elliot came and stood next to her. 'Who does he think he bloody is,' he muttered. 'As for her, that bloody woman in bloke's clothes.'

She didn't meet her husband's eyes, but even though their bodies were not touching, she could feel his anger.

Anthony looked for Abigail. He was seething inside. Elliot Beaven had a quick temper and although the drink might have slowed him down, the Russian wasn't much better.

He found her nibbling at a baked potato, its black skin shedding soot over her yellow kid gloves.

'There was no call for what you did,' he seethed, barely able to keep his voice down.

'Oh,' she said pertly, her teeth nibbling and her gaze fixed on the potato's fluffy interior. 'What did I do that was so wrong?'

People eating, drinking, laughing and talking loudly surrounded them: he kept his voice low. 'You know damn well what you did. You could have started a fight. You know what Igor's like when he's been drinking. And you've got some idea of what Beaven's like too.'

After throwing the potato skin into the fire, she wiped her gloves and glared at him. 'So do you, Anthony.'

He frowned.

'He's a jealous man, a violent man. And before you try and deny anything, just remember that he's as likely to take his jealousy out on his wife as on you.' She stared directly into his eyes. 'I think you should avoid walks in the dark from now on. Don't you?'

She quivered with anger as she stalked off. By holding her breath, she kept most of it inside her, but hot tears threatened behind her aching eyes.

She knew he wouldn't follow her. Hopefully her outburst might make him see the error of his ways. It could not – it must not – happen again.

'The fire. It's so hot,' she said to Beth's husband, patting at her red cheeks and trusting it was an acceptable excuse.

'Shouldn't be here then, should you.' He too was munching at a baked potato, his teeth skimming the skin to get the last bit of whiteness.

'Why not?'

'Well, it's not your battle. Won't change anything for you, will it.'

Elliot shoved the skin into his mouth and swallowed.

Abigail raised her plucked eyebrows. 'On the contrary, I will have the satisfaction of knowing I have done some good.'

He shook his head and laughed. 'You can't live on satisfaction.'

'I don't need to.'

She eyed the way his eyebrows met above his nose. His hair looked black in the firelight, though she knew it was reddish. It draped against the collar of his jacket. In the glow of the fire, he looked demonic.

He eyed her sidelong. 'No. That's for sure.' He wiped his hands on his hips.

'Someone has to organise things.'

'I dare say, but we've got Anthony. We don't need you.'

'I've got a car.'

It sounded trite to her ears, to Elliot's too, it seemed. Puffing out his cheeks, he spat the words out. 'You've got a car! What the bloody hell has that got to do with anything?'

His mockery made her see red, but her retort was sharp and self-assured. 'I run messages. I take people to places they're needed.'

'You've got a car,' he sneered. 'You've got a lot of things, and that's the bloody trouble. Some people's got lots, and some people's got naught.'

'But some of us care. We'll fight for the rights of man, just like they did in Russia, and it cannot be—'

The man's glower stopped her.

'What would you know, with your smart car and big house?

Just because you saunter around like a man, do you really think you're achieving anything?'

In response to the disturbance, Igor walked in between them. His eyes were red but he seemed to have sobered up enough to voice his opinion.

'I heard you,' he slurred, his thick arms lying heavily on their shoulders. 'And I tell you this, we did not fight just for ideas. We fought so children could have bread in their bellies. We fought to rid the country of a man who had absolute power over us. Little Father, we called him, and while he lived in grand palaces and collected great art works and dressed in fine clothes, we dressed in rags and collected dandelion roots to eat, perhaps flavoured with a little pigeon meat if we could get away with snaring one. Peasant farmers like my father were the lucky ones. They had some sort of security. But there were others who could be bought and sold like cattle dependent on their skills. They were serfs, a breed that this country of yours has not seen for five hundred years! And it doesn't matter whether you are a man or a woman. Starvation makes everyone equal!'

He bent his head so that his eyes were level with hers. 'Go home and get yourself a husband. There must be a man that'll have you.'

Her face reddened. 'Of course there is!'

Elliot smirked. 'Blimey. He must want something.'

Abigail turned on him. 'He does! He wants someone else's wife.'

She glared tellingly to where Anthony was handing Beth another hot potato wrapped in one of his gloves.

She saw understanding register in Elliot's eyes, saw them flicker and stare.

She turned away.

'Won't you keep me company?' Igor shouted after her.

No. No, she could not. She had sowed a terrible seed in Elliot's mind and it was Beth who would reap the results, perhaps even Anthony.

She had to warn them, do something to make amends. But what?

Just like on the night she'd got scared and left Anthony to the thugs employed by the carrying company, she couldn't stop her legs from running. She ran past them and didn't stop until she'd got to her car.

Leaning her head against the steering wheel, she burst into tears.

* * *

Without saying a word, Elliot knocked the potato out of Beth's hand and dragged her away.

Anthony was taken by surprise. 'Elliot! What are you doing, man?'

Beth tried to prise his fingers from around her wrist. 'Elliot!'

He paid neither of them any heed. His jaw was set in a firm line. His eyes were as steely as the toecaps on his best boots.

Anthony was left speechless staring after them. *What's happened?* he asked himself. He looked around him for an answer, his gaze automatically searching for Abigail. She was not near the fire and beyond the firelight there was only darkness and few places to be comfortable – except for her car. He walked quickly in that direction.

She was dabbing at her eyes when she got there. Resting his arms on the roof, he peered in at her. 'You've been crying.'

She jumped at first, then sniffed and attempted an excuse. 'I just got something in my eye.'

He could see she was shaking. His expression darkened. He

knew that look very well. Abigail always looked like that when she'd done something wrong and didn't want to own up to it.

'What have you done, you stupid bitch!'

'Anthony!'

But he was already striding back to the fire, the quay and the narrowboats moored there.

Frightened and feeling guilty for what she'd done, Abigail ran after him.

'I didn't mean to say it. I was jealous. I saw you with her earlier...'

She didn't need to go on. Anthony clenched his fists. Even though she pawed at his arms, he remained stiff with apprehension.

What would Elliot do? He could only guess. All he could hope for was that he could get there in time and stop things getting too bad. He would have to deny that anything happened. He would have to lie. He would also have to ensure that the two of them were never alone again.

* * *

Elliot flung her down into the cabin. Her hip hit the side rail. She fell flat on the cabin floor, hitting her head against the range.

Her mother was sitting there, Pamela sleeping in her lap. 'No, Elliot. Please,' her mother said, as Beth fingered the bruise rising on her forehead and smelled singed hair.

'Take the baby with you tonight,' Elliot murmured, his eyes hard with vengeance and not leaving Beth's face.

Her mother shook her head. 'No. No, I'll not do that, Elliot Beaven. I will most certainly not!'

Never in her life had Beth seen her mother rear up as she did. In her stout shoes, she was still not much above five feet two inches. She stood defiantly, daring Elliot to force her to leave.

Elliot's stance remained the same. 'This is nothing to do with you, Ma. 'Tis between me and me wife.'

''Tis everything to do with me and every other wife who's borne a life of misery. You'll not touch my girl, Elliot Beaven. I swear I'll swing for you if you do!'

Beth remained on the floor. She looked at her mother, then at Elliot. She didn't ask what she was supposed to have done. She knew the answer. Someone had seen her alone with Anthony. That same someone had told Elliot.

Someone called his name.

Beth recognised Anthony's voice. She tried not to look relieved. To do so might provoke him further.

The clumping of heavy boots heralded Anthony's arrival. Elliot glared at him. 'Get off my boat!'

Anthony's eyes swept over all of them before going back to Beth's husband.

'Not until I'm sure that everyone isn't likely to get hurt – any more than they already are,' he added after he'd noticed the bruise rising on Beth's forehead.

Before, there had been camaraderie between him and Elliot. He realised from the look in the man's face that their friendship, which had been based on working together, had slammed against the buffers.

'You'll stay away from my wife,' Elliot growled.

Anthony began his lie. 'Your wife soothed my wounds a while back. I cannot help but feel a respectful admiration for her.'

Elliot was unmoved. 'Oh! Is that all it is? Do you expect me to believe that?'

Anthony shook his head and lowered his eyes. 'I don't know

what you've been told and who's been telling it, but it's all lies. Can't you see that, Beaven? Can't you see that now?'

Abigail shouted from the quay, 'I didn't mean it, Mr Beaven. Honestly I didn't.'

'Then why did you say it?' Elliot shouted back.

A pause followed, a sniffle, then Abigail, more strident this time as though she'd regained her self-control. 'I wanted Anthony to take more notice of me – as a woman. So I pretended... I want to go with him to London, you see – as his wife... and be like you and Beth...'

Anthony could hardly believe his ears. Even Elliot's angry jaw slackened in surprise.

Beth hid her eyes behind her hand, wincing when her fingers touched the sore spot.

Abigail was showing her true colours. She felt sad for her, but also a little envious. Without appearing to, she eyed Anthony from between her fingers. He looked as though Abigail's confession had taken him completely by surprise. She felt compelled to say something. 'Didn't you know?'

He met her look only fleetingly and shook his head. 'No. I thought she was just a—'

'I know,' Abigail interjected. 'You thought I was just a bloody good help... like a bloody good bloke but smelling of perfume.'

The atmosphere in the tiny cabin had grown perceptively less explosive. Both men looked awkward and unsure of what to do or say next. Pamela chose that moment to wake and cry for her food. Beth got to her feet.

'Well, I don't know about the rest of you, but I'm off to my bed,' said Elizabeth Dawson after she'd handed Pamela to her mother. Anthony tipped his hat as he stood aside to let her past. She paused in the narrow opening and addressed him. 'I suggest you do the same and take your woman with you whilst the going's good.'

He looked surprised but nodded. 'No hard feelings,' he said to Elliot, reaching down to shake his hand.

Elliot was subdued, a world away from the man who had been stewing with anger a moment earlier. He shook the offered hand and even managed a brief grin. 'Better get and sort her out,' he said.

Anthony caught his meaning. 'I'd better. Who'd have thought it?' He shrugged and then his expression turned serious. 'See you in the morning, Beaven. We've still a battle to fight.'

'And a war to win,' said Elliot, echoing Anthony's favourite saying.

The air between Beth and her husband stayed electric a few moments after everyone had left. Beth rocked the baby; Elliot stood very still as though he was thinking things through.

'Put the baby down,' he said suddenly.

Beth didn't dare disobey. She did as ordered.

He hit out and caught her cheek. This time, she slammed back against the framework of their cubby-hole bed.

He began taking off his belt. 'Time you were in the family way again. That should keep other blokes away from you.'

Whilst Pamela gurgled in the wooden drawer that was her bed, her mother stifled her sobs. If only I were free, she thought, and wished she was. But unless something drastic happened, she'd be an unhappy wife for the rest of her life.

24

The days dragged on. September was coming. A kind of truce had been reached and some boatmen were thinking about leaving. Anthony fought to dissuade them.

Most of them took the same view: 'They've promised to look at our wages and conditions.'

Anthony was adamant. 'We haven't got an agreement in writing. Not yet. Once I'm waving that bit of paper over your head, you can call it a day. But not until then.'

Abigail was proud to stand at his side. He'd treated her differently since her outburst over Beth Beaven. She caught him looking at her with a puzzled expression in his eyes. She asked him what the matter was.

'Nothing. I was just thinking about how helpful you are.'

'Are you going to say that I'm your right arm?'

He grinned. 'You mean like a wife.'

She found herself blushing. Inside her heart was dancing. 'I am available.'

She realised that it was not quite the right thing to say. Oh yes, she was available, as opposed to someone who was not, someone he still glanced at longingly. She wondered if he dreamed of her.

He was furtive, but sometimes she saw his eyes straying to the boat on which Beth was teaching the children to write their name. Her own eyes wandered there for a different reason. Beth was suckling her child at the same time as instructing her pupils. All the sweetness of their earlier friendship was souring – at least as far as she was concerned.

'We need to keep watch,' Anthony said to her and Igor. 'Spooner, the company representative, told me he'd be back tomorrow morning, but I wouldn't bank on it.'

The earlier elation of having reached an oral agreement had melted away. No signed agreement was drawn up. The delay went on and the men were beginning to grumble.

Abigail watched Beth with the children, the former glancing uncertainly in her direction then immediately switching to Anthony the moment he appeared. It hurt like mad. Oh why did they have to carry on like this?

Elliot was sleeping off the beer he'd consumed the night before. The local pub landlords donated it, their contribution to the fighting fund.

'Keep watch on the gate,' Anthony said to her. 'I don't trust any of them. Mark my words, they'll try something. Watch for coppers. Watch for any gang of blokes that look as though they mean business.'

She did as ordered. The gate he referred to was sandwiched between two warehouses. Most of the canal trade came and went through it. At present, only lorries were coming in, driven straight into the sheds for unloading. Then they were away again, the warehouse doors shut firmly behind them. The yard was left silent in between the opening and shutting of the rattling doors and there was hardly a soul in sight. Even the policemen who had been manning the gates seemed to have disappeared.

The day wore on, hot and humid, the sort of weather when no one wanted to move too much because the slightest effort resulted in floods of sweat.

Leaving her vigil by the gate, Abigail stiffened her shoulders then marched into the shade of the warehouses where sprawling bodies smelling of dirt and stale beer were taking advantage of the coolness. Like rows of floundering fish, their mouths were open but, unlike fish, they snored loudly. She wrinkled her nose. They looked disgusting. Bristles grew profusely on their unshaved chins. Pigs in clothes, she thought.

'Isn't it time you men had something to eat?' Her voice echoed against the red-brick warehouses, the high walls and narrow gullies amplifying the sounds.

Some shifted. Some continued to snore.

'Come on. Grub's ready.'

She began kicking the soles of their boots. Snorting like real pigs, they shook themselves into some sort of wakefulness.

She gave an extra kick to a man who had broader shoulders than anyone else. Bull-necked, reddish-brown hair and hands that seemed always to be clenched into fists. Elliot Beaven was hardly a handsome man.

He grumbled and mumbled expletives as he roused himself. 'Mr Beaven. You're alive.'

He got to his feet then stretched to his full height. The smell of him and the solidity of his body almost made her shiver.

'I thought you might be hungry,' she said. 'They're doing a fry-up over there.' She pointed to where a group of uniformed Salvation Army was dishing out thick rashers of fatty bacon that dripped and sizzled as they were passed from pan to plate.

She managed to attach a bright smile to resistant lips. 'You've got to keep your strength up.'

Later that day, she shared out clothes she had brought with her in the boot of her car. She told herself it wasn't guilt that made her give Beth the best of what she had brought. 'This will suit you,' she said, holding a skirt and a neatly fitting jacket against Beth's slim frame.

Beth had barely looked at Abigail since the eventful night.

The suit thrilled her and reminded her of her favourite green skirt. It was patched and darned, but still she wore it. She was wearing it now. *Abigail is not your friend*, said a small voice in her head. 'You can't get round me with a second-hand costume,' Beth said grimly.

'I'm not trying to,' Abigail lied.

Beth's look was steady and her voice was stiff with accusation. 'Oh yes you are. You saw me with Anthony. You mentioned something about it to my husband.' She raised her hand palm outwards as Abigail started to protest. 'Don't lie. I know how you think, Abigail. Keep all you want to yourself; only give away the stuff that you're finished with.'

'Please,' Abigail said plaintively. 'I'm sorry. Really, I am.' Beth found that being stubborn was difficult to maintain when faced with such a beautiful shade of green. She snatched it, rolled it up and tucked it under her arm. 'It'll do as dusters!'

Abigail had so wanted to make amends. She'd hoped Beth would be more amiable, but tried not to show her hurt. 'Do as you wish.'

* * *

Anthony Wesley looked towards the ugly oblongs of warehouses and the main gate and frowned. The number of vehicles, horse-drawn and otherwise, entering the yard had increased and filled him with a sense of foreboding. The horse-drawn vehicles went in and out, but the lorries disappeared into the cavernous doorways and didn't come out again. Yet if goods, crates, sacks or raw stock was being unloaded, how could they have room for lorries as well?

'No lorries have come back out,' he said.

'Perhaps they still will.'

He shook his head. 'It's too late in the day.'

Abigail gave a quick nod of understanding. It was evening. None were likely to come out now. Most had been of the high-backed sort covered in a long oblong of tarpaulin.

Goblin Coombes came rushing along to say that a man named Len Green, who worked in the warehouses and was sympathetic to their cause, wanted to speak to him.

Anthony nodded a quick greeting and shook the man's hand. 'You have something to tell me?'

'I don't know but I ain't been allowed near the place all day. They told me to go home early which is strange enough, but they also said I'd still get paid. Now that's a turn-up in itself! But I don't know why they're only unloading in the sheds. They normally only do that when it's perishables and it's raining.'

'Only when it's raining?'

Beth was standing nearby and overheard.

'How many of the lorries that arrived went into the sheds today?' asked Anthony.

'All of them,' said Abbie. 'Did they reload?'

'They went, then they were back again. The same lorries!' Len Green's rock of a nose wrinkled as he sniffed the night air. 'I can smell stew cooking,' he said. 'Irish stew like the sort my old woman makes with lamb and carrots and big, juicy dumplings. Where's that coming from, then?'

Beth heard him. Although Elliot had ordered her to keep away from men's business, nothing would stop her from getting involved and she'd told him so.

'We've little left for stew ourselves. The cooking must be coming from down in the warehouse there.'

With a half-baked laugh, she said, 'P'raps they're setting up a soup kitchen for us folk.'

Anthony's arms dropped to his sides as a terrible realisation fell upon him. 'They're feeding someone, all right. Come on!'

Anthony was running, Abigail right behind him and more gathered behind as they sensed that something momentous was happening.

'Gather round!' Anthony shouted.

Those merely talking in groups obeyed instantly. Others, asleep on the grass, raised tired heads on cupped hands. Still others grunted as their compatriots shook them or thrust a steel-toed boot into their ribs.

Anthony stepped up on to a convenient crate and a crowd of expectant faces turned towards him. 'It looks as though our demands are about to be met with force,' he said and nodded pointedly towards the sheds. 'There's food cooking down there and they're certainly not laying on a feast to celebrate our victory. I believe those sheds are now full of men paid by the company to break this strike. Whether they're police or not is of no importance. They're here to try our mettle and we have to be ready to take them on.'

The hush that descended took him by surprise. He had expected them to shout, raise their fists and promise defiance or at least ask each other's opinion as to whether to give in or go on. As it was the silence was so suffocating, he almost prayed for noise.

In other circumstances, Beth would have been proud when her husband stepped forward and spoke his mind. But she was no longer the innocent girl she had been. She knew Elliot Beaven too well. His words were bravado, and his politics were a belief in his fists. She watched as he shouldered his way through the men who parted without comment until he stood at the front of them.

'I've come this far and I'm willing to go further.' He turned round to the grim-faced men behind him whose eyes were glassy and whose stomachs rumbled with the promise of more and better food but not yet, not until this thing was over. At least the fields in the quiet places held rabbits, pheasant and pigeon. Moorhens scuttled amongst the reeds and the odd vegetable could always be lifted without it being noticed. He read their minds. 'We've all survived this far. If we give up now we're beaten for good. If we're left with nothing else at the end of this, at least we'll have our pride.'

Anthony was grateful to Elliot for his plain language. 'Small gains can grow into big ones,' he said. 'But I'll not stop anyone from leaving who's got no guts left to fight. Leave now. No one here will hold it against you.'

A middle-aged man with a dark moustache and smoking a pipe stepped forward. 'If it's all the same to you all, I'm pulling out. My wife's expecting, you see, and it hasn't been easy, her being of a refined—'

Elliot rounded on him. 'Come on, George! We've all got wives and although yours might be a bit more la-di-dah than ours, that ain't no reason to turn tail, is it now!'

Out came the pipe from George Melcroft's mouth and at the same time he jutted his chin towards Elliot so that they were almost nose to nose. 'Are you calling me a coward? Go on! Say it, Beaven! Say it and I'll knock you to the ground, you bloody swine!'

'Hold on there!' Anthony jumped down from his crate and shoved himself between the two, his greater height and his broad, sea-going shoulders easily separating the two faces that glared so fiercely at each other.

'We're all in this together,' shouted Elliot. 'No one should leave.'

Rumblings of approval from the gathered men echoed his statement.

'Wesley said we all had a choice and I'm making mine,' said George. 'Is that not right, Mr Wesley?'

Disappointed but not a man to break his word, Anthony nodded. 'It's your choice. George Melcroft, isn't it?'

'Yes,' said George.

'Then do what you must do, George, and thank you for all you've done.'

It was bedlam from then on. Everyone busied themselves or merely panicked. Abigail, who had admiringly watched Anthony's handling of the situation, was now as animated as everyone else. 'Women and children to the school boat,' she shouted, Pamela bouncing in her arms.

Someone asked what was happening. It was George Melcroft looking too embarrassed to go, too nervous to stay.

'There's men in the sheds. Another battle's brewing,' Beth explained.

George puffed thoughtfully on his pipe. His pale eyes were almost hidden by the deepness of his frown. 'Well, we won't be staying around to see it. We're going.' Clenching his pipe at the corner of his mouth, he began to tinker with the engine, greasing the input before firing her up.

Abigail heard. Her fingers folded over the boat's side rail.

Her jaw was firm and her eyes were angry.

'You can't give up! Not after all we've done for you!'

'I didn't ask you to do anything for me. I can do what I want for myself,' said George, head bent over the engine, fingertips smeared with oil.

George looked too tired to have either a young wife or a baby on the way. 'She wants to go,' he said wearily. 'She just wants to go. Don't ask me why. She's hardly come out of that blasted cabin since we got here and she sulked all the way on the journey.' He looked round pleadingly at Beth. 'But I felt that I had to come. I really do believe in what we're doing. We all have to stick together in this, don't we?'

Beth tossed her head as though she was totally indifferent to it all. 'If she doesn't want to see me, she doesn't want to see me and that's it.'

George shrugged again.

Something inside Beth snapped. 'Let me have a word with her!' Before George could stop her, she swung her legs over the side and rapped repeatedly at the cabin door. 'Carrie! It's me, Beth. You can't leave, Carrie. Everyone will think that your husband is a coward. How will he ever hold his head up again? Have you thought about that!'

There was no reply.

'Let her be,' said George.

Abigail leaned against the side of the boat, arms folded. 'I can't believe it! To give up after all this!'

George continued to ignore her.

So did Beth. Again she rapped on the door. 'Carrie! Come out! Surely you'll say goodbye to an old friend?'

A small voice sounded from within. 'Is it just you out there, Beth?'

Beth glanced at Abigail's back. She was leaning against the side of the boat, apparently uninterested in what was going on. She decided she didn't count.

'Just me, Carrie.'

The small door creaked open, the pale wood glowing in a sudden burst of sunlight. Carrie came up out of the cabin. She looked pale and slightly nervous.

Carrie pretty lips twitched with a smile, then froze as her gaze fell on Abigail.

Abigail was staring, her mouth and eyes wide open as though someone had slapped both cheeks and then punched her in the stomach.

It was Carrie who spoke first. 'Abbie.'

'Caroline!' Abigail's voice and body shook in unison. 'I didn't know...' The words stopped but her mouth remained open.

Carrie bit her lip. 'I thought you might be gone by now.'

'You knew I was here?'

Carrie nodded.

'You really were on the narrowboats,' said Abigail. She remembered the lies she had told their father.

'You know I always liked them,' said Carrie.

Abigail shook her head. 'But why? Why did you leave?'

Carrie shivered. 'I couldn't stay at home, Abbie.' She lowered her eyes. 'He... he... loved me too much.'

Abigail nodded. She remembered being jealous that her father doted so much – too much – on her sister.

'I didn't realise just how far things had gone,' Abigail said. A wry smile momentarily brightened her face. She shoved her hands in her trouser pockets. 'Hence my reason for dressing and behaving the way I do. Once you'd left, I had to save myself from him. And I did.'

Carrie smiled. 'You always were the wisest of the Gatehouse sisters.'

'Sister!'

At Beth's exclamation, they both turned as if seeing her for the first time.

Carrie sighed. 'I think we have some explaining to do. Do we have time for tea?'

'I thought you were going,' said Abigail, throwing an enquiring glance in George's direction.

Carrie shook her head. 'It was my decision. I thought we should go before you discovered how I'd ended up.' She lowered her eyes. 'I thought I'd embarrass you.'

'Never!'

Abigail climbed on to the boat. They embraced, staring at each other and holding hands.

'We'd better be quick having that tea,' said Beth. 'Things are happening.'

She glanced at the growing melee of running people, shouting women herding the children towards the school boat and the others beyond.

Mindful of the mounting crisis outside, the story was told hurriedly.

'I was innocent for a long while. I thought all fathers loved their daughters in that way. I found out otherwise when I followed him to a house in Portland Square. The house was a tall, narrow building in the Dutch style. I knocked on the door and as I waited, I planned what I would say once the door was open.

'As it turned out, I didn't need to say anything. "Are you the new girl?" asked the woman who answered the door. She was frightening. Even now I remember what she looked like and how she was dressed. She had a severe hairstyle, wore a black dress, and had glittering eyes. She reminded me of a governess, the horrible sort you only read about. I presumed she was expecting someone for the job of scullery maid or something. Instead, I was taken on a tour of the house. Rich reds and thick brocades were everywhere and so were young women – very young women in a state of undress. So too was our father.

'In that moment, my eyes were opened. I realised also that his love for me was not always...' She paused and exchanged an understanding glance with her husband. 'Proper. I knew nothing about such things up until then. Seeing him with these young girls threw my mind and my world into turmoil. So I went to where I always went when I wanted to be alone. I ran through the garden and down to the water meadow, threw myself into the grass and cried into the wildflowers that grew there. After that, I followed the towpath until it was night and I couldn't walk any more. People from the narrowboats are by no means overburdened with wealth, but none refused me a morsel to eat or a cup of sweet tea. They kept asking my name but my mind was a blank. I couldn't remember exactly who I was. I didn't want to remember, I suppose. Then I met George.'

Husband and wife gazed at each other in adoration and caused a flutter in the hearts of those listening.

Carrie continued. 'He mended me. Bits of my former life came back, but not entirely. Not until I saw my sister at Market Drayton.'

Abigail's eyes met hers. 'You saw me there?'

Carrie nodded at Beth. 'We were buying the material for your wedding dress. Remember? And suddenly I disappeared?'

Beth acknowledged her nod with a curt one of her own. 'I panicked. I felt ashamed.' She hung her head.

A wealth of emotion passed between them. 'So,' said Abigail. 'Are you still going?'

Carrie's eyes met her husband's. He smiled down at her. 'We'll stay, girl. If that's what you want.'

Carrie eyed the baby girl sleeping so peacefully against Beth's breast. 'That's what I want.'

Shouts and the sound of marching men filtered into the tiny cabin. Beth was first to get to her feet.

'Carrie. Will you take care of Pamela for me? I want to be part of what's happening.'

Carrie willingly took the sleeping child.

Abigail looked distracted for a moment. She was thinking of her father, thinking of how best to expose the man he really was. She heard someone saying something.

'I said, are you coming, Abigail?'

Abigail nodded brusquely and got to her feet. 'Yes,' she said. 'First things first. Let's get this over with.'

Throngs of people were running this way and that way. 'What a pickle!' cried Abigail. 'Let's get them organised.' Beth ran with her, gathering the children as she went.

'Quickly, children. This way! This way!' From one brightly painted boat to another they ran, shouting, dragging children and women from cosy cabins and their sparse evening meal. 'Get them all in one place!' she shouted. 'Take them to the school boat quick as you can.'

Everywhere, feet were running, heavy boots tramping through the dust and pitted quays.

One woman clung to Abigail's arm, a length of children in diminishing sizes clinging in turn to their mother and their siblings, trailing out like a bonnet string behind her. Another child clung to her other hand, the small fingers sticky with stale jam and her clothes smelling of coal dust.

'Come on! Come on! Run as fast as you can!'

They obeyed, running as fast as their scrawny legs could carry them. The school boat filled up quickly. The residue tumbled into an empty butty boat, thin legs poking out from beneath hanging hemlines and ragged trousers.

A large tarpaulin had been thrown over the central strut that ran from prow to stern, forming a huge tent the length of the boat. Frightened children grizzled as mothers held them close in the dank darkness, work-worn hands gently smoothing tangled hair.

'Will you read to us?' asked one small mite in a voice quivering with fear.

Although she was as scared as they were, Beth rubbed his dirty hair and exclaimed what a good idea it was. 'You wait here and I'll get a book then I'll be back.'

Packed with women and children, it wasn't easy to climb into the school boat. She took one of the books from where she'd left it on top one of the crates. Her mother was seated nearest the door, a small child asleep in her lap. Beth passed her one of the books brought in by Abigail.

'Read this to them,' she said. 'Ali Baba. They'll like this.' Outside, the heat of the afternoon was turning into amber sunset. Midges spiralled up and down in clouded columns and leaves hung languidly from the trees as if waiting with bated breath for what might happen next.

Most of the men had been organised into groups around the muddy periphery of the pounds. Anthony was marching in between the two, directing his lieutenants to where he wanted them, overseeing them all and wondering how he would get through the night – how they would all get through the night.

He looked imposing and totally committed. In her heart, she knew that after this, she would never see him again. There was no point in saying goodbye, but at least she would remember the way he looked tonight.

He stood with one arm outstretched leaning against a tree. From the trunk, the end of a washing line hung down like a very skinny snake. Anthony was flicking at it nonchalantly. She guessed he was thinking deep thoughts.

She didn't mean it to happen, but suddenly, he saw her. 'I haven't seen you all day.' Although he smiled, lines of tiredness circled his eyes.

'You're a busy man. Besides…' she shrugged and shook her head. 'Once this is over, I'll be off on the boat and you'll be off to London.'

He didn't deny it. What he said next astonished her. 'I want you to leave Elliot.'

'He's my husband,' she said then realised it sounded alien, as though it had no place here with them among the trees and the gathering twilight.

He kept his gaze fixed on a spot where Elliot was lining men up like a squad of soldiers, wooden staves and boat hooks rather than rifles over their shoulders.

'Promise me you'll think about it,' he said.

'I can't promise you anything. You know that.'

She turned abruptly away. The smell of him, the grass, the trees, the wild plants was still with her when she went back to the pounds. She'd never forget him.

She went to collect Pamela from Carrie, beating a quick tattoo on the window. 'Carrie! Come on. You'd better come with me.'

There was no reply. Perhaps she's gone to a boat, she thought, and started to make her way there herself.

* * *

Carrie was standing rocking backwards and forwards on the path that led to the copse where Beth had lain with Anthony.

'Shouldn't you be with the other women?' Robbie's lengthy shadow fell over her. 'I don't like you sitting up here. You could get hurt and so could the baby.'

'Pamela's fine. Aren't you, Pamela?' she said, jiggling the child up and down.

'I didn't mean that one.'

'No,' she said, eyes lowered, 'I didn't think you did. But the answer's the same and it's no business of yours anyway.'

'But it's—'

She glared up at him, her face flushed and angry. 'It's none of your business!'

'Caroline?' Abigail appeared on the path. Robbie looked surprised, Carrie relieved.

'I think you should be with the others on the butty.'

Abigail eyed Robbie suspiciously. What was he doing here with her sister? 'I'll take you there,' she said.

Robbie winced beneath her steely gaze. There was something about her that terrified him.

Oh well, he'd harboured affection for the woman, and if it hurt this much, he'd never do it again. Shrugging off the concern, he shoved his hands in his pockets and made off back down the path. Even if Carrie didn't want to know, there were plenty more fish in the sea.

* * *

'Here they come, lads!'

In a heaving wave, men with staves came rushing out of the warehouse. Just as Abigail had predicted, a private army had been paid to crack heads and break the strike in any way they could.

'Hold your ground,' shouted Anthony from the island in the middle of the compound. Thankfully they had the advantage of being on higher ground.

Elliot stood beside him along with Igor. Squashed between them and Ferdy Smith, a man who had fathered an army of children, was Goblin Coombes, his chest already heaving in expectation that he might be able to brain one of the strike-breakers or burst his lungs in the process.

'Charge!' shouted Anthony.

An avalanche of bodies fell down from the hill and went

crashing into the baton-waving thugs coming up from below them.

'Every man for himself!' shouted Anthony. It was debatable whether anyone heard him.

Staves and batons rose and fell on capped heads, around ears and against bodies already weakened by lack of sleep and malnutrition.

The fighting spread, some men running, others chasing, groups beating at each other, solitary men beating at three or more, but all the time, the superior strength, the greater brutality of the carrier men beat down the good intentions and high hopes of the boatmen.

Back in the boat, the women were strangely silent, their eyes full of fear. Even when the sound of men fighting finally came closer, they remained silent. Each of them knew that the men with staves who had been secretly ferried into the warehouse were now free to do their worst.

What can I say to them? thought Beth as she eyed their frightened faces. Can I really tell them not to be afraid? I am, so what right have I to tell them not to be?

There was a sick churning in her stomach and the muscles of her legs felt suddenly wasted. Where was her strength? She had to tell them something, give them a few words to keep them going.

'I'm going to read to you,' she said, and felt helpless saying it. Until now, she had sat with a book cradled in her lap. She'd always been able to think things through when she was reading a book. She read out loud. In her mind she pondered her problems.

Anthony had asked her to leave Elliot. It was out of the question. Life stood in the way. Despite her inner turmoil, she had to do something to prevent panic, her own as well as those she was with.

Scared eyes stared at her. They were waiting. She had to do what she could.

'I'm going to read a story called "Ali Baba and the Forty Thieves".'

* * *

Once she'd escorted her sister and Beth's baby on to one of the boats containing women and children, Abigail turned her attention back to the battle.

The fact that she had found her sister had left her drained of emotion. All that mattered was winning this battle then winning the one against her father. She wanted to destroy him, just as surely as he'd destroyed many young women over the years.

The dust cloud kicked up by fighting men settled on her clothes, stuck to her face and dried her lips. Personal discomfort could be ignored but she could not ignore the staves that rose and fell over the heads of the boatmen.

A man fell against her and attempted to push her to the ground. She fought back, kicking and beating at him with a stick. He was flaccid-faced and had a broken nose, but that wasn't who she saw lying there. Every man she hit today had her father's face.

'Bitch!' he shouted.

'Yes,' she snarled, 'I am,' and landed a well-aimed kick into the soft, fragile tissue that hung between his legs.

'Missus! Yoohoo, missus!'

Spiky Pike, the boy who had helped her with the books, was calling out to her and dragging a very little man behind him. The man had blood running from his head and appeared to be having problems with his breathing.

'What happened?'

'He's out of puff,' explained Spiky.

She took hold of the little man's other arm. He was surprisingly heavy, probably because he was a little misshapen and had a very large head.

'Let's sit him here.'

They sat him against a crumbling wall that seemed only to be held up by the thick ivy growing over it. He groaned, large pale eyes rolling until only the whites were visible.

'Oh my God!' she muttered.

'Not God. Goblin Coombes. At yer service, missus,' he said, and passed out.

'He took one hell of a whack,' said Spiky.

'There's bandages in the boats and there's more in my car down by the gate,' said Abigail. She pursed her lips. In the car was no good. She wanted bandages here and now! 'Fat lot of good that is!'

'Pardon, missus?'

'I need a bandage for this man.'

Spiky rummaged in the back of his trousers. There was a loud ripping noise.

'Will this do?' A piece of almost white material fluttered from his outstretched hand.

She took the piece of shirt tail, noted that it felt warm and a little greasy and tried not to guess at the last time it was washed. Carefully she began to dab at the scarlet gash on Goblin's forehead. He groaned and closed his eyes.

'Is he gonna snuff it?' asked Spiky with interest rather than remorse.

Abigail got to her feet. 'No. He might not have the looks of a thoroughbred but he's got the constitution of a carthorse. He'll live.'

She got up and walked the length of the wall, then leaned against the damp moss, closed her eyes and took a few deep breaths. A cool breeze blowing up from the canal scattered her hair on to her face. She turned to greet it and the trees it blew through. She prayed that not too many would get hurt. The bushes to her right rustled. At first she put it down to the night wanderings of a fox. Then she saw him.

He wore a black trilby and there were bruises down one side of his face. Perhaps it was because she was tired that she didn't recognise him at first. But the face was familiar and so were the bruises.

Harry Allen!

Not taking her eyes off him, she eased away from the wall. Her mind worked quickly. This was trouble and here she was alone except for a skinny boy and an injured dwarf. Now was the time to be brave.

Feeling her way slowly along the wall, she kept her eyes fixed on Harry as he moved closer to her, bristling with revenge. Eventually, the wall ran out. There was nothing left to lean on except a pile of fallen stones.

Spiky piped up from the other side where he squatted with Goblin Coombes. 'What's up, missus?'

'Nothing. Stay where you are.'

It appeared Harry hadn't heard. 'Want to bash my brains in again?' he growled. 'Want to have another go at me, do you? Well not this time, Miss bloody Gatehouse. This time, it's my turn. And have I got some bright ideas in mind for you. I want you to be nice to me, Miss Gatehouse. I want you to give me some pleasure before I give you some pain. Some real pain!'

Abigail continued to walk backwards, searching for a way out. 'I'll report you to my father.'

'What do I care!'

'You'll lose your job.'

He lit a cigarette, throwing it away again as though he had all the time in the world to play cat and mouse with her.

'I don't think so. In fact, he's been most generous, most generous. Especially after I said I would have to report the matter to the police, and I mean it wouldn't look very good for someone of his standing to have a daughter arrested for grievous bodily harm, would it? You're a disappointment to your father, Miss Gatehouse: a grave disappointment. Won't even get married, so I hear. Well, I can understand that. Women get first-night nerves, don't they? Well, I'll take you through that, Miss Gatehouse. I'll show you all there is to know.'

It would have been so easy to interrupt his tirade, to shout at him, or scream blue murder for someone to come along and help her. But all the while he talked, she wrapped her hand around a loose stone, assessed where Spiky was, and mentally measured how far she had to run before Harry could catch her.

He was quicker than she'd thought. He grabbed her shoulder, and although she knew that those behind the wall might hear them scuffling, she controlled the urge to scream.

Claw-like, his other hand hooked into the neckline of her blouse. The buttons spun off into the undergrowth. Her blouse was ripped to the waist and one strap of her camisole hung loose. If it had been darker he might not have seen her bare breasts and she would not have seen the lewd intent in his eyes.

But she held her ground, her breathing surprisingly even. She calculated what he would do next and what she would do to him. He came forward to where she wanted him, pushing her back against the wall, his body hard against hers. His breath smelt of onions. His skin was as oily as his hair.

'There,' he said as he licked his lips and cupped her breast. 'I knew you were a real woman underneath those stiff clothes.'

As he bent his head to her breast, she clutched the stone tighter and chose her moment. Unseen and unexpected by him, she raised her knee sharply. At the same time she brought the stone down hard upon his head.

His body jerked and his eyes opened wide in surprise. Eyes bulging and hands shielding his groin, he grunted and buckled forward before crumpling to the ground.

Abigail closed her shirt and smoothed her jacket.

Spiky came out from behind the wall and glanced at Harry. 'Crikey! Have you killed him?' His voice was full of admiration.

'Unfortunately not. Come on. Let's get you and your friend back down to the compound.'

'Can you hear anything?' Spiky asked.

Abigail's blood ran cold. 'Silence. That means the fighting's over.'

She was less careful getting the delirious Goblin Coombes safely down than she should have been. She had to know what had happened, not just whether they'd beaten the men off, but what had happened to Anthony. Hopefully, he was now the hero of the hour.

The low hum of subdued voices made her ache inside. Where were the laughter and the shouting that would have pronounced a successful defence? The answer hurt.

Only a few days before, the compound had throbbed with celebration. Now those that had rejoiced were stumbling with heads bent, blood running down their faces, broken arm held by the good one, broken leg dragging along behind.

Women struggled along with stumbling menfolk hanging from their shoulder and crying children scrabbling at their skirts all coughing because the fighting had stirred up so much dust and the days and the nights were still so dry.

A man with a notepad was running in and out of the throng, his face flushed, his voice high-pitched and excited. Another man ran along behind him, tripod and camera tucked clumsily beneath one arm.

By the main gate in front of the company offices was a fleet of blunt-nosed ambulances, white and ghostly under the feeble lights of the wharf. White aprons and stiff veils fluttered busily like night moths as nurses ran in among those who'd been injured.

Carefully, she set Goblin Coombes down and a nurse took over.

Instead of feeling less weighed down, her body sagged. How could this have happened? Sweat trickled from her eyebrows and down her nose. She mopped it up with the back of her hand then wiped it on her waistcoat, which had been quite clean but was now as dusty as any man's.

Leering oafs carrying staves eyed her curiously as if they had half a mind to find out what she was made of. Deterred by the look in her eyes and the scattering of police, who had only lately reappeared, they veered away, watching from a distance as they talked in huddled groups.

Children scattered as the victorious oafs continued to patrol. People, nurses, police and dogs milled around everywhere as orders to go back to their boats rang out over their heads.

Tired but defiant, Abigail searched the crowds, asking where she could for news of Anthony. Her head felt hot, bursting with a hotchpotch of conflicting emotions. She had to see how her sister was. Did she still have Pamela? But most of all she wanted to know where Anthony was – perhaps hurt, she thought with sudden panic, or perhaps arrested.

A black car drew up at the bottom of the steps leading up to the offices and a figure she knew got out and took off his hat. He mounted the steps, went into the office briefly then came out again.

Recognizing Penmore, she edged away, finally hiding herself behind the open door of a conveniently placed ambulance.

She ducked out of sight as he glanced in her direction. What was that weasel doing here? Suddenly, there was more noise, someone shouting, a voice she thought she recognised.

Penmore, who had been sneering triumphantly, turned to face it. The sneer wavered as he saw two policemen supporting a third man between them.

'Abigail Gatehouse did it.'

Harry Allen! Careful not to be seen, she peered up through the oval of glass set in the ambulance door.

Surprisingly, Penmore's attention wavered suddenly. He was looking beyond Allen and frowning at a slim figure with a serene face and silvery blonde hair. Carrie, wrapped up in helping everyone she could, did not appear to notice him. So far, Penmore looked as though he wasn't too sure of who she was. If he was left looking at her too long, though, he would be in no doubt and then he would tell her father. Abigail did not hesitate. She leapt out from behind the ambulance door.

'Penmore, you rat!'

His attention reverted to her. Out of the corner of her eye, she saw Carrie glance at her, then at Penmore, and the colour drain from her face. Briefly, their eyes met. *Hide, Carrie. Please hide!*

'That woman's mad!' shouted Harry Allen, his hand clutching his crotch as blood trickled down over one eye and one cheek. 'This is the second time she's attacked me. Last time, I kept my mouth shut. This time I won't. She attacked me, I tell you. The woman should be locked up!'

Abigail noted the swift look that passed between the wharfinger and Penmore. She saw the latter speak to two policemen, his head bobbing abruptly as if he were a blackbird searching for fleshy snails. The policemen kept her in their sights as they walked over to her.

It occurred to her to run there and then, but she couldn't do that. Carrie needed time to hide. Hopefully, George could get her away.

A burly policeman with pink cheeks and a ginger moustache cut in a straight line despite the curvature of his lips stalked over to her with his hands behind his back, two subordinates flanking him. Milky-blue eyes looked down at her from either side of an aquiline nose.

'Do you deny you attacked this man?'

'Nearly killed me, she did!' shouted Harry.

She lifted her chin high and affixed her most arrogant expression to a face that had lost most of its makeup and was smudged with dust and running with sweat.

'Do you know who I am?'

'No. Who are you?'

'Abigail Gatehouse!'

He nodded to his younger colleagues, who immediately stepped forward. 'Abigail Gatehouse. You're under arrest.'

25

Beth craned her neck, pushing through the sobbing women and battered men. Where was he?

A hand grabbed her shoulder. 'Beth!'

Her face dropped as she turned and faced her husband. 'Elliot!'

If it wasn't the man she was looking for, she didn't show it, especially when two burly policemen tried to take him.

'Spare him, please! He's got me and the baby to take care of and another one on the way.' She patted her belly as though it were really true.

Elliot's jaw dropped in amazement. Luckily, he didn't ask her why she hadn't told him before. Lies were justified.

'Tell them you need to be with me,' she whispered, her fingers clawing over his threadbare coat collar. Hysterics followed. 'Please! Don't leave me. Please stay. My babies! Have pity on my babies!'

'Now, now there, missus!' Strong, masculine hands peeled back her fingers and dragged her off him.

She brushed at her eyes and the damp hair that clung around her face as she watched him being taken. What a sorry sight he looked. His shirtsleeves were hanging off, and he stumbled as they took him away.

She saw him roll his shoulders in an attempt to shrug them off. They handcuffed him then and her heart went out to him. Poor Elliot.

Poor Elliot? Strange, but she'd never thought that way about him before.

He struggled again and glanced at her over his shoulder.

For once in his life, he looked helpless.

'You'll be home soon,' she shouted after him. He was bundled in the back of a Black Maria along with the other men. She was left with the other women staring as the vehicle trundled away.

A strange emptiness descended all over the compound. The men had left women who could please themselves but couldn't remember how.

For what seemed like an hour, but must have been much less, all eyes stayed fixed on the gate through which their menfolk had left.

The police began to move them away from the main gates, clapping their hands and shooing them away like stray dogs. 'Now come on with you, off to your pots and your pans. There's nothing for you here!'

They lingered defiantly. Babies squalled in their mothers' arms; children squabbled, cried for food or attention or both. Their mothers were numb, turned in a moment to blocks of wood. The children cried and, eventually, so did the women.

Like the rest, Beth dragged herself back to where the boat sat cold and quiet. No smoke rose from its iron chimney.

Beth barely noticed. She rubbed at her aching bones and asked herself whether it was all worth it. They'd got nothing. No wage rise, no earnings over the past weeks, and before very long, they might not have a boat. The carrying company was a hard master.

* * *

Night came, the darkness silvered by a full moon. The water glistened and the trees were black against an indigo sky. After gathering her books, she went along to *Sadie G*. Carrie had Pamela in her arms and was cooing and feeding her thin porridge. George was with her.

'I managed to escape,' he said to Beth before she even had a chance to ask him how he wasn't arrested. 'Told them I'd been here all day and no one was around to see me come on board and state otherwise.' He looked sheepish but also slightly pleased with himself. 'Excuse me while I get the engine ready. We'll be out of here as soon as I can get the motor running.' He left.

Carrie asked, 'How many men have been arrested?'

'Quite a few. I saw them being loaded in the Black Maria. They've taken Elliot, but I didn't see Anthony. I wonder where he is.'

Carrie glared at her. 'You're talking about your husband, Beth. What's Anthony to you?'

'Why are you snapping at me, Carrie?'

Carrie paused, put down the porridge and began rubbing Pamela's back to bring up her wind. 'You should know why.'

Beth shook her head.

'Abigail told me. She saw you with Anthony.'

Beth sank down on to a stool. 'I didn't mean for it to happen.' It sounded lame. She tried to understand herself why it had happened. And why hadn't she felt guilty until now?

Carrie emphasised the point. 'He's not your husband.'

Beth heard the accusation in her voice and saw it in her eyes.

She couldn't help but retaliate. 'And what about the father of your child?'

Carrie looked incredibly superior. 'That's different.'

'Different? How can it be?'

Carrie took a deep breath so that her breasts seemed to rise closer to her collar. 'I wanted a baby. I didn't want him.'

Beth was speechless. 'But you committed...'

She couldn't bring herself to say the word. Carrie said it for her.

'Adultery. No. I don't think so. I love George and him alone. But George cannot father children and I cannot injure his pride by telling him so. Having one, a little baby like Pamela here, will complete our happiness.'

Amazed at the ease with which Carrie matched morals to suit her circumstances, Beth slapped her hands on her knees and took a deep breath.

'Well, there's one difference for a start. You love George and he treats you very well, respects you for who you are and what you are. Elliot wants me to fit the mould he's prepared to accept. He doesn't want me to read, but he doesn't want to read himself. He accuses me of being unfaithful, even though the event he refers to happened before I married him.'

Carrie looked shocked. 'It happened before you married him?'

Beth looked down at the floor. 'I tried to fight him – Harry Allen – but he was too strong.' She shook her head mournfully. 'I couldn't stop him!' Suddenly her head was in her hands and the tears began to flow. 'My life is empty, Carrie! I need someone like Anthony.' Her hands fell helplessly into her lap. 'Anthony Wesley fills that gap, Carrie. Suddenly, here's a man who's interested in me! I've watched my mother downtrodden by my father. I've seen women trying to gain some happiness and only ending up with the same drudgery. I wanted my moment, Carrie. I wanted to love and be loved for once in my life. Please, please, don't hate me for that.'

Carrie looked back at her with a mix of sadness and confusion. Then she reached out and clasped one of Beth's hands in hers. 'I don't hate you, Beth. I was merely worried about you. And you're right. Under the circumstances, I can hardly blame you. We all have to escape and find some happiness.'

Beth nodded and took Carrie's one hand in both of hers. 'Thank you for being a friend. Thank you for understanding.' She got up and leaned over to kiss the head of her daughter. 'I'm going to make sure my daughter gets a better life than me. I don't know how, but I'm determined. Somehow, I'll manage it.'

The two women looked at each other in mutual understanding.

* * *

She let Carrie take care of Pamela that night.

'I'm enjoying it. You rest. We two will be fine together.' George too seemed as besotted with the child as Carrie.

Placing his pipe to one side, he could be seen bending over the baby and speaking in a language that only babies might understand.

In the absence of anyone else, Beth felt it her duty to reassure women that their men would soon be home, and to reassure men that their fight had not been in vain.

Injured men who had escaped arrest sprawled on the ground or leaned where they could, nursing their injuries. Everywhere she went, despair hung in tired faces, broken limbs and in the very air they breathed. No one had seen Anthony or knew where he was, although one man accused him of running away.

Suddenly, she could stand it no more. Hurrying away from the compound, she made for the trees, the fields and the church upon the hill. Holding her skirt high, she scrambled up through the bracken and into the small copse. The air was less depressing, the perfumes given off by the wild flowers hanging like a scented veil. A night breeze rattled the leaves on a silver birch. The moon came out from behind a cloud and etched the trees in silver. That was when she saw him.

Anthony was slumped with his back against an ivy-covered wall. He was slouched, his head held in his hands.

She paused, hardly able to believe that this was the man who had stood like a general commanding his troops. Now he looked broken.

'Anthony!'

Her voice quivered with emotion. Without touching him or seeing his face, she could feel his exhaustion and desolation.

At first, there was joy in his eyes when he looked up and saw her. It didn't last.

'We've lost,' he said. His words seemed to take flight the moment they were out of his mouth.

She threw herself down at his side, took his head in her hands, raising his face to meet hers. Inwardly, she groaned. There was a cut in the corner of his mouth from which blood trickled through stubble and dripped off his chin. She stared at the congealing flow, preferable to meeting the sadness in his eyes. She reached out and gently dipped one finger into the gathering blood. She forced herself to swallow her sobs before she spoke.

'There'll be other battles,' she said softly. The moment and the emotions connected with it flooded her thoughts and drove out reason. 'And there'll always be you and me. I've had feelings for you from the time you were lying there battered, bruised and dirty.'

'Shh!' He raised his finger to his lips.

The words had tumbled from her mouth without forethought, without plan because she was with him at this moment and for now that was all that mattered.

He raised his arms as if to hug her. She stepped back.

'I can't. We can't.' Sobs threatened, but she held them back.

His hand dropped to his side. He seemed to think a moment then reached for her again. 'Help me up.'

The hand she took was warm to the touch.

He struggled to his feet. 'You're right, of course. We both have our different duties. I have to take the consequences with the men I led, Beth. You have your duty as a wife. I have mine as a leader of men. I've been thinking about things. People with wealth and power on their side beat us today. If you can't beat 'em, join 'em, as my old mother used to say. So that's what I'm going to do. I've got to get power in order to help those who have none. London and the politics there are where I have to be. Abigail's right on that.'

'Yes.' Choking back her emotions, she helped him back down to where the last of the men were being loaded into the ominous black vehicles.

A policeman recognised him. 'Oi! You!' He was snatched from her immediately and roughhoused into the back of a Black Maria. Their eyes met one last time before the door closed. She was alone. Drained of energy and devoid of company, she made her way back along the wharf.

Sleep didn't come easy that night. Visions of Elliot and Anthony floated around her dreams. She imagined running away with Anthony, Pamela clutched in her arms. How would Elliot feel about that?

But he'll still have his boat! He loves his boat! The sentiment was all part of her dream.

* * *

The next morning, she found what breakfast she could and by lunchtime, she was making preparations to visit the police station and find out where they had taken the two men who were most prominent in her life.

Just as she was about to leave with Pamela in her arms, she heard a brace of footsteps from the wharf. A sick feeling wriggled in her stomach. The police were probably rounding up the last of the troublemakers. Just after the footsteps stopped, the light from the doorway was obliterated by a familiar figure. Battered but unbowed, Elliot had returned.

Dark shadows hung beneath his eyes. His shoulders were stooped as on a man twice his age. He opened his mouth to speak. At first there was nothing. He cleared his throat and tried again. 'I've lost the boat, Beth. We've got to pack everything up and get out right now.'

* * *

Abigail Gatehouse was sure that it was Penmore who peered at her through the small flap of the cell door.

'Penmore! Get my father! Get him right now!'

She threw herself at the door, smashing against it at the very moment that the flap was slammed shut.

'Penmore! Get me out of here, you disgusting creature! Get me out of here! Get my father! Get him!'

But her father did not come. Where was he? Where was Anthony? Where was the union?

She felt so alone. Silence rang in her head like a funeral bell. Prisons were like tombs; once inside you were dead to the outside world. It was almost as if no one would ever hear her ever again, and they certainly could not hear her through the thickness of the walls. The prospect frightened her.

Sinking down on to the grey blankets that covered a mattress no thicker than a crust of bread, she thought of the events that had led here. Did she regret any of it? No, she decided, but for the first time in a while, she wanted to be home. Would her father come to get her out? And had Penmore told him about Caroline?

She thought carefully about the consequences. He'd always been so determined to find Caroline. She'd thought it purely out of obsessive affection, but that absurd love had hidden, darker secrets. And Caroline had told her everything.

Just wait till I see him, she thought to herself. I'll throw it all in his face. He'll be totally disgraced. Despite the chill surroundings, she threw back her head and smiled triumphantly at the ceiling. If only he'd come through that cell door right this minute...

Each time she heard the sound of hollow footsteps from the corridor outside, her hopes were raised. But her hopes were dashed. He didn't come and the fact that he didn't began to worry her.

Shivering, she pulled up the collar of her thick, tweed jacket. When that failed to warm her she bundled herself in the rough grey blankets from the bed. The cell was freezing; its lack of heating was not helped by the tomblike coldness of the white, tiled walls. What worried her most about being here was that the others arrested had been thrown ad hoc into cells: four in one, three in another, perhaps two in another. But she was alone. At first, she presumed she'd gained privilege because of who she was. Later, she'd heard the police sergeant say that she was to have a cell of her own because she might be a danger to herself and to others.

My father is punishing me. That's what it is, she decided. She was being treated like this on her father's orders because she had made a fool of Gilbert and she was still involved with the union. The fact that she'd now brained Harry Allen twice did not seem quite so important as the other two shortcomings. But first as last, she would not go quietly.

Fed up with waiting, she began shouting and banging on the door. When the metal flap was let down and food pushed through the opening, she took the cheap tin enamel plate and threw it at the door. The food stuck momentarily before trickling to the ground in an orange and green mess of stew and vegetables.

'I don't want your swill. I don't want anything from you demons, you who would take the food from the mouths of babes. You who'd deny the working man his wage; deny his wife the means to buy their daily bread!'

Her voice held. It was a strong voice and needed to be because she did not stop shouting. *She would not stop shouting!*

The fact that no one came antagonised her even more. What were they trying to prove? Was this what it meant to be kept in solitary? And this was the punishment her father had decided on to dampen her spirit and make her behave like other daughters behaved? Well, it wouldn't happen!

Deciding on the reason only seemed to strengthen her resolve to annoy these people as much as possible. By annoying them, she was annoying her father.

When darkness came, she was still alone, her voice weakening but not dying completely. Her throat became dry. Words had poured out like bullets, ricocheting against the cold white walls.

No one came, and as midnight chimed on the town-hall clock on the other side of the street, doubt began to filter into her mind. All her life she had slept alone, and all her days she had put her trust in her own strengths, her own confidence. But being in a dark cell was different than being in one's own bed.

Surrounded by a mess of her own making, the spilt food, torn blankets, and an upturned bucket, she now felt terribly isolated. The cold intensified so although the blankets were torn to shreds, she gathered them around herself. I must look like a beggar on some street corner in Cairo or Calcutta, she thought, and was thankful she could not see herself in a mirror. When her voice was too hoarse to cry out, hunger and tiredness began to take over. Her head flopped on to her right shoulder; her nose snuggled down into the mouldy blanket despite the smell of mothballs and old sweat.

She did not hear the flap open. She did not see the eye that watched her.

Eyelids that might have been weighted with lead ingots were slow to open as the cell door opened. Limbs tired from standing and running turned to jelly. Thick fingers grasped her upper arms, jerking her to her feet.

'Let me go,' she croaked as they slipped the sleeves of a jacket up her arms. 'Let me go!' she rasped again as the cell was flooded with light.

They wore white uniforms. Police don't wear white, she thought to herself. I must be dreaming. She struggled as her arms were passed across her body and a kind of high collar was pulled tight around her mouth.

I'm dreaming, screamed her mind. *Please, let me be dreaming! I'll wake up soon. I know I will!*

She was bundled out of the cell and along chill, drab corridors. She still clung on to the hope that this was a nightmare brought on by hunger and little sleep.

When they finally got to the street and she saw Penmore standing near the open doors of the ambulance, she doubted her own sanity. A face was watching her from the window of a long, black sedan. She recognised her father.

'I want to wake up now,' she said to one of the men in white, but the gag around her mouth muffled her words.

The man exchanged a small smile with his colleague. The

other man spoke to her. 'Don't worry. We'll put you to bed and you can wake up somewhere safe.'

She didn't understand. 'What does he mean?' She wrenched her neck round and saw her father watching, his face devoid of expression. He tapped his chauffeur on the shoulder and turned away. The car drove off and suddenly she was very afraid.

26

'The strike achieved nothing!'

Anthony Wesley was leaning on a desk with his arms folded, staring down at the smouldering ashtray where Alistair McCrea, union convener and potential Labour MP, had just doused another Woodbine. He hoped he'd light another soon. The smell of tobacco was far preferable to the stench of the police cell that had saturated his clothes.

'I'd supposed the company had some integrity. Obviously I was mistaken.' Anthony kicked at the leg of the table and wished it was Archibald Gatehouse – or even that sneak, Penmore.

McCrea came around from behind the desk and patted him on the shoulder in a fatherly fashion. He admired this young man and it pained him to see his dejection. He was determined to do something about it and decided some useful advice would not come amiss.

'You're wasting your chances, Anthony. Why don't you try for a Party position? I'll be needing a good personal aide once I make my stand for Parliament. How about it?'

Anthony looked at McCrea. He hadn't expected to get an

opportunity at the heart of the Party just yet. The older man was well respected. There was more than a good chance he'd get nominated for the vacant seat, an opportunity that had arisen by virtue of the previous incumbent dying in office.

'Do you really mean that?'

'Of course I do. And why shouldn't I? You have all the attributes I require. You've a quick mind, good health, and you believe in what you do. Besides, a good-looking young fellow like you, it's only a matter of time before you get the offer of a good seat.'

He looked beyond Alistair's head to the trees growing in the town square and the mix of people, trams, horse-drawn drays and motor vehicles going about their daily tasks. He remembered what he'd said to Beth. By obtaining power, he could help those that had none.

'So experience in your department will give me the credentials I need?' he said, wondering what exactly Alistair had done in the movement to get him where he was in the first place.

'You need to attend to a few basic requirements first. A wife would be useful. The electorate likes to see a stable background, good family life. It would equalise the more disruptive element of the activist factor. Even better if you can marry a girl who knows a few people.' He saw Anthony's sudden distaste and reacted immediately. 'I'm only saying it as it is, Anthony, without the idealism. Put the ideology on hold until you've got the power – a bit like the Party, really. Will you think about it?'

'Of course I will.'

He thought about it a lot on the way back to his digs above the Black Sheep pub. The more power a man had, the more influence he had over people's lives, the more he could help them. Although there was some pricking of conscience about leaving union organisation behind and stepping more into the cut and thrust of things, the idea of being able to get more done was irresistible.

It was power, Alistair's power, that had got him out of the hands of the police. There was a fine, of course, but nothing that couldn't be easily met.

* * *

The next day he walked to the town square. The grit from sooty chimneys fouled the air. He breathed it in. Some folk liked the countryside, the smell of grass, the stink of farmyards. He loved the city and the bigger and busier, the better. London, he decided, would suit him well.

Shoving his hands in his pockets, he made his way to the police station, where he enquired about the other men. Some had been fined and a few of the more belligerent had been sent down for a while.

On the tram that took him to the dock gates, he thought about the future and tingled. Alistair was offering exactly what he wanted; in fact, he wanted it so much, it hurt. Wonderful plans to put the world to rights whirled inside his head. He had few reservations and was surprised at just how mercenary he became at the thought of putting them into operation. Politics would add gravitas and respectability to his struggles on behalf of the working man. So too would a wife.

Abigail! Behind every great man was a strong woman. He found himself overcome with affection for her and guilt at the way he had treated her. Yes, she had sometimes been terrified at the situations he'd landed himself in, but she'd always come back for more.

Could I live with her? He couldn't help smiling to himself.

Could she live with me?

A dark-haired flower seller chose that moment to turn round and offer him a bunch of violets. She was not as pretty as Beth.

'Violets, sir?'

He shook his head and looked away. Best to forget Beth. Best to help her and her kind from a distance. The more he thought about it, the more he realised just how far he could go with a woman like Abigail at his side.

As the tram neared the canal compound, he thought about not getting off but going round the circle and back into town. When it came to a standstill, he sat in his seat though his heart beat like a hammer on an anvil.

He would not seek Beth. He would find Abigail. His mind was made up, or at least he thought it was.

Just as the tram started to move off again, he leapt to his feet, pushed through to the platform at the bottom of the spiral staircase and jumped off on to the slippery wet cobbles.

* * *

An air of desolation hung over the compound now. All the camaraderie, the feeling of fighting for what was right, had melted away. So had most of the boats, but not, he saw with rising spirits, the *Agincourt*.

The door was tightly closed.

'Beth!' he shouted. 'Beth! Let me in.' Stubbornly, the door refused to open.

It occurred to him that Elliot had already been released. He shouted his name.

'They're gone.'

The voice came from the next boat. Carrie Melcroft took him by surprise.

'Where have they gone?'

She eyed him thoughtfully, one arm seemingly supporting her belly, one resting beneath her breasts.

For a moment, he had the distinct impression that she didn't want to tell him. He tried another tack. 'Why have they gone?'

'They got thrown off the boat. The company said they would not employ Elliot because he'd assaulted Harry Allen.' Anthony eyed the painted flowers that ringed the windows.

'Elliot loved this boat.' He shook his head sadly.

Carrie had made up her mind to say nothing. A marriage was a marriage, after all. The sadness in Anthony's eyes changed her mind. 'I think his father is a lock keeper. He has a cottage somewhere.'

Anthony thanked her. 'I'm glad they're all right,' he said and turned to go.

A fine white hand clutched at his sleeve. 'Is Abbie all right?' Her eyes were full of anxiety.

He frowned. 'I presume so. She's at home, surely?'

Carrie hung her head. 'My father came to see me. He was angry – and afraid.' Her expression was resolute when she looked up. He couldn't help admiring her face. It was perfect, arched eyebrows above large, childlike eyes. 'You know she's my sister.'

Anthony stared at her. 'I had some idea, but she was secretive. She never seemed to want to talk about it.'

'Beth tells me that Abbie loves you. Is that right? I'd like it to be true. Abbie deserves someone special in her life.'

He wasn't sure she was telling the truth, though her expression seemed sincere. It was just something about her eyes...

'What did your father want?'

'Me.'

She swallowed. He sensed she was shivering. Her face was drained of colour and she seemed to be studying her feet. What was wrong with her? For a dreadful moment, he wondered whether she was experiencing the pains of birth. Nervously he waited, unsure what to make of the situation. Carrie explained.

'He blamed Abigail for everything and said he'd had enough of her antics, that she had a big mouth and that he'd teach her a lesson.'

'What did he mean?'

'He tried to tell me that she's been charged with attempted murder and wasn't worth worrying about. He wouldn't admit that he'd ever done anything wrong – I mean, when I was a child,' she stammered.

Anthony was tempted to ask what exactly Gatehouse had been guilty of, but sensed it caused Carrie pain to speak of it. 'I presume he had no intention bailing her out,' Carrie added.

Just how evil was Gatehouse really? 'I'll see if she's still at the police station.'

He took leave of her and caught the next tram back into town, his mind reeling with possibilities.

The police station was drab and smelt of stale sweat. The sergeant was not helpful. He peered balefully at him through a square opening no more than two by two. 'Nothing to do with us, sir.'

Anthony fiddled with the brass bell on the counter. A notice above it said *ring for attention*. He kept ringing it, determined he would continue to irritate if he didn't get answers. 'Her name is Abigail Gatehouse. Could you check again, please?'

Begrudgingly, the sergeant did just that. 'Nothing, sir.'

Anthony was vaguely aware of a door opening behind him.

The new arrival had a large black moustache that appeared to be directly attached to a hooked nose.

'Can I help you, sir?'

'I hope so. I'm looking for a Miss Gatehouse.'

'Ah!' said the man as though the name answered everything he'd ever wanted to know. 'She was the lady arrested for assault on a gentleman named Mr Henry Allen.'

'Ah!' said Anthony in an intentional parody of the police inspector. 'So you do have her here!'

The man shook his head authoritatively. 'No, sir. We could not press charges, on the grounds of her mental condition.'

Anthony's blood turned cold. 'Mental condition? Since when has strong-mindedness been regarded as a mental condition?' Fearfully he tried to imagine just what sort of trap Abigail had got caught in.

'Nothing to do with us, sir. You'll have to check with the family as to how they are dealing with her.'

Gatehouse! He had to see him.

* * *

There was a long wait at the railway station so he bought a paper from a newspaper seller with no legs. The poor man sat on a small wooden trolley and used a brick placed against the wheel to stop it rolling away.

A great, black, steam engine chuffed into the station. Never had a journey taken so long. He willed the engineer to throw more coal into the boiler, for the shiny, black locomotive to charge forward like a war-horse rather than plod on as if ploughing a ten-acre field.

Although it would have been more sensible to eat supper and find a bed for the night, he ignored his grumbling stomach and sore eyes. Abigail was top priority. He had to find out how she was and what he could do for her.

The gates of Pearcemore Park were closed so he climbed over them, walked up the lengthy drive and banged the big brass ring against the coal-black door.

Again and again he knocked until black windows exploded with light.

The sound of bolts being drawn preceded the opening of the door.

'Anthony Wesley to see Archibald Gatehouse.'

'It's very late, sir,' returned the bony-faced man who appeared in the gap.

'I don't care. I want to see him now!'

The servant looked taken aback but still managed to look down his nose. 'Please leave here immediately before I call the police.'

Anthony thrust one strong arm against it so both the door and the man were flung back into what he gauged was the reception hall. Footsteps sounded from above.

'What the devil is all this noise about? How dare you barge into my house like this! Who the devil are you, sir?'

The blustering voice could only belong to one person.

And there he is, thought Anthony, his eyes blazing.

Archibald Gatehouse, the man who wanted to pay pennies to those who worked for him whilst he gathered the pounds, was standing halfway down a curving staircase.

'I'm looking for Abbie. Where is she, Mr Gatehouse?'

'What's it to you?' A shower of spittle flew from his mouth. Anthony felt disgust, but did not show it. He hadn't needed Carrie to tell him why she'd run away. She'd been young and pretty, and Gatehouse, judging by what he'd heard, was the worse kind of lecher there is.

'It's a lot to me, Gatehouse, and a lot to you if you don't tell me where she is.'

The other man guffawed but there was a hint of puzzlement in his eyes. 'Now what can you mean by that?' he thundered.

Anthony glanced meaningfully at the bevy of servants, all dressed in an array of unattractive nightwear, and all listening intently to whatever he had to say. 'I think we should discuss this in private. Reputations are so easily ruined when business – both personal and otherwise – is discussed in public.'

'Who is it, dear?' The voice was high and set his teeth on edge. Abbie's mother.

Gatehouse blinked. 'Everything's under control. Get back to bed.' He turned back to Anthony. 'In the study, I suppose, but you'd better not be wasting my time, whoever you are.'

Anthony almost crowed out loud, pleased that this obnoxious man knew his name but not his face.

Gatehouse made his way down the stairs.

'I'm Anthony Wesley,' said Anthony, half expecting to see Gatehouse stumble at the mention of his name.

Just as he had supposed, Gatehouse stopped in his tracks. He looked stunned. 'So you're the one who she's been colluding with, and against her own father.'

For a moment, Anthony thought their interview was at an end. But Gatehouse, obviously curious, led him into a room lined with books, dark and smelling of beeswax.

Anthony spun quickly round, taking Gatehouse off guard. 'Where's Abbie?'

'And what business is that of yours?'

'She's a dear friend and I owe her a lot. I want to know that she's all right.'

'You! If it wasn't for you, she'd be married and settled, and not causing embarrassment to her family.'

Anthony strolled over to the desk, fiddled with a letter opener then picked it up as he might a dinner knife. 'I think you could cause enough embarrassment to this family without Abbie's assistance,' he said, his eyes following the letter opener as he scraped it along the soft green leather top.

'What do you mean?' said Gatehouse, his eyes now following the course of the knife.

Anthony enjoyed torturing him, making him wait to see whether he'd cut through the sleek leather. He didn't need to look to know his face was turning puce, to see the fear in the arrogant eyes.

'A certain establishment. You've been seen there. Does your wife know?'

'Get out!' shouted Gatehouse, half-rising to his feet. He glanced nervously towards the door.

'Does your wife also know about your unnatural affection for your daughter?'

'How dare you!' Gatehouse exploded.

Anthony felt as though he'd grown ten feet tall. He had seen the fear in his adversary's eyes; he knew then that he'd guessed right.

'You see, I did some checking before I got here. You're a wicked man, Mr Gatehouse. You like young girls. The house you frequented; your daughter followed you there. That's when she realised how wicked you were.'

The blood drained from the other man's face. *I've hit the right spot! I've got him!*

In the midst of triumph, a feeling of nausea rose from his stomach. Imagine, he thought, this obese, sweating, red-faced man with a slim young girl barely an adolescent. He swallowed his revulsion, forcing himself to stick to what he'd come for. 'So where's Abbie?'

Gatehouse slumped back in his chair, his face pale, beads of sweat trickling down his brow. He ran his fingers over his sweaty forehead. 'She could have gone to prison.'

The excuses were expected. Anthony waited for him to explain.

'She almost killed Harry Allen. Do you know that?'

'Would the world be a worse place without him, I wonder?'

'But he could have pressed charges. There would have been a trial and then how would I have looked? One daughter running away, one daughter in prison.' He hung his head. 'It doesn't bear thinking about. If she'd have just got married like other respectable women...'

Anthony couldn't believe what he was hearing. Everything Gatehouse was saying put the blame squarely on Abbie's shoulders. What did he actually know about respectable women?

Anthony took in the opulent surroundings. It was a big house. There were plenty of places to hide. 'I'm going up to get her and I don't want anyone stopping me,' he said, turning and making his way to the stairs.

'She's not here! We had to put her somewhere safe until things died down. Anyway, it will give her time to get her mind in some sort of order.'

Anthony remembered what the police officer had said. A mental condition. His blood froze.

It felt good to squeeze the fat man's throat.

'Please,' Gatehouse spluttered, taken off balance by the sudden attack.

A red mist had burst like a dam before Anthony's eyes. 'I would dearly love to throttle you, you bastard! I would dearly love to squeeze your throat until your eyes pop from your sockets. Now! Tell me! Where is she?'

27

He didn't care that it was four in the morning when he arrived at the wrought-iron gates and saw the sign that sent a shiver down his spine.

Reverlow House, Institute for the Insane

Not expecting to get an answer, he rang the bell and heard a clanging from the porter's lodge. No one came. Well, he certainly wasn't going to wait for dawn!

The gates rattled as he heaved himself up, his feet finding an easy foothold among the swirling patterns of rigid leaves and iron roses. The drive to the main building weaved around scattered bushes and ancient trees. He took the short cut, uncaring that the ground was soft beneath his shoes, the grass soaking his trousers.

A faint light was fanning out from the east by the time he made the main door.

He pulled the bellpull and from within the high old building he heard the ominous ringing, but there were no footsteps, no lights, no sign that anyone acknowledged his arrival. He rang more firmly but still there was no response.

'Come on!' He pulled more aggressively for the third time. 'Answer the damn door, will you!' he shouted. 'What is it? Are you all deaf in there? Are you all dead?'

* * *

Abigail was staring at the bars crisscrossing the window in a pattern that was loosely described as Gothic Revival. The walls were white, the floors bare and all windows and doors were stone-framed and fashioned to ape the pointed arches of a medieval abbey.

Every night since her arrival, she had stared at those bars, willing herself to wake up from the nightmare of a place of strange sounds where only the whitewashed stone matched the clinical coldness of uniformed staff.

Every morning, she stared at her reflection as she combed what used to be silky, red hair now lying lank and lifeless against her head. Without makeup, her face was too pale, her eyes too round, the pupils lighter than the dark lines beneath them.

'What am I doing with these mad people?' she had demanded.

They'd stripped her, dressed her in a stiff, cotton gown and locked her in a room with two souls who looked to have every right to be there.

'You'll soon settle in,' they told her. 'And you won't be lacking company.'

As though she had anything in common with these creatures! 'This is my father's doing!' she shouted. 'He doesn't want me to tell anyone what he's been up to and why my sister ran away. He likes little girls! Yes! That's it! He likes them too much. He's a monster, do you hear me? A monster!'

'She's suffering from delusions, the doctor says. Leave her a while. She'll soon adjust.' Their indifference filled her with horror. So did the fact that money could buy anything, including a doctor's lies.

The creatures who shared her room had simple faces and vacant eyes. One of them grabbed hold of her hair and pushed her against the door. Bad breath covered her nostrils and uncut nails dug into her scalp. 'What have you done with my friend? You can't stay here. That's my friend's bed! Where is she?'

Abigail fought to control the woman's claw-like fingers. She felt pity for her but she was also frightened. Eventually she hit her to the floor.

'You've hurt me,' the woman wailed.

The other woman did not appear to have noticed her. Bereft of expression, she sat on a narrow bed. The mattress looked terribly thin, the blankets patched and smelly. She cradled a rag doll, rocking backwards and forwards, backwards and forwards, and forever humming, morning, noon and night. Sometimes she spoke to the doll as though it was a flesh-and-blood child.

'I want to go home,' Abigail said to the attendant who brought their food. 'I want to speak to my parents.'

'This is your home,' the woman had answered. 'You're ill.'

'Ill! Of course I'm not ill. Do I look ill? Do I sound ill? I'm not like these two.'

'No,' said the nurse. She had the stink of mental anguish about her. 'You're not like them at all. They've never tried to kill anybody.'

Abigail stared after her as the truth dawned. Harry Allen was the excuse given for placing her here, but not the real reason. Her father feared anyone finding out the truth. Carrie would stay quiet for her family's sake. Abigail, he knew, would not.

Fear ran like ice through her veins. She had not expected him to do something so drastic to protect himself.

An unrelenting future of white rooms and white uniforms was all she could look forward to.

Sleep deprivation was self-destructive, she'd read. At least if she was mad herself perhaps she wouldn't notice how dreadful things were. But it wasn't just that keeping her awake night after night. It was the noises, the sounds of disturbed people sleeping, dreaming and crying for things they couldn't have and had never experienced.

There were also the sounds of a building settling down for the night as though it too was about to sleep, confident that its inhabitants were safely locked away behind its thick walls and stout doors.

Tonight, she heard a bell sounding. It rang again and again. Someone should answer it, she thought, and wondered why they didn't. Someone should be on duty and aware of anyone screaming or crying or even of the doorbell ringing. But the attendants were as human as anyone. Duties were sometimes neglected in favour of a good night's sleep or a rendezvous in a shared bed veiled in darkness.

Abigail sat up, listened to her roommates, hearing only the sound of their drugged breathing. That was another reason why no one was on duty. What was the point if all the patients were given hot drinks laced with something calming before bedtime? Her roommates drank Abigail's every night. They slept like logs. Abigail stayed awake.

The bell rang on. Someone was determined to be heard.

Perhaps she could see who it was.

The floor was cold beneath her feet. She shivered as she reached for her dressing gown and slippers. Quietly but swiftly she went over to the windows. Down below, something moved.

The figure was familiar, one she'd long dreamed of. But could it be? She rubbed at her eyes. 'I'm dreaming.' She looked again. 'I'm not dreaming!' Her spirits soared.

Anthony!

Sliding her hand through the bars, she wrenched the catch and pushed the window open.

'Anthony!' Her shout was a strange mixture of loudness and the hushing sound mothers use to soothe frightened children. At first, he looked around him, not sure of direction.

She said it again and this time he looked up. 'Abbie. I've come to get you out,' he shouted back.

'That's... that's... absolutely marvellous,' she said, tears streaming down her face. Her old sarcasm returned with a flourish. 'Now how do you propose to do that, Sir Lancelot? Full-frontal assault or have you brought me a pair of spare wings?'

'Abbie, you've never been an angel, so why start now?' When he disappeared again, she was overcome with panic.

Just as it threatened to set her knees shaking, he reappeared. This time he had a ladder. Slowly, too slowly for her liking, he climbed closer and closer. Finally, they were facing each other.

'Abbie.'

'Anthony,' she said through her tears. 'I never thought...'

Suddenly, he leaned forward and kissed her. 'Of course you did. You're always glad to see me, aren't you, Abbie?'

He didn't give her time to reply. In his right hand he held a crowbar.

'This shouldn't take long,' he said. 'The metal's pretty rusty on this side. That's the problem with cast iron. Wrought iron's a lot stronger, you know, but cast iron can disintegrate quickly, depending on the quality, of course...' He went on talking as he tackled the bars, his voice hushed.

'That's it,' he said at last as the bars gave way with a grating crunch of rusted metal against crumbling stone. 'Now just wait there. We don't want to wake anyone, do we?'

Before he'd reached the bottom of the ladder, Abigail had cocked one leg over the window ledge and found the first rung.

'Well, that's Abbie for you,' he muttered to himself.

Eventually her toes touched the ground and he was looking her over as though she was a bag of dirty washing. 'Not your style,' he said with a grin, indicating the voluminous attire.

To his surprise, she did not respond. She shook slightly, and it wasn't because it was cold.

'Are you all right?'

She nodded. 'I am now.'

Her eyes flickered towards the bleak building and swiftly away again.

'It was horrible. Don't ask me about it.'

'I won't.'

He sensed something had changed but he wasn't sure what.

He tried again.

'Welcome to earth,' he said more gently. He wrapped his arms round her and closed his eyes. She gripped him just as tightly, whispering his name.

'You can't imagine how worried I was,' he said.

'Stop looking so pleased with yourself! You're no Sir Lancelot rescuing Guinevere.'

He pretended to be hurt. 'If I go down on my knees...'

'We don't have time.'

He glanced up at the dark windows to the right and left of the top of the ladder. 'We have to go.'

Keeping low, they darted off through the shadows. 'I want to confront him,' she said as they ran.

'Your father?'

'Who else?'

'Do we have to?'

'I most certainly do!'

He knew from the tone of her voice that nothing would stop her.

* * *

It was midday before they reached Pearcemore Park. She flounced past the surprised butler. Anthony followed, stunned again to awed silence by the opulence surrounding him. The reception hall alone was double the space most people lived in.

'Who is that disturbing my Sunday lunch, Baxter?'

Baxter's jaw hung open a while before he spoke. 'Your daughter, sir.'

'Caroline!' His joy was obvious. Abigail smarted.

He stopped in his tracks when he saw her, the joy freezing on his face.

'What are...?' He looked past her to Anthony. 'Why did you bring her here? What are you after? I'll not pay you. I'll not be blackmailed!'

He sweated. His face was red and his eyes darted nervously between the two of them.

Anthony's dislike deepened.

It was Abigail who spoke. 'I'm here for two reasons. Number one: I want some decent clothes.' She indicated the nightgown she was still wearing. 'This isn't quite to my taste. I also want you to put this right, Father.'

He blustered again as he had with Anthony. 'It was for your own good. A young girl like you should—'

'Make things right, Father,' she said. Her mother looked tearful. Abigail felt sorry for her but as things were, she could not bring herself to make peace. Her mother *must* have known how it was with her father. She had done nothing to curb his behaviour.

Her father's eyes flitted around and there was an uncharacteristic paleness to his face.

He nodded. 'Yes. I'll do that. I'll instruct the institution that you are quite cured and they are not to pursue you.'

Anthony watched silently. He couldn't take his eyes off either the father or daughter. Looking at the father, he was beginning to understand why Abigail dressed and acted the way she did: to protect herself. He found both his admiration and his affection for her growing.

'I'll get some fresh clothes,' she said to him.

Whilst Antony waited, his eyes held her father's. 'Do you know how I'm feeling, Gatehouse?'

There was no response. His expression stayed the same; the pomposity was still there. He didn't want the likes of him in his home.

'Then I'll tell you, sir. I want to physically beat you.' Gatehouse jumped without his feet leaving the floor.

'But what good would that do,' Anthony continued, his hands curling to fists in his pockets. 'What you did will always hang over you. It will always be there.'

It was hard not to punch the man's face to a pulp, but he held himself back. What would that prove? What would he gain? Satisfaction, he thought. That's all. Just pure satisfaction. Upstairs in her room, Abigail bundled trousers, shirts and even a dress into a bag. Her maid tried to help, but she wanted to do this for herself.

For the last time ever, she looked out of the window and took great gulps of air. There were men outside cutting the grass with great, long scythes. They glanced up and she waved. A man alighted from a car. He looked like her father's lawyer, or perhaps one of his bankers. The look on his face was similar to her father's: pompous and without warmth.

He too looked up, saw her and raised his hat.

The old Abigail, the one who liked to shock, re-emerged from where she'd been hiding.

She smiled: one act of bravado beneath her father's roof. The breeze disturbed her nightgown and the stink of carbolic. Beneath it, she was naked. Standing before the window, inviting attention, she pulled the nightgown off over her head and flung it out.

All the men, those scything the grass and the pompous man from the car, looked up in amazement.

'I'm free,' she shouted, naked as the day she was born and waving her arms above her head. 'I'm free!'

She danced around the room.

When she came downstairs, her mother was slumped in a chair. Even her father looked shocked.

'Am I missing something?' She looked searchingly at Anthony, then at her father for signs of a broken nose or a cracked jaw.

'It would be ideal for her to get married, but you...' Gatehouse began.

'I have prospects,' said Anthony quickly. 'I've been offered the chance of a political position. Eventually, I'll get a seat in the House of Commons. Be in no doubt, Mr Gatehouse: the Labour movement has only just begun.' He had adopted a serious expression, the sort he considered would command respect. 'I shall have grave responsibilities and feel that Abigail would make me the perfect wife. She has a taste for politics. I think we would do well together.'

Abigail was speechless.

'If that's all right with you, Abbie; what do you think?'

Her mind raced. His proposal was far from romantic, but she didn't care. They were made for each other.

'We can do great things together,' she said, in a forthright manner, the sort a political speaker might use.

'Well, that settles that, then.' He picked up his hat.

'I think so.'

'Is that your only piece of luggage?'

'It's all I need.'

The conversation was between them alone. They were cocooned in their own world. No one else mattered.

28

Limewashed walls shone slightly yellow in the fragile sun of late April. The blue slate tiles of the cottage roof looked wet even though it hadn't rained for weeks.

Elliot's father had opened and shut the lock on the Kennet Canal for some years now. Orchards and woodlands framed the cottage, roses climbed riotously around the front door, and marigolds blazed like flames against the windows. Against the walls, lilac blossom too big for its own good nodded on skinny stems, its old-fashioned perfume lying heavy on the air.

There was a vegetable garden at the rear where Josiah Beaven grew peas and scarlet-flowering runners, and a host of tomatoes, carrots, green cabbages and purple-flowering broccoli. Petals from the orchard blew like pink and white snow along the towpath. Among the trees, two or three pigs grunted as they gobbled up what remained of last year's apples and last night's meal that had been deposited over the fence for their benefit. Hens clucked and pecked in a wire-netting run, and a few geese honked as they strutted around the yard before dipping their heads beneath the fence and joining the rest of the menagerie in the orchard.

Beth loved the place. If she could have married Elliot purely to live in his father's cottage, she would have done. He was a different man here, gentler, as though the soft blossom, the natural smells, had some effect upon his disposition and his mind.

When they had lost the boat two years ago, he had broken down, cried like a baby. She and Pamela had cried with him, the baby's little lungs bellowing as if she knew their lives had changed forever.

Six months after that, Carrie, with George and her new baby, Arabella, passed through.

Beth introduced them to her own new baby, Elizabeth, named after her mother. 'And I'm expecting another,' she said.

Carrie congratulated her.

As the men leaned over the lock, talked and peered into the water, the women made themselves comfortable at the kitchen table. Beth had made tea.

Carrie drew the shawl over the face of her sleeping child. 'I hear Robbie's joined the army.'

'Yes. Milk?'

'Yes, please.'

Beth added milk to Carrie's cup. 'I'm glad.'

Beth looked at her over her raised teacup. 'Did he try to see the baby?'

'No. I think he lost interest.'

'He wanted to see the world. That's what he told my father.' Beth sensed there was something else Carrie wanted to say and instinctively knew what – or rather whom – it concerned.

'You've seen Anthony Wesley.'

Carrie nodded, sipped and finally raised her eyes. 'Anthony is married.'

'Oh! More tea?'

'Yes, please.'

Her throat was suddenly dry but she tried not to show it. 'Good luck to him and her whoever she is.' The tea helped her throat. She'd presumed that was all, but she could see by Carrie's face that there was more.

'He married Abigail. He's my brother-in-law.' The tea slopped in the cup as her hand shook.

'I never thought Abigail would marry. She had plans for making her way in the world by herself.'

'Don't be fooled by my sister's bluff exterior,' Carrie said, nestling her baby against a breast swollen by motherhood. 'She's soft in the middle. I should know; she looked after me for years when we were small.'

'I wish them luck,' said Beth. 'Tell them that if you see them.'

Carrie sighed with relief. 'I'm so glad you're over him. You *are* over him, aren't you?'

'Yes! Yes. Of course I am.'

For days afterwards, Beth threw herself into anything that might make her joints ache and her brain tired.

The pigs needed cleaning out, the hen house too, and there were flowers to gather in the orchard and put in old jam jars and painted buckets they'd brought off the boat. Anything, even scraping the pigsty, was better than thinking about Anthony and Abigail.

Beth heard her father-in-law calling her. 'Time for tea.' His voice was bell-like. After he'd called her, he called his sons. Four o'clock, never a minute earlier nor a minute later. Josiah Beaven was a man who respected time and kept to it.

Widowed almost fifteen years ago, Elliot's father didn't mind making tea or cooking even though there was now a woman in the house. He was used to it, and judging by the straightness of his walk and the way he held his chin, anyone criticising his independence was likely to get short shrift.

Wiping the sweat from her eyes, she shut the door to the sty behind her.

In the warm glow of the afternoon light, when shafts of sunlight gleamed through the trees, father and son walked together. With her children, she enjoyed the long grass and the sweet smells of this place that had brought such calm to her life. She looked at her children beneath the trees and her daughter chasing passing butterflies. Carrie's news about Anthony Wesley took her thoughts back to the dreams she'd shared with him. She'd wanted to open a school for the narrowboat children.

'What a dream,' she murmured to herself.

Ahead of her, the two men stopped in their tracks as the sound of someone talking came from the direction of the hen house.

Like them, her eyes followed the angular figure of Gareth Beaven, Elliot's brother. When she'd first come here, she'd assumed he was talking to the pigs or the geese. Only those who knew him realised he was talking to his dead comrades.

Josiah Beaven thrust the stem of his unlit pipe into his mouth. Like his son and daughter-in-law, his eyes followed Gareth's shambling form. A black-and-tan dog followed, head almost pressed against the young man's calf.

Clearing his throat, Josiah tapped the bowl of his pipe out on a fence post. 'The old dog still follows him everywhere.'

'Two of a kind,' said Elliot.

'Aye. Both shell-shocked. Even when he hides himself away in the chicken coop, the dog waits for him outside. Until he's better. Until he's himself again.'

The old man spat on to the weeds that flowered white and yellow in three-foot-high clumps beside the boundary wall.

'And no word on the pension,' said Elliot.

'Fit enough, they say. When he's up before the board, he gives little sign of anything being wrong – in his body. They say the condition I'm describing is that of a malingerer!' He scowled and spat again. 'Coward, they means! But they don't say it. Not in so many words. Not to my face! They just imply – that's the word – imply that he was lucky not to be shot.'

Elliot shook his head.

His father turned to Beth. 'You reading to him has done a great deal of good,' he said to her. 'Helps him forget, it does – as best he's able.'

'Glad we could help,' said Elliot. 'Ain't that right, Beth?'

'It is. In time I think I'll be able to get him to write, especially once the children start learning.'

The men nodded at her and each other. Then they were off in deep conversation as they disappeared through the cottage door. But she was not ready to go back inside and neither was her eldest child, who was already running towards the orchard.

There was a sudden movement of her skirt. The dog was looking up at her with misty eyes, his old tail wagging slowly. She gently rubbed his head. The tail wagged faster.

'Max!'

Gareth was standing next to the stable block at the corner of the orchard. People avoided being alone with him, thinking he was mad because he talked to his old pals who'd gone 'over the top' and become part of the mud of no-man's-land. He was staring at her, his brows dark and deep over his eyes and his mouth grim.

She looked down at the dog. 'Let's see your master, shall we?'

Gareth had turned away by the time she got there and was stroking the muzzle of a skewbald horse, one of the sturdy sort used for generations to pull thirty-ton loads along the waterways of England. Keeping one was a sentimental act on Josiah's part.

Instinctively, she said nothing but did as he did, appreciating the velvet-soft muzzle. A cold shiver ran down her back when she looked into Gareth's haunted eyes. She had forgotten how alike the brothers were. The only difference was the white streaks among the dark-red hair.

With a broad smile she said, 'I like horses. Do you?'

He hesitated. She looked up at him and briefly felt like an intruder in his world.

'I like all animals.' His voice was shaky and there was a faraway look in his eyes.

'What about people?' she asked softly; loud voices frightened him.

'Depends. Depends...'

He hesitated, as though knowing what it depended on but being unable to identify the right words. 'Depends what they're wearing. Khaki. And red,' he added suddenly, his voice high and thin. 'Red. Like poppies in a field. Fallen flowers! Fallen flowers!'

His voice rose like a battle hymn then faded away.

Beth's smile froze on her lips. What was he seeing as he gazed off beyond her and the cottage, the fields and the woods? And all the time, his fingers rapped – rattatty tap – on the stable door.

She laid her hand over his and softly began to sing a lullaby she sang to the children. Although her throat was dry, she kept singing, willing her voice to be soft, the words gentle.

Like a door with rusty hinges, his mouth creaked into a smile. The distant look in his eyes disappeared. It was as if the man himself had just returned.

'Beth,' he said with gentle surprise as if seeing her for the first time. 'Is Elliot with you?'

She nodded, her eyes filling with tears because he had forgotten that they'd been living here for quite a while now. Some days, some moments, were better than others.

His gaze landed on her hair. 'I like your hair. It's black.'

His touch took her by surprise. She stepped back and he looked frightened as though she had slapped him or pinched him.

'It's all right,' she said, instantly regretting it. She reached for his hand and laid it flat on her head again. 'It's all right, Gareth. It's all right.'

When he smiled, it turned to laughter and she laughed with him. Like the sunny day and the deep blue sky, he was reborn – at least for the moment.

Suddenly, Elliot's shadow fell halfway between her and the cottage door. He had a strange look on his face.

'I don't care what you think, but I'm going ahead and doing it anyway so listen to what I've got to say!'

'I don't understand.'

'The old man's retiring. Wants me to take over. He'll help when he can, but his bones are going. There's Tommy Brown who helps out now and again. I'll train him up. And our Gareth will be able to help out – in time.'

Arms crossed in front of him, he looked at her as if inviting her to protest.

She nodded thoughtfully, her eyes fixed on his. 'You, Gareth, the children, your father, and me all living here together. Is that what you're saying?' she said, hardly able to keep a straight face, hardly able to believe this answer to her prayers.

'Aye!'

She clapped her hands together gleefully. 'It's a wonderful idea!'

'It is?' He looked surprised.

'So what made you think I'd be likely to protest?'

He shrugged. 'You was born on the boats. I wasn't sure…'

She kissed his cheek. 'Everything is going our way. Even the weather.'

29

On a day at the end of October that year, the skies turned black and someone in heaven turned on the biggest water tap ever made. Gutters, drainpipes and downpipes gurgled with the heavy rain that drummed on the corrugated roof of the hen house. Beth came back from feeding and cleaning out the animals with her hair matted to her head. Excess water trickled down all their faces, dripped from noses and saturated cottons and woollens until everyone smelt of wet sheep. By early evening, the sky was the colour of lead, relieved here and there by rebel pockets of cloud that dared be a shade lighter. Beth lit the oil lamp, its amber glow glancing around the simply furnished room as she carried it from the window ledge to the table.

An evening meal steamed on platters of pure white Staffordshire. Elliot reached for bread to accompany the bacon-hock stew already in his mouth. Tonight, they were alone. Gareth and Josiah were attending yet another tribunal about Gareth's pension and the walk back from the station would take longer in the rain.

Beth spooned the last mouthful of mixed-up vegetables on to

Elizabeth's little pink tongue. Pamela was old enough to feed herself.

All was well with the world. Elliot was a better man than he had been.

'I hear the village school's to close,' he said suddenly.

Beth looked up in alarm. 'Why?'

'Old Miss Pratt says she's too old to run it any more, so them children remaining will have to walk to Cheveney instead.'

'That's four miles away!'

'That's right. Some won't bother.' Since reading to Gareth, Elliot's attitude to reading and writing had changed drastically.

'I'll have to teach ours myself, but what about the boat children?'

Up until then, the narrowboats passing through had been able to stop at the junction half a mile further along. The children had only needed to walk five hundred yards to the village school. Cheveney was much further for them to go.

Elliot looked up, saw her expression and put down his cutlery.

'Don't even think it! Teach our own. You can't take on a whole schoolroom. Besides, there's us to take care of.'

That night, she stared at the ceiling, thinking about that old dream about teaching the narrowboat children. Just a dream. She tried to sleep. The dream refused to go away.

* * *

Winter was wetter than autumn. The cottage was lit by a mellow light and warmed by a roaring fire.

It was just after supper when the warning bell sounded. It hung in the lock and was used to alert the lock keeper by any boatman wanting to go through. The boatman merely reached up and gave it a tug.

Elliot took his fob watch from the pocket of his black corduroy waistcoat. 'Don't that man know the lock's closed at six?' After glancing regretfully at what remained on his plate, he reached for his cap and his jacket then opened the door and bawled out for Tommy. 'Damn that boy! Gone rabbiting again, I'll be bound!'

Beth checked the sash that held Elizabeth in her chair.

A blast of wet came in from outside as Elliot opened the door. 'Let me help you,' she said, wiping her hands down her apron in a business-like fashion as she got to her feet.

'No. Stay here. It's my work, not yours.'

Elizabeth chose that very moment to regurgitate her food and send it running down her clean smock.

'Oh, Lizzie!'

Elliot lingered by the door, as though he was thinking something through.

'Get on and close that door, Elliot. This place is getting damp,' she said as she mopped up the mess.

'You're a good wife, Beth. I think I should say that. And I ain't always been the best of husbands; I think I should say that too.'

For a moment, neither the words nor the meaning registered. When she finally stared at him, he just smiled, winked and closed the door behind him. It touched her heart. Later that night, she would remember it more clearly.

What was left of the evening light seemed to go with him as the lamp flickered on the last drop of oil. With the slamming of the door, a great silence descended.

Beth looked around her. The walls were lumpy, the furniture old but comfortable. This place had become home, and yet she found it hard to rid herself of an odd feeling that everything was about to change.

Ten minutes later, she looked up from clearing away dishes. She'd heard something, had half fancied it was a scream, but couldn't be sure. A gutter gave way just above the scullery window. A torrent of rainwater gushed over the panes and bounced off the window ledge. The weather was making her imagine things. She bent back to the dishes.

The rain was drumming on roofs, doors and windows. She sang as she worked. A sudden hammering at the door startled her; she dropped a dish. She left it there, apprehension returning.

A soaking-wet woman stood there, the hem of her skirt sticking to her legs, streams of water trickling from her face. It was the wife of the boatman wanting to pass through the lock.

'He's trapped under the boat. He slipped! He went right under! There was nothing we could do. Nothing!'

She ran through the pouring rain, screaming all the way across the yard to the lock. Elliot's father and Gareth chose that moment to return and heard her, both rallying to her screams.

She vaguely remembered the boatman telling her what had happened.

Blinded by the rain and the wind, Elliot had lost his footing on the side of the lock. He'd slipped into the rushing flood of water. The lock was barely wide enough to take the width of the boat. The water released into the pound had been rising quickly. The boat had risen with it. At first Elliot's head had showed above the surface, but not for long. Trapped between the side of the lock and the side of the boat, he had been hit on the head and gone under. Fully laden, the boat sealed him in the water. Nothing the boatman could have done would have saved him.

* * *

They buried Elliot in the little churchyard up on the hill where the church spire looked westwards to the Severn and the Welsh borders and north-eastwards to the honeycomb-coloured cottages of the Cotswolds. Everyone from the boats attended the funeral.

'What will you do now?' Carrie asked her.

Beth took a deep breath because she needed to answer and she was determined she would sound positive despite the daunting possibilities.

'Elliot's father has lost the heart to continue. Gareth isn't really...' She was going to say *interested*, but that wasn't true. Gareth did what he could when he could. 'I'll run things until they find someone else to take it over. I'm sure I can get a boy...' She was going to say *a boy like Tommy*, but he had disappeared after the accident. 'I'm sure there's a willing boy somewhere to help with the lock.'

Carrie nodded. 'I wrote to Abigail and Anthony and told them about Elliot. I hope you don't mind.'

Beth threw her a sharp look. 'But they were too busy to come, I suppose.'

Carrie's expression was strained. 'I don't think that's the case, Beth. I thought about writing to them before I actually did, I wasn't sure how you'd feel about it so they might not have got the letter yet.'

Beth desperately wanted to ask her on what day she had actually posted it, but pride stilled her tongue. Instead, she looked at her mother, who was sitting on a cracked and mossy tomb singing to a contented Pamela.

A gruff voice said, 'Time we got round to giving him a send-off.'

At one time, Beth would have cowered at her father's voice and his shadow falling darkly across her. But she was numb inside. Nobody like him would ever hurt her again.

'You mean the pub?'

'Of course I mean the pub, woman. Singing hymns wets a man's appetite.'

'Does it now.'

'Don't give me that sarcasm!'

'Don't bully me. Not here in this place! Not in any place! Not ever again! I have my own life and I don't need you to tell me the rules I should live by just because I'm a woman.'

Bewildered by her onslaught, he stepped back, slipped on the wet grass and tumbled back on to a flat-topped tombstone. She couldn't help the wry smile and cheeky comment. 'You can lay around there if you like, but I'm off in the warm,' she said. Her father-in-law and Gareth went in with her.

The range in the cottage kitchen was four times the size of the sort used on the narrowboats. She had arranged chairs around it so those feeling the graveyard chill could dry out before its convivial glow.

'He's gone looking for the pub,' she said to her mother. 'I'll just have tea.'

Her mother nodded.

'So will I,' said George Melcroft who, although he smiled and bounced Pamela on his knee, had no eyes for any baby except his own – or the one he believed to be his own.

'She's growing,' Beth said to Carrie and her friend looked pleased.

30

The smell of breakfast had escaped from the kitchen and up the stairs, encouraging her to rise early and sit ready in the dining room. She liked her coffee hot. Anthony liked it tepid. The pot had cooled by the time he appeared. Whilst she waited, it was her habit to open post addressed to Mr and Mrs Wesley. Some men might not approve, but Anthony had never suggested she should do otherwise.

One letter above all others this morning caught her undivided attention. Carrie had written to her. Her fingers ripped at the cheap white envelope. When she saw what it said, her heart began to race and the old jealousy awoke from its sleep. Her marriage was happy. Nothing must upset their lives now, not even the death of someone they'd once known. And who was he anyway? A nobody.

Abigail sat upright, her coffee untouched. She had one question in her mind, one question she had never thought to have to face. What would her husband do if he knew Beth was free now? She got up and went to the mantelpiece.

Anthony's passion for the little boat girl had been powerful to the point of obsession. She wasn't sure that a marriage certificate would be enough to stop him straying. Even Edward yelling for his breakfast failed to interrupt her concentration.

'Nurse!' she heard Anthony call. 'The baby's crying.'

Abigail Wesley, who had been Gatehouse, was the mother of a handsome baby boy: an amazing fact. Just as amazing was the fact that she was standing here by the fireplace dressed in a dress of pale turquoise silk trimmed with bands of pink and lemon. She also wore silk stockings and high-heeled shoes – even before breakfast!

The letter shook in her hand. She shivered. What a lonely future she might have had if Anthony and Beth had followed their hearts the same way she had followed hers.

Quickly, just barely pre-empting that moment he entered the room, she shoved the letter behind the clock. Abigail didn't like the clock very much but it was a gift from Gilbert. There was something very satisfying about giving it a place in the sitting room when Gilbert would have preferred a place in her bedroom.

'Isn't it working?' Anthony said casually nodding at the clock before shaking out his newspaper.

'Yes!' she said brightly. 'Of course it is. I was just looking at the walls and wondering what colour I should have them repainted them in the spring. Eggshell-blue I think, or perhaps *eau de nil*.'

'Look all right as they are to me.' His eyes stayed on the headlines and the articles he needed to know about. He sat in the big armchair by the window that looked out across the lawn to the privet hedge and the copse beyond.

Abigail eyed him appraisingly. If clothes made the man then they had certainly done the power of good to Anthony since he had married her and entered politics. Always an impressive presence, he now looked more professional in his sharply cut suit and crisp white shirt. A silver pocket watch dangled from his waistcoat.

He is now the type of man people would trust with their nation, she thought decisively. She bent over him and kissed the top of his head. 'Enjoy your breakfast, darling?'

He laughed a low morning laugh that hadn't yet grown large with the day. 'You're beginning to sound like your mother!'

'Oh no! I don't, do I? I never meant to get like that,' she said and for one wonderful moment she had an urge to turn back time. Again, she was single and wearing mannish clothes, pretending to be something she wasn't. A bit, she thought, like the principal boy in the pantomimes she'd taken part in at school.

A female hand rapped smartly at the door. 'Beg your pardon, Mrs Wesley, but young Edward is ready for his breakfast, and if you remember I did say I had to see my sick mother. The brake is already here,' said the nurse.

'I'll be right there,' said Abigail. To Anthony she said, 'I'll be back to hear what you've been doing all week.'

Anthony grunted, his eyes fixed on the newspaper headlines that shouted out about cutting the miners' wages, cutting any man's wages in industries feeling the bite of a failing economy. But what about the bites taken out of a loaf of bread? One penny less meant one less loaf, one less mouthful of food for a famished child in a poverty-stricken family!

'Have you read this?' He looked up to find that the door had closed and he was alone in the room.

Having no one to discuss the situation with, he flung the paper to one side and sprang out of his chair. 'Well, that's enough of that!'

Thrusting his hands into his pockets, he slowly strode to the fireplace where he rested one arm on the mantelpiece and stared down at the brass fender, polished by a slip of a girl before he got up.

Reading of other people's suffering caused his own wealth – or rather his wife's – to lie uncomfortably on his mind. Perhaps it was self-punishment that made him place his leg so near the fire and hold it there until he could stand the heat no more. Whatever made him do it, the result was that when the heat did get too much, he clenched his fist, flung out his arm and hit the clock so hard that one of the gilded cherubs went clattering down into the grate.

'Best place for the bloody thing!' he exclaimed. Then he sighed. Not being a man who liked seeing things broken, he reached down to pick it up. After glancing over his shoulder to see if the coast was clear, he attempted to stick it back where it belonged.

It wasn't really that difficult because the little chap's feet were still attached to the clock. The snapped legs fitted easily into place. It was now just a question of keeping him there. He shifted the clock round slightly so he could get a better grip, and as he did so, the letter and its envelope fell forward. He frowned. The one thing he could say about his marriage was that he and his wife were honest with each other. So why hide a letter?

His fingers brushed the cheap paper. One simple question rose in his mind. What or who was the one thing to incite her distrust?

Fold by fold the words within were exposed to his gaze. The secret of who it was from and what it was about became clear.

His eyes first went to the bottom of the page.

Love, Carrie

Her sister! That fact in itself was no reason for her to hide the letter. He read from the beginning and the past flooded over him.

He closed his eyes. What should he do? Burn it? He couldn't bring himself to do that.

When he reopened it, the words leapt up at him and sank deep beyond his mind and into his heart. Beth's husband was dead. According to the date on the letter, he was buried by now and Beth was alone.

Alone and available. But he wasn't!

The paper crackled as he crumpled it in his hand. He threw his head back. *Why didn't I wait? Why didn't I wait!*

So obsessed was he that he did not hear the door opening or soft footsteps on thickly woven rugs. When he finally opened his eyes Abigail's gaze met his. She looked troubled, frightened even.

He did his best to lick the dryness from his lips and quell his anger. 'Why did you hide it?'

'I was going to tell you.'

He swallowed. Despite the firm set of her jaw, her fingers were tangled tightly together in front of her and her knuckles were white. She was lying.

There were a lot of things he wanted to say, things he wanted to shout and scream at her. But he was not that sort of man. Anger was something he thought about before acting and he certainly never got angry with those he loved and who loved him. And he did love Abigail – in his own way – but not in the same way as Beth. The passion, as his wife had guessed, still raged within him.

'It's none of your business!' blurted Abigail. 'Her own people will take care of her. You have your own family to think of, and of course your career. There's no time to go to other people's funerals.'

Shoulders stiff with tension, she marched towards the window and stared at the neatly tended borders laid out by a gardener to her explicit instructions. Perhaps he was right. She was getting like her mother and all the other old hens who clucked around her. She had the lifestyle they had, the servants, the comfort. Something of that old hunger to put the world to rights had died the moment Anthony had slid a gold band on to her finger.

Anthony was astounded. 'Other people!'

He'd never heard her talk like this before. Where was the woman who had pleaded passionately at union headquarters to be allowed to help those worse off than her, especially women? How could she be so callous and why, for God's sake, hadn't he seen this side of her before?

Suddenly, he was angry. Not just with her but also with himself for being so blind, so impatient to have the career he wanted, that he had married a woman who meant something rather than one who meant everything.

Hands clenched, head bowed, he joined her, standing behind her and looking over her shoulder. 'Your attitude to the poor and uneducated might have changed, but mine has not. I owe Beth my life, I think. I cannot discard her friendship as easily as you can.'

She wanted to shout at him, *Friendship? It's far more than friendship!* But she controlled herself. Instead she said, 'I just think you have more important things to do.'

'She'll be upset and worrying about how she'll cope,' Anthony went on, his voice as steady as ever although he was boiling within. 'When I was physically hurt, she helped me. Now she's the one who's hurting, though hers is of the emotional kind.'

He paused. Abigail remained stiff and silent though her cheeks were reddening and her eyes were moist. The cause, he hoped, was regret at her attitude. He couldn't bring himself to be civil, so he turned away. Head bowed, he reached for the door handle.

Hearing it turn, Abigail spun round, eyes blazing with jealousy and fear. 'Where are you going?'

For a moment, he said nothing. His voice was low, resolute. 'I have to see her.'

'No! No, you are not going to see her!'

Not a muscle moved in his face. Neither did his eyes blink or his lips part. He told himself that the cause was right. Beth needed him.

'I will be back in time for supper.'

Such an even voice. Such a broad back, she thought, as he turned to go out of the door to another woman.

From the very first, she had ached with jealousy over every woman who had ever looked his way. With Beth, it had been different. He had shared his love of literature with a girl who had owned fewer than a dozen books in all her life.

Growing on her turbulent emotions, jealousy at last got the upper hand and exploded into anger.

'You still love her, don't you?'

Stiff as marble, he stood in the doorway. He had a certain look in his eyes and she recognised it for what it was. She had stated the truth and it was there in his eyes. The truth skewered her heart.

Cold words erupted from hot anger. 'If you visit her, Anthony Wesley, you need not come back to this house! *My* house,' she added and immediately wanted to bite off her tongue.

When he looked at her, she shivered. Then he was gone, the door closing slowly behind him.

'And don't come back!' Some semblance of the old Abigail returned to sustain her. She stormed over to the fireplace, rested her elbows on the mantelpiece and dug her clenched fists into her eyes.

'Come back,' she murmured, clenching her teeth so tight it hurt.

She hit the clock with her elbow; the cherub with the broken feet toppled, fell and broke in pieces.

31

The mangle was a luxury Beth much appreciated. Because the breeze was stiff and sending clouds scurrying like sheep across the sky, she knew the rain would keep off, at least for the next few hours. Clothes and towels blown fat like bulging cheeks were already hanging on the line.

Her skirt blew tight around the slim waist that had reappeared following the birth of her youngest daughter. At times like these, with her hair tossing around her face and the smell of budding bluebells coming from the woods, she almost felt like a girl again.

She paused a moment and shielded her eyes, gazing far off to a field beyond the copse. Ted Bertram, who farmed the land immediately bordering the canal, had purchased a mechanical tractor. Like any man of his age – he was around forty – his new toy was irresistible. She could hear it now, its loud drone like a very large bee. He was ploughing up and down the field. The sound seemed to fly towards her then change its mind, turn at the last moment and fly away again, the process repeated over and over again.

Another sound came to her. For a moment, she stopped

sticking pegs on to clothes and turned towards the canal. She saw no boats coming into the pound. Shaking her head, she turned her attention back to her washing. It was only the tractor. A boat skipper would ring the bell and Gareth and the new boy, Spiky Pike, who had been such a trooper at the strike, would deal with him. But the tractor was making a lot of noise. It was hard to tell.

Whipped by the breeze, the washing flapped and cracked, flying upwards then falling back as the passing zephyr lost its breath but once replenished did the same again. The sheets especially were tossed to the sky and she laughed at them. They reminded her of the curtains being pulled back at one of the little picture houses she'd visited. She'd sat in stunned silence and watched black-and-white people silently live black-and-white lives. Would that life were that simple!

As the sheets blew upwards, she thought she saw someone. The sheets fell back again. She narrowed her eyes. Was she mistaken? No, there he was again.

She knew him!

Quickly flinging her pegs into the wicker wash basket, she looked again. Flanked by billowing sheets, she saw him there, his dark hair tossed by the wind, his blue eyes smiling.

'Anthony!'

Face tense with emotion, he threw his arms around her and held her tight.

'I heard,' he said softly.

She closed her eyes, but not for long. *Now it's him that's married*, said her conscience.

He brushed her hair away from her face, and used his thumb to trace the fine lines around her eyes.

'I've got wrinkles,' she said, staring up at him, trying to work out whether he was a dream or for real.

'I love them.' He kissed them gently. 'Because they're part of you.'

'I wasn't sure you'd come. You heard what happened?'

He nodded. A nerve twitched in his cheek and she sensed it hadn't been that easy to leave Abigail and come to her.

'What will you do now?' he asked.

Dark and long, her lashes fluttered nervously over her cheeks. 'I've had an offer of marriage.' She nodded in the direction of the noisy tractor. 'The farmer, Ted Bertram. He's asked me to marry him.'

'You'd marry a man you do not love?' He sounded hurt that she'd even considered it.

She looked up at him to see if what she'd heard was in fact a mistake about to be corrected. There was no doubting the fact that he was horrified. Disbelief replaced her affection for him. She let her arms slide away from his and stepped back.

'Anthony! You know from experience this is far from being a land fit for heroes. Well, it isn't exactly milk and honey for women either, especially widows. I have to do what I can for me and my daughters.'

'Daughters! Two?'

'Three.'

Should she tell him about Elizabeth? Would he guess? She decided not to on both counts. Men were more naive than they'd ever admit to.

'I have a son,' he said almost as an afterthought. 'Beth, you know I had to see you, but I can't...'

'No. You're married to Abigail. You can't!'

As she regarded the strong jaw, the broad shoulders and the expressive eyes which sometimes seemed grey, sometimes blue, she knew that whatever passion had existed between them would not be rekindled. It wasn't that she wanted to lose him, but she could not possibly make Abigail's life a misery. She didn't deserve it.

The wash basket fell over as she took another step back. Unwilling to continue looking into his face in case she did weaken, she went down on one knee and began gathering up the fallen garments and scattered pegs. He followed her, his fingers picking pegs from among blades of grass. All the time, his eyes stayed fixed on her face.

'I can't just forget you, Beth. I can't.' He covered her hands with his.

Again, she retrieved them. The pegs scattered into the wash basket as her chin jerked forwards.

'I didn't say you have to forget me. If you've come here offering me the chance to be your whore – your mistress, I believe the polite term is – then forget it! From here on I am a woman, no, a person in my own right. There is no man now to lord it over me. I will do what I want to educate and assist them less fortunate than myself and somehow, I will raise the money to do so. No, you're right: I will not marry the farmer, but that doesn't mean to say I'm hanging around for you!' She looked pointedly down at the shabby green skirt she'd once been so proud of. Faded, roughened by much wear and tear, it was fit for nothing except for working in. 'And believe me, there are quite a few who are worse off than me,' she added with a toss of her head.

Anthony's jaw dropped and a hurt look came to his eyes. She immediately knew the reason why. The pedestal she had put him on was far too high above other men. Deep inside, he was no different than they were.

She sighed. 'I know I'm lecturing, but I can't help it. This is the way things are. Women, to a greater or lesser degree, are appendages to their menfolk, the busy bee in the background who keeps the fires lit, the food cooked, the children clothed and the kettle forever on the boil – and that applies both literally and to the more intimate side of a relationship! In your case, that's Abigail's job now, not mine.'

Anthony looked away, his gaze taking in the whitewashed cottage and the grassy hill behind it. Blossom fluttered from the apple trees, and beneath them, the grass was speckled with pimpernel, bluebell, cowslip, and all manner of other flowers he could not possibly identify.

'I know a place... This is a lovely place. Shakespeare would have known a place like this.'

'It is, and it's my place. Mine and my children's.'

'I didn't mean to insult you, Beth, or take things for granted. I would never do that.' A wet sheet floated behind his back as he dug his hands in his pockets and dropped his head forward.

Beth resisted the urge to reach out and touch him. It would have been so easy to comply with anything he had to say if it meant holding him close again and hearing him recite beautiful words into her ear. He was looking at the grass beneath his feet. If he had looked at her, even sidelong, she would have fallen.

She convinced herself that the moment of passion was now under control. What he said next took her completely by surprise.

'I'm willing to give up everything, Beth, if you'll have me. Any chance of a political career I'd gladly let pass for you. Much as I love my child, much as I respect Abigail, them too I would forgo. I can't marry you and I can't see that Abbie would let me have a divorce. And she has plenty of money. Her father died. But I'm willing to give it all up for you, Beth.'

She shook her head.

'Drat it!' he looked sheepishly at her, smiled sadly and shook his head, his hands still buried in his pockets. 'I couldn't even offer you respectability. It would be just us against the world.'

She looked at him steadily, wondering at a weakness she had never seen before. Now she was stronger than he was.

She took a deep breath and told him her feelings. 'At one time, I would have gone with you, Anthony. But not now. Things have changed. You're married. I'm alone and rather than grieve at what might have been or kick over the traces and live with you, I intend throwing my passion in another direction.'

Anthony raised a thumb in the direction of the noisy tractor. 'You don't mean you'll reconsider...?'

Beth shook her head. 'Do you remember when I told you about setting up a schoolroom in a little cottage beside a lock?'

'Yes. I do.'

He looked at her sidelong. Her resolve was not strong enough yet so she made a point of looking down into the washing rather than into his eyes.

'That is what I want to do. The carrying company can fit a self-operating mechanism on the gates.' She glanced up then looked down again. 'Seeing as Abigail owns the company now, she could arrange for that to happen. That would mean I could stay here. Gareth, my brother-in-law, is strong, though sadly disabled by the war. He could work those gates by himself. Besides, his father could help when he wanted. After all, the Lloyd George pension doesn't run to all that, does it? And I could run my school. It would be a very good arrangement.' Beth felt pleased with herself. Night after night, she had thought out what would be best for her children, for other children and for herself. Looking after Gareth, a man with every ounce of violence knocked out of him, would help her achieve her ambition.

'I think it could be arranged,' he said slowly, already planning how to make things up with Abbie.

'I would need to be paid to teach them. The boat people could pay a little, I suppose, but they've not much as it is, so what about the union? I hear there's funds for educating them that need it?'

He looked at her as though seeing her for the first time. It had not occurred to him that she had stored up everything he'd ever said at those meetings held in draughty church halls and smoky pubs. Now she was turning it back on him, using it as the basis of her demand.

For a moment, the expression on his face was virtually unreadable. Then he laughed and shook his head as though he was the biggest fool ever born. 'And there was me wondering how you'd cope without a man to bring home the bacon. You're the one who should be going into politics, not me!'

My, but it had been so long since she had heard him laugh. The anger she felt about his ideas for their future melted away. 'Teachers never get married, you know,' she said suddenly. 'Those that do stop being teachers. It's a vocation, you see: a way of life. I'm willing to accept that because I want to improve the lives of a lot of people. They deserve it.'

'I think I can arrange it all, given some time.'

'I don't have much time. The lock manager has given me notice to quit.'

'We'll see about that! Or rather, Abbie will!'

He took a few steps back towards the canal where the top of a gentleman's cruiser showed just above the parapet. It was hard now to see him go, but although she knew regrets would remain with her, her dream would replace the gap he had left in her heart.

'It's funny,' he said. 'Abigail was the one who was out to change the world for women when we first met and you were the one with a husband and everything. Now it's the other way round.'

He could have said more but he knew now what he had recognised in Beth when he'd first met her. All people were moulded somewhat by their early life. Some accepted their lot and cowed down to what they were supposed to be. Others looked up, saw the stars and wanted to give them to other people.

'I'll do everything you want.'

He waved at her from the boat, backed it out and turned it round. He didn't look back. What she had asked for was possible and he could get it done. Besides, it would mean they could keep in touch and one day... who knows.

Beth watched him go. He wasn't hers to have and yet that did not lessen the pain. If he arranged everything she had asked for, which she was pretty sure he could, then she would still see him on occasion. It would be enough.

She looked around her. As Anthony had said, it was a pretty spot. The colourful boats that had plied the canals for over a century were steadily disappearing. Rail and road transport were replacing them fast. The world was changing, but at least when she was old and grey, she would have memories of those times. She would remember the people, the hard work and the poverty, but she would also remember the hidden places, the secret banks where the wild thyme really did blow in a fresh spring breeze.

MORE FROM LIZZIE LANE

We hope you enjoyed reading *Trouble for the Boat Girl*. If you did, please leave a review.

If you'd like to gift a copy, this book is also available as an ebook, hardback, large print, digital audio download and audiobook CD.

Sign up to Lizzie Lane's mailing list for news, competitions and updates on future books:

http://bit.ly/LizzieLaneNewsletter

Want more gritty, heartbreaking historical sagas from Lizzie Lane? Why not explore her brand new *Coronation Close* series...

ABOUT THE AUTHOR

Lizzie Lane is the author of over 50 books, including the bestselling Tobacco Girls series. She was born and bred in Bristol where many of her family worked in the cigarette and cigar factories. Coronation Close is her latest saga series for Boldwood.

Follow Lizzie on social media:

- facebook.com/jean.goodhind
- twitter.com/baywriterallat1
- instagram.com/baywriterallatsea
- bookbub.com/authors/lizzie-lane

Sixpence Stories

Introducing Sixpence Stories!

Discover page-turning historical novels from your favourite authors, meet new friends and be transported back in time.

Join our book club Facebook group

https://bit.ly/SixpenceGroup

Sign up to our newsletter

https://bit.ly/SixpenceNews

Boldwood

Boldwood Books is an award-winning fiction publishing company seeking out the best stories from around the world.

Find out more at www.boldwoodbooks.com

Join our reader community for brilliant books, competitions and offers!

Follow us
@BoldwoodBooks
@BookandTonic

Sign up to our weekly deals newsletter

https://bit.ly/BoldwoodBNewsletter

Ingram Content Group UK Ltd.
Milton Keynes UK
UKHW042259110723
424969UK00004B/98